The Sun at Eight or Nine

The Sun at Eight or Nine

Ouyang Yu

PUNCHER & WATTMANN

First published in 2025
Published by Puncher and Wattmann
PO Box 279
Waratah NSW 2298

http://www.puncherandwattmann.com

A catalogue entry for this book is available from the National Library of Australia.

ISBN 9781923099487

Cover image by Zhao Baokang
Cover design by David Musgrave

Printed by Lightning Source International

This is a work of fiction. Unless otherwise indicated, all the names, characters, businesses, places, events and incidents in this book are the products of the author's imagination and should not be identified with any persons living or dead.

Australian Government

This project has been assisted by the Australian Government through Creative Australia, its principal arts investment and advisory body.

The world is yours, as well as ours, but in the last analysis, it is yours. You young people, full of vigor and vitality, are in the bloom of life, like the sun at eight or nine in the morning. Our hope is placed on you.

—Mao Zedong[1]

When parents are revolutionaries, their children should succeed them. When parents are reactionaries, their children should rebel.

—Madame Mao[2]

It really is a catastrophe. So many millions of people suffered from dire poverty. So many millions of them died with deep regrets. So many families fell apart. So many kids became hooligans. So many books were set on fire. So many places of historic interest and scenic beauty were destroyed. So many tombs of the sages were dug up. And so much crime was committed in the name of revolution!

—Qin Mu[3]

---

1 Qtd here: https://www.marxists.org/reference/archive/mao/works/red-book/ch30.htm

2 Based on the original Chinese couplet: "父母革命兒接班，父母反動兒造反": https://zh.wikipedia.org/wiki/ 血统论

3 His original Chinese words are here: "这真是空前的一场浩劫，多少百万人颠连困顿，多少百万人含恨以终，多少家庭分崩离析，多少少年儿童变成了流氓恶棍，多少书籍被付之一炬，多少名胜古迹横遭破坏，多少先贤坟墓被挖掉，多少罪恶假革命之名以进行！"

To the memory of a lost revolution, and youth.

Author's Note

The Great Proletarian Cultural Revolution (1966-1976) is one in which Chairman Mao Zedong reigned supreme in China. Under him, things unprecedented in history took place. Workers, peasants, and soldiers were in power. Professors were removed from their teaching posts. Leading cadres, as capitalist roaders, were removed from their positions. University entrance examinations were suspended so that secondary school graduates, instead of taking the examinations and going to the university, went to the countryside to learn from the peasants. People with foreign connections, e.g. relatives overseas, had to cut off their relationships or suffer being dubbed *jieji diren* (class enemies) engaging in *litong waiguo* (having illicit relationships with foreign countries). Foreign books, in the original or in translation, were burned or recycled. Political oppression and persecution led to multiple deaths. Recent findings point to a death toll of at least 3 million, if not more, during that period.[1]

And yet, many more have survived. Ordinary people managed to lead ordinary lives and survive despite pain and suffering and adversity. Zu, for example, is one young man who lived through those hard times. This story is about him, as a teenager who lived in the heyday of the Revolution, as a secondary school graduate who settled in a village and as a twenty-odd-year-old who succeeded in going to a university when the Revolution ended.

---

1 See 'Death Toll and Mass Killing from Cultural Revolution': http://factsanddetails.com/china/cat2/sub6/item1813.html (accessed 21/11/17)

Contents

Book I. 'Little Low Heavens'[1]

'In *liaozhai zhiyi*, or *Strange Stories from a Chinese Studio*, no distinction exists between the living and the dead,' Dad said to Zu. 'A woman comes to the man, wakes him up and sleeps with him. Then she tells him: I died 500 years ago. I now come alive because I realise you are the right one for me. Or a woman dies of sadness or anger. But she doesn't die in her death. And, with a breath of love, the man manages to bring life back to her and they lead a happy life ever after. Most are dreams. A lot are fantasies. But everything seems real, are real in fact. The book, you know, was not published till 50 years after Pu Songling, the author, died. Like one of the characters or many of the characters in his book, he comes alive half a decade after his death and eternally tells his stories, the people not interested in him or in publishing him long dead, with no hope of ever coming alive again. That's life. That's death, if you know what I mean.'

As if by magic, of the Pu Songling kind, Zu comes to me and says, Wouldn't it be better if I'm allowed to tell my own story, if only for once, for one chapter perhaps?

With Pu Songling in mind, I allowed, not without a degree of fear, that this kind of storytelling might incur a similar fate to his, and following is Zu's story.

---

1 This title is based on a line taken from a poem, 'Spring', by Gerard Manley Hopkins: http://www.poetryfoundation.org/poems-and-poets/poems/detail/51002

Chapter 1: Who's Zu?

He was an ugly-looking man. Not that he was not handsome. He had a face that was clean and white. He had eyes that were double-lidded, a well-regarded quality for both men and women in his culture, to such a degree that those with single-lidded eyes, to enhance their looks, were inclined towards having an operation on their eyes, to make them double-lidded. He was short, shorter than most, but taller than a few, such as Chao, a middle-school classmate. Zu and Chao once had a chat about what future girlfriends they would have. Chao specified that he would have someone shorter than him, or at least about the same height, never one inch taller. Why? said Zu.

Because, said Chao, it just doesn't look decent when your girlfriend walks alongside you and looks taller. People will talk. They will look down on you, treating you like a midget. Worst of all, girls would never lower themselves to someone lower than them.

But what about love? said Zu.

What about love? said Chao.

Isn't love something that can overcome everything? said Zu.

You are not realistic, said Chao.

Realistic? What do you mean? said Zu.

Oh, you have to consider the facts of life, such as how people form their relationships and in what ways. Girls simply don't go with men shorter than them. I know that for a fact, believe me, said Chao.

Well, then, said Zu, unconvinced.

Being short was not the only negative quality that made him unlikeable in the eyes of his girl classmates. It was his teeth that were not only protruding but also gappy. People didn't look at him; they looked at his teeth, the same way they looked at someone limping or someone with a huge birthmark that darkened part of his or her face. One day, while he was walking down the street with Dad, Dad found it odd that he never spoke a word, keeping tight-lipped. This boy, Dad said, such a strange boy, which he heard but didn't make a response to. They walked into a local Xinhua bookshop, the only one in town. There, little Zu saw under the glass counter a row of Mao's books, white covers with enlarged red letters and Mao's profile gold-stamped, featured prominently on all covers. But he did not recognise the language, as it wasn't English although it looked like it. He could only recognise the three words, Mao Tse-tung.

What language is it, Dad? said Zu.

Albanian, said Dad.

Why Albanian, not English?

Because we are in a very good relationship, China and Albania, came the answer.

Then, I'll learn the language, said Zu, full of hope.

No, you won't. You don't learn that language.

Why?

Because it's a small language, too small.

But the bookshop is full of them, Zu looked around him and pointed at the stacks of Mao's volumes in the small language.

I'll tell you when you grow up because you won't understand it now. But this is not the language to learn in any case.

Out of the stack, though, little Zu spotted a newly published three-volume set of *The Romance of the Three Kingdoms*. He was so excited that he wanted Dad to purchase a set for him. He could see that Dad was hesitant, between willing and unwilling. Then Dad said something that delighted him; he said, 'I'll buy you a set when you grow older.' It was a promise and he was pleased with it. He came to know years after that Dad had never carried out that promise; he had either never intended to, promising for the sake of promising, or he had clean forgotten it.

People may have never commented on his teeth, but it was Zu who hated the look himself. When people grinned and revealed their white even teeth, he shut his mouth and looked grim. When classmates laughed out loud, their teeth hanging out like display products, he shut his mouth and brooded. It was only when Dad opened his mouth and spoke, he noticed something similar: his teeth were white and even but slightly protruding in the upper front, the shape of which he had somehow inherited. But that's where their similarity ended. Zu kept thinking of a day when he would lose all his teeth, replaced with a mouthful of beautiful fake teeth, like the woman in the film, with ravishing beauty, but the teeth, like his life, were stuck with him. Bulky, unclean and stinking, they got tiny bits of food, meat and vegetables that refused to be cleaned up by a mere toothbrush once a day, so he had to use his index-fingernail to scrape the tartar, tooth by tooth, inside and out. If his right one couldn't reach the depths, he would use his left, before putting the little bit on one fingertip till it amassed into a pile of pale excreta. And he would smell it before he trashed it, as he liked the pungency of the smell. This was strange because if it were from someone else, he would have been disgusted with the sight and smell.

祖

Zu's early teens. In the middle of the Great Proletarian Cultural Revolution when there was sheer chaos. Work in his mother's *danwei* was indefinitely suspended. Every staff member was left to his or her own devices, having nothing to do, but somehow keeping busier than ever, with their own domestic chores. Uncle Zhu was learning to do haircuts by first trying it on his own kids, then doing it for the kids of the other staff members, all for free. Uncle Li raised chickens that were overrunning the *danwei* compound. Uncle Zhang was into playing card games with his neighbours. Uncle Zou had daily Chinese chess with anyone who was willing, right beneath the Chairman Mao portrait in the middle of the corridor facing the main gate entrance. Zu's mother did nothing. She complained, behind a closed door. She was careful not to make any criticisms in public, not even a 'public' consisting of two people because the other non-Zu-family person might end up informing against her. There were plenty of lessons to be learnt. One heard of a Mr So and So who went around carrying a fountain pen and a notebook in his pocket, pretending to be extremely interested in what others had to say about current affairs. Once he caught a remark out of the ordinary, criticizing the government, particularly the Great Leader Chairman Mao, he would memorise every word of it, go home and meticulously

14

record every detail before reporting it to the revolutionary committee that was in power. Whoever made the remark or remarks would see their own downfall. Pretty soon, people got the hang of it and they would shut their mouths and say nothing.

Behind the closed door, though, Mother was fierce. She was openly critical of the System and everything it did: the replacement of the existing management with a revolutionary committee consisting of non-professionals, such as workers, peasants and soldiers, the three corners of the society that Chairman Mao wanted everyone to trust and believe, with whole-hearted support; the suspension of classes at school when kids were 'forced', in her own words, to learn from the peasants and workers by spending days, sometimes weeks, in the fields or factories, learning things that had nothing to do with book knowledge; and, worst of all, the waste of time, talent, and energy at work, where no one did anything decent and reputable, raising chickens, for example, leaving the place messy and smelly, covered with shit that she hated. But there was nothing she could do about it. The only thing she could do was keep her own small room of 6ft x 6ft, spick and span, where a desk by the window, a double-bed in a corner and a single bed by the door, with half of the bed underneath the desk, was all she had. In a corner between the bed and the wall, was a stack of suitcases full of clothes. Underneath the bed was box after box of necessities, such as bars of soap, stowed away for daily use. In summer, when cotton quilts were no longer needed, they were put up on the wall and hung, big and bulgy, from the nails there.

From early on, Mother observed that the boy had a temper. As he grew up, he became more tempestuous. In her memory, there were happier times when the boy would listen to whatever she said and would follow her advice regarding schoolwork. He wouldn't say no, reading a book length-wise, with his face turned towards the wall, lying in his quilt in his bed, when Mother came over and stood the book up so that he felt uncomfortable having to twist his neck to read the lines properly. Years after, he realised why Mother did that; she did that because she stood by the bed and thought the boy, lying down, ought to read the book the way a standing person should do. How wrong? But he didn't say no.

He just read it length-wise, as told.

It was the Cultural Revolution that turned everything upside down. People formed into two main fighting factions, the Rebels and the Royalists. But Zu's mother and father stood in the middle, supporting neither, because they were the least powerful people, father being classified as a Kuomintang leftover and mother being automatically reduced to a lesser social position. On more than one occasion, Zu overheard Mother sigh and say, in Father's presence or behind him: I wouldn't be in this sorry situation today if I had not married you. Zu could see that Father never got angry. Instead, he would laugh it off and say: How can you say that? How can you say that? Hahaha.

The existing system was being pulled down, right from the top. It was down with everyone and everything. No one knew what was going on. But every day it was in the news that some top officials were toppled, like a lawn being mowed, top down, and ripped apart. Bureau Chief Wang, of the *danwei* where Mother worked, was given the combined job of a cleaner and rubbish-collector. Zu witnessed him doing his work diligently. No one else paid any attention to this bureau-chief turned cleaner/collector and he had no one to talk to, either; he was not supposed to. Zu watched him cleaning the windowsills in the meeting room on the second floor, with a mop. He watched him carry water in pails and pour the water into the huge wok to boil before filling scores of thermos bottles for the office staff. And he went around reading big-character posters that went on every wall and any pasteable surface. Things private became transparently public. A section chief was exposed to have concealed his personal history of having been a Sanqingtuan (Kuomintang Youth League) member; a colleague had been found to be a soldier once fighting for Kuomintang till it was defeated when he turned coat before liberation; a fallen Party secretary reputedly had had many *pipan* (skin stumblings), a euphemism for sexual liaisons, because of his manipulation of his powerful position and good looks; and diaries galore were exposed, page after detailed page of personal grievances, ills or behind-the-back bad-mouthing, as a result of raids on these people's homes or anonymous reports. As the saying, *renren ziwei*, goes, this seemed a dangerous time for everyone.

Zu, like the rest of the crowd, went out and looked at the big posters. He didn't read them. He just looked. He understood little of the connections between the present and the past. And the atmosphere of rebellion, coupled with the fact that he was in his mid-teens, made it impossible for him to read between the lines. He had wanted to become a Red Guard. That desire grew stronger with Mu's urgings. Mu was a big girl, big for a pre-teen. She took Zu to the street; together they watched how the Red Guards demonstrated and demolished anything that was classified as feudalistic, capitalistic and revisionist. These included shop signs that featured dragons and classic calligraphy, and road signs that were found to be too traditional and archaic, all replaced with names like Revolutionary Street, Workers Road or New Fours Road. There were books from the Soviet Union that were confiscated and burnt. While Mu found all that exciting, Zu, for some reason mysterious to himself, remained cold. He didn't think; he couldn't possibly think clearly; he just found everything overwhelming, and exciting, too. His was like a moving eye, that kept being blasted, bombarded and blasphemed, as it went from street to ransacked street, from temple to destroyed temple, and from book to burnt book. A conversation between Mu and Zu ensued.

We must join them, said Mu.

Yeh, sure, said Zu.

What? You don't sound enthusiastic, said Mu.

It's not that, said Zu.

It's what then? said Mu.

I heard there's an age limit, said Zu.

So? said Mu, edging closer to Zu.

We're too young, said Zu, moving away from Mu on the bench they were sitting on.

Even if that's the case, we can still follow them, said Mu.

Follow them? said Zu. I don't know how. They might reject us. He had wanted to say, 'My family background might disqualify me.' Instead, he kept those words to himself.

Oblivious to what was going on in his mind, Mu went on, You can follow me, then.

'Follow you?' Zu thought to himself. Then he replied to himself, 'No. Why would I follow a girl like you?' Again, he swallowed those words.

He didn't go because he was afraid; he was more afraid of the girl than the Red Guards. He didn't know why he was afraid. But he was sure he was not comfortable in her presence. She was pushy; she was openly flirtatious; and she wasn't very pretty, either. The first time they went out together to 'join' the Red Guards, Mu stole a finger to hook his right hand. But the touch itself was so anathema to him that Zu instantly withdrew his hand, pretending, as he did, to scratch an imaginary itch on his right cheek. On another occasion, when he was watching the Chinese chess game in the hall of his mother's *danwei*, she found him and got so close that he had to edge away from her till his bottom fell out of the edge of the bench, nearly causing him to fall. Frowning, he cursed under his breath. But Mu giggled.

What's the matter with you? said she.

I just want to see the game, said he.

All right then, said she, looking away as if she didn't care.

祖

If my character were alive he would come out of this novel and say to me: But there's so much you haven't written about me. Like what? I said to myself, not believing a fictional character could have had that power of anti-depiction, subverting a writer's authority. But, like the stink bug that just now came to perch on the French window that separates my room from my balcony, offering me an opportunity to take a couple of photos of him with my mobile phone, and disappeared without a trace when I took another look, the fact that my character becomes alive with an accusation suddenly charges me with a memory of him that gets lost somewhere in the thick of writing. This is a young teen who was into wearing tattered clothes. When he went beyond a certain age, all the old clothes were too short for him. His trousers had to be lengthened with the bottoms of trouser legs, cut off from the trousers his father had

18

worn and discarded. Mother carefully measured them and sewed them together so that they fitted well. But the colours didn't often match. The same was true of his outer garments, whose sleeves and hems had also to be lengthened and joined with the old stuff, stitch by stitch with Mother's neat needlework. These trousers and garments were full of holes, too, but that were all patched over with pieces of cloth that were different in colour and texture. People looked at him curiously when Zu walked down the street. His classmates didn't openly laugh at him even though the girls giggled at the sight of him walking into the classroom like a moving bundle of tattered patches. He was ashamed of those patches and the lengthened parts but there was nothing he could do about them. He had to wear them as there was no other choice. Mother's words, on the other hand, acted as a prop for his spirit, her words came in a quoted common saying that goes, *xiaopo bu xiaobu*: People laugh at the holes, not the patches. And she added, 'As long as you keep clean, there's nothing else to worry about.' After that, Zu felt better and more composed when he wore those pieces of patches outdoors. He even felt proud of himself because he was different. After all, he was clean and he was well organised, that is, well patched up and more sightly than those who wore new clothes that were dirty. He believed that he was also following Mao's motto that stipulates in these words, *jieyue nao geming* (one ought to be frugal when engaged in the revolution). If he had read 'soul clap its hands and sing, and louder sing / For every tatter in its mortal dress,' of W. B. Yeats' 'Sailing to Byzantium', he might have felt even prouder. But those were the days when no such literature was accessible in China.

Chapter 2: The Revolution

Mum was beginning to take things home, things she saw that could be turned to good use. A piece of wood that belonged to a smashed chair, or a desk that survived the *wudou*, or the factional conflicts. She would, her eyes avoiding those of Zu's, murmur, 'I've pinched something.' Zu kept his mouth shut, feeling ashamed. He knew Mother was someone who considered herself above things like that. She would not, for example, go through the *houmen*, the backdoor, by bribing anyone in a powerful position to promote her own interests. She emphasised, time and again, the virtues of studying hard, of self-reliance, and of not seeking anyone else's help in difficult circumstances. She would say, to the degree that Zu felt his ears had become callous, 'Grandpa is a man of dignity. He comes from a family of book fragrances, that is, a family of *dushu ren*, scholars.' Although nothing more was said, the idea somehow stuck that they were distinguished from people who were not *dushu ren*. And that made all the difference. It was a time when the theory of *dushu wuyong lun*, knowledge being useless, went viral throughout the country as nothing was worth reading anymore. Books right back to the beginning of times were denounced as being feudalistic, all rubbish; books from the West, all bourgeois and capilalist, corrupt and corrupting; and books from the Soviet Union, downright revisionist that were not truly Marxist and Leninist in nature, entirely against Mao Zedong Thought. The only book that remained to be read was Mao's book, *Quotations from Chairman Mao Tse-tung*, commonly known as the *hongbao shu*, a book of red treasure, or the Little Red Book. Zu, along with his other classmates, had to hold it in front of them with three fingers—the index-finger, the middle-finger and the wumingzhi, the nameless finger, or the ring-finger—on the cover, and the rest of the fingers behind it, to show that they were signifying *san zhongyu* (three loyalties), loyal to Chairman Mao, to Mao Zedong Thought and to Chairman Mao's Proletarian Revolutionary Line. And, in doing that, the hand gesture meant four 'infinites', infinite worship (*wuxian chongbai*), infinite love (*wuxian re'ai*), infinite belief (*wuxian xinyang*) and infinite loyalty *(wuxian zhongcheng)*.

Zu followed all the rules and regulations, but rebelled against them at heart, particularly after what his father had revealed in an anecdote he told about loyalty. In or about 942 AD, Liu Chang, last emperor of Southern Han, decreed that the only way that ensured that officials would remain loyal to him was that they must be physically castrated, or there would be divided loyalties because of their ties to their families, wives and children. As a result, over 20,000 were castrated.[1]

He kept his mouth shut because his father told him never to tell anyone else about it, just keep it to himself. He thought it over and decided not to follow the trail of the castrated by also turning into a castrated person. This had the effect of not revealing his ugly teeth and serving the purpose of self-protection, turning him into a sarcastic and whimsical, somewhat bitter boy, good at observing funny details. On one occasion, in a school sports event, he remarked that a PE teacher was so delighted with the achievements of his students that he had moved 10 steps away from where he was standing without realizing what he was doing. The remark made all the students around burst into laughter, although, at other times, his jokes failed to impress as they were actually veiled attacks. Once, in an open-air political meeting, everyone, thousands of them, gathered in the glaring sun to celebrate May 1st Labour Day. Firecrackers were being sent off, creating suffocating clouds of smoke that suffused the crowd on the square outside the Great Hall, the only place for social gatherings, theatre plays and political meetings in Yuwang Town, and Zu found himself uttering a remark that shocked his classmates, who were covering their mouths and noses against the onslaught of the smoke. He said, This is sheer *wuyan zhangqi* (pandemonium). As soon as the words rolled off his tongue, he regretted them, fearful that he might end up being taken to task, first by his political instructor, then by the school authorities. He recalled how a girl in his class had been suspended from classes by the school as a result of her surreptitiously putting down '3 Loyalties and 4 Infinites', instead

1 See Sun Yinggang, *suitang wudai shi* or *A History of the Sui Dynasty, the Tang Dynasty and the Five Dynasties*. Shanghai People's Publishing House, 2015, p. 174.

of a formal 'Three Loyalties and Four Infinites'. That, in the eyes of the authorities, was tantamount to committing an unpardonable crime against the beloved Chairman Mao. For days after, Zu dreaded similar consequences although, as luck would have it, nothing happened.

At home, it was Zu and Mum, living together, but separately, for Mum was always busy at work, even after dinner. When he heard what I had written about in that period, Old Zu pointed out that I might have made a mistake, as that would have been much earlier and that my arrangement of events and details seemed to have muddled sequences of time and space. Still, he didn't think that was a problem as there isn't, and there shouldn't be, a specific pattern one should adhere to. Even though every mother goes through similar changes in a pregnancy, the babies they deliver greatly vary in weight, size, length, colour of hair, of skin, of eyes, not to mention racial, cultural and ethnic origins. At a loss as to what to do because of his intervention, I went on, relying on the mnemonic material I was provided with.

It was actually earlier than that, perhaps as early as Zu could remember. A baby, perhaps 2 to 3 years old, was standing in the bed, too big and empty for him, in that tiny room that was large enough to contain only the bed and nothing much else, with an electric bulb hanging by the bedside, over a wooden box serving as a tabletop, bare of anything. In a moment of terror, he saw someone looking at him, right opposite him. His first reaction was speechless. He stood watching. Someone was also watching, standing. He stepped forward, unsteadily in the soft bed. That figure, in the windowpane, was also stepping forward, towards him. He was scared, in fact so scared that he burst into tears, watching the figure, lit up by the bulb, as if in a pale aura, menacing, advancing, terrifying.

'Mama,' he cried, his voice sounding hollow, unusually loud in the quiet of the night, accentuated by the absence of responses. 'Mama!' he raised his crying voice to another level. 'Mama, mama.'

No one answered. The night was gathering around him, compressing the room into a tiny space of three: baby Zu, the bulb, and the figure, facing him facing the face, whose mouth was moving, in imitation of his own. But no sound came.

He stood crying till his legs could no longer support him when he fell headlong onto the bed. In that instant, the figure was gone. Still, no one came to soothe him in his troubled sleep that, as described in a poem shown me by Old Zu, held 'a dark street strewn with corpses, glittering like florescent lights / with nose-choking smells of blood' where the baby 'is running naked, alone, in the sunlight of blood'.

In fact, his mind was a mess, worse than the poem. As soon as he fell asleep, his mind turned into an enormous cave, echoing with noise of all kinds.

When he woke up, time had marched into the Cultural Revolution, but not till he danced, naked, one night, in the bed, by the side of Mother, quoting a word she had often used in her talks with her colleagues, or with Father, *zhuanqian*, making money, as he turned around in his nakedness. Was it like that? said baby Zu. The word '*zhuan*', had the homophonic meaning of 'making' and 'turning'. In his young mind, Zu had inadvertently associated the act of making money with that of turning money as if money could be made by a mere act of turning.

Mother laughed and said, But *zhuan* is not turning; it is making. Who told you this word? You should never think about this.

Inside the quilt, the boy was lying on top of his mother, cupping her breasts with his tiny hands, feeling aroused, his little dick so hard against Mother's cloth-covered crotch that he felt an unutterable sensation stirring inside him. After something that seemed to last forever, he fell into another sleep, this time more sweet and blissful.

On one occasion, Old Zu made a seemingly casual remark about sex being bred and fermented between mothers and their sons. When I said, 'I'm sorry?', he had already changed the topic to something else about current politics. It was too late when I recalled this minor detail again. But, in that instant, another detail emerged. Don't ask me where I secured the detail. A writer's mind is a hoarder whose source is mysterious, sometimes beyond his own comprehension, to which no footnotes could be attached.

It was a winter morning, at 3 a.m. A long line had formed outside the only butcher shop in town and the line was so packed that one person was pressed against the back of another. This at least served the double-purpose of preventing any queue-jumping and keeping warm. It so happened that there was a girl, about Zu's age, standing right behind him. But for her presence, Zu would have found this endless queue, this cold darkness, impossible to endure. Clinging to the two meat coupons, Mother's and his own, of one *jin* (half a kilo) of pork, their monthly ration, he remembered Mother's taunting words that he ought to have been out in the queue as early as 2, sometimes even 1 a.m., to be at the front, or else he would have failed to get anything, as happened on a previous occasion, for the shortage of pork in storage meant meat ran out before half the queue reached its destination: the chopping board with the fresh pork. 'If you get up too late, you won't get anything. Then all is wasted,' said Mum.

It was for this reason that little Zu got up at half past two and went to the butchershop in Shengli Street, along a deserted lane, unaccompanied by Mum, who was too tired to rise that early. On arrival, he was shocked to find a quite long queue had formed already and he quickened his steps to join in. This was the age of coupons as everything was rationed; there were meat coupons, cloth coupons, rice coupons, vegetable coupons, soap coupons, sugar coupons, salt coupons, cotton coupons, cooking oil coupons, tofu coupons, cigarette coupons, indeed, coupons for everything. But, of all those coupons, the meat coupon was the most treasured, the pork being the mainstay of one's subsistence.

Zu grew up using these coupons. He used them as he was directed by his mother, to go to the market to buy foodstuff, vegetables, tofu or soap, as he was doing now, back to bosom, his back against the bosom of the girl, standing right in front of her in the packed queue, whose warmth began affecting him in a way that made him feel dangerously comfortable. Even though his hands were cold, his feet were cold and his ears were the coldest, his loins were somehow warm without him knowing why. In fact, they were so warm they turned hard. More than once, he had suppressed a growing desire to turn around and hold the girl full frontal in his arms. Instead, he stood there, moving inch by elongated inch, patiently waiting in the total darkness, impatiently wanting to yell: What is it going on here? Why does the queue seem to get longer and longer? Why is it so dark that it never ends?

He heard himself yelling these words, chucking them towards the night sky and the people in the shape of a long snake, but the words refused to come out. They were held within, like inmates in the prison cell of his heart, the same way the erecting desire was being retained, like a pig whose head was roped up that was running amok, ready to break free once the rope was broken. The only exchange of a few words between them was (he said) 'It's so cold' and (her) 'That's right', (his) 'You do this often?' and (her) 'Yes, every month', and (his) 'This is my first time' and (her) 'How lucky you are'.

In an instant, in his mind's eye, he saw himself turn around, his arms wide-opened as the girl let herself received by his hot kiss and the two became united in a fire in which two flames merged into one, consuming each other. Instead, after what seemed an eternity, he heard himself say to the man behind the counter with what little that remained of the pork for sale: Can I have that fat piece, the one over there?, pointing to a strip of pork with much skin and white fat. Never for once had he dared turn his head back to look at the girl full in the face. All he was aware of was a warm body pressed against his back and not for once did he bother who it was that his own front was pressed against. It was the first time the young teen had come into the closest contact with a woman, with his back.

Chapter 3: Fishing, and the Shoe-tongue

After being shown what I had written above, Old Zu, now in his late 80s, mumbled something I could barely hear but that was unmistakable: This is sheer crap. Then, words came out of his toothless mouth, with a full set of dentures (I could see them moving as he spoke), 'If I were BSJ, I would have scrapped the whole thing. Lies, all lies.' Then and there, I decided not to bother showing him anything I'd written so far. It's not worth my while, I thought to myself. If it's all 'lies', let them be. Let him die for all I care and let the lies live.

In fact, the little town was full of lies like that, lies of a life that were real but that sounded surreally unreal when fully revealed, either by the living mouths or in the execution posters. In summer, the done thing, as the local customs would have it, was putting the bamboo beds out in the open, in the courtyards, on the open tops of the multi-story buildings or on the pavements. Boys were cautioned to be careful of a man prowling at night who would prey on the fast sleeping boys by taking out their erect dicks and sucking them dry, one by one. That caution had left Zu sleepless for nights on end, his hands involuntarily cupped around his balls for self-protection. But he dropped his guard as soon as he was overtaken by sleep and nothing seemed to have happened along the line of the story.

The next day when he went to the Yangtze and swam in it, he was shocked by what he found. It was with Jian, a boy much younger than him, whose dad had died of icteric hepatitis. Zu recalled his dad had called him a 'hypocrite', a word he didn't understand the meaning of but could vaguely guess at, when he said something about not wanting to live in this small town but would prefer to move elsewhere. Jian's dad, deputy bureau chief before his removal from his position and final death, chuckled and said, 'You are a hypocrite.' But Jian, the younger boy, was helpful. When they went out together, fishing in the Yangtze, Zu would play the fisherman boss and Jian would act as his deputy. Around the corner, behind the wall of a wood stockpile, where a slope of rocks jutted into the water, Zu sat at the top of the slope, just beneath the wall, and chucked his line and hook, with a wriggling earthworm, usually black, into the water. Because the water was alive with minnows, it was a quick and easy job of catching them by simply thrashing his line at the surface of the water and pulling it up. There it was, a long shiny piece of live flesh, flapping, jumping and wriggling, was hooked up. Then began Jian's job of unhooking the fish, stringing it up with a thin thread, putting the string of fish in a pool of water so they wouldn't go dead and dry in the sun, and putting on another earthworm before Zu chucked it into the water again. Sometimes, when the line got tangled up, Jian would put it out of the entanglement as he had nimbler hands than Zu while Zu would sit there, half-reclining in the sun, enjoying himself watching Jian unhook fish after fish with infinite patience.

Then, when things got slack, no fish biting, Zu and Jian would strip bare, slip into the murky Yangtze waters and swim. The surface of the water, suntanned and sun-heated, was warm to the touch. But when he pushed it off as Zu swam ahead, it felt like peeling off a warm watery skin, underneath which the water was cold. Meters away from the bank, he would do *caishui*, treading water, by standing up, quickly moving his feet up and down as he hit the water with the flat of his hands. Thus, he felt the full impact of the coldness coming up from the depths below while the black hair on his head, directly struck by the heat of the noonday sun, felt like burning. He would then turn around, lying on his back, chest up, facing the sun, the sky and the drifting clouds, with half-closed eyes, soaking his hot hair in the water, enjoying the moment of pure pleasure. After the two got tired, they would swim back, climb the stony slope and sit down on it. While Jian ran to a shade, away from the sun, Zu would sit sunning on a flat stone till his dripping skin completely dried up and turned brown. He would repeat the same process by getting completely wet and drying up again till lunchtime when they would walk home, barefoot, Zu with his fishing rod on his shoulder and a string of minnows in one hand, and Jian giggling, and tagging along, with half of the caught fish.

This love of fishing went back to Uncle Liu, a tall man with a long face who spoke perfect Mandarin. Married to Aunt Chen, opposite Zu's one-room abode, across the narrow passageway, he would, from time to time, visit Aunt Chen from Wuhan, the provincial capital. When Zu wondered what he did, Mother would shut him up by saying, Kids don't ask questions about daren, adults. Don't be so inquisitive. But he found out anyway. Uncle Liu worked on the railway although he looked nothing like a railway worker. Refined in his manners, he was soft-spoken, and kind. When Aunt Chen was at work, he would go out alone, fishing. Each time when he returned, there would be fish, mostly crucian carp, palm-long and palm-wide, alive and thrashing, in absolutely silver loveliness. Zu would watch him cleaning up the fish, one by one, by the side of the well at the end of the passageway, and wonder what had happened to his fishing rod because he had never seen him go out with one. Uncle Liu said, laughing, I don't need one. When I arrive at the place, I just cut a bamboo and turn it into one. Even more amazed, Zu, wide-eyed, wondered aloud, But why didn't you bring it back? No need, said Liu, smiling his infectious toothy smile. Too cumbersome. If I go fishing again, I'll cut another one. Zu grinned, then quickly closed his mouth, realizing how ugly a sight his teeth might present to Uncle in contrast.

It was at this time that Aunt Chen had another visitor. This happened after Uncle Liu left because Aunt Chen's single room was as small as the one Zu and his mother shared, with room enough to fit only two people at any given time. Slightly older than Zu, this girl was homely looking and had a temper. Zu never spoke a word to her nor did she speak to him, not even exchanging a glance with him. But he could see that the girl would often refuse to eat, apparently for no reason at all. Or she would hide herself in the communal bathroom next to the cluster of little rooms where they were living. This bathroom was a roofed shed squeezed between a long wall on one side and a row of one-room staff dormitories on the other, each room containing one family. In summer, men and their kids, male ones, would come here with pails of hot water and cold. They came with towels and soap, laughter and noise. Zu preferred to wash himself alone when they were all gone although he would occasionally do the bath amidst the crowd, with the steaming and greasy bodies of the adults. These adults would energetically scrub each other's backs as they were cracking jokes and laughing, about anything from the size of a particular dick to the intensity of the factional fightings. Old Zu told me later that he had no memories of anything said and he said to me that I could write any way I liked, making things up as I went, as long as it was as entertaining as *Tom Jones*, which Somerset Maugham suggests is one of the best ten novels in English literature. I thought to myself, without voicing it to him: But Maugham is not a serious writer in the strict sense of the word, not as funny as Laurence Sterne with Shandy, not as dark as Hardy, nowhere as adventurous as B. S. Johnson, not even half experimental as Richard Brautigan, and certainly not as pessimistic as E. M. Cioran. Still, I went headlong into it, with stuff that seemed to come from nowhere, and everywhere. In the only one bath he took, Zu stood gazing at the naked skins around him, forgetting the towel in his hand, until someone scooped a handful of water and poured it onto his little dick. It shrunk instantly, dampened by the cold water. This came from Uncle Zou who liked to play a practical joke or two. Watching the boy's embarrassed, and pained, look, Uncle Zou reached a hand out to touch his shoulder, in a friendly, soothing gesture. But Zu turned pale and brushed his hand off as he muttered something abusive, audible enough for everyone to hear.

This boy is so uncouth, said one.

His mother ought to kick his arse, said another.

He needs to thoroughly rinse his stinking mouth, said a third.

Looking sullen and feeling hurt, Zu refused to take the kind words offered by Uncle Zou who tried to joke it away by saying: It's all my fault. There, there, there's a good boy.

After that incident, Zu refused to have any more baths with the crowd; instead, he would wait till everyone was gone and do it alone. When Mum asked why and suggested it might be a good idea that he go with the flow because to be sociable was to be desirable, he got cross with her, not with words but with silence. At the back of his mind, there was the thought: What does she know? And there was the answer: She doesn't know anything. The boy, in his early teens, was growing into a full-fledged rebel. He learnt to say abusive words from watching his dad, who, on one of his rare visits back home, while chatting with someone on his way back to the *danwei*, said something to this effect: His mother's cunt! And followed that with another curse word, A dog fucker! In the darkness, Zu watched his dad in awe and wonderment, disbelieving his ears that such words could have flowed so freely out of his respected mouth. He didn't ask, he remained silent, and he learnt. Presently, though, he got his due punishment. In an inner courtyard, with a *tianjing*, or sky-well, surrounded with family-rooms on all sides, kids were running around, chasing after each other. Attracted by their war cries, Zu joined in the fun, his voice being the loudest. In fact, his nickname was *Zhagang*, an explosive water vat, because he had a voice that was throaty and loud, to an ear-splitting degree. When he got frustrated or overexcited, he'd be a real terror for the sheer decibels of the sound. Just as he was enjoying his own noisy moment someone came over and kicked him on his shin. It was such a hard kick that he was instantly crippled. He bent double, cursing for the pain of it, when another kick came that sent him flying. He knew who it was but he dared not hit back and did not have the strength to hit back because it was a boy much older and stronger than him. It was Da, Hei's older brother, a man of few words who hated the kids' noise. He was reading at the time and his patience was wearing thin till it got to an explosive stage when he heard Zu raising hell with his loud voice. This was a boy that he disliked, one with huge protruding teeth, a bad temper and an ability to read books faster than anyone else, a quality that disgusted him most, particularly when he needed a quiet time to read. When he reduced the boy and his noise to total silence with his kicks, he went contentedly back and resumed his reading.

But Zu learnt nothing from his mistakes. He went on to become more rebellious. When the spirit of the time was captured in the words *dadao* (down with), with anyone on top, such as Liu Shaoqi and Deng Xiaoping, and when the Red Guards smashed up everything that was considered capitalist, feudalistic and revisionist, indeed, anything that was traditional, Russian or Western, it was not surprising that Zu became easy prey to the tempers that were running high, the spirit of the time striking a chord with his temper and temperament. At the primary school he was graduating from, it was Zu's teachers that became the target for attack as students were encouraged to write criticism, right from the start of the Revolution. Teacher Li, a young woman who liked to dress up prettily in each and every class, was denounced in student criticisms as being petty bourgeois, with a head full of bourgeois sentiments. Although she never taught his classes, Zu could tell from watching her movements on campus that she was pretty in her bright-coloured and flowery dress, always with a bright and welcoming smile. After she was denounced, she turned into a totally different person: a tall figure in black, with an embittered face, walking around the place like a ghost of her former self. When he entered into the middle school, Zu met another woman teacher, a music teacher with stunning looks. Even though she wore grey clothes, her sparkling eyes and the lovely features of her face would set his heart pit-a-pat whenever he saw her on campus. The teacher, whose name he didn't know, paid no attention to him. But that did not stop him from dreaming of her and he welcomed opportunities to run into her if only to just glance at her beautiful face or even her back, the shape of which was more than enough to settle the teenager's troubled mind. It was odd that even in the intensity of the Revolution a developing body with a learning mind was more attracted by the opposite sex than what it knew itself. And it began with the ankles.

The boy, I assume he was 10 or 11, was into something he just knew he liked, without knowing why, without even knowing he didn't know why, which is why he never even asked himself why. He just looked at the exposed ankles of the girls in his class, particularly from behind, the posterior part of it, and he liked what he saw: the white stems of them, fleshy or thin, like a piece of moveable jade. He hardly looked at the faces of the owners of those ankles; instead, his eyes would follow the curvature of an exposed posterior ankle whenever and wherever it appeared. These, in turn, found their way into his many and varied dreams and may have led to his first nocturnal emission in the office across the corridor from his mother's office in the bureau building, according to Old Zu. For some reason mysterious to him, he was put up for the night there, in an unused office room full of furniture and stuff. When he woke up from a dream in which he literally holds an ankle in his hand, examining it like a piece of art, cold and fascinating, he felt uncomfortable as he found he was wet underneath. He couldn't possibly have wet the bed; he never did since he was little.

He took his dick in his hand and it felt sticky and the wet spot wasn't huge the way piss spread after one wet the bed. He wondered what it was. Then it dawned on him that this must have been what adults referred to as *yijing*. He quickly wiped himself clean and put the stuff away, a bit like a blob of phlegm.

Shortly after, things took a nasty turn. The next day, a team of Rebels stormed the bureau building. Young men, armed with rifles and looking utterly serious, went searching door by door for what was occupied by the Royalists. The staff of the bureau turned out, standing downstairs in the courtyard, Zu among them, next to Uncle Zou and Vice Bureau-chief Yang, a veteran who had fought against the Americans in the Korean War. Only a few days earlier, he had nipped all the budding flowers of a watermelon seedling that Zu had planted in the back of the communal bathroom. Zu loved growing little things, particularly the seeds of watermelons. In the pre-refrigeration days, on a hot summer day, when a watermelon was bought, Zu would put it in a *bing tietong*, literally an 'ice iron pail', actually a metal pail, filled it with cold water from the well, a common practice in cooling the melon. When night fell, and bamboo beds were put out, in the corridor, Zu would take the melon out of the water in the pail, already lukewarm, put it on a chopping board, and, with a kitchen knife, cut it into mouth-watering slices that he would devour with his mother, sharing them with whoever happened to be there. Then, from the heap of black seeds left, meant for washing up and sunning dry before being fried with salt and turned into melon seeds for cracking, he would pick one or two. Mother was kind enough to allow him, knowing that the boy would plant them and see them grow, although she would laugh off the boy's hope of reaping any melons.

Zu ran to the back of the bathroom where there was a strip of land, overgrown with weeds, between the row of staff dormitories and a wall, and dug a hole in the ground as he weeded the ground around it, removing the broken bricks or roof tiles that lay scattered around. Then, carefully, he put in the two black seeds, shiny and slippery, into the hole, and backfilled it with the soil dug out; he put in two, not one, because the one he put in last time didn't somehow sprout. After he poured in water from a tin can, he left them there and went back each and every day till two tender shoots broke through the crust of the earth, each with a bud on top. He watched the process of germination with fascination and imagined, gazing at the vine with young green leaves spread, that the budding flowers would one day turn into tiny little melons. And his heart gave a wild leap when, all of a sudden, a tiger pounced upon him, taking him completely by surprise. It's a human tiger with a smiling face, and kind words: Aren't these flowers lovely? He said as he pawed them, breaking each flower from its stem. In an instant, all was destroyed, the yellow flowers lying beheaded in a sorrowful state. The tiger, who was Deputy Bureau-chief Yang, left with these stern words: Don't you ever grow anything in here. The sunshine that had suffused the boy's heart was now gone, leaving darkness there, perhaps for life.

The team was led by a tall young man with a rifle in hand. He stopped outside a door, took hold of the doorknob and turned it. It refused to open. He stepped back, raised a foot, shod with a huge iron shoe, and kicked at the door. Once. Twice. Thrice. The door opened. The men rushed in. When they came out, the tall man had a pair of brand-new leather shoes in his hand. All the eyes were raised and the attention was focused on what he was going to do with the shoes. From where he was standing, Zu saw with open-eyed wonder how the young man was taking out a short dagger, from under his broad belt, and, with it, cut off the beautiful shoe tongues, one by one, of the leather shoes in pair, never worn, before carelessly chucking the tongue-less shoes onto the floor.

Zu watched all this with fascination. He wanted to laugh but dared not. He didn't understand why the man with the rifle should cut off the shoe-tongues instead of simply chucking them into the rubbish tip. He found it so regretful for the man to lay waste to a pair of shoes that was waiting for its owner to step into when he came home and the spectacle of him finding the pair without the tongues would have pained the owner immensely.

The rifle the man was carrying reminded him of something he had seen. Only a week before, he had seen Uncle Yang climb the wall outside the communal bath, onto its roof, while hugging a rifle. His movements were agile and soldier-like. When he jumped off the wall, minus his rifle, hidden away somewhere, his feet were dropped where Young Zu's watermelon seedling was, flattening it. With a huge palm held out towards him, Yang the Boss said, Don't ever tell anyone I've been here.

Chapter 4: He Swallowed Himself

She must be the most pretty woman in town. He watched her go down the street, in shoes that were different from what most women wore. From what people said about her, she was an actor with the local *wengong tuan*, literally, Literature and Art Work Group, but realistically, Song and Dance Troupe, a local performance troupe that ran all kinds of shows from eight model plays to anything meant to promote and spread Mao Zedong thought. But this woman actor was the only one in Zu's eyes that was worth looking at from one end of the street to the other, through the dense crowd till she disappeared. And long after she disappeared, her image would stay alive in his mind: a short but slim figure, big eyes, a big round face that was white, hair curled and wavy. It was also an image that hurt. The boy was the silent type. His eyes watched and followed and held. They noticed things. They saw that his attention was never returned. The woman acted as if he did not exist. Her eyes skipped him, looking past him, over him, and through him. It was said that she was a singer. And that she danced. Even though he had never seen her perform, Zu was able to imagine her on stage in various colours of attire, chief among them red and blue.

It was at this time that Zu became acquainted with Mongmin, a student from a next-door class. From the very minute they came into each other's acquaintance, Mongmin bragged, about his ability to *shouyin*, masturbate, among other things. This is what he said when they wandered about on the school sports ground. 'Let me tell you this but don't tell anyone else that I told you so. We did it all the time. We *shouyin*ed, you know. It's something all the boys do. There's nothing wrong with it. In fact, we did it collectively. It was only last year, right in a little grove of willow tress by the river, that we did it. I was the one who took the lead, shouting "1, 2, 3," when each and every one of us, pants down and cock in hand, rubbed and pushed it, facing the flowing waters that glimmered on the other side of the grove, till the thing came streaming out, thick and sticky and shining, white as white cotton flowers, collectively in a rush. But of course I was the one who came out first. It felt wonderful, what do you think? Otherwise, we did the job by ourselves. I don't know about them; whether they do it in their own time or for their own pleasure, I have no idea and don't want to know. It's for them to decide if they want to do it or not.'

Emboldened by what Mongmin described, Zu tried it on himself, a few days after he had that conversation. Lying half-inclined in bed, he was stroking himself, amazed by its hardness as it raised its head to an all-time high, when a woman came into view, with a round, whitely powdered face, the eyes embedded in them like gems seen in an American film. In a moment of bewilderment, he was not sure whether it was the *wengong tuan* woman in heels or the woman he had seen years earlier in a foreign film, with looks so stunning that he was struck not only speechless but was left wondering about the beauty days after he had seen her. It was a cleansing experience for him. He was with his Mum and Dad, sitting between them in a front row. He didn't understand a word of English spoken nor did he understand the Chinese characters in the subtitles. The woman's face, though, was open right in front of his eyes, like a ravishing flower, a landscape of such rarity his eyes were riveted on it for as long as it stayed on the screen. It was like all his life-force was being sucked out in that instant by the wonder of that face. Never again would he experience the same rarity of beauty in his life. But as he stroked himself he thought he was watching the two women merging into one, a local Chinese actress and an English-speaking American woman, twisting her body as she came towards him from afar, in shoes that looked strangely alluring, and, without knowing it, he climaxed, his right hand flooded with hot cum, sticky and white. Horrified, he looked down at his guilty hand and felt sorry about the profusion. Then, in an act that he was to regret and wonder about late in his life, he swallowed all his cum in his hand, licking each and every finger clean. At first, the pungent smell of the cum made it hard for him to swallow. But the thought of this associated with the two most beautiful women in the world helped him ease into it. Without the watching eyes of his parents, he found it much easier to do all the swallowing and cleaning, seemingly without a shred of bad conscience.

Chapter 5: TV in the Sky

Every time he went down the street, past the printing factory, Zu was puzzled by something new that appeared on top of its building. It was a bare stick standing straight in the air, with a row of tiny thin sticks, a little like a stove grate. He had heard about TV. But would people put a TV set on top of a grate-like thing like that? Would they be doing that even in the middle of a winter like this? How would they watch it then, standing around and raising their heads to look at the grate on top of the building? He could see something shiny along the bars of the grate. They must be icicles. In fact, eaves everywhere were hanging with heavy icicles, some as thick as a rolling pin, particularly in the mornings before sunrise. Roofs were covered in thick snow, white and clean. But where people walked it got dirty and dark. For much of the winter vocation, Zu stayed in his mother's office, near the office stove, with a long pipe of white metal, going upwards and bent at a right angle, that went across the room near the ceiling and out of the window through a hole, acting as a chimney. When he was little, he remembered, Mum had sat him on her lap, took out a long ruler and asked him to produce his left palm. When he hesitated, fearful of the consequence, Mum yelled into his ear, Do it! Then she held his hand out and hit the open palm, punctuating each hit with a, 'Do you dare do that again!' He held back his tears that were surging to the eyes and wrestled the sharp pain to the ground, so sharp he was nearly choked with it. After that, he was an enemy of his mother. His tempers grew as he grew up, emulating her, adopting her choosiness about things, her quick tempers that flared like lightning without warnings or reasons, and her abhorrence of things domestic. She didn't cook; in fact, she hated cooking. She smoked and complained about her bowel movements. She complained about the stinking toilet in the corner of the bureau premises. She was unhappy about the burden of childbearing. She, though, liked to chat with her male or female colleagues, and would occasionally wax sentimental about the boy.

But Zu didn't like her sentimentality and he hated the way she would suddenly become emotional, cuddling him with endearments, getting him to sing, 'Honghu shui, lang da lang', a popular revolutionary song, singing of the guerrilla warfare before liberation. Mum was washing his feet for him, having put him on a stool next to her, and she started calling him 'Brother', an endearment that never failed to please him. But as soon as she switched off to the song, humming it in a low tone, and, hit by the idea of getting the boy to sing in unison with her, the boy turned nasty. He did not know how. He found the woman a nuisance. He disliked either the lyrics of the song or the tone of her singing voice. His sudden silence puzzled his Mum, then upset her, when, she said, scolding, 'Why are you so glum? Didn't you see Mum is getting tired washing your feet for you? Next time, you'll have to do it all by yourself. No one is doing that for you again.' In that instant, Mum turned into another woman, morose, unpleasant, remote, so remote she dumped him next to her in bed, not allowing him to be near her. The distance only a few centimetres away but felt like vast and long. Shortly after, he was put on a bed on his own, with half of it underneath the table.

Zu never told anyone of his curiosity about the television in the sky. It was not his secret. It was more like something he assumed everyone already knew about, a box sitting on top of the grate on top of a roof, for everyone to look up and gaze at its screen. What an idea! In this small town with a population of 10,000-odd people, no one had seen a real physical television set. They might have heard of it on radio or read about it in the newspapers. They also talked about it as they were doing now, sitting around the stove, keeping warm and heating up sweet potatoes, their smell now wafting in the room.

They say television has arrived here, Uncle Liu said. To Zu, everyone was an uncle and he was raised to call anyone older than him by a decade either *Shushu* (Uncle) or *Ayi* (Auntie). If he failed to do that, he would be considered a rude boy with no manners.

Ah, yes, said Uncle Zhang. He was the dismissive type about anything new. What is that going to do to us? Taking a deep drag on his cigarette and puffing it out in a rolling smoke much resembling a white cloud, he answered his own question, Not much.

Who knows? Uncle Liu said. But I heard it can do a lot more than the movies. In future, each family will own one, people can watch it everywhere, even in the comfort of their own homes. I thought it a great idea.

But how? Zu wondered to himself. Do they have to watch from a telescope or climb onto the roofs of their dormitories to watch if each television set is to sit so high on top of the grate-like antenna?

Well, I don't know. Wouldn't a book serve a much better purpose as it is so easily portable and keeps you company wherever you go, in fact, anywhere, in bed or in a toilet? Would a television set serve the same purpose? Would it give you page after page of words, nothing but words, mere words or wonderful words, words that lead to words, words as we voice them daily, words that are enough with words and that are content to be nothing but words? said Uncle Zhang as he picked up a sweet potato and began peeling it, transferring it from one hand to another, in a quick succession of heat dodges, till he successfully broke it in half, passing the bigger chunk to Zu. Seeing the soft yellow inside exposed and smelling the sweet smell, Zu grinned as he took the offer from Uncle Zhang and 'ah'ed, instantly scorched when he sank his teeth into it.

As the staff members were chatting about TV and other things, Zu was busy eating the half sweet potato, liking its bright yellow colour and sweet taste, strengthened by the heat from the burning coal underneath, particularly the bit on the inside of the skin. Apart from that, he enjoyed the way Uncle Zhang seemed to be chanting something mesmerizing about the difference between words and something no one had yet set their eyes on, let alone watch a program on it. Just then, he heard something by Uncle Zhang again, thrown his way, Boys like him. They'll know how to watch and how to deal with a future of pictures. Not for me. I'd rather stick to my mahjong, oh, no, I meant my books.

That little slip of tongue that might have caused heads to roll did not register with Zu, his thoughts already wandering far off, to a future in which no words existed, replaced by pictures that dominated the world, pictures that became alive on what people were watching on top of that grate-like antenna and women, like the one he saw in the movie and the one he saw on the street, walking straight off the screen, stunning fairy queens that came directly at him, taking him instant prisoner and delighting him with their many and varied ways, for he already was a full-fledged young man with muscles and many private parts— an expression that Old Zu told me about—that gave them no end of pleasure.

But Old Zu had no memory of those revelries. He didn't blame me for inventing them, although he did not praise me, either. 'It's really up to you guys to work it out,' said he. 'But the stupidity is the same, I mean that non-understanding in regard to the advent of a new technology in the town, as the one I had when I went to Vancouver.'

I said, 'What happened?'

He said, 'Oh, now that I'm about to be no more, I can tell you what it is or was.'

Then he told me of his experience traveling on Skyline in Vancouver with a group of colleagues. As they went further away from the city, the landscape became more barren and bleak, with wall after wall of graffiti and occasional writings sprayed on the walls. Among these, he spotted the words 'BODY' and 'BODY WORKS', and that gave him a mental pause. So this is the real West, wild, wild West? And this is what it's all about, 'BODY' and 'BODY WORKS'? 'Where do I find them?' he wondered to himself. He had heard about corruption in the West and about the Westerners' general depravity in things related to sex, and he had been inoculated against all that in meeting after study meeting, to prepare against the onslaught of Western depravities before they left China, in which one read detailed material about Western corruption and how to fight it. Then this, so in your face, so blatant, and so irresistible. Written right on the wall! He wondered how to find the bodies and felt ashamed of thinking so but was led on by it from one imagined body to another.

I was to feel sorry about it because I interrupted him with quite an improper question that went, 'Were you able to find one eventually?'

There was no answer as he discontinued the email communication.

Chapter 6: The Three Lines

It's literally called *sanxian*, three lines, and variously referred to as *sanxian jianshe*, the construction of three lines, or the Third Front or Third-line Construction. What is it? I don't know but you are welcome to Google it. I was a boy of 15 at the time. Mum was away at work in the Third Front. No one knew what it was about. Everyone talked about it, in a secret sort of way. Hush, hush. Military. Trucks. Construction with a big C. Everyone rushed there. I went there with the uncles on a school holiday. Not one of them I knew. But as soon as I was introduced, they treated me as one of their own.

Oh, he's Zu's son, I know, one uncle said.

Such a big boy, hey! said another as he held out his hand and tried to pat me on my head. I ducked and dodged, frowning.

We were going there by truck. You must understand I have been dead for many years. What death does is that it erases memory. I don't recall whether we went there by train or by truck. We just went. The night before we left, we were in a huge hotel room with dozens of beds. An uncle, whose name I forget and who can be given any name, say Zheng Xin, spoke to me across the space from his bed, You must go with us to Shiyan to see what's going on there. They had flies this explosive that they'd explode and send clouds of black wings all around you and over you as soon as you got near a pile of shit or a broken piece of watermelon. Oh, there were so many piles and pieces you'd be amazed why you don't have them here and pretty soon you'd start wishing you'd have them here, too.

I watched Zheng talking and heard them laughing. In that laughter, I could sense a mockery at my ignorance and inexperience. I ignored it and went on listening to him talking, this chain-smoker of a man whose phlegm-filled voice matched his smoke-yellow face with a pair of eyes that stared and bulged, never smiling himself, in an utter seriousness that made his plain words seem more funny than they were.

Then we arrived. We arrived just like that. But, of course, it was something I had never seen before. There was only one road with traffic going either way, like two rivers running in reverse. The road was lined with mountains, tall mountains of green slopes. There was so much dust on the road that, sitting in the front seat of a Liberation Truck, as I did, one could not see much in front of him in the dust raised by the buttocks of the truck before and the truck before that truck. The road, in fact, was wrapped day and night in the dust that made it hard to breathe, worse because everyone smoked, including Mum. I had asthma and I was asthmatic throughout.

I met Mum in the Command Centre where she introduced me to everyone as Bin Bin. I met Wang Siling, Commander Wang, a fat and short man. I met a lot of other people Mum introduced to me. They were adults whose circles I didn't move in. I stepped aside and felt pleased. Then came this handsome young man. Mum said, Call him Fan Shushu (Uncle Fan).

I said, in a low voice, looking away, Fan Shushu.

The man burst out laughing and said, He's so shy!

We soon became friends. The trees in the valley around the Command Centre witnessed us walking side by side, appreciating the scenery and the birdcalls, sometimes lingering on the basketball court in the valley where, instead of playing, we talked about poetry. I had nothing to show him because I had written little, and the little I had written was once laughed at by Hong, a tall classmate of mine. Though he wrote little poetry himself, Hong said that the repetitive lines were funny, judging by what poetry he had been taught in class. Unlike Hong, Fan had heaps to show because he wrote profusely. But he mainly wrote in the classic style, with rhyme and rhythm, which was nothing compared with the classic poetry by Li Bai, Du Fu and Bai Juyi. When I said so, I found his face turning blue, displeased, and he defended himself fiercely, saying that his poetry was about the present, not the dead past.

The next day when we met again, he gave me a folded piece of paper. He wanted me to read it not in his presence. As soon as he said that, he went away. I stared at his back, his big hair encircling his square face, as he disappeared in the distance.

It was a didactic poem exhorting me to keep trying my best in everything I did and not to forget the good advice from people older or with more experience or both. I put it aside after that and didn't give it another thought. But I would occasionally take it out and read it again and again.

The summer holiday was soon over and it was time to return to my hometown again. One day before my departure, I stood by the roadside and watched them count the trucks they said were heading back to the provinces. These were all Liberation canvas trucks, with dark green oilskin canopies. I looked at them without interest, without any curiosity. I just thought: Oh, these trucks, heading home. And tomorrow my truck would also take me home. But just then a man next to me offered, You know what's in there?

I said, Obviously.

What? said he.

Aren't they going home in these trucks? said I.

Yes, it's 'they', said the guy. They are all going home, all dead.

All dead? said I. But I didn't see a single one.

He looked to one side, then to the other side, and he looked behind him as well. When he made sure there was no one around, he went to the back of the truck, lifted a corner of the dark green tarpaulin and, looking back, said to me, See here.

I was on my tiptoes and I craned my head. But I managed to see only a spread of darkness in that instant in which the corner was lifted. Judging by the waviness of it, one would assume it was a stack of bodies even though I did not smell a single smell of bodies.

Afterwards, I left the mountains and went home in a truck through the dust storm raised by the other trucks.

祖

I must say this authorial invitation extended to a character did not seem to work, for two reasons, one that memory is not trustworthy as, in most cases, it turns into a mound after years of wear and tear, and mental weathering, not to say emotional, as what was the hardest hit the mind tends to forget the quickest, and the other that the 'I' that is the character is often not a very good writer and the story coming out of his or her mouth is often not very well embellished, meaning not 'literary' enough, in the words of a German reader I once came across.

Instead of expanding or embellishing Zu's own story after he came back from death, I thought I might just let it stay as it is till edited or revised. You never know what might happen later on; you might even cut the crap by half.

祖

But he came back one night in my dream and says to me: You are such a liar. I don't blame you for writing my story in the first-person narrative, not even in the second or the fourth, as long as it sounds real. And when your imagination runs its course, you just need to relax and sit back, doing nothing as everything will happen by itself, like right now when I enter your mind.

I stopped dead in my writing tracks, listening to him giving me a talking-to, my tongue so tied I could not find anything to say. I just listened as he related his story.

祖

I would have been 15 or so when Mum's colleague, a soldier-like man, commented on me by saying, 'The boy is so shy; he looks like a girl.' Another uncle, also Mum's colleague, commented on the quantities of food kids like us could consume. This was a northerner and he said in a typical northern accent: '*Ban da xiaozi, chi si laozi*'. To this day, even after I died 40-odd years ago and have learned a dead language, that of death, a language no one living would want to learn, I still find it hard to translate into proper English. Literally, it means 'A half-big little man will eat (to) death an old man.'

The meaning, though, is clear enough to this writer, as it means that a boy in his mid-teens could consume so much food that his dad would die of hunger with no more food left to eat.

At the time, I was with Jan, the youngest son of Mum's old friend Mother Zhou. He was about my age but much taller than me and whiter, with eyes twice the size of mine. But when I made the remark that he'd make a handsome film actor in the future he got upset, more so than I had thought he would be. He hated my guts for saying it. He never told me why he hated the idea, nor could I guess where this disgust with a performance career came from. But we kids were like that. We hated playacting of any kind, and found it unnatural. Intolerably sissy. When we were herded together in military forms in middle school in an auditorium to watch the performance of revolutionary songs and dances in celebration of Party's Day or National Day, we would make vicious comments on the girls and boys that appeared in it. We found them ugly, to say the least, with a propensity for obscenity the way they moved their bodies so close together. Sure enough, a girl in our class fell in love with her art teacher and they made love underneath the stage in the auditorium so many times that they were caught in the act one night and were expelled from the school.

Jan came to visit me from time to time when I was with Mum before going to the Three Lines and would sometimes stay for the night. This was in a huge building of many storeys, made of dark green granite, that people said belonged to the foreigners in the past. Mother said it was one of the foreign settlements by the Yangtze; could have been the German or the English ones. Mum's headquarters, or the headquarters where Mum was working, was based there. Jan was my only playmate. To while away our time, we'd race upstairs to the top floor, making noise that echoed in the hall, mostly unoccupied. Or we'd lean against the tall and large window, looking at the narrow street down below with people shrunken to the size of ants. This was right in the centre of Hankou where traffic was busy day and night. On one occasion, the whole city entered into a stage of alert as part of a campaign aimed at getting rid of the mosquitoes across the city. What they did was block all the sewer outlets, light a fire with poison in it and, in a couple of hours, when the smoke carried through the entire sewage system, the mosquitoes were killed to the last one. Jan and I were watching from a window how the city was shrouded in a bluish smoke and we were amazed that, afterwards, not a single mosquito was left to bite us for nights on end.

And, on another occasion, a number of criminals, on their way to the execution ground, were paraded on a truck through the city centre. Each one of them had a long strip of wooden board on their backs, the piece of board sharpened in the shape of an 'A' at the top and painted white, with large characters written in black top down. One was an 'Active Counter-revolutionary' and another a 'Murderer'. As the Liberation truck went down the street, people crowded and thronged to see them. I was watching from the window, so all I could see was a sea of black-haired heads and the pieces of white wooden board on these condemned. Jan went there by himself and came back to report that one of the guys was actually happy as he was laughing, with no tears on his face. He saw how the guards behind him twisted his arms so hard that his face twitched and distorted in pain, but he could not make a sound because his mouth was gagged with a dirty piece of rag.

'It's awesome,' he said.

When he gave that description and said the word 'awesome', Jan was in a bath with me and we were both naked. Darkness was falling. The dark-green granite walls were around us, hard and cool. A shaft of waning light was struggling through the tall narrow windows. All was quiet. Only the leaking water in the pipe somewhere down below. The two naked bodies were soaked in the lukewarm water. Jan had sunken into a semi-stupor, not aware that I was gazing at his penis and, as I was doing so, an expression, often used in the math classes, 'the lowest common denominator', came to mind. I smiled at the expression and reached out for it with my hand.

Jan instantly drew back as if my hand was a snake. Stop that, he said.

Stop what? said I. I didn't do anything.

I saw your hand coming.

I was just comparing.

I know yours is bigger but mine is not bad, either.

How do I know? As I said so, I recalled how I had masturbated in the past and swallowed my own cum. But he was not the one to reveal that secret to.

Can you do me again? Jan said as he further relaxed himself, extending his arms outside the tub and stretching his legs past my head to reach beyond the tub and hold against the wall, his tiny denominator hidden amidst a black grove of hair.

The warmth of the water did not seem sufficient to induce an erection. But I rubbed it till it took on the look of a bullet and swelled. Never as proud and virulent as my own but nevertheless filled a half-handful.

As I kept rubbing it, my own subsided to a shrunken fist of flesh, and, as Jan uttered small cries of moaning, I went faster till the thing exploded, ejaculating stuff that was white, sticky and slimy, much resembling that streak of something curly in the egg white, oozing out of the egg yellow.

Watching Jan's closed eyes and distorted face, I stood up, weary and disgusted. I towelled myself dry and went away, leaving him enjoying himself in the after-taste.

Chapter 7: Jianhua

What Zu forgot to mention was the fact that he had actually spent nearly each and every summer in Hankou, during the Great Proletarian Cultural Revolution, when he was a boy of forbearance. I say this because I know that while he was walking with Uncle Zhang on their way to the railway station, on a scorching afternoon, his face was sprayed with the saliva coming out of the uncle's mouth whenever he coughed and spat. They were walking side by side, he on the leeside, the left side of his uncle. When Uncle Zhang, a habitual smoker, cleared his throat ever so often and spat, the wind would blow it his way, spraying Zu's face with shards of the spittle. The little Zu said not a thing. He did not even frown nor did he ever raise a concern asking the uncle to stop spitting. Squinting his eyes in the sun, he simply wiped his face clean with the overlong sleeve of his blue hand-me-down coat. Nothing he was wearing was not hand-me-down; this included his trousers and shoes; they were over-large on him and were patched up here and there. That did not make him ashamed of himself; instead, it did him proud. On this occasion, though, he wore better clothes, still hand-me-down, that had the least number of patches, because he was going to spend a summer holiday in Hankou with his Guma, his father's sister. Uncle Zhang said, What does your Guma do?

Buzhidao (don't know), said Zu.

And your Gudie, Guma's husband?

Buzhidao.

You've got to learn not to have three don't knows for one question, cursed Zhang as he spat.

Zu looked up at him, wiped a tear of a spittle from his eyelash, and kept his mouth shut, wondering nevertheless how much longer this was going to last. But Uncle Zhang went on, Your concerned mother entrusted you with me and asked me to take you there. She's also concerned that you might make trouble. Nowadays there's trouble everywhere. Big trouble.

He spat sidewise just as a wayward wind blew across. Zu's face was sprayed once again, even though he ducked, but not in time to dodge it. He wiped it and Zhang went on, The two groups are fighting with each other tooth and nail. Many have died. This is why your mother wanted me to take you to Hankou, to just escape all that violence. It's sheer pandemonium. And you have got to be careful when you are there. Avoid the bad people. Be good and listen. Always listen to the adults.

Zu listened and kept wiping the drops of phlegm off his face. He said not a word but just tagged along, watching with more interest how the local porters flew down the slopy roads, pulling their long hand-held carts, loaded with goods piled up like small mountains. The roads were uneven, mostly flat but sloped in places. They would start like in a racing match, speeding up as they ran, till they built up enough inertia when they literally flew, their feet off the ground, and the hand-held carts behind them acting like an engine, propelling them forward headlong. And as they did so, they yelled out in a long series of war cries full of excitement and pleasure. This was a sight that never ceased to please Zu, whenever he went through the river town by the name of Echeng on his way from the ferry to the railway station.

祖

Guma's was a family of five that lived in a spacious *yanglou*, a Western-style building, in Chezhan Road, or Railway Station Road, formerly known in its two sections as Rue Clemenceau and Avenue de Marcilly in the days of French settlement more than a century ago. The Dazhimen Railway Station, first built in 1900 and one of the oldest ones in China, was on its Northwestern end while the Yanjiang Dadao, the Riverside Avenue, inside of the embankment on the Yangtze, was situated on the Southeastern end, with Zhongshan Dadao, Sun Yat-sen Avenue, cutting right across Chezhan Road. This was one of the busiest areas in Hankou, a city of commerce and industry, second only to Shanghai in importance, with five foreign settlements, the French, the English, the German, the Russian and the Japanese going back as early as 1861. It was awesome for Zu to set his eyes, for the first time, on a city of sun, colour, people and noise, with streets that seemed to be pouring traffic in all directions, day and night.

The dinner he had the night of his arrival was one that made him as uncomfortable as the spray Uncle Zhang had made over his face, but in a different way. Guye, his paternal aunty's husband, was strict enough. He stopped him talking as soon as they sat down around the table, although Aunty was kind enough to offer a placating smile. Zu's face turned ashen, realizing that he must have made a mistake, but did not know why he was in the wrong. He could see that everyone was lowering their heads and was saying something in a low voice. Without knowing why, he followed suit and also lowered his head. But he looked sidewise either way and saw the moving lips. He wanted to laugh but, remembering Guye's stern face, he held his lips tight. Then they started eating and that's when he found he had much less freedom of movement or that of choice than at home. The eyes that looked at him were not encouraging. The chopsticks he was holding in his hand were suspended in the air more often than put down in any particular bowl until he no longer knew what to do, to stop eating altogether or wait for Guye to give the order as to which dish to go for first. This torture was over when he rose as he put down his chopsticks and the empty bowl and when everyone else seemed to heave a sigh of relief. It was not till then that Aunty began picking a piece of fish from a bowl of dish half-finished and put it over the rice, also half-finished in Zu's bowl.

After dinner, he was introduced to the boys, the one with a monkey-like face called Bi De (Peter) who grinned at him, revealing a row of pointed teeth, and the other, a tall, handsome but silent fellow by the name of Lu Jia (Luke) who left as soon as he said Nihao, and the third one, the youngest, a boy of thirteen by the name of Jianhua, Building China, who scowled at Zu, with thick lips hanging out of his mouth, from which was oozing something shiny. Instead of saying 'Nihao', Jianhua scowled and growled at Zu, making him frightened. Just as he was turning to go, Jianhua made a sound from his oozing mouth that sounded as if he was asking where Zu was going and who exactly he was. Bi De giggled and said, He's uncle's son, from Yuwang Town.

Where is that town? Jianhua demanded, deep from his throat.

Zu was about to open his mouth and say something when Bi De winked at him to stop and said, It's a town on the Yangtze.

Town on the Yangtze? What's that mean? said Jianhua.

A town on the Yangtze is a town on the Yangtze. Nothing more, nothing less, said Bi De, spreading his arms wide, palm-open.

Out of the corner of his eye, a timid Zu saw that Jianhua wasn't happy with the answer. He stared at Bi De, making a strange noise akin to the barking of a dog. And the way he stared was almost as if his eyeballs might roll out of their sockets any time. Bi De pulled Zu to one side and said, Let's go back to our bedroom.

祖

A few days into his living in Chezhan Road, Zu found his paradise, right in the middle of Zhongshan Dadao. Every morning, at about 9 o'clock, a water truck would come down the street, sprinkling water in a spray of white misty rain as it sang the melody of the song, 'The East is Red and the Sun Rises.' Zu, leaning over one of the short, fat stonewalls that separated a row of street-side columns forming a long shopping corridor, watched as he listened to the music. As soon as the water truck turned up, he could see street urchins show up from nowhere. And they ran after the water truck, getting themselves wet in the spraying water, unlike the pedestrians who would dodge it this way and that, the second they heard the upcoming music of the song from the truck. There seemed so much fun in running after it than dodging it, Zu thought.

The next day, he went up there early after breakfast and waited. There were people coming and going in the roofed shopping-corridor by the side of the street. Most of the shops were not yet open. Outside the columned corridor, Zhongshan Dadao was busy with traffic. A smell that had recently become familiar to Zu rose, attacking his nostrils with a mixture of morning heat, domestic sinks of washed-down food waste, pungent pong of *matong*, horse-barrels or night-soil buckets, filled with piss and shit, and that of an occasional sharp smell generated by the friction of the wheels of a car or a truck on the road, as it came to a sudden screeching stop, as well as the incessant dust that was raised from the asphalt road. When the water truck came, all this would change. The world became cleansed, the road turning blacker with the water, and the air devoid of anything pungent or putrid. As he sat there watching and brooding, a shrill voice called, Come on!

He turned and looked. A boy, about his own age, but much thinner, came running, right in the middle of the road. He was half naked, wearing shorts, red shorts, and he was followed close at heels by the water truck that sang and sprayed, scaring people away in all directions except the red shorts boy. Because the water truck went at a slow pace, making sure it cleaned up all the spots where its sprinkling water could cover and reach, the boy took his time, turning around to face the truck, with both his arms raised, in a triumphant gesture that seemed to say to the driver: Come on! I dare you to run me over!

The truck seemed blind, bent on its purpose of doing the daily cleaning job for the city streets, taking its time, too, as it went down the street. The boy then deliberately slowed down and went to the side of the street, not far from where Zu was sitting, in time for the truck to go past him when the water from the side of the truck hit him on his naked chest, then the back, with a sharp flapping, spluttering noise. Then he was in the shower, running in the shower and chasing after the truck in the shower, till he was tired and drenched with the morning truck rain when he came back and, eyeing Zu, said to him, in the local city accent, It's just fantastic.

Really? said Zu, in a voice that imitated his accent.

Xie, let's assume it's Xie, immediately sensed the difference, not just from the accent but also from the manners and the way Zu was dressed, and said, You from the country? Where?

Zu looked at him. A fish of a boy with the eyes of a fish, too. Zu didn't say a word. He just stared.

Xie didn't push him for an answer; he'd already got the answer. And he said, Can you join me in the fun next time?

So it was agreed that they meet the next morning at the water truck time.

祖

Back at Guma's place, Zu's life was less happy. Uncle had a stern face. He was critical of nearly everything Zu did. Zu was bad-mannered; he didn't address people properly; he didn't even address people. He had only one thing to praise and that praise Zu could remember even in his old age, while he had forgotten all the bad things Uncle had ever said. According to Old Zu, Uncle once remarked on Zu's ability to organise his own clothes by putting them in a neat pile, saying, This boy will have a neat, organised future. Whatever that means, I don't know. But when I checked with him, Old Zu refused to be drawn out.

Lu Jia, the older cousin, also had an unsmiling face, like his father. He hardly ever said anything to Zu, apart from a 'nihao' in the morning if he happened to see Zu and another 'nihao' in the evening when they met for dinner, which was rare.

Bi De was home much of the time. Zu found him likeable because he was someone he could approach and tell about his own problems, e.g. his rhinitis. Bi De, on learning that, grew very concerned and said, That's no good. Then, with a roll of his eyes, in which Zu noticed much white, Bi De said, I know a way to treat this. He then lowered his head and whispered into Zu's ear. At the time, both of them were lying on a bamboo bed, out in the courtyard in front of the house, half naked, with only shorts on, enjoying the cool after the dark. As he listened, Zu was ashamed that he had a hard-on because his lying body was so close to Bi De from behind. He immediately withdrew to the edge of the bamboo bed till he felt safe and the erection subsided.

What Bi De told him was, Go and smell your own shit in the toilet. The more you smell it, the better you'll be treated. Because the way Bi De said that was utterly serious, no suggestion of even a smile on his face, and because he was a few years older than him, Zu regarded him as a big brother and trusted what he said. Subsequently, he carried out the experiment. When he shat, he lingered and smelt hard what was generated from his own shit. He felt better. His nose no longer itched. It didn't seem dry anymore. But, after a few attempts at it, his doubts grew for he could see that Bi De was a man who could crack a joke without smiling, as if he were talking about the most serious matters in the world. Although he never told Zu what he had suggested was a mere joke, Zu had worked out for himself that he must have meant it for a joke, not to be taken seriously. Besides, the smell of shit was good for a change, but was not sustainable. One would have had to make a strenuous effort in practising it till one was convinced that he had somehow cured himself of the condition. Such was not part of Zu's temperament, as he soon grew out of this adopted method of treatment.

Bi De, more approachable than either Lu Jia and Uncle, was certainly much less aggressive than Jianhua, for Jianhua would often throw tantrums for no reason at all. When Zu came home late for lunch after wandering around the block, drenched to the bones, Jianhua, looking at him in disbelief, would yell at him, Where have you been? What have you done? How dare you do all that without letting me know?

Zu, frightened, stood near the entrance, hesitating, not knowing whether to enter or run away. But he met Jianhua's eyes and saw that they were glazed, lusterless, his growling only a threatening sound. Emboldened by the discovery, he went in, almost on tiptoes, sidling along, ready to turn and run if he saw any attempt on Jianhua's part to attack. But Jianhua's bark was worse than his bite, as he stared at him and kept staring as if his eyeballs couldn't roll of their own accord. Then, he did something that shocked Zu.

Jianhua had been holding a broom in his hand, like a weapon, which he now released his hold of and let fall. As he did so, he loosened his trouser belt. The next thing he let fall was something that caught Zu totally unawares. It was Jianhua's dick, which he exposed on full display for Zu's view. A gleeful giggle emitted from Jianhua's mouth as he saw how horrified Zu was, as he quickly retreated into the darkness of the hall. The ugly sight of Jianhua's dick left such a bad taste in his eyes and his mind, that, for days subsequently, Zu never saw Jianhua without thinking of his flaccid hanging cock along with his grinning, agape face, and he lived in constant fear of him doing the same to him again. To prevent from being caught sight of again, Zu would sneak out as soon as he had breakfast, often before Jianhua got out of bed, and, no sooner had he gone out of the forbidding premises of the red-brick walls and the foreign façade of the house where he shared accommodation with the family, than he would be out on the street, at large with himself again.

On the other hand, he was uncomfortably sympathetic to what he would regard as pure misery that Jianhua was living. The bib he wore was forever wet and slippery with his saliva that kept oozing out of his twisted mouth, from which an indistinct babbling sound would issue. No one knew what he was talking about when he opened his mouth, from which a string of unintelligable words rolled that hardly made much sense. Though he was limited in his ability to produce meaningful speech, his mood swings were unmistakable to anyone present. If he was angry, he would yell. If he was unhappy, he would yell, too. But if he happened to be pleased, which was rare, he would chuckle to himself and didn't seem to enjoy sharing it with others. On one occasion, when he saw Jianhua pleased, Zu also felt pleased, so much so that he offered a smile to him, only to be rejected with a 'what-the-fuck-are-you-doing' rebuttal in the form of a howl. Quickly, Zu hid himself away and ran out onto the street, coming back only when he made sure that Jianhua was not seen anywhere, probably in one of those epileptic fits again that Zu witnessed, in which Jianhua was lying on the floor, wriggling in pain, his mouth ringed with a white foam.

祖

It was on a clear autumn morning that a stranger whose face was familiar to Zu came. When told it was his Dad, Zu refused to acknowledge it. He had grown so used to the life here, the freedom to roam the streets in the neighborhood, the acceptance by Bi De, a serious joker of no smiles, the rejection by Jianhua who had never chatted coherently with Zu on anything so far, and the curious recognition by Uncle impressed with Zu's refusal to let the cleaning maid in the house put his pile of clothes away in a closet, that he refused to go. When Dad, the stranger in a pair of leather shoes whose yellowness offended Zu's eyes like something so pretentious, pulled Zu to him, meaning for him to go, Zu pulled the other way. And, in that instant, there was an audible click somewhere in the arm, Zu's arm. Later, when he was taken to a local doctor, it was found that his arm was out of joint.

Chapter 8: The Zhou Family

Sandeli was a neigbourhood where Mother Zhou lived. As far as Zu knew, she was Mum's best friend. Whenever they went to Hankou, Mother and Zu would stay in Mother Zhou's place. Even though it was dark, narrow and small, cluttered with things, and meant for living by no more than one person only, her family of five happily lived together there, with a constant source of immense warmth and friendship. Uncle Cao, Mother Zhou's husband, worked in an antiques shop in the middle of the city. Mei, their daughter, and Kang and Jan, their sons, spent most of their time at school. Mother Zhou was the person who would wait and wash and cook and pick up after them. She was a large woman, with a broad face and heaving breasts. She smoked with Zu's mother, also a smoker, while Zu, unable to sustain an interest in their endless conversation about the kids, their school, Uncle Cao's constant back pain, Zu's father's regular need for an operation on his bladder cancer, and numerous domestic matters, would go out the door, turning left, through a dark hallway, with a hole in the corner where the cluster of families living in the same building would wash their clothes, their vegetables and their night pots, out by the main door, into a lane that led to a wider lane where, if you turned right, you'd walk a few metres right into the busy traffic on Jianghan Road but for the inverse U-shaped iron bar that served as a stop to the pedestrians. That's where Zu would spend much of his day, loitering and watching.

He'd sit there alone, on the iron bar. It was cold. Soon, it grew warm underneath his bum. People walked to and fro. Cars, trucks and trams streamed past him in both directions. Bicycles wove through the traffic and the pedestrians. He watched but his eyes were unfocussed. In the eyes of the pedestrians, this was just an urchin who had nothing to do. Only he knew that he had no one to play with. At night, it was better when Uncle came home from work and when Mei, Kang and Jan came home from school. At a time when television was non-existent, there was little to do after dinner but sleep. In a room where everyone slept— Uncle Cao and Mother Zhou in one bed, Mei in another, and the three boys in a bigger bed—the only thing left to do was tell stories. After the first few nights, Kang, whose broad face took after his mother and whose familiarity with the ways of the world took after his father, recognised the ability in Zu to tell stories. As soon as they got washed, the three boys, always the first, would creep under their quilts, lying side by side, and Zu would start telling stories, mostly from the books he had read. He would skip the plot by plunging right into details. He had just finished reading a Russian novel, titled, *yongan*, or *Courage*, and was absolutely blown away, particularly by Dong Ni Ya, possibly Tonya, a girl who grows up living in a toilet, goes on a long-distance train to Siberia to join the others in a Communist Youth League City, falls in love with Sergie, and gets spurned by him but, inadvertently impregnated, carries his baby.

What sort of a girl is that, living in a toilet? said Jan.

She's poor, you know, said Zu.

Oh, yes, said Kang.

You are not interested, said Zu.

I'd rather sleep; I'm tired, said Kang.

What happens? said Jan.

She's a very bad-tempered girl and she's a loner, too, said Zu.

Bad-tempered? I don't like bad-tempered girls, said Jan. But is she pretty?

Pretty? I don't think so, said Zu. According to the book, she doesn't seem a pretty girl. Her whole family is living crowded together in a corner of the toilet. People pay no attention to them. When she grows up, she is ignored and laughed at. Then this Sergie seduces her. For some reason, she is described as a woman full of anger and coldness. But then she is seduced.

I know girls are like that. They pretend to be cold; they assume a wooden face. But their hearts are full of hot desire. That is why when a handsome man appears on the scene, they get seduced, said Jan.

Listening to Kang's snoring getting louder and louder, Zu said, That's kind of true. As he said, he thought of Mu, the fat girl in his mother's unit who'd never see him without trying to accost him and get close to him; even when they sat together, she would edge for physical closeness that would invariably make him uncomfortable and try to move away.

Did you read that book? said Zu.

What book? said Jan.

The one your father hid away in a box that I found?

Not that one, said Jan.

But it's an interesting one, said Zu.

Interesting? I didn't see anything that was interesting, said Jan. It's just a boring medicine book.

No, it's actually not, said Zu as he whispered something into Jan's ear, in no time setting him laughing out loud.

Don't make such a noise, boys, said a voice. It's from Uncle Cao, Jan's father. The old man coughed and said, Kept awake by the two boys talking.

Soon enough, the two boys fell asleep. For a long time, there was only the traffic from Jianghan Road outside.

祖

The household had a newcomer shortly after the arrival of Zu. His name was Ding Gong. In one glance, Zu took him in: a country yokel who could hardly speak a word in the Wuhan dialect, the urban speech. The dialect he spoke was the Guangji variety that no one in the Zhou household could understand except Uncle Cao, because Ding Gong was one of his nephews. Hardly anyone paid attention to him although Kang, Jan and Zu were all kind towards him. Zu offered him a smile; he smiled back and said something that Zu could not understand. Kang and Jan exchanged a glance and smiled, too. At dinnertime, Zu noticed, out of the corner of his eye, that Ding Gong ate in total silence, his head lowered, raised only when spoken to. But it all sounded like mumbling, hardly intelligible. At night, while Zu was telling stories to Kang and Jan, Ding Gong lay in a makeshift bed next to them without a sound. Zu had a terrified feeling that he was dead, so in the middle of one night he tiptoed to his bed and stood listening. There was absolutely no sound. It was almost as if Ding Gong wasn't there. In the total darkness, Zu could barely make out the mound that Ding was. He held his hand out to where Ding's head was supposed to be lying, to test if there was any breathing, when a figure rose out of the depths of his bed, like a ghost, with a shriek that woke Kang and Jan up. Zu stumbled back into his bed and he crept under his quilt, trembling all over.

Shortly after, Ding Gong's condition got worse. He refused to speak. He didn't look at anyone. Zu found it hard to catch his eye. When he tried to, Ding Gong simply turned his head. There was no way turning his head back like one does to a globe. He might fly into a rage. His gloomy face resembled a burnt-out light bulb, darker by broad daylight. During the day, he slept, refusing to rise even for his meals. But at night he stayed awake, not reading, as Zu would do during the day or part of the evening by a lamp. Ding Gong would just sit there, his knees drawn up, his face between them, with a vacant look on it. No one paid any more attention to him, a lump of flesh in the darkness. But his condition got Mother Zhou worried. Time and time again, Zu saw, she went up to him and talked to him in a quiet, gentle voice, one that Zu was jealous of, because she never spoke to him like that.

One night, after Kang and Jan were asleep, Zu overheard a conversation between Mother Zhou and Uncle Cao about Ding Gong's condition.

Was it because we didn't treat him well? said Uncle Cao, in a very low voice.

I don't think so, said Mother Zhou.

He didn't seem like that before, and as far as I know, he seemed always happy in his village.

I'm beginning to wonder if the contrast between the city and the village is a shock to him, said Mother Zhou. Because I notice he has grown less and less happy. He's not even smiling anymore.

He's such a strange boy, sighed Uncle. I don't understand what happened.

I'm wondering if it's because he found us too rich for him, said Mother Zhou.

Oh, no, cut in Uncle and said, but our own life is no better than anyone else's. It's no cause for concern.

Well, actually, I think we are not doing badly, said Mother Zhou as she dropped her voice to a low pitch, so low that Zu could hardly hear anything anymore. Then a heavy drowsiness fell upon him as he drifted away into sleep.

祖

Back in the school and this was the first Diary Display Day. Master Peng was tall and gaunt, with a face full of smiles when he set his eyes on some of the pretty girls in the class, but that turned dark when he saw a few unruly boys, particularly Zu, who had been known for his argumentative manners and unpredictable tempers. He had been spotted wrestling with another boy during recess, only to be wrestled down on his back, on the ground in less than a minute, and he had been reported to be wasteful with food and not admitting his sin; as a result, a class-wide criticism had been initiated of his wonton behavior, prompting him, the headstrong boy, to write a self-criticism as well. Mr Peng, however, was so pleased with the quality of that piece that he read it aloud to the rest of the class as a typical example of good writing, despite his concerns with the boy's reported behavior and his other acts of rebellion, including that of talking back when a teacher made negative comments. Mr Peng liked his writing more than his person and, because he was a fair-minded teacher, he never let an opportunity go without demonstrating it, when he saw that there was worth in a student's writing. A month after he had assigned the students the task of keeping a diary in a notebook they were urged to buy, he collected them and read them. Once again, he was impressed with Zu's writing, so much so that he decided to launch his first day of diary display, prominently featuring Zu's diary along with a number of other good ones.

It was in fact more a one-class affair than a Day. But it was overwhelming for Zu as he could see that his classmates, boys and girls, were crowded around the rostrum before the blackboard, one girl literally picking up the diary and starting reading, her head bent over it, as she turned the pages. It was a pleasing sight as he knew in one glance that this was the most reticent girl in class. In all the group discussions he organised as the *yuwenke daibiao*, the representative of the Chinese-language classes, Zu had never for once seen her open her mouth. He had wondered why. But he dared not raise a question although he did, on a number of occasions, raise his brow. Indeed, he once ventured a mild criticism, aimed at her, without mentioning her name, saying, While everyone has spoken, there's still someone who seems to refuse to say a single word.

All eyes were directed towards this girl, whose name was Yingying, and who hung her head even lower after the remark was made, appearing submissive but one suspected that it was more stubborn than demur. The grey of her khaki clothes seemed suggestive of a deeply buried anger, ready to burst out, but that escaped Zu's notice.

Chapter 9: Keeping Watch at Night

Chinese New Year's Eve, when Mother Zhou's place was deserted. There were only three people: Mother Zhou, Uncle Cao and Zu. The fire was lit, on which sat a wok of boiling oil. From a large bowl, Mother Zhou took a handful of minced meat, mixed with chopped ginger and water chestnut, among other ingredients, and she, through the hollow formed by her holding hand, squeezed one meatball after another, which slipped silently into the wok. The balls sunk to the bottom of the clear, boiling oil, and came up to the surface in no time, with a sizzling noise and a mouthwatering smell that drew attention from Zu, whose head was bent over a book.

Would you like to have one? Said Mother Zhou.

Yeh, said Zu, his eyes fixed on the bobbing and rolling meatballs in the oil, having removed themselves from the page he had been reading without understanding.

Are you still preparing for school? Uncle Cao asked with concern, Still early days. No?

If it were his own mother who had said this, Zu would have turned away in disgust. But Uncle was kind. His voice was soft. And he was caring in his own nonchalant way.

No, said Zu, it's just a book I'm reading but don't quite understand.

Have this one, said Mother Zhou as she picked up from the oil a big round meatball turning brown and put it in a small white bowl. Mind the heat.

Before she finished her words, Zu had already picked up the ball and put it in his mouth. The second he did so, he 'ah'ed, and spat it out, his lips and the tip of his tongue scorched instantly. All eyes were focused on the ball that was rolling and kept rolling till it stopped under a table. While Zu was agonised over the pain caused by the scorching ball, Uncle lost no time in retrieving it from under the table, took it in the hollow-heart of his hand, blew the dust off it, wiping it clean with his fingers before putting it in his mouth. Zu could see his mouth extended with the ball in one cheek before it returned to its original shape.

祖

'If you keep going you'll see the Tong Renxiang, or the Bronze Statue, in front of you, in the middle of the road when you reach Liuduqiao.' The message, from Mother Zhou, kept repeating itself in his mind as Zu, warmly wrapped up in a cotton coat, went along Jianghan Road. It was dark. The streets were lit up in patches. A cold wind was blowing. There weren't many people on the street. Those who were out were walking in hurried steps as the festive occasion gave them an urgency of homecoming. Soon, the street, otherwise busy with traffic and pedestrians day and night, was becoming deserted. Zu kept walking, his thoughts full of the Bronze Statue and the family near it where Jan, Kang, Mei and the rest of the extended family were enjoying the Shizitou, or Lion-heads, a delicacy, among other things. According to Jan, this was very tasty. Whenever he talked about it, Zu felt jealous because he had not had it before. On one occasion, he even took to laughing in Zu's face for not having had such a simple thing that they would eat on a daily basis, when in fact it was only on Chinese New Year Eve that they would have their once-in-a-year opportunity to have a taste of it. With that in mind, Zu walked in more brisk steps, the image of a lion's head somehow interconnected with the head of the bronze figure of Sun Yat-sen, the figure standing on a pedestal, dark with the passage of time, used as a road sign to point out the way.

As he kept going and thinking these thoughts, he was haunted by a feeling that something might have gone wrong somewhere, and he became hesitant. This sense of hesitancy did not stop him in his tracks. Instead, it kept him going, stopping from time to time to observe the surroundings. The streetlights, like the occasional flowers in a field, dotted here and there, seemed to grow dimmer, until the traffic became almost non-existent. 'All gone home for the Big Dinner,' thought Zu, 'and yet, I was walking further away from home. "Further away?" "Further away from home?" My home wasn't here. My home was elsewhere. I was going to Mother Zhou's extended family, with her mother and father, and her own kids.' But the bronze figure was nowhere to be seen.

And there was no way to call Mother Zhou to tell her where he was and ask whether he'd been walking in the right direction in an age devoid of electronic devices. Zu's sixth sense or the seventh was starting to tell him: 'Turn back. You have long gone past the crossroads where you need to turn.' Prompted by that warning sixth or seventh sense, Zu, for the first time, stopped.

Something touched his face, cold and windy. It felt like a raindrop. It wasn't wet. But it was warm. Felt warm. And seeped into his skin instantly. 'What is this?' He wondered, as he raised his head and saw a sky of insects, falling like shadows of flickering lights. In a moment of bewilderment, he thought that he had returned to the summer when the air was alive with the *liangliang chong*, light light insects, or the fireflies. But this was winter. It dawned on him that these were snowflakes that were falling. They were emerging from the dark depths of a vast sky, flickering and swaying as they fell, lighting up instantly in the sparse streetlights and disappearing the second they touched anything, from the telephone poles, the tree leaves, the branches, to the pavestones on the sidewalk. They were delightful to watch and exciting to taste. He was actually sticking out his tongue to receive the wayward flakes that seemed to refuse to accurately land on the tip of his tongue. When he finally caught one, he was thrilled with its instant taste of tastelessness that tasted like the very taste of melting.

He turned back from the darkening street with millions of *liangliang* insects flying above his head and around him, and retraced his steps all the way back to Sandeli. By the time he arrived 'home', Mother Zhou was astonished to see a fat walking snowman standing at the doorstep and cried out in a voice that was quite touching, What happened? Come in quick!

Chapter 10: The Book

When everything is as it is, as it is seen around one, can one move beyond the mere seeable and feelable, twenty, thirty or even forty years ahead of one, when nothing seen now is in existence any longer? Can one dream a dream that far down the track, even long after one dies? That was one of the thoughts that frequently occupied Old Zu's mind. If he could deliberately dream a dream fifty years ahead of time, he'd have done so without an effort, long after Mum was gone, as he was doing now.

He has arrived at the compound of the Bureau, encircled by a row of dormitory flats on one side and the two-storey building of offices on the other, facing the staff canteen across the compound. Nothing seems to have changed in nearly half a century except that the place is overrun with people, people sitting around their tables and eating, people whose faces show no sign of recognition as he threads his way through them till he's blocked by another eating crowd. Unable to move ahead to the corridor that leads to his home, he raises his eyes above the crowds in the direction of the well, from which water had been drawn in a pail to cool a watermelon down on many an occasion in summers when he was little. There is a gap and he heads for it, managing to get through.

The darkened room looks all grey. A figure sits there with its face turned away from him. He recognises straight away that it's his mother. And he can sense that his mother is aware who's behind her. But she seems determined not to turn around and say anything to welcome him back. The grey light that suffuses the tiny room, Zu can see, is coming from a hole-like window in the wall. But she's eating, in silence, sitting upright. He starts wondering aloud if he can have something to eat, too. Without a word, Mother passes a large bowl to him. Instead of waiting for him to take it in his hand, she puts it on a wooden board his head high. When he reaches to pick it up, he can see that nothing is left in it except the colour of soy sauce in patches that have stained the inside of the bowl. He wonders if he should go and wash it. But he's afraid that Mother might be offended by this unfilial act. His mother mutters something under her breath, too faint to catch but loud enough to detect that it's a complaint. He says nothing, having learnt to say nothing in her presence, particularly when she is cross. He says to himself: Can I take this and get a meal? His mother turns around, the dream instantly shattered there and then, into unrecognizable and unrememberable fragments that remained impressions not even words could depict.

祖

The book was huge. It weighed like a pail of well water with a watermelon in it. Zu had to hold it in his arms when he went to his bamboo bed under a vertical trellis for grapes that stretched from one end of the compound to the other over a passageway. There, he would lie down on his belly, his head lifted above the book, turning the pages. It never occurred to him how this book had found its way into his hands. All he knew was that it was a gift from his grandmother, his grandmother living with his uncle somewhere in Liangdaojie Street in Wuchang, *jie*, street, pronounced 'guy' in the local lingo, a bit like the Danish word 'gade'. We'll have more to tell about him in Denmark forty years after. Right now, he was lying there, head over the book, his little hand turning the pages, reading with concentration. A Shushu who happened to come by—there were a lot of Shushu who came and went by his bed—would stop and ask with concern, Won't this hurt your eyes if you keep them so close to the pages? He would ignore that and keep reading, absorbed. Other kids, like Jian, Hei and Qiao, would cluster around him and ask him questions, their black-haired heads around him, trying to peer at what he was reading. But they couldn't make head or tail of it. The pictures, though, were what interested them, pictures, drawn in black and white, of an emperor riding a chariot, followed by a large entourage of richly dressed officials and court ladies whose looks were gorgeous, of dragons and phoenixes, and of soldiers with swords and spears charging into the enemy ranks, also armed with swords and spears, all on horseback, trampling the corpses under foot.

When the summer vacation was over, this book was put away and stored somewhere on top of a stack of firewood and *fengwo mei*, honeycomb coal briquettes, in a corner at the end of the dark corridor, soon forgotten. The bookish 'Big Head', a nickname given him by the boorish Qiao, a playmate who, often silenced by Zu's knowledge, was known for his rough ways of manhandling the kids outside the Bureau and coming out the winner, would be seen walking side by side with the latter to school. But an argument soon put an end to this. Just as he walked down the steps in front of the Bureau at the main entrance, with a schoolbag on his shoulder, Zu saw Qiao approaching him.

Can we be friends again? said Qiao.

Zu looked away, didn't say anything, still feeling hurt.

When Qiao repeated the question, he simply said, 'No' and went quickly down the steps, leaving Qiao bewildered and shaking his head, sighing audibly.

It was all on account of an insinuating remark Qiao had thrown his way the other day about Zu's mother being a 'landlord's daughter' when they were both fishing on the Yangtze. This hurt Zu's pride very much. He knew his mother was not born into a landlord's family because he had heard her mention that she was a city girl who had suffered a lot in the early days. He knew Qiao said this because he was proud of his own father's revolutionary heritage as someone who had fought the Nationalist army in the mountains in southern Hunan, even though he had been a poor peasant turned bandit before that. As time went by, Zu's number of friends decreased. He no longer spoke to either Hei or his older brother because of the former's bullying and the latter's physical assault in that kicking incident. He resented the big and stout Two Dragons, a nickname given to an older boy for the excess amount of snot hanging out of his nostrils, in the shape of 'two dragons', who held himself superior to Zu because of his calligraphic skills that Zu was found lacking in. The other smaller kids, like the Guo brothers, Zu had little interest in. He found them a nuisance and once even came to blows with them both on a hot summer day. He was wearing shorts when the younger brother jumped at him, slapping hard on his naked back. He was so angry that he rushed back into the dark corridor, grabbed hold of an iron paperweight and rushed back as he threw it towards the older brother. Big Guo ducked for cover so that the flying object hit hard on the wall, missing him by the inch; both quickly ran off. Afterwards, when he thought of what had happened, Zu broke into a cold sweat. If the paperweight had hit Big Guo on the head, he would probably have been killed instantly.

This boy, the mother realised, had been a social misfit right from the start. Zu was independent, that's for sure, but he was willful. He always must have his own way or else he'd throw tantrums. When Chen Ayi, from across the narrow aisle, commented that he seemed behaving well lately, Mother was not so sure because she knew in her bones that the boy would only be peaceful with a book in his hand. Once he was with his playmates, he'd invariably get into an argument that led to the breakup of their relationship. Seeing his friends leave him one by one, she grew concerned. But when she conveyed her concerns to him, the boy would simply say, 'Why would I care? It's not my fault.' This stung her so much that she said, 'If you behave like that, you'll remain friendless till you are utterly alone in the world.' Zu retorted, 'If it's utterly alone, it's utterly alone. Let me be. I'm not afraid.'

Although Zu's mother knew little of what psychological and emotional change the boy was going through, she suspected that this might have something to do with the arrival of Lijiao, Chen Ayi's younger sister, a wisp of a girl with a strong will.

Zu had learnt how silence could be used as a weapon against a mother's authority by watching Lijiao behave. He and Lijiao never spoke, even though they were door to door across the narrow aisle. This was a glum girl, hardly ever smiling, easily given to outbursts of temper. On many an occasion, she would storm out of the door and stand in the empty bath shack, where male stuff members and their boys would have bath in the evening on hot summer days. When Aunt Chen went over and tried to persuade her back by pulling at her arm, she wrenched her off with a toss of her head, refusing to speak, refusing to move, her whole person a pillar of staunch silence. Chen Ayi came back, forcing a smile at Zu as she went by, who stood aside, watching, and as he watched he could see her two prominent *huya*, tiger-teeth or canine teeth, standing out, with much of the red gums exposed. Instantly, the boy got the hang of it and began to somehow admire the girl's negative strength. By not speaking, not moving, not eating the meal prepared, she had her own way till Chen Ayi buckled under her will.

There's nothing I can do about him, said the mother when she was sitting in Chen Ayi's room, chatting with her as she always would whenever there's something that troubled her. He's so stubborn.

I think it's fine, said Chen Ayi.

You do? Why?

Think of Lijiao, my younger sister, said Chen Ayi. When she was here, she was full of tantrums, refusing to eat and to help, getting upset at the slightest provocation. I dared not scold her. I dared not even laugh because she'd get hurt, thinking I was scoffing at her. It was probably because it coincided with a time when she had her first periods, so she's moody and all that. But she's better, much better now at handling her own emotions.

Does she? said Zu's mother.

Oh, yes.

I'm wondering if the boy goes through a similar period to the girl's. He's often agitated, and restless, like he's having a period.

Ha, ha, ha. You think?

I'm serious. You know how it's like. The boy has nocturnal emissions. I notice them and wash them ever so often. Although I never say anything, I did once tell him not to play with his little thing.

Did he listen?

Or perhaps he didn't do it deliberately.

He can't help it, I guess.

He hardly ever listens.

Or he does but he doesn't show it, you know. Boys will be boys.

No. But he's not like the other boys and he fights with them all the time. Then he deserts them. Or they desert him.

That may be because they like to tease him and irritate him.

That's true, too. The boy's simply too bookish for their liking.

He'll grow up one day, like Lijiao.

How's she doing these days?

Thus, the conversation went on.

The only friend Zu had, though, was Luo, a thin-faced boy from an adjacent province, now living with his uncle as his adopted son because his uncle and aunt had no children. One day, Zu went to seek him out in his room, really a room with a bed and a table. But he was not there. He knocked on the door. There was no sound from inside. He knocked again and listened. There came a creaking noise from within the room, the creaking of a bed as a body turned in it. Then a sleepy voice said: Who's that? But I'm asleep now.

'Asleep?' Zu repeated the word as a smile stole to his lips. If he was asleep already, how could he be talking? If he was talking, he's not asleep. So weird. When he told his friends about this little incident, they all burst out laughing. One said, This guy must be talking in his sleep. Another said, He's very funny. A third said, No but it's just his way of not wanting to see people. Despite what they said, Zu liked Luo all the more for it. He told Mum about it, too, wondering if he could invite him home. Mum immediately said, But you like the ones like that, don't you?

What did you mean? said Zu.

The kids who follow you and listen to you, said Mum.

But that's not true, said Zu, tacitly agreeing with what she said but refusing to see the truth.

You fight all the time with other kids who belittle you or tease you. Is that right?

Zu fell silent, resentful. He went to his can of worms, a used milk can in which he had put a chunk of earth and kept a number of thin red worms that he had found outside in a corner, in the wet shade of the bath shack. These came handy whenever he felt like fishing. Mum watched the boy pick up the worms one by one and wrap them up in a piece of newspaper. She said, 'Are you going fishing again?' The boy, bent over the can, did not reply. She said, 'But each time you come back, you get nothing.' Again, no reply. Mum went away, muttering to herself, 'Don't know what's the matter with this boy.'

祖

The summer morning was fresh. It was a Sunday. No one around. Only two boys sat on the edge of a lotus pond, fishing, each with a large lotus-leaf on his head, shielding him from the glare of the sun. The pond was thick with lotus-leaves, large and small, large over small, and large and tall. Dark shadows were everywhere under the bright sunlit leaves. The water underneath was cool, clean, with an occasional 'tsip', 'tsip' of a fish coming up for air before it quickly disappeared. The two boys, Zu and Luo, sat apart from each other, each intently watching their floats. While Luo was a novice, Zu had learnt a trick or two. If the float started bobbing, he would hold his breath and his rod, not lifting it for fear he might scare the fish off. He would only lift it if the float went flat, an indication that it was a *jiyu*, or crucian carp. But if the float suddenly went down, it would be a big-mouthed catfish with whiskers that swallowed the worm, hook and all, and you only had to lift your rod to get it. He knew all this, but he lacked patience. It was always too early or too late, not least because he had also brought a book with him. The book lay at his side, unread. It was always like that. When he went out, he'd bring a book, whatever he could lay his hands on, but forgot to read or had no time to read it.

Luo, on his part, wasn't particularly keen on fishing. He just went along because Zu had asked him. Indeed, the latter had insisted on it, saying all the good things about fishing, when Luo said, I know all that. I probably know more because crucian fish are good for postnatal women when they need milk to suckle their babies. Before he could even finish his words, Zu took hold of his hand and dragged him along, protesting and blabbering. But Luo did not have the slightest idea of how to even fix a hook with a worm wrapped around it, with the tip of the hook going all the way through the body of the worm without breaking it in half, not even after Zu showed him how. He managed to break a few worms into pieces and, picking up a fat black worm, he said, I'd just use this one. In one glance, Zu knew that it was not the right kind of worm for the crucian fish, and he would never catch anything in a lotus-pond with that. But he said nothing and went on to get his own ready before casting the line and hook into the clear water.

After a while, Luo got bored, his eyes tired from watching the unmoving float for a long time, and he found the sun too hot for his liking. He literally gave up when he grabbed hold of the unread book, lying close to Zu, and went to a tree nearby, to sit in its shade. A few pages into it, he found it hard to contain his delight as he exclaimed: This is a great book!

Zu immediately shushed him, saying, Don't be so loud. You'd scare all the fish away, his eyes fixed on the bobbing float till it popped up and went flat when he lifted his rod with a quick swishing sound. But there was nothing, only an empty hook, the worm gone, eaten whole by the escaping fish. Zu got upset and said to Luo, just do your reading quietly and don't disturb me anymore. Luo looked up from his book, remotely and resentfully, but didn't say a word. What he found interesting was the bit about a king in ancient China. This king was born into a very poor family that decided to drown him then and there because they couldn't possibly afford to raise him. Just at that moment, an old aunty came and saved him by taking him out of the water. He thus earned a pet name, called Poliu, or Aunty Saved. He looked up from the book spread open on his laps and looked towards Zu, intent on his rod under his large lotus-leaf hat, wondering aloud if it was time to go home for lunch, not aware that he had meanwhile caught two crucian fish, each about an index finger long.

As they walked home together, he started talking about Poliu when Zu cut him short, saying, I know all that. In fact, I know more. This Poliu, when he grew up, was often seen in the shape of a huge lizard in his sleep, ablaze in a red aura. Observing this, a fortune-teller said that he would have a great fortune and future down the track. Sure enough, he ended up becoming a king.

When the boys arrived home, Zu's Mum laughed and said, Just as I have predicted. But she made busy preparing a lunch for them two, cooking an aluminum pot of fish soup after cleaning them up, with the roe and maw in it. When it was ready, the soup was white like milk and tasted wonderful. Zu's mother sat watching the boys eating, feeling happy and content.

祖

The big book disappeared without a trace when the Cultural Revolution came. When his Mum was away at work on a Sunday, Zu looked everywhere for it in the tiny little room. He opened one leather suitcase after another, three of them, all stacked one on the other in a corner, between the big bed and the wall. They were full of clothes. Decades after, a similar thing happened. In a shack outside the main house, also in a corner, in another country, where Old Zu was living, tens of thousands of miles from his native country, there were a number of carton boxes containing books, one of which had letters from his mother. In preparing to write a novel, I asked him about these letters, written to him while he was in the country. But, according to him, the letters were nowhere to be found. Eventually, when he had to give up, he could not forgive his memory that he had kept a bunch of Mum's letters, so vivid and tangible he could reach for them any moment should he need them. While the suitcases returned no big book of his, it was a memory that came haunting him, of a story Grandma had told him. When the Japanese bombed Hankou in 1944, a man caught fire in the street where she lived. She saw him jumping up and down, wrapped up in a fireball, till the fire swallowed him up and reduced him to a skeleton in a pool of cinders.

But is there anything he could do to save himself from that? said Zu.

Oh, yes, Grandma said. Instead of jumping up and down, he should have rolled on the ground. A few rolls and the fire would have been put out.

Little of Jiajia, Homehome, or Grandma, was made known to Zu, whom she called by his pet name, Binbin, except that she had moved from Kaifeng to Hankou after the death of Grandpa. According to Mum, she was a woman particularly picky about the things she ate. She didn't touch mutton or beef. She preferred pickled vegetables to fresh ones. She

74

ate congee instead of steamed rice. In fact, she loved books more than food, her highly myopic eyes with an old-style glasses further proof or a direct result of it. Apart from that, if there was anyone she liked best it would have to be Binbin, her step-daughter's son, a wild boy with a curiosity for knowledge and a passion for books. When she decided to give him that book as his 10th birthday present, she had hoped that he would grow up a scholar like her dead husband who had died of starvation, living as a village scholar writing letters for the villagers and helping them understand the written deeds or contracts. She was pleased to receive a short letter from the 10-year-old, thanking her for the 'big book' that he couldn't understand much of, and she hoped that the boy would be one day become a truly knowledgeable person despite what her step-daughter had said about his temper tantrums and being a social misfit.

There was a story that she told, in her heavy Henan accent, from that book, titled, *Sanyan Erpai*, about a bad boatman on a river, working with a mute pole-man. One day, this boatman met two passengers, a man and his wife, and got it into his head that he'd somehow get rid of the man and make the woman his wife, so he asked the man to come along with him to cut firewood in the mountains. When they both carried a pile of firewood on their backs and came down the mountains, he saw his chance and took it, raising his axe and hacking at the back of the man's head till he fell dead, covered in blood. He went back and told the man's wife that they had encountered a *Dachong*, Big Insect, or a tiger, on their way, and it took the man's life, while, fortunately, he managed to escape. The wife refused to believe him, saying that she wouldn't believe it till she would go back and find her man's bones. The boatman, as a result, had to retrace his steps with her but he took a different path till they encountered another Big Insect. Instead of attacking the woman, the tiger set upon the man and ran away, with the back of his clothes in his mouth, to enjoy the man as his evening meal. When the woman came back she saw something blocking her way. It turned out to be her man, who was bloody all over and seriously injured, not dead yet. She heard his story of attack and took him back to the boat. It was not till then that the mute pole-man started opening his mouth and telling them how wicked the boatman was and how many bad things he had done. As soon as he finished, the pole-man shut up, going back to his former self.

The core story, of how a tiger could single out a bad man to eat was as impressive as mysterious, not least because of the fact that the mute man could tell his story and go back to being mute again. Such power of storytelling stirred up a desire to tell his own stories one day. But life in Zu's mid-teens had suddenly changed with the arrival of the Revolution. There were no more classes as the Gongxuandui, Workers' Propaganda Team, entered into his school, and became the substitute teachers, teaching the students to do the farm work or factory work. Instead of studying the textbooks, the students studied Mao's Little Red Book, of which every passage had to be memorised. They had to do Zao Qingshi and Wan Huibao, asking for instructions from the great Chairman Mao in the mornings and reporting to him on their own daily conduct in the evenings, for days and weeks on end. They had to receive education from the peasants, workers and soldiers, who formed part of the Workers' Propaganda Team, and worked in the factory workshops, in the rice paddies, or training on the sports ground like soldiers. If he was physically weak and bad at doing physical labour, Zu had shown that he was adept at writing about these experiences as part of the writing assignments set by his teachers.

Meanwhile, he was turning rebellious and the first person he rebelled against was his own mother.

Chapter 11: Down with Mother

Not long after Lijiao, to whom Zu had never spoken a single word, only aware of her rebellious silences, went back to Wuhan, Zu began acting strangely, in his mother's eyes. He had few words. Or he said nothing. When Mum asked him to do this or that, he'd just do it as if he had no problems. But Mother could see that he was not willing. He didn't smile, his lips pressed tight together, tighter than when his father once saw him when walking together down the street. Apart from not saying more than necessary, he had an ulterior motive of his own. He had bad teeth, so bad that they were ugly to look at, with his front teeth large and protruding, something that he was never comfortable with. When he looked at the photo he had taken with his dad, in the local photographer's studio, he felt ashamed of his looks, his eyes half closed, his big teeth exposed, hanging outside above his lower lip, standing beside his dad like a simpleton. Unhappy with his own teeth, Zu, throughout his teens, developed a compulsive need to smile as little as possible, speaking only when absolutely necessary. And he went further by trying to hold his upper teeth with his lower teeth, hoping to somehow pull them back, an exercise he practised daily when he was alone, till one day when his mother said to him, Why, but yours has turned into a *wa kozi* face.

According to Old Zu, this expression, a local one said in the local dialect, was hard to explain. The closest match would be the word 'concave' as in 'concave mirror'. After that explanation, I now understand that Zu's mother actually talked about a concave face when she referred to it as 'a wa kozi face'. Formerly a round moon face, and now, a concave face, which came as a surprise to her. Zu shut his mouth and didn't say a word. Instead, he turned away in disgust, pretending to be upset, to the chagrin and puzzlement of his mother. He, too, saw the difference in a mirror. His chin seemed to have become slightly extended. And if he looked at his own profile, he'd see his face in the shape of a crescent moon. And he blurted out, without knowing what he was doing, I hate myself! I hate myself! I hate myself! No one had heard him talking like that. But the seed of self-hatred had sowed itself, embedded in a corner of his mind and heart. How long would he have to live with those teeth like that? A lifetime of big ugly teeth? The thought was scary enough for him to recall a conversation he had had with other kids in his little room. Hair said, There's a guy who goes into a bathroom and shuts the door behind him. One hears him brushing his teeth but, at the same time, he is also whistling. Guess how he manages to do that. Zu, along with the other kids, couldn't work it out despite their many wild guesses till Hair said, It's such an easy thing: He removes his false teeth, brushing them and whistling at the same time. No one believed him, least of all Zu, because, not having seen such a thing, he refused to believe it possible. A heated argument ensued amidst heavy smoking till Hair said, Not only have your faces all smoked yellow, but the light bulb seems to have turned yellow, too. Zu could not suppress a smile when he raised his head and saw that the bulb was indeed quite yellow around midnight.

If he hated himself for his own teeth, no one else seemed to take notice. Among his classmates, no one was perfect. Huang was too fat. Jiang was slit-eyed. Xian had lips like two horizontally placed fingers and his brows were like that, too. Wei was the opposite, his brows and his lips as thin as the blade of a pencil-sharpener. Flat Head got his name because the rear part of his head looked as if it had been chopped off. Hua's face was shaped like a gourd. Xu walked with a limp. Tu's head was so big he looked like a walking head. Hei had a tongue too big for words. When he was struggling with putting words one after another in a clear order, he was described by some as speaking with a carrot in his mouth. Zu had a big head, too, and went with the nickname Big Head where he lived. But no one called him that at school or was even aware of it. He knew, though, that his mother didn't approve of his looks. She had literally said that she wished he were a girl. She loved his white creamy skin, putting her head down on it, touching it with her cheek and kissing it, uttering small sounds of 'Umhmg mmfg'. But Zu hated it, more and more so as he grew older, with the Cultural Revolution turning headier, involving the old and the young. By now, he had long forgotten one remark quoted by his father from *Shenyin yu*, or *Words, Uttered in Moaning*, a book written by Lü Kun, a Ming-dynasty writer, which goes, '*yi wuxin wei nei, ze wushen yi waiwu ye*'.[1]

What did that mean? said Zu.

If I regard my heart as internal, then even my body is a thing external, said Dad.

What does that mean? said Zu.

Well, paused his father before he said, trying to put it as simply as possible, a heart is all one has and the most important thing. In that sense, even one's body is secondary, something that can be discarded, as long as one keeps one's heart whole.

Zu thought of it long and hard after that. But he could only grasp the meaning in terms of his own physical appearance, his looks external, discardable, but his heart internal, always there, more important than anything else outside, eternally hidden, untouchable and who knows if the heart is not also the mind? How can one be sure? When he thought of this, Zu had an enormous admiration for Dad who seemed to have a ready answer for everything. When he was little, Dad had got him to read a classic story, which was succinct and easy to understand. But the meaning was completely lost on Zu. If something made no sense, Zu would simply dismiss it as unimportant, not dwelling on it, although Dad insisted that it was a wonderful story about human cruelty. When I asked Old Zu what exactly the story was, he said he could not remember and all he could ever remember is the fact that it's a story about a brother planning to kill his own brother and succeeding in it to secure his place as a king. It took years, according to Old Zu, for him to understand the message but by then he had lost the plot and the story.

In Zu's father's few visits to the town where he and his mother lived, Zu would chat incessantly with his father, about anything and everything. He once even told him of his meeting or failure in meeting with Luo because of his excuse that he was sleeping, and that's when Father quoted a poem in English by a poet by the name of Walter de la Mare as he said, That's exactly what the poet wrote in the poem,

---

1 See Lü Kun, *Shenyin yu*(《呻吟语》). Shanghai University Press, 2012 [1593], p. 46.

The Listeners[1]

'Is there anybody there?' said the Traveller,
Knocking on the moonlit door;
And his horse in the silence champed the grasses
Of the forest's ferny floor:
And a bird flew up out of the turret,
Above the Traveller's head:
And he smote upon the door again a second time;
'Is there anybody there?' he said.
But no one descended to the Traveller;
No head from the leaf-fringed sill
Leaned over and looked into his grey eyes,
Where he stood perplexed and still.
But only a host of phantom listeners
That dwelt in the lone house then
Stood listening in the quiet of the moonlight
To that voice from the world of men:
Stood thronging the faint moonbeams on the dark stair,
That goes down to the empty hall,
Hearkening in an air stirred and shaken
By the lonely Traveller's call.
And he felt in his heart their strangeness,
Their stillness answering his cry,
While his horse moved, cropping the dark turf,
'Neath the starred and leafy sky;
For he suddenly smote on the door, even
Louder, and lifted his head:—
'Tell them I came, and no one answered,
That I kept my word,' he said.
Never the least stir made the listeners,
Though every word he spake
Fell echoing through the shadowiness of the still house

---

1   See the poem here: https://www.poetryfoundation.org/poems-and-poets/poems/detail/47546

From the one man left awake:
Ay, they heard his foot upon the stirrup,
And the sound of iron on stone,
And how the silence surged softly backward,
When the plunging hoofs were gone.

See, said Dad. That's what I was reminded of when you knocked on the door. Zu said nothing, so awed by this strange poetic experience that he wished he would one day do the same.

祖

With the arrival of the Cultural Revolution, even the English classes were turned into shoutings of slogans and proclamations of love for Chairman Mao.

Repeat after me, said Mr Wen, a teacher of English, long live Chairman Mao!

Long live Chairman Mao! echoed the students, in voices that didn't sound very much like the real English.

Now, pay attention to the correct pronunciation and repeat after me, said Wen. Long live Chairman Mao, the great mentor, the great leader, the great captain and the great steersman!

This time, no one could follow him, not even when he wrote the words down, on the blackboard as 'The great mentor, the great leader, the great captain, the great steersman, long live Chairman Mao!'[1] No one, that is, except Zu, who not only pronounced each word correctly but also said the whole thing without stop that the others found breathlessly difficult. Wen was so impressed that he gave Zu 100 out of 100 in the final term examination, with four sentences required to be written in English, the two above and two more, including 伟大，光荣，正确的中国共产党万岁！万岁！万万岁！ (*weida, guangrong, zhengque de zhongguo gongchandang wansui, wansui, wanwansui*), which literally means, Ten thousand years, ten thousand years, ten ten thousand

1 See the slogan here: https://library.ucsd.edu/dc/object/bb8977365r

81

years to the great, glorious and correct Chinese Communist Party! But Zu rendered it as 'Long live the great, glorious and correct Chinese Communist Party!'

When Zu showed the results at home, his dad shook his head and said, This is terrible. How can they possibly do this? This is not English. This is just slogans.

Shush, Zu's mother said. Don't be so loud. You will be a bad influence on the boy if you keep saying things like that. Turning to Zu, she said, But you've done an excellent job.

Zu wasn't pleased; he was pleased with his mother but not with his father. He knew Father was right. But his non-praise left him disconsolate. What would he have done to win praise from the old man? It was easier, he found, for a woman to please and praise although Mother wasn't like that, as she would always encourage him to do better, criticizing him only when he did wrong, sometimes very harshly, so harshly that he would argue with her and talk back. She was mostly concerned with the boy's growth and health problems, particularly his asthma and rhinitis. She laughed out loud on hearing the boy talk about Bi De's treatment. But she advised that the boy needed to use the nasal drops on a daily basis, which would stop the itchiness. She cautioned him not to pick his nose so often, least of all pulling out his nose hairs, saying that it would cause bleeding, even brain damage. When the boy lay on bed, having an asthmatic attack, she lay by his side, listening to that whooping noise in his throat, sounding like a saw sawing through a rock, or a cat constantly purring, as one of her colleagues jokingly put it, and feeling the boy's pain as if it were her own, without being able to do anything except pat him on the back and coax him to sleep, hoping the sleep would ease the pain of breathing.

The boy tried hard to sleep but couldn't, his asthma rolling him like a wave, grilling him like a fire, kicking him like a football, suffocating him like a heavy wet blanket. He was this reed, drifting on a lotus pond devoid of any lotus flowers or leaves, on a desolate winter day, through a gap in a fallen embankment, into the wintry Yangtze till he was engulfed by the brown waters that came rushing downstream. He was down in a cave, a bottomless one, climbing downwards along the trunk of an ageless tree, into the cold abysmal depths. Were the voices he heard those of apes or snakes or tigers? He was plunging into them, headfirst, like a fish. It was not the blood-flooded street he was running along in his early childhood nightmare. It was a different world altogether, a world in which he was the only one left, going on his solitary journey, unaccompanied. When he woke up, he found his mother asleep, her arm across his chest, and, gently, he removed it and fell back into sleep again.

祖

In the heyday of the Cultural Revolution, when everything seemed possible, cutting classes, storming a school library to take the books for one's own possession and/or selling one's own books deemed dangerous at a cheap price at a paper recycling station, Zu did things that he would never have even dreamt of doing. He poured a bowl of hot water onto a feeding pig in the bureau's pigsty and was thrilled to hear the pig shrieking until he was mildly reprimanded by the toothless chef Zhou, who said, Boy, you should never have done that.

Why, said Zu. It's just a pig.

It's not just a pig, said the chef. It's human; it's like a human. And it feeds humans.

Even when he ignored that remark, Zu remembered the pitiful look the pig took at him and the awful joke that didn't work. He was swept by a feeling of guilt, mixed with sadness and repentance, only to forget it completely till years after when the chef's word sank in. But, shortly after that incident, he was plunged into another one in which he, instigated by Uncle Zou, found himself shouting a slogan that took him by surprise. It was after a struggle meeting in which Bureau Chief Wang, now a kitchen hand and general cleaner, was struggled against, with attendants shouting, Down with capitalist roader Wang! Down with his evil capitalist road practices and corruption! And down with his capitalist thought!

Now, said Uncle Zou. It's time you did something.

Like what? said Zu.

Do you dare shout 'down with'...?

Down with who?

Well, what about down with your mother?

Why, I am not afraid, said Zu, thinking of a motto Mao had said, which goes, *geming wuzui, zaofan youli* (It is not sinful to revolutionise and it is reasonable to rebel.)

Then, say, 'Down with Mrs Zu!'.

Down with Mrs Zu!, said Zu.

Say it louder.

DOWN WITH MRS ZU!

Haha, haha, hahahaha, said Zou. Well done. There's a good boy.

No one else praised Zu for his courage. Instead, people shot angry glances his way. Some shook their heads and others simply turned away in disgust. Sensing the antagonism, the boy left without a word, feeling somehow vindicated and cleansed.

As soon as Mother got wind of this, she said to Zu, You don't have to live with me if you don't want to.

Why? said Zu.

You know why, don't you?

No, I don't.

You really don't or are you pretending?

No. I never pretend.

Why did you say that?

Say what?

If you don't tell me honestly what you said, you'd better leave.

I didn't say anything. But if you want me to leave, I'll leave. You think I want to live with you forever?

As he said so, Zu made for the door. But Mother grabbed hold of his arm, wouldn't let him go. The boy turned around and hacked at his mother's arm, with the lower edge of his open right hand. Mother 'oh'ed, and said, 'Don't do that; it hurts. You know you are so heavy-handed.'

The boy broke free and didn't return.

祖

On the third floor of the building housing the bureau, there was a meeting room, which had fallen into disuse for a long time. It's a place Zu had rarely been to as it was very official, only meant for the staff. That night, after he refused to eat dinner and left home, pissed off, he climbed the cracking stairs, broke through the door and put a plank against it in case someone might push in from the outside. He was hungry. But he tried not to feel it. Instead, he paced, the way an adult did, from one end of the room to the other, around the tables put end to end in the middle of the room. When he paced back to the long bench against the wall near the door, he sat down on it, head bent low between his knees as a thought came to him: 'What if they can't find me?' For a moment, he was scared. Then he dismissed the thought. 'Didn't she say she didn't want me? Then she wouldn't have me and wouldn't want to see me.' He raised his head as his eye fell on a hole in the ceiling. Stuck through the hole was a wooden ladder rested on a table. He wondered why he hadn't seen this before. He stood up, went to the table and climbed onto it. Hesitating momentarily, and looking through the hole at a portion of the darkness outside, he was not sure what to do. Almost instantly, his mind was made up as he climbed the ladder, rung by rung, till he was half out of the hole, his head feeling as if it were swimming in the air. Up above, there was no cloud in the sky. Around him was a dark-red roof laid with large wavy tiles that spread all over the place. Down below, there must be the one street running from east to west but nothing could be seen from where he was standing on the ladder, half within, half without. Placing his hands on the outer edge of the hole, he raised himself up till he was completely out.

The wind that blew on his face was cold. But the feeling was free, that he was able to find his way to this height never reached before. He had to be careful because one slip underfoot might cause him to roll off the roof and fall down onto the street below. By now his legs were trembling so much, from both fear and cold, that he found himself squatting instead of standing. Down at the edge of the tiles, there was the gable with a gap in it. He moved towards it, bottom down, feeling it slippery. A sudden thought that the gable might collapse under his weight gave him such a fright that he decided to turn back, climbing, hands and feet, over the tiles till he reached the opening.

Something noisy caught his attention. It was the sound of approaching footsteps, and it must have been the people who were searching for him. He quickly came down the ladder, wildly casting around for a spot to hide. He made one decision after another: Not under the table, too easily seen. Not outside on the roof, too easily traced up the ladder. Not behind the door. Not even behind the heavy window curtain which didn't hide his feet. As he looked around, up and down, and everywhere, a smile came to his lips as his eye fell upon the space below the bench, large enough to cramp his little body in. When he crept in and curled up, he had peace of mind and he felt safe, but only for the moment. He felt exposed because one would immediately spot him lying inside the cramped space. There had to be something to conceal him from view. He crept out and found a piece of plywood from a pile of them in a corner. When he crept back in again, he pulled the piece towards him, like a makeshift windowpane, and made himself snug within the tiny space. He was trying to sleep but the approaching footsteps made it impossible. He was determined to stick it out no matter what.

Soon, the footsteps stopped outside the door. A man's voice was heard saying, Did you check in here?

No, came the answer.

Zu recognised from the voice that it was the good-looking moustached man who had a good relationship with his mother, often coming to their room for a visit. He held his breath and listened. There was a pause, in which no one spoke. Then a voice said, Where's the switch? A torchlight, turned on, was scanning the wall till it stopped, fixed on one place. Zu heard a click. But there was no light. A muffled curse. The swinging of the shaft of light from the torch. More swinging till it went up and fixed itself where the ladder was. A voice, Can he be outside there? Another voice: It's not impossible. A third voice, You go and have a look.

Then came a creaking noise as footsteps went up the ladder. A short while after, the creaking noise of the footsteps coming down the ladder, reporting, The boy wasn't there.

Where could he be then? A woman's voice, almost in tears. It's Mother's voice. Zu recognised it right away. Exactly what I wanted, he thought. I want to hurt, an inner voice said. I want to hurt badly.

The adults stood together, talking, and discussing what to do next, not far away from the plywood that stood beside Zu, hindering him from view. As they went away, conducting another search somewhere else, in the compound of the bureau, Zu was swept by a sense of triumph and euphoria. Suppressing a desire to shout in an announcement, 'I am here but you can't find me', he turned on his side, facing the wall, trying to snuggle up for a sleep. But he was prevented from doing so by thoughts of fights with his mother in the past, against her wanting him to behave like a girl because she did not have a girl, against her constant complaints about his answering back, about his untidiness, about his bad temper, which was actually an inheritance of her own bad temper. He wondered why she was always so quick-tempered. A word was wrongly said, and she would flare up. And she was stingy with her praise, too, hardly ever speaking highly of him in the presence of those critical adults, her colleagues, even when they sounded welcoming and encouraging. There were better mothers as he could see. Qiao's mother, for example, was a kind woman who would cook, do the laundry and be busy around the house every day without ever being seen throwing tantrums, without ever even complaining. 'But my own mother,' Zu thought, 'she's in many ways like a man, smoking cigarettes, chatting with her male colleagues and playing ping pong with them, even going away on business with them. She hates doing domestic chores. She wants me to do my own, folding my own quilt, washing my own clothes, doing my own dishes, and asking for street directions on my own, which I dislike most. She thinks I have too thin a skin. No guts. Knowing that I don't like to ask strangers for street directions, she insists I do, saying that I need to learn to behave like an adult. But what's that got to do with that?'

The more he was thinking, the more he wanted to become crazy, the way the girl next door did, the way Jianhua did, and the way Ding Gong did. If I want to be crazy, can I force myself to be crazy? He thought. He closed his eyes hard, so hard he saw stars sparking behind his eyelids, as he also tightened his fists till they hurt. But his head remained clear; he could hear silence around him, no traffic at this late hour of the night, no sound of anything. He opened his eyes and saw darkness around him. Wouldn't it be better if one went completely crazy, if one had no idea what one did or said, completely unrestrained by anything? Could he choose to go crazy like Hua Ziliang, the Communist prisoner in the novel, *The Red Rock*, who conceals his true identity and pretends to be a madman for twenty-odd years before he manages to escape? For what purpose? Just to escape from all the restrictions Mother had been placing on him?

While wishing to go wild, he didn't forget to pull himself together in an effort to fight against the cold. Curling up, he drew into a ball, in a fetal position, wondering what to do next, and finding that he was actually wanting to be found out. If he stuck out to the morning, he would have to creep out and find some food. Then, only then, he would have to go home again as he always did, having nowhere else to go. He thought of Jian's strange stubbornness in refusing to leave after he had been beaten up by a boy next door, sitting in front of the boy's dormitory, with a big stone in his hand, vowing to brain him should he dare come out; Zu ceased to show interest after a day or two, but Jian was still there, himself almost turned into a rock to which no one paid any attention.

Hours went away. It must be past midnight now. No one seemed to care, and it was care that Zu found himself hankering after. He had lost track of time and had thought the day was about to break when the footsteps came back again. All his senses were keyed up. The footsteps were now becoming louder and louder, with a sense of urgency, but no accompanying voices. Pure footsteps. For a moment, Zu thought they were first raindrops, raindrops that were hitting the roof. But they stopped abruptly outside the door. He waited, with abated breath. The door opened as a shaft light directed itself straight towards the plywood by his side. In that instant, he knew, the game was over. A man came over, removed the plywood and said, That's him there.

Zu crept out, stood to his feet, his head lowered, avoiding the torchlight, and acting as if nothing had happened, while the man, along with the search group members, said not a thing and quickly left. In that instant, a fleeting thought came to him: They must have all been exhausted.

Chapter 12: The Foreign Ship

Xanadu loomed large in the distance after the rain, a huge one in the eyes of Zu, huger in Jan's eyes, something neither of them had ever seen in their lives except in pictures or the movies. The place was Yangluo, a town on the Yangtze, where the river bent in a circle as it winded its way eastward, forming a natural river harbour. It was well-known that corpses of people who had died upstream would float down and concentrate here because a perennial whirlpool here sucked all the bodies in and threw them up onto a sandbar, where they piled up and rotted away.

There was not a single body that could be seen when they arrived. The sandbar was a stretch of brown lying between the bank and the flowing river, dotted with ships at various stages of undressing, a word that came to Zu's mind when he set his sights on them and that he shared with Jan, who ignored it as he was absorbed in the daunting look of the ship. When Kang wondered if they'd like to climb up on board, Zu jumped at the idea. But Jan hesitated. He stared at Zu running towards the ship across the strip of the sandbar and stop at the lowest rung of the rope ladder, raising his head to look at the bottoms of Kang halfway in the air beside the huge body of the ship, he himself resembling a tiny dot against the faint pink of the lower part, normally under water, now exposed in its full time-bleached glory.

Kang had reached the top and had climbed over onto the deck, waving to Zu and Jan for them to follow him. Zu got his hands on the rope ladder, his right foot on the lowest rung, when the ladder started swaying from side to side, so much so that he could not hold it steady. He stepped off and stood aside, looking up helplessly at Kang at the top.

When you climb the ladder, don't look down. Look up. Always look up no matter what, said Kang.

Zu did so this time and felt better, climbing up one rung after another, stiffening himself against the swaying. The higher he climbed, the easier going he found it. When he reached the top, he looked down, forgetting what Kang had told him. Instantly, he felt dizzy, so dizzy that his legs weakened and he was trembling all over, almost to the point of releasing his hands. It was at that moment that Kang took hold of his forearms, one hand each, and pulled him up on board. Zu fell in a heap on the deck but instantly stood to his feet, feeling quite ashamed of himself.

More comfortable now, and leaning against the railing, he looked down for Jan. But he, trembling a while ago, was nowhere to be seen.

祖

Kang had gone to a meeting with his mates about the dismantling work to do, leaving Zu on his own while advising him not to run around as the ship was a maze in itself, where one would easily get lost. Following Kang's advice, Zu went around the deck gingerly, admiring the funnel with a broad blue ring on top above a white building of four floors with many windows. There were no flags identifying the ship and even if there were, he wouldn't know what they stood for. He went to stand against the railing and had a look towards the river, but failed to locate the whirlpool where bodies were said to pile up. This section of the river, and from this height, was white and placid, running smoothly towards the East, unlike his hometown one that was brown and turbulent. Occasionally, he spotted something bobbing in the water. He thought he had seen a dead body but a workman who happened to go past him corrected him by saying that it was a river pig. A river pig? wondered aloud Zu. Can a pig swim?

It's not a pig in the pig sense, the man said, laughing, it's a river dolphin.

A river dolphin? As he watched the man disappear below the deck, Zu went to the other side and saw the town with its black-roofed houses, cut through by a long straight street that led to the green fields in the distance, fanning out in a landscape dotted with bright tears of lakes, meandering creeks, and trees everywhere. He got bored and thought of the hole through which the man had disappeared, as he went there and lowered himself by a ladder.

Along a narrow aisle Zu walked, looking from side to side as he went along past the crew's quarters. Through a round hole, he saw a tiny room with a double bed, with no bedrolls. He turned the doorknob. Amazingly, the door opened. His nostrils were met with a pungent smell he couldn't identify but that was evocative of a foreignness he had experienced when reading novels like *Oblomov* by Ivan Goncharov. Was this a Russian ship? A thought flitted across his mind. But the words on a glossy magazine lying open on the small table beneath the porthole didn't look like Russian because they were not the ones he'd seen among his father's dozen Russian books he himself had managed to sell at the wastepaper recycling station. Ignoring what he couldn't understand, Zu plunged into the magazine, only to find page after page of foreign words, with occasional pictures of cities and buildings standing in the skies and people with foreign faces nothing like those of his own people. Then he realised what the pungent smell was, as it came from a bottle that must have contained perfume, almost drained to the dregs, lingering in such a pungent way that he nearly fainted, for a brief moment, when the beautiful woman in that film came back in his mind's eye. Already, this created a double effect on him. While his little birdie was gaining an erection, his throat started making a whooping noise, first signs of another asthmatic attack. Quickly, he left the cabin and, standing in the aisle, he felt a shortness of breath and suppression in the chest. He was instantly disillusioned. How could one have lived in such a cramped space and set adrift in a sea, perhaps for days, weeks and months, without seeing the land? And such stinking perfume would have killed him more than once. He recalled the story his mother had told of a male colleague of hers who had a mysterious weekly asthmatic attack that not even his doctors could work out. When they eventually did, they found it irresistibly funny because the man met his girlfriend on a weekly basis and when they met his girlfriend would dress up and spray herself all over with perfume, which triggered his asthma attacks.

That story led to him recalling another story, told by Uncle Cao over dinner on a Spring Festival day that had impressed Zu in the moment, but that was soon forgotten, only to re-emerge with the perfume-induced asthma. According to Uncle Cao, a married man in his work unit had fallen in love with an unmarried woman, causing much talk behind their backs. Uncle Cao tried hard to persuade the man out of it and was convinced that he was successful because the man had nodded his approval to everything he said, to the effect that he could make his marriage last if he tried hard enough to solve the problems between him and his wife, and stick to her regardless for, after all, they had met, fallen in love and got married out of their own volition, not through arranged marriage. But, Uncle Cao said, his face written all over with despair and inevitability, that the man changed his mind after the talk, gained a divorce and married the new woman despite all the bad-mouthing among his colleagues and friends. Was there a moral? The moral, according to Uncle, was that a man and a woman will do anything they think right, regardless of whatever people say, even if they all think it wrong.

His wanderings below the deck, aisle by aisle, corridor after corridor, left Zu hankering after a life elsewhere, drifting around the world, beyond the familiar and the daily, into a world of unknown, so unknown he could never be reached again. Afterwards, when he shared the experience with Jan, the first thing he asked was, Were there beautiful women in the magazine you read?

What did you mean? said Zu, surprised.

I mean they say the sailors have all sorts of womenly things because they can't bring their own women with them out at sea and they have to somehow sate their lust.

You should have come up with me and that way you'll get an eyeful yourself.

But I wasn't particularly interested.

You what? You didn't have the guts.

No, that's not right. I didn't feel well at the time.

You think I believe you? said Zu, to himself at heart.

Instead, he said, Oh, that. Yes, I did see a woman's lace panty, a black one, along with a crumpled black stocking, just one, not a pair. Don't know what that's meant for.

Oh, I know, said an eager Jan. They must have used those to wank themselves with. How wonderful it would be to have those things handy. They are lovely to look at, aren't they?

No, said Zu. I didn't take a close look. But I found them disgusting, smelly even.

You should have brought a few back for me.

If you had had the guts to come up with me, you could have gathered heaps of them for your own use.

Don't say that, said Jan, annoyed. You should have kept an eye for me as a favour in return for Kang's kindness in bringing you here.

That had an effect of shutting Zu up, not wanting to say any more, although resenting it.

They were now lying on the bed together. A shaft of winter light struggled through the dirty window across Jan's pallid face that was wan and full of desire.

What? said Zu, with concern.

Can you do me again?

You get it off then, said Zu, with impatience, while patiently waiting.

When Jan stripped off his pants, his dick was exposed. It was tiny, the size of a pin, or almost, and cold to the touch. Soon, under Zu's dexterous fingers, it raised its head, to the size of a half-pen, and as hard. As he rubbed it up and down, Jan began moaning, his mind's eye bristling with virulence of images that Zu had brought fresh to him, fishnet tights that wrapped women's legs like slippery, smooth fish-skins, perfume that was so foreign the mere smell of it would bring on an erection, and those faces that were powdered and perfumed, white to the point of snowflaking. Then he came, uttering a delirious cry of ecstasy, and sat up, looking at Zu's fingers smeared with the sticky stuff. Then, he did something that took Zu aback. He grabbed hold of Zu's wrist and, pulling it towards his mouth, he began sucking the semen off his fingers, one by one, till all was licked clean. Then, without a word, he went outside to the sink in the dark hall. Zu heard the noise of water running and Jan's rinsing of his mouth. When he was done, he did the same, washing his sticky fingers clean, again and again.

Chapter 13: A Fish for the Father

Father was not far away. But he was never present. After Round Wind, the small town on the Yangtze, he was moved back, to a labour camp called May Seventh Cadres School in South Lake. Mother never visited him, either in Round Wind or in South Lake. She always said to the boy, 'You go and see him.'

But how? said the boy.

Bizi dixia jiushi lu, said the mother.

The boy knew that and he hated that. 'Yeh, the road is under your nose. So what? But I don't like to ask people. It's beneath my dignity to act like an ignoramus asking people, always asking people, for directions.'

Yes, the road is under your nose. If you open your mouth and ask, the road is right under your nose, too, said his mother.

This made the boy uncomfortable. If he was asked to do something against his will, he'd resent it and fight against it. But after that experience of escape and capture upstairs, he became wiser. He was mumbling something about the distance when Mother said, It's one hour or two on foot. Won't take long.

The boy packed things up in an old schoolbag of military green, with his toothbrush and toothpaste, a face towel, an enamel mug, and a couple of books, and went on his way. It was high summer. The cicadas were loud. And the road by the riverbank was dusty, one Zu knew by heart, that would lead to South Lake. There was an ox cart, piled high with rice straws, plodding along the road, followed by an old peasant. When he passed him, Zu thought of asking the man how far it was. But he stopped himself asking the question that he had been rephrasing in his mind a number of times, from 'Please can I ask how far it is from here to South Lake?' to 'Master, is it far from here to South Lake?' He hated all the formalities; he'd rather follow his own nose and go his own way. In the end, he overcame his shyness when he saw someone, another peasant, shouldering a hoe, going in the opposite direction, by saying to him, 'Please tell me if this is far from South Lake?' As soon as the words came out of his mouth, he regretted it. He should have said, What's the distance between here and South Lake?'

But the man's answer took him by surprise, *Yipao di*.

Yipao di? One cannon place? Vaguely, Zu remembered it was a reference to 10 *li*, or half a kilometer. But why a cannon? What has that got to do with the distance? And how far? Those were the days of nil telecommunications. He couldn't possibly check a map on his non-existent mobile phone, nor could he call home to find out; his mother wouldn't know anyway. His reluctance to ask people for directions may have predated the latter-day reliance entirely on one's own, assisted with the technology, easy even for someone in his early teens to use without bothering to ask anyone for assistance. Zu, though, had to live with the forced need to lose his dignity by asking.

Bareheaded, under the full glare of the summer sun, and without a bottle of water, he walked with an increasing sense of fatigue, wondering why it was taking this long. There was hardly any traffic. The dust, the sun, the road, and an occasional man or woman who happened to pass by, not even travellers in those days of little tourism, but people from nearby villages. A long embankment on his right separated the Yangtze River from view, and the willow trees on either side of the bank formed a roll of green smoke, extended far into the distance. On his left, there were rice paddies grown with long rice stocks ripening in a rich yellow, its scent carried in a breeze that was wafting in, a sight familiar enough to a boy born and bred in a country town. He walked for what seemed an hour or two before he could not resist the temptation to ask another peasant coming down the road.

Yipao di, the man said, without even looking at him before he went on his way.

Zu started hating the word 'yipao'. God, he sighed to himself inwardly. 'I've probably done two "pao" and there still is another "pao". Oh, I see. They must have meant the distance a cannon shot would cover.' He was pleased with this new discovery of what it must have meant, all by himself. But the ancient cannon could not have covered a long distance, as 5000 metres wasn't really far. Or was it? 'Wouldn't this take me into the night before I wasn't even halfway? I should perhaps never have set out like this in the first place,' he thought.

Just as he, tired and thirsty, was almost on the point of giving up, the scene changed as the road turned left and joined an embankment road across a lake. There were more people walking in either direction. Far in the distance, he saw the back of a girl walking. [I realise that I actually made a mistake because Old Zu, after reading it, said that it's not in summer that Zu paid the visit to his father but it was in the middle of a winter that he did that. I guess I may have put him in a summer because I happened to write about it in a summer, too, a Chinese summer more than a thousand kilometers away from his then home, even though I wrote it also by a lake. That somehow helps because of the reflections of trees and birds in the water. Would I care to revise it so it's winter instead of summer? I'm not sure. Perhaps yes, perhaps no. Or, perhaps let's put it this way. Educated readers may not simply look for a straight story with no reflections of another story that is wrongly told. And they may forgive mistakes made for the simple reason that no one can avoid making mistakes, particularly in one's teens when one is a mere wavelet swept hither and thither by one's emotions, or in one's old age when one's memory is but a hole in which nothing remains but slippery stuff that turns this into that and vice versa. Do we want something as perfect as the skeleton of a Marlin caught in the old man's skiff that is mistaken for a tuna by a female tourist? Can we possibly correct that female mistake? I'm sorry about this diversion and let's just keep following the narrative line no matter what.]

As Zu later recalled and told a friend, that experience of gazing at the behind of a girl walking in front of him gave him a rare insight, that even though the girl was in her mid-teens she looked like an adult, well formed and beautifully figured. As he went past her, Zu was deeply impressed. He didn't know why this was so, but he went on in a more brisk step. He felt warm and realised why he had constantly asked how far it was. He was tired because he had put on too many pieces of clothing, including a red woolen sweater that Mother had knitted by her own hand. He took that off by the roadside, and put it on top of the bag he was strapping across his shoulder. Just then, he thought to himself, I'm feeling hot. I'll wash my hands and pat my face with water, then wipe it clean off the sweat. So, he put down his bag, along with the red sweater, and, squatting, he put his hand in the water. He had hardly put out his hand than he withdrew it because, in that instant, he saw the back of a fish, a big fish, lying in the water motionless.

Holding his breath, he squatted and watched. The fish was in a small pool, built on three sides with concrete walls, with one opening that led out via a narrow water trough to a lake in the distance. Because the water was down, the trough was left high and dry, and the level of the water in the pool was low, with part of the dark-green back of the fish exposed, half sticking out of the water. Zu put his hands down into the water and, with an outburst of energy that came from he knew not where, he scooped the fish from underneath him, holding him, fish and all, in his arms, dripping. Curiously, the fish remained motionless till Zu relaxed his vigilance when it began flapping, moving in a violent manner that made it so slippery that it threatened to come out of his arms and did, falling on the dusty embankment road where no one was watching.

Zu jumped over the fish, much the same way a goalkeeper did in a soccer game, and got him in his arms again, his own face touched with a pinch of dust and a sensation of the cold fish skin. Because he wasn't able to cover the remaining distance, holding a fish in his arms like that, he decided to wrap it up inside his schoolbag, putting its contents on top of it and got on the road again.

祖

When he arrived outside the May Fourth Cadres School, Zu was tired out. Menfang, the doorman, went to inform Zu Sr. of his son's arrival. The first thing his dad said to him was, What happened? Why did you get yourself covered in dust?

Without a word, Zu opened his bag as he said, grinning, to his dad, See? A big fish.

His father took a look and grinned, too, saying, But where did you get the fish? Looks quite big.

He's dead now, Little Zu touched the fish and said, But he's quite alive when I caught him. Then, as if waking up from a dream, he wondered aloud, But where's my red sweater? It didn't take long for him to realise that he had lost it, somewhere on the way, perhaps where he caught the fish. But his memory failed him as no detail could exactly be pinned down to any specific incident on the road.

The May Fourth Cadres School wasn't exactly a school. Wikipedia makes this clear enough in an entry that goes,

> The May Seventh Cadre Schools (Chinese: 五 七 干 校) were Chinese labor camps established during the Cultural Revolution that combined hard agricultural work with the study of Mao Zedong's writings in order to "re-educate" cadres and intellectuals in proper socialist thought. In practice, they were closer to forced labor camps.

In Zu's day, one'd have to live half a century to learn what Wikipedia was. And when Zu was there, all he could see was a row of doors in a building of red bricks and red tiles. Behind one of these doors lived his father with a number of other uncles, in what was called *shangxia chuang*, up-and-down beds, or bunk beds, made of wood.

After Father went to the kitchen and asked the cook to make a soup of the fish, he came back with the boy and said to the man sitting on the upper bed mending his clothes with a threading needle in hand, The fish reminds me of a story.

A story? The man said without raising his eyes from the clothes he was mending.

Yes, Father said as he saw Zu lie down in his bed, without a sound. He went on, thinking he might be tired, about a man in an ancient pen-notes story telling of his own experience in turning into a fish and acquiring the freedom of swimming around like any other fish till he feels hungry, so hungry that he swallows a bait knowing there's a hook hidden inside it, when he is hooked and drawn up, taken to the kitchen, with his head put on the chopping block, despite his repeated attempts to stop the fisherman from chopping his head off.

Oh, the man patching up his clothes said. I seem to have read that story a long time ago. It's an example of reincarnation. But the man loves life so much he is reluctant to leave.

What's reincarnation? said Zu, in a weak voice.

For the first time, Senior Zu realised something had gone wrong. He turned around and saw his boy lie there, breathing with difficulty. His hand went instinctively to the boy's forehead and felt a rising temperature there. Leaning over the boy, he said, Are you all right?

The boy didn't say anything; instead, he turned his face to the other bed next to him, closed his eyes and fell into a sleep so profound that no one, not even his father, could wake him up.

When he did, near midnight, Father was still there, sitting on the edge of the bed, watching him.

He woke up with a smile, and said, What time is it?

Father glanced at the Enicar on his wrist and said, Oh, it's 11.38.

Then he said, How are you feeling now?

I'm feeling very hungry and thirsty, said Zu.

Don't be so loud, Father said, pointing to the other beds around them. He went to the table, took the thermos bottle, poured the hot water into a bowl, half filled with the ginger soup, and brought it back to the bed for Zu to drink from.

Where's the fish? said Zu, feeling better.

Oh, they've turned it into a white turnip soup that I've shared with the other uncles here.

Is there anything for me?

Oh, yes, plenty. I've kept a bowl of it for you.

Can I have it now?

While the boy was eating the soup, his father was sitting and watching, a book that he'd been reading laid aside, by the kerosene lamp. But you haven't answered my question about the reincarnation, said the

100

boy.

Oh, that, said his father, instantly remembering a story about a Buddhist abbot who, after being discovered having an affair with a maid, decides to die sitting cross-legged, only to be reborn some thousands of kilometers away on a river where a woman dreams of having a sexual intercourse with him and becoming pregnant afterwards.

Oh, it's just like the story I told the uncle sitting up here about the fish when you arrived, he pointed to the bed above and said.

I wonder if that fish is what I turned into after I fell asleep.

Now, don't you talk nonsense. Have a good sleep as I'll have to sleep, too.

祖

The fields in winter were wild, bleak. Stubbles only, brown-coloured. And it looked as if it were going to snow, so the cadres were told there was nothing to do but study in their dormitories, where they gathered around a small fire, talking about the fish the boy had caught and how delicious the soup was.

How did you catch it? a black-faced uncle said to the boy.

I just did, very easy, scooping it up from the water, said the boy, who looked more himself than yesterday after a night's sleep and a big bowl of ginger soup.

The lake is full of fish, a young man said who looked like someone who had just walked out of an ancient story, ready to do battles with the fish. although not as many as the *Beidahuang*, the Great Northern Wilderness.

Oh, yeh, said an old man, gaunt-looking and chain-smoking. Fish there are for the taking by the scoop. But the boy's fish tasted real good yesterday.

We ought to get the boy to catch more for us or perhaps we should go out together, the young man said, winking at Zu, who took an immediate liking to him.

All the while, Father sat there without a word, like a piece of wood, not looking at anyone, either. Nor was he reading one of his books. He just sat there, his eyes glazed. There was no way of knowing what he was thinking. When the study session began, with the reading of selected excerpts from Mao's work, followed by group discussions, Father's face became a show of endurance and torture although a smile, like a peel of paint, was frozen there. After a while, little Zu got tired listening to the men talking about their labour experience in praise of Mao's words and fell asleep again, the only option he had because Father wouldn't allow him to go out in the cold.

祖

Back home, Zu was hesitating as to what he should tell Mum about Dad and things that had happened to him on the road to and from there.

Did you easily find your way to the school? said Mum.

Oh yes. It didn't seem to take long, said Zu.

Did you have to ask people a lot on the way?

No.

I know you didn't. Remember what I said?

I know.

Anything happened on the road?

Hum, yes. I got a fish.

Fish?

Yes. I caught it.

Big one?

Big. Very big.

How big?

This big, said Zu, indicating the size of his left forearm, when straightened, from the elbow to the tip of the middle finger.

What did you do with it? said Mum.

Didn't do anything; just got Dad to get it cooked.

Oh, how's Dad?

He's fine.

Did you pass my letter onto him?

Yes, I did.

Has he got something for me?

Oh, yes, I forgot. Here it is.

Mum opened the envelope and took the letter out of it. She read it without a word and put it back in the envelope.

There's something I forgot to tell you, Mum, said Zu, hesitating again.

Yes. What's it?

I, I, I lost something.

Something? What's that?

The new red sweater you knitted for me.

Oh.

I didn't dare tell you because you might be angry with me.

That's fine. But how did you lose it then?

Zu went into detail about how he caught the fish and how it was too late when he found that he'd lost it because he had already arrived at the Cadres School. As he went on about this, he kept saying how he should never have lost it.

But Mum cut him short by saying, 'It's not a problem. Don't worry about it. I'll knit another one for you.'

In his heart of hearts, Zu was grateful. For the first time, he had something kinder from Mother than criticism and he felt warm-hearted.

Chapter 14: Night Talk

That summer, before they started their first term in the middle school, Zu and his friends, Qiao and Jian, went to *xuenong*, to learn from the peasants, in a village by the Yangtze, called Riverside Village. They got up early and headed straight for the cotton fields. It was a scorching summer day. But they went bareheaded because they had no idea of what the sun would do to them if they didn't have any protection. After a full day of cotton-picking, each and every one of them was left suntanned short of having a sunstroke. But Zu was hit the hardest, much to his own satisfaction, because he had been waiting for this opportunity to get suntanned till he turned into a black fish, so to speak. Instead, he was all red, looking like a red-faced Guan Gong, the Deity Guan in a Guandi Temple, as Qiao put it.

One year older than him, Qiao had much experience. As soon as he realised how hot the morning sun was, he borrowed a straw hat from a peasant and asked if Zu would like one. Zu refused it right away. He was not afraid of the sun nor was he afraid of the sunlight. Both were one to him, a source of strength and pleasure. He had heard that people could copulate with the sun at its strongest but doubted the truthfulness of the legend; the peasants looked to him like masses of dust and soil rolled into one, nothing romantic in them. He spent his rest time poring over a fairy book in which a man is struck down to the ground facing the sky. But when the sun is out, he is able to fight back by gaining his feet and throwing the monster off him, eventually crushing the monster and vanquishing him. He admired such heroes the same way he admired Danko, in a story by Maxim Gorky, a revolutionary Soviet writer, who, with his flaming heart, leads his people out of a dark forest onto a beautiful plain. Although he had never actually seen any such likes in real life, he was so deeply moved that he could never forget the way Danko holds up his heart that lights the path forward, particularly towards the end where one of the people treads on his flaming heart, extinguishing it as he goes forward.

At night, when all was quiet, the three boys were excited over a topic that none of them had any experience in or knowledge of. Lying in their own respective beds, in a room with no kerosene lights on, they freely talked about things that came to mind and one of the first things was how women gave birth to their kids.

I think they just squat and shit them out, said Jian.

You mean the way they open their bowels? said Zu.

I suppose, said Jian.

I think it's their men that put something inside them and make them breed kids, said Qiao.

Oh, I know, said Jian. Like a dog that climbs on top of another dog. I once saw that happen in the wilderness.

Or a cow, said Zu.

I don't know, said Qiao, but it's certainly not like the animals that just shat their young from their anuses.

Ow, I hate the sight of the bleeding anuses, said Jian.

I heard that they come out from where they piss, said Qiao.

No, that's not right. It's not possible, said Zu.

That's because you think their holes are as tiny as your own, said Jian.

But certainly not as big as the size of a kid, said Zu.

I don't know. I haven't seen one, said Jian. All I have ever seen is the naked back of a woman when she squatted. The one I pointed out to you the other day, you remember?

I know. I was horrified that you had the guts to notice that.

But didn't you like that?

Didn't like what?

The naked bit?

Not the way you did, nor the way Lu Xun described.

What did Lu Xun describe?

Lu Xun said that a Chinese man is so obscenely imaginative that if he sees a bar of naked flesh on a woman, he is led to imagine the rest of her body and pretty soon he'll want to go to bed with her and have kids, illegitimate kids.

Oh, I know that one. I happened to hear Zu's father talking about it one day.

But you have to read the essay to know the intensity of a man's imagination. It takes only seconds for a man to see the naked back of a woman's hand to imagine the birth of an illegitimate child.

But that's only part of human nature, as Confucius says.

Still, I am fascinated by the way women can just squat and give birth to their children like they are opening their bowels.

Like the hens laying eggs, hahahaha.

Hahahahaha, that's right.

Kaff, kaff, kaff.

Oh, someone was coughing outside and probably overhearing us, said Zu.

It's that old man there, said Jian.

Yes, it must be the old man, the guy who told us which field to go to and pick the cotton, said Qiao.

A short silence ensued before the conversation began again.

Guys, do you want to get married? said Zu.

Of course, I do. As soon as I turn 16, said Jian.

But that's not even the legal age, said Qiao.

What's the legal age then? said Zu.

18 perhaps?

It's so easy. Just go and grab a woman and it's done.

Then have kids like laying eggs?

I can't work that one out, really.

You mean doing kids like shitting?

That's right.

Don't worry about it. You'll know it all soon enough.

You sound as if you knew everything already.

That's because I do, said Qiao.

At that, the other two boys seemed to see him winking wickedly and laughed uncontrollably, without any more detail they could imagine to add, too young yet for that sort of thing.

Pretty soon, they fell asleep, one by one.

106

The dawn showed bright on the window, shafting its lights on the sleeping faces of the three boys, who would have squandered the morning in their blissful sleep after the long rambling chat that took them deep into the night but for the old man's constant coughing, which came closer as he went up to their door and stopped. He put out a hand and was about to knock on it when he decided not to. Instead, he said in a gentle, enquiring voice, Boys, time to get up, as the sun is hitting your hips now.

No one stirred, all sleeping on, oblivious to the man's gentle enquiry, the cocks' crowing and the birds singing around them. Zu, however, was the first to hear something near the door that sounded like someone talking, like last night, and was about to pick up where they had left off when he realised that it was the old man outside. With a start, he woke up and said to the voice outside, Getting up now, as he pulled up his shorts, ran to the door and opened it for the old man.

I heard what you were talking about last night, said the old man.

Did you? said Zu.

Oh, yes, you boys kept me awake nearly all night.

Zu 'he-he'ed.

It's not good, said the old man.

You think?

Not good at all. Boys of your age should never talk like that, said the old man.

I thought it was all right. After all, no one else knew.

But I heard it all. And I just wished you would somehow stop. But you never did.

We did, actually. We fell asleep.

Please don't ever talk like that again, said the old man as he walked away.

祖

On their way home, the boys were silent. Qiao glanced at Zu from the corner of his eye and knew that he was sullen. Jian went looking for the grasshoppers and would string them together on a long blade of grass when he caught them. Then, he would show it to them. But seeing neither was interested, he grew upset and chucked the thing into a rice paddy by the roadside. Then, all of a sudden, they began complaining about how miserable the day had been, causing them to shed their skins in the blistering sun. Jian was feeling itchy all over. It must have been the bed they had been sleeping on, said Qiao, because there were bedbugs.

Talking about the bedbugs, said Zu as he spat out a blade of grass that he had been holding between his lips, I was reminded of a story I had read.

What is it? said Jian, without any interest, whose eyes were focused on any hopping grasshoppers.

It's a very simple one, said Zu. According to this ancient storyteller, a louse is a determinant of life in a person. When a louse crawls towards a dying person, the person will come alive. When it leaves, the person dies.

Yeh, said Qiao. I've seen street-side beggars covered in lice and they bit them one by one with a popping sound as if they quite enjoyed it. And these beggars never die, it seems.

Perhaps they feed on the lice, said Jian.

Thus chatting, the boys found their way home, sooner than they had expected. And the first thing Mother said when she saw Zu was, What have you done to yourself? You look like a sun-dried shrimp!

Chapter 15: Unrequited Loves

According to Old Zu, in an undisclosed email he sent me, Zu, throughout his teens, fell in love with numerous women. He had sexual fantasies he couldn't put a name to. But he watched faces from afar that fascinated him and held him in thrall. Even though there were no women, before or after, that could ever match the intensity of the stunning beauty of the woman in the foreign film, there were others, about his age, that fired Zu's imagination and propelled him along the fall-in-like-close-to-love lines.

Ming, for example, was such a girl. She was in the same class as Zu. They never spoke to each other. It was not the done thing, for a boy student to speak to a girl student or vice versa unless absolutely necessary. But chances for the absolutely necessary were nil. Still, eyes were the freest things. They roamed. They wandered. They even dreamed when looking. They were the active apparatus of a heart hankering after what it found lacking in itself. They, to put it simply, wanted to feed on what they found visually nourishing.

There wasn't anything particularly striking about Ming. She didn't have large bright eyes. Nor did she have a figure with romantic curvatures. She was petite. She had an oval face and her eyes were two slits. But she had a calm smile that was appealing. And the way she walked, swaying slightly from side to side, as she came from the opposite side, had such magic in it that Zu felt that his own heart was being swayed from side to side, too. Their eyes, the four of them, would often meet in their wayward wanderings and separate, only to come back again, like two travellers who walk away, impressed, after the first meeting, and hanker for more. There was no physical contact. Absolutely none.

By now, the country had seemed to have entered into its purest time in history. Brothels were wiped out. Concubinage became nonexistent. Affairs were made almost impossible to exist because of the density of human cohabitation. If there was anything that happened outside the norm, ordinary people, least of all teens like Ming and Zu, wouldn't possibly know. Dark spots of history would remain unknown to its present residents till long after its passage, like a sky we look at without knowing what's happening on the other side till we have the vehicles to reach beyond. But the walls were thin when Zu was young and the voices of lovemaking were so muffled by the selves engaging in the act that they instantly turned themselves into silences, leaving no traces in history, or the written part of it.

When Zu fell in like with Ming, it was at a time of *fangkong dong*, or air-raid tunnels, that were being dug in accordance with Mao's demand to the nation for *shen wadong, guang jiliang, bu chengba* (deep tunnels, extensive storage of food and no hegemony) as a strategic stance against the potential Soviet Revisionist invasion. Classes were suspended and students were turned into diggers, working underground day and night in constant fear that nuclear weapons might be used on Chinese cities, wiping them off the face of the earth. Like groundhogs, Zu and his classmates were burrowing deep into the earth, in wet and cold conditions of semi-darkness, lit at regular spaces with a yellow bulb, with one student hacking away at the stone and earth in front of him and another student putting the accumulated earth in a bamboo dustpan, passing it onto a third student in a relay, till the earth-filled dustpan reached a spot right underneath the opening in the ground where there was a rope with a hook at its end. When someone pulled the rope at the other end, this dustpan would ascend to the top before it was dumped on a growing hill of earth nearby.

Zu, neither the monitor nor a class leader, was the hardest-working man in the front. Knowing that he had come from the most abject background, with a father that was a former Nationalist Party official and a mother that was a landlord's daughter, his only chance for survival, for excelling among the rest of the crowd, was to devote himself to the hard work no matter what. So about ten metres under the ground, in a tunnel that was two metres high, he was swinging a pickaxe at the white clay that formed much of the wall in front of him. He had never worked in a coalmine. But he suspected this wasn't much far off from it, in that you dug and took out whatever you had dug in a place that was uniformly night, the only difference being the yellow earth with streaks of white clay all around you. He had no thought or emotion. He became one with the pickaxe in his hand. He hacked and pried and dug. And he stopped, to wipe the sweat off his brow, only to start again.

Towards the evening, when everyone had gone home, and he was taking the last dustpan of freshly dug earth to the shaft for someone to pull up to above the ground, he heard a voice speaking to him at the top of the ladder and recognised straight away that it was that of Ming's.

Is there anyone down there? the voice said.

Oh, yes. I am. I am, said Zu. His heart was set afire the instant he heard the voice, so gentle it sounded like drops of rain falling into a parched mouth.

Can I draw this one up? said the voice.

Yes, yes, just do it, said Zu. For some reason, his voice sounded harsh and unkind.

The voice stopped, the owner of which seemed hesitant, before she resumed, saying, Sure, sure, I'll do it.

Even though he could not see the face from where he was standing ten metres down, the voice with its gentle firm qualities came to him like the offering of a helping hand in times of distress, an invisible hand that swept his heart-waves to a surging height, only to drop them again.

It was soon over, with the dumping of the earth in the pan. And the next day was one of the many similar days in which glances were exchanged, thoughts were thought but no action was taken. The physical boundary was never crossed for a single time even though Ming was marked as one Zu would be living with should there ever be a chance. In these metaphysical times, love was not a word that suited the lips. He had never, for example, heard his mother or father ever utter the word to each other or in his own presence, even though his semen-saturated dreams would often feature torrid scenes of naked — as if it's the past tense of a verb 'nake', my apologies — bodies engaging in flesh warfare, no traces even recallable afterwards except those of the semen that needed to be cleaned up.

祖

He had never seen a kangaroo before. But his heart, he dreamt, was like one that hopped from one girl to another, not a butterfly of colour, but a dragonfly that skipped and skidded. Not even that. But more of a dragonfly-kangaroo, whose tiny eyes would never stop scanning the landscape of female humanity. This inner kangaroo went about its business secretively, surreptitiously, skipping most faces that it considered beneath its notice, dwelling on a few adorable ones before it went further, beyond its own class, to the other classes, until it stopped, its feet touching the ground, its nose smelling the air and its eyes turning, thinking, still surveying.

Nothing could have been further from the truth, I imagined Old Zu saying. There was no such kangaroo. There was only the knowing through looking and the looking that led straight to knowing. You saw someone you liked and there she was: you liked her regardless even though you knew it was more than impossible that you'd ever have a chance.

This was a girl much discussed amongst the boys, such as Hei. He could sit there talking about her for hours, saying how big her eyes were, what curly, raven hair she had, and how lovely she walked in those elastic steps in and out of school. More than once, his enthusiasm made Zu wonder if Hei had fallen in love. But when he asked him, he would adamantly deny that he was. He went so far as to say that he wouldn't bother about the bitch as he would go for someone much better. On Zu's part, though, he liked Juan—that was her name—well enough, for her moon face of queen-like qualities and her plump shape in red or green garments that were quite eye-catching. But this girl never returned his glances, not on a single occasion. Frustrated as he was, he was not someone foolish enough to stick to his goal, but one with a sensible heart that knew where to eye the next one.

While he let others read his diary pieces on display, Zu kept another diary, a parallel one, in which, for fear of what his innermost thoughts might be revealed to the others, he'd put down fragments of his ideas or sentiments associated with the girls he'd dreamt of after seeing them. White River, for example, was such a girl from next class. It was a name that he liked and he gave it to the girl he fantasised about. In one entry he wrote, 'I saw her standing before a wall, reading.' In another he said, 'But days are too long without her.' More entries came, in long hand, thick and fast. 'I like her face, white and creamy.' 'Her hair is so black and long, her eyes dazzling like the night.' 'Her dad, a big shot once, is now down and out.' 'But she's beautiful.' 'So cold, though.' 'Never looked at me.' 'I wish I had the power of eyes that could pull her into my arms.' 'I wish she were mine by mere wishing.' 'I've dreamed so hard and long. But I have never managed to dream her into my dream existence.' 'Am I wasting my time waiting?' 'Why but I can never pick up enough courage to approach her and say to her, "I love you!"' 'My heart beats so fast it hurts my chest.' 'But I've never had a hard-on like Jia.' 'I shall never do anything physical to her. Just love. The purity of it all.'

This 'love', to Zu, was sheer agony and madness. Mum was concerned. She said, But what's happening? Why don't you eat?

Not feeling like eating, said Zu.

Did you not do well in exams? said his Mum.

That's not it.

What is it then?

Don't know.

Perhaps fallen in love? Mother's voice became suddenly quiet, sweetened.

No, no, no, no, no, denied Zu vehemently.

I know. I know. A mother knows what her son is thinking of, said she.

Pulling a long face, Zu turned to go when his mother said behind him, Let's have a talk when you have time.

For some reason, the promised talk never eventuated because the girl suddenly disappeared. Some said she had transferred to another school far from the town. And that was that. After a time, the girl went out of his mind, like a fire that had extinguished itself.

Then Pei came on the scene. She was Mother's friend even though she was about Zu's age. That in itself seemed to make her a patronizing senior, an older sister even. When she spoke to Mum, Zu felt it was as if she were talking to an equal, laughing along the same wavelengths. Then, as soon as she turned to see him watching on the side, her smile softened and her voice gentled, much the same way she had seen a much younger boy, dismissing his seriousness as a joke, taking no note of the dark brooding emotions underneath the veneer of politeness.

She had come from a poor family background. Zu could tell that in one glance, as he did when Mother and he paid Pei a visit over New Year's Day in Hankou. Her father sat in a corner, with a claw of a hand, picking peanuts out of a mess of other little things. And her mother went about the household chores with a bent back, both in a tiny, cramped space, squeezed between their neighbours, all living in their tiny snail spaces in which they shared their tap water, their cooking facilities and their toilet. That, though, seemed to make Pei even more lovely. With a green shawl around her neck, she was like a rose bursting into flower in a dumping ground, basking in the admiring eyes of a Zu who could not stop following her with his glances, glimpses, gazes and rhetorical embraces and hugs, thinking that in doing so he might succeed in attracting something back from her in a mere look. Nothing like that happened. She helped her mother clean up a space in the bedroom-kitchen, one separated from the other by a window, and joked with Zu's mother about what she and Ping, her boyfriend, had done in a recent rehearsal their art and literary propaganda team had put on. In that rehearsal, according to Pei, Ping and the other actors had made music on instruments made of tools used at the construction site.

Zu was fascinated. As a matter of fact, he had watched one of these performances in his town. In a time when only eight model works of revolutionary opera were shown, and one was allowed to see, apart from two or three films prominently featuring women characters, e.g. women protagonists playing a leading role, to pave the way for Madame Mao's taking over from her husband, there had been nothing so revolutionarily avant-garde. The performance was staged at Dalitang, or the Great Hall, the only ceremonial place in town for celebration or condemnation. When the actors appeared on the stage, with their saws, spades, shovels, axes, hoes, bowls, chopsticks and tree-branches, the audience burst out laughing because they thought they must have come to a wrong spot: was this supposed to be a stage for musical performance or a display of their working muscles?

As soon as the stage was set for a work scene in a forest clearing, people were amused, with a sigh of relief, to find that on a wooden bench, carved out of a tree trunk, was laid a row of large porcelain bowls, normally used for containing cooked rice, or dishes, now filled with water, with reflections of lights from the ceiling of the theatre. A man, square-shouldered and square-faced, in a white shirt and earthen-coloured shorts, sat behind the bench, with two bare sticks in his hands, made of tree-branches, resembling a pair of chopsticks, and began hitting the edges of the bowls lightly, like taps of first rain on a dry roof of a hut in the mountain, that turned into thuds of something bigger and heavier, like the gravels that spilled out of a running tyre. Then he became more dexterous as a streamlet ran off his hands, bubbling, tinkling, leaping, and even sighing, as if weary of its own vital force or surprised at its own creativity. Bowls of water served as piano keys, with do, re, mi, fa, sol, la, ti, do sweeping across the audience like a cool breeze in a hot summer, delighting their eyes and ears, and loosening their minds in an imaginary landscape of post-revolutionary zeal.

Zu knew that it was Ping because the way he looked and acted matched Pei's description. He was full of a helpless jealousy, liking the music he produced but disliking his person, feeling at the same time thankful to her for this ticket that allowed him to come in by the entrance without having to climb the wall as he did on many occasions before. He was never good at it, and had to be helped up the wall by Qiao or Hei. Even though it was something shameful—climbing the wall without a ticket, like in guerrilla warfare, he had done it without feeling so because that's what teenagers did in those days. Now, though, he would proudly walk through the entrance, without trying to dodge the inspectors.

The programs that followed were nothing short of amazing. One actor sawed at a wooden barrel that looked like one of night soil, with a tree-branch, to produce a number in *Swan Lake*. Another ran around the stage hitting at a hoe, its wooden handle, a spade, a sickle, even a bamboo basket, with a small hammer, to create a piece of music that sounded like the song, titled, *zaofan youli*, or 'It Is Reasonable to Rebel', based on a quotation from Mao Zedong. And, then, when it came time to do an ensemble in 'Internationale', the musical group of this wild nature burst forth with a chorus of voices mixed with music invented on their agricultural tools and pieces of construction equipment, drawing wave after wave of applause from the audience and eliciting ceaseless admiration in Zu, himself a spontaneous composer of unsung songs, having received no training whatsoever except an ability he had acquired all by himself of reading the numbered musical notation, with which he was able to record songs heard over radio from North Korea and to blow the mouth organ with Russian songs he had learnt from the numbered musical notation books, a most loved one being '*shanzha shu*' or 'The Hawthorn Tree', which began with these tunes, 66162, 6717326. 63312, 67171721. 555432, 66712123, 111235, 4327326.

Would one be a composer without being able to play any instrument except a mouth organ? That was a question Zu frequently asked himself but that he himself could never get an answer to and no one else could answer it, either, because he had no personal knowledge of any professional musicians where he studied or lived. There was one student in his school whose father was a prefectural commissioner but who, without any musical training or instrumental skills, managed to be selected and recommended for training as a composer in a musical conservancy in the capital city of the province. Zu, a lover of music and musical composition, watched this with interest, curiosity and jealousy. He wished he had a powerful parent to help him climb the social ladder. He had none. All he had was a passion that propelled him to do things that would never probably come to anything the same way he had love that seemed to be doomed to failure right from the start.

Then the news came that Pei and Ping were getting married. Zu, a frustrated teenager, was able to comfort himself with a remark he had prepared for himself for all occasions, Oh, I don't really care. Pretty soon, Pei had also gone out of his life. The last he had heard of them was a remark Ping had made when he said that he'd like to be an acoustic designer in a theatre if he went to university and the fact that Pei had changed her name from Red Education to Mengying, Dreaming Shadows.

Book II. Broad Sky Country

农村是一个广阔的天地，在那里是可以大有作为的。

毛泽东

> The countryside is a vastness of land and skies where
> much could be achieved.
> Mao Zedong

Chapter 1: Building a House

Zu would always remember the day when he was sent away from home to *chadui luohu*, literally, to insert oneself in a production team and settle down there as part of a household. The expression had been hammered into every school-leaver months before their departure, in and outside the classes, that they must answer the great call of Chairman Mao that 'the countryside is a vast heaven and earth where one can become well achieved.' At the age of 18, Zu was imbued with enough revolutionary spirit to actually long for a bright future in the countryside where he could do great. Many of his hopes had been dashed at school. For example, when he entered the middle school, quite a few of his schoolmates had joined the army as part of the effort in the Kangmei Yuanyue War, the Anti-American War in Support of Vietnam. But, because of his family background, with a father being an ex-Kuomintang Party member and a mother from a middle-class family of book fragrance, e.g. scholars, his application to join the army was rejected. He'd never forget a remark made by a classmate that people like him, with his kind of class status, would never have a chance. Still, he kept up a long correspondence with Qian, his closest childhood friend, son of a factory worker, who was serving in a corps of signals based in Inner Mongolia and from whom Zu knew much that life in the corps wasn't as interesting as he thought it was because Qian revealed that he was suffering from insomnia as a result of working constant night shifts. Then, when everyone in his class had become members of Communist Youth League, he was excluded, again because of his questionable class status. On more than one occasion, he heard his mother complain under her breath that his father should never have been as stupidly honest as he was, confessing that he fitted the *chengfen*, the class status, of being a KMT government official, instead of just a government staff member, a neutral term that would at least not harm the boy if it did not benefit him. In the end, on the advice that Mother gave him, Zu filled in his application for the Youth League membership, with his mother's chengfen of a staff member. Shortly before he left the school, Zu became a member, an acquisition that raised him a peg or two above his tainted background in the eyes of others and explained his enthusiasm for the future.

After an evening walk with friends on the Yangtze embankment, he came home and recorded his revolutionary thoughts in a longish poem, part of which goes, in my translation, 'As successors to the revolution / we shall inherit the brilliant achievements of our forefathers' // 'And we shall go to the countryside! To labour, to fight / to temper a red heart and to roll in the mud.'

His mother accepted the fate the only way she could, with acquiescence and resignation, along with the thought that Zu was not the only one, among millions involved in this nationwide campaign, known as *shangshan xiaxiang*, up the mountains and down the country, that poured the middle-school graduates from cities and towns into the countryside, as sons and daughters of nearly every one of her colleagues had to go to the countryside. Her concerns for the boy, though, were real. Although he grew up quite independent, always living on his own, managing to have his meals in the staff canteens and washing his own clothes, while she was away for long spells of time on business, the boy was quite unsociable and at times anti-social, even anti-familial, with a bad temper into the bargain, unlike Qiao next door, son of a colleague, who was sweet-tempered and respectful to all the adult staff members in the work unit where she worked, despite the constant trouble he had made outside the unit. The times were partly responsible for that as rebellion of the young was encouraged against the old traditions and the families carrying those traditions. The bad temper, though, was more of a family issue than anything else. In her younger days, whenever she was in a bad mood, she would find it irresistible to take it out on the boy, making him cry, then hugging him to soothe him. As the boy grew up, she watched him with concern that he was building muscle, getting so physically strong that he would not only talk back but also fight with her. On one occasion, she meant to hit him like he was a little boy but he held her hand in a tight grip that she could not get out of. It was not till she cried out of pain that he let go. She looked at the boy in a new light and wondered what sort of a person he might grow into. On the eve of his departure for a village called Clear Water Village, about 50 kilometres from the town where they lived, she helped pack up the boy's luggage, a roll of his quilt and bedclothes, all washed and starched, smelling fresh and new, into which she thrust two large bars of brown soap and a bag of white sugar. As she did so, she wondered aloud if she should also prepare a jar of fermented bean curd and pickled white radish, and a salted fish, all Zu's favourites. Zu was reading and ignored it. When she asked him again, Zu said, It's all fine by me. Why so complicated?

What did you mean by 'complicated'? his mother snapped, flaring up. What do you know about being 'complicated'? It's not like going to visit your relatives in Wuhan for a few days. It's like, like——, she stopped, choking on the words, and said, 'going forever, with little hope of ever coming back.'

That's even better, said Zu, without raising his head from a notebook he was reading.

Even better? Said his mother. Then why am I doing this for you? Why don't you do it yourself? Piqued, she put down what she was doing and lit a cigarette, saying, Is this what you want to tell me after all those years of hard work bringing you up? You are so ungrateful.

I can actually grow up entirely by myself, said Zu, as a thought swept across his mind that he did actually grow up by himself in the absence of either his mother or father.

That's just getting more *buxianghuale*, said the mother as she suddenly calmed down after a few puffs or perhaps because there was something in what the boy said that made sense. What are you reading? said she.

Nothing.

Show me.

No.

Show me!

No!

They wrestled, she wanting to snatch the notebook from the boy's hands and the boy clutching it so tightly that the mother couldn't succeed in snatching it off him, till she sighed and said, You are such a stubborn boy. I don't know what to do with you. If only you listened.

The boy ignored her, his eyes fixed on the ending lines of a prose poem he had written a few months earlier: 'Ah, today! Why are all of us so excited? Why are we braving the cold wind thus? Oh, I see, it is because the wind has brought messages of spring to the earth, blowing them right into the heart of everyone.'

I know, the mother said resignedly. It's your poetry again. What's the point of writing poetry? You don't have the experience. You haven't met anyone. You are so unworldly. Think more of how you can start a new life there, living in peace with people and not throwing tantrums at the slightest provocation.

Yes, not like you, said the boy.

Sighing a deep sigh, his mother pretended not to hear that and went on packing what remained of Zu's luggage till she was done, when Zu said, I want to take this with me. He pointed to his notebook.

All right, said his mother. Do whatever you like as long as you don't get me angry.

祖

The next morning, Mother and Son went together to the school. There, in one glance, Zu saw the campus packed with schoolmates, their parents and staff members. They stood in a circle around a number of Liberation trucks. Across the campus stretched red banners that featured slogans like 'Farewell to the Revolutionary Educated Youths who Go up the Mountains and down the Countryside' and 'Chairman Mao instructs us: the Countryside is a Vast Heaven and Earth where One Can Become Well Achieved.' When he climbed onto the back of a truck and took in his luggage, Zu noticed his mother looking at him and the other parents helping their kids onto their designated trucks. One or two women parents started sobbing and looked away when they realised people were watching. The male parents were standing by, just watching, like it was a show. It was not till then that he realised that he had been put together with people that were not his classmates. A lank young man by the name of Len grinned at him, showing two rows of teeth that bulged at the front. Zu grinned back and thought: He's got teeth better than mine. Next to him was another young man whose name was Han, with a large handsome face and a brazen air, trying to accost a tall girl who smiled by way of an answer. Zu said nothing. He just wanted to leave. And when Cui, a short girl with two short pigtails, greeted him and said that she was happy to be in the same group in the same village, Zu was surprised. 'Why was I bunched together with these strangers,' he thought. As the truck started in motion, his heart sank at the thought that the future might not turn out well. He was so absorbed in his own misery that he did not hear his mother's parting words as she shouted in the wind, Be a good boy! And always behave yourself!

祖

On the very next day of their arrival, the village welcomed them by building a house for them.

It's a *mingsan anliu* that they were building. Of the three young men, Zu was the youngest, with the largest head. Han was the oldest, with the handsomest face. And Len was aged somewhere in between, with slightly protruding teeth. Pan Da, head of the production team, was telling them to work harder, in his usual loud voice that sounded unusual to the three new arrivals from the city, 'Hey, what's your name? The white face! Stop laughing like that. Do something. Catch!'

As he yelled his criticism, Pan, wearing a large straw hat that concealed half of his face, so sun-tanned it looked dark-red, threw a brick up in the air, in the direction of Han, the 'white face', who, standing on the one wall that had risen from the ground, took it as it flew into his arms, catching it without bumping it against his chest. The grey mud-coloured brick, twice as large and as thick as a standard red brick, broke in his hands. Han let go of the two broken pieces and cursed.

Pan De, a Korean veteran, pulled his face, with a wry smile, and said, 'City boy, no good,' as he climbed the wall and said to Pan Da, 'Throw me one.'

Grinning, as if he'd won, Pan Da picked up another huge earthen brick, weighing about a kilo or two, and, in a half-squatting position, with bent knees, the way you did when you rode a horse or shat, balanced a brick in his hands before he sent it up, horizontally upwards. It's not a throw, less still a chuck. It's more like a give, a give-forth, the way you hold out a plate full of dish, except that in this case it's sent with a force that seemed to have grown two invisible hands that held the brick all the way up to the catcher, Pan De, who, not grinning but looking grimmer, took it without exhibiting the least sign of exertion and put it next to him. It's like welcoming a golden carp home after it jumped all the way up over the dragon gate.

Or, as Zu, the outsider, put it, 'It's like a boat that sailed right into his arms, steady and stable.'

Han took a look at him and gave him a push.

It was not a harsh push. But it was not a gentle push, either. Zu 'ah'ed, swaying from side to side, his arms swinging, before he fell, as a fleeting thought came to him: I'd break my head, if not my heart, falling like this.

He broke neither. Instead, Pan Da came rushing over and took an armful hold of Zu, saving him from the downward plunge into a pool of muddy mortar. As he did so, he breathed a blast of foul smell into his face, saying, 'Hey, how come you are so light, like a butterfly!' With that, he pushed him up, back to where he was standing, like the fast rewinding of a modern-day videotape, not invented then.

Or perhaps this is all imagining that instantly took place inside Zu's head as he stood there watching, admiringly, how he himself took one brick after another and fitted them in place on the rising wall, easing himself into the work till he was so skilful that he won praise from both Pans, less from De who hardly had anything good to say about any of those students who had newly arrived in the village. In fact, he hardly had anything to say about anyone except crack hard jokes, a trait Zu was soon to discover.

祖

By lunchtime, the empty ground in front of a wall-like slope of Green Hill was no longer empty. Four walls, fully erected and regularly spaced, waiting for the roofs and tiles to come, stood in parallel. And on the wide side, there were two other walls that joined them, the front one with a door and one window on either side, and the back one with a single door. Sitting at the table, Pan Hua, the village elder, explained to the students from the city, 'This is what we locally call a mingsan anliu, Bright Three and Hidden Six. Right now, as you can see, the three spaces formed by four walls and two walls on the wide side are the so-called Bright Three. After lunch, when a number of partition walls come in, they are further broken into six smaller spaces, forming into six rooms, and that's what's called Hidden Six, including one for the kitchen at the back, one in the middle as a hall, and two each on the side as bedrooms for the five of you.'

When he said 'five', Zu cast a look around, remembering the two other girls that he had only met a day or two ago. The one, Cui, had curly hair and smiled a lot. The other, Xi, was tall and paid no attention to anyone. Where have they been? He wondered to himself.

Just then, the door of a neighbour's house opened. Out came a string of ringing laughter, followed by two girls, one in a bright flowery dress and the other, a white blouse atop a black skirt, each holding in their hands a large plate of food, walking in elastic steps towards the dining table. They had been helping cook the lunch at the back and now it was time to serve it.

The table was soon covered with plates, of large dices of red-braised pork swimming in shiny lard, of fried eggs, of tofu stir-fried with bok choy, and, of course, a red-braised fat-head, a local fish variety known for its enormous head disproportionate to its body. The eaters, all the villagers involved in the building of the house, surrounded the table and the food, chopsticks at the ready.

It was not till then that Zu noticed something. He could see that no one on either side of the table moved a finger. He was hungry. He wanted to eat. But something held him. One glance around the table assured him that everyone was waiting intently and impatiently for something to happen. Just as he was about to point his chopsticks to the fat-head, no longer able to endure the terrible rumblings in his empty stomach, he saw the old man with slit eyes, sitting across the table from him, whose name he didn't know, tapped the fat-head fish with the tips of his chopsticks, before sinking them into it and coming out with a torn piece of white flesh. Someone whispered into his ear, saying, In here, you have to wait for the oldest person at the table to move his chopsticks first, then you can start eating.

Before the words sank in, Zu saw the chopsticks raised around him like a falling forest of trees, all pointed at the fish, so dense he couldn't get a chopstick in edgewise. People ate with a deafening noise that made him ashamed because Mother had always chastised him for making noise while eating. He managed only to eat a few mouthfuls before the plates were cleaned up, as if wiped with a mop, the fish skeletal, and even the rice barrels emptied to the bottom. The only expression he could think of describing this was *fengsao canyun*. That is, people ate like a whirlwind that swept the remaining clouds.

When all left, Zu, his hunger barely allayed, stared blankly across the empty plates at the wall of Pan Da's house on the other side of the village pond, with a slogan by Chairman Mao, written in red, that says: Great Leader Chairman Mao Teaches Us: Eat Liquid When not Busy; Eat Dry When Busy; Eat Half Liquid and Half Dry at Normal Times, Mixed with Sweet Potatoes, Vegetables and Turnips.

祖

Nightfall was not a gradual dark. It was fairly sudden. After everyone ate, the girls went out. They loved to get in touch, to visit their neighbours and to gossip. Clear Water Village was so small it had only 40 households, lining the bank of the Clear Water River, actually a creek. On the other side of this small creek, there were paddy fields that extended far beyond. A mud road, flanked by a thick growth of cogongrass, known as

Bamao, ran along a tributary of the Clear Water River in the direction of the city. Afraid of the gathering darkness in his own room, shared with Len, Zu stood in the doorframe of this newly built house that smelled fresh whitewash and unpainted doors and looked towards the road where it disappeared into the darkening cogongrass. A poem came to mind from *The Book of Songs*, that went, 'Her hands are like soft young-cogongrass, her skin is like congealed fat, her neck is like young longicorn, her teeth are like gourd's seeds, her head is like a cicada and her brow is like a moth. Isn't her smile pretty! Aren't her eyes beautiful!' That's exactly what my girl should be like, Zu thought to himself.

The arrival of a village young man, Lin, however, made it impossible for Zu to engage in any such amorous thoughts. Lin was about the same age as Zu but he had large, calloused hands, a thin figure much like a reed. He stood there, watching Zu talk, looking bewildered, even a little dazed, a silly smile on his face that curled his fat lips, revealing two rows of uneven teeth, rimmed with too much gums. Their conversation ran something like this.

What's your food like, said Lin.

It's fine, said Zu.

I can see it's not fine.

I don't mind.

You city boys can't take the rough, I'm sure.

No, we can take anything. If you don't believe, ask him.

A group of village urchins were gathering around them, their dirty little faces opening up in wide grins, particularly when Han came out of his room that he kept entirely for his own use, looking so smart that one teenage girl, known as Niqiu, a loach fish, precisely because she looked like one, 'ah'ed in admiration, revealing a mouthful of white teeth.

No, Han interjected as soon as he came out of the house. Food here is awful. The fish tasted like mud. They were so stingy with their salt and oil. And the vegetables tasted like they were boiled in water.

See, Lin said, not pleased with the criticism but pleased with his own correct guess. Like I said. This is the way. You've got to get used to it.

Look at you, Han said. You can't even wear your own Liberation Shoes properly. And your lower mouth is open, too. Is that also the way here?

Before he even finished, Han burst into a raucous laughter as he inhaled a last take on his burning butt before he flipped it out above the heads of the little ones in a deft little movement with his right thumb, index-finger and middle-finger. The butt drew a rascally circle in the air before it jumped to its death in the pit serving as the rubbish tip in front of the house.

Zu took a look and saw that Lin's shoes did not seem to be a pair. Instead, both looked like they belonged to the right foot. How uncomfortable it must be to wear shoes like that, he thought to himself. But, he suppressed the thought with another one that immediately followed: Perhaps that is the way here, too. He could see that the kids had clothes too long on them. Those clothes, handed down from their parents, were obviously expected to grow with them till they grew out of them. A boy even wore what appeared to be altered from a woman's *duijin* garment.

Lin, not to be outdone, scoffed at Han's face with a sneer, as he made as if he was going to button up his trousers but changed his mind as his index-finger found the button missing. Darkness gave him a hand, too, concealing much of the detail. With one remark, Lin hit Han hard. He said, Your face is so white that the sun will make you cry when it turns it black.

But Han had already turned, ignoring the remark as if he hadn't heard it, and went into his own room, to examine his face again, in the mirror that he had hang on the wall above his desk the minute he moved in. He loved the mirror because it served as a daily proof of his handsomeness.

Zu stood and chatted a bit more with Lin till the latter said, The mosquitoes here are so thick. I'll have to go. Can't stand their bites.

Zu loved the word, 'thick', as it's not something he'd ever heard anyone use in the town he came from when describing the mosquitoes. They would say, There were too many mosquitoes. Their thinking so logical.

Chapter 2: The Vinegar Incident

At night, Zu put the mosquito net down around him. This was a round, green-coloured one that hung from one of the rafters and radiated around him. When he tucked it in by the four corners, Zu created a cozy space for himself. The net was handed down from his father, Zu Senior, an accountant. When he was a five-year old, Zu remembered, Dad had lived in a collective farm, in a tiny room with a round mosquito-net by the side of a huge yellow earthen road, with deep, dry tractor ruts. In the room, Dad kept a chicken and when it laid an egg, it cackled, and when Dad reached for the egg inside a box by the bed, it cackled even more loudly as it ran away in a great flurry. One morning, Dad asked little Zu to get the egg out for him. Zu was afraid that the chicken might make a stir. He waited till it was gone, making sure it showed no sign of coming back to attack him if he picked up the egg. When he did, he was delighted. The egg was new, almost white, except for the stain of shit from the chicken. And it was warm, too. *Baba*, he called out, from the box. *Baba*, he called again. But no one answered.

That was all Zu could remember, of that little farm incident, still warm and white in his memory.

There was no ceiling in this room or the rest of the house. When he raised his head, Zu could not see the moon as Li Bai did in that poem of his, so simple and yet so moving. All he could see was the rafters and purlins put across each other, beneath the tiles, like a human rib cage. He had helped lay the tiles during the day by playing a relay role, passing dusty tiles in piles of four to five and, in the process, dropping a few and breaking them below him. Whenever that happened, he laughed, reminding himself at the same time that he must be careful enough not to let things fall again.

Just then, something emerged out of the bowels of his memory. Though it had happened only a few years earlier, it felt like long ago enough to be a thing of the past.

It was a churlish evening, followed by a restless night. Mother had cooked the meal, a bowl of noodle for each; Father, as usual, was away in Round Wind, a small town miles away upstream, on the Yangtze. There were no dishes, only two bottles of soy sauce and vinegar. Mother and son ate in silence, under a bare bulb, in a room that contained only the basic things necessary for a living: a bed, folded quilts, a smaller bed half concealed under the desk by the window, and a stack of suitcases squeezed in a corner between the bigger bed and the wall.

The food tasted so flat, said Zu. And not sour enough.

Mother did not say anything in reply. Instead, she took hold of the vinegar bottle and, aiming its mouth towards Zu's bowl, upended all the remaining vinegar on top of Zu's noodle as she said, again and again, You want it sour? You have it all. Now eat it, eat it, eat it!

Zu was taken aback. He had known Mother to be a tempestuous woman, but not vicious, not as vicious as this. He did not understand. He raised his face in pain, looking at Mum and mumbling something about too much vinegar. But Mother's voice came, resolute and determined, You wanted it and now you must have it, regardless.

A taste assured Zu that this was sour beyond belief; it was venom and it was vitriol. But he had to eat it, regardless, which is exactly what he did, forcing all the soured noodle down his throat while opening his mouth to breathe out what seemed smoke from the vinegar-lit fire.

Years, about 50 years after, in another country, I reach into the depths of my memory and look the boy in the eye. I say: Did you know why your Mum was so upset with you?

I can see the boy had no idea. And I have no idea, either, even though I wonder about the coincidence of a woman's period and her long separation from her husband in a time when such things were a part of one's life.

[An inter-textual insertion: When I checked with Old Zu, his answer was that he recalled having written an essay on the same subject. But because this was so long ago, and as he was in another country, on another continent, he'd have to take time trying to find it. As soon as he found it, he'd let me know. Please see below a pre-novel piece he wrote a decade or so ago.]

My 40-odd Diaries: lost, and found here

It would be good if I could bring them back, at least some of them if not all.

7 February 1996. I do not know why this date stays in my memory. It was such a hot day that when I went out in my Camira I wound down the window on my side. Strange to say, I did not let my right arm hang loose outside the door the way most Aussies would do in a similar situation. I would have lost it if I had done that for, half an hour later, a car smashed into me on the driver's side, turning my car into an instant write-off.

I was lucky enough to survive the accident but what followed was worse, a mental accident with a lasting impact: the 40-odd diary books that I had kept some twenty years earlier never eventuated after they were mailed from that country. I waited and waited. Nothing. I rang Australia Post a few times, was even directed to the dead letters office but, again, nothing.

It was a nothing year in more ways than one. After I secured my doctoral degree the shattering of my dream of a better future became total. I could not find a job I had wanted: teaching English in a university and eventually becoming a professor. It is not till now that I realise that the judging panels in those days must have somehow resembled the Dictation Test administered in the early days of this country, designed to fail whoever It wanted to fail. I did not have the right face. Nor did I have the right accent. The reality had brought me down to the earth.

By then I had just turned 40, unsuccessful, unhappy, unfulfilled. Little I wrote could get published. The harder I worked, it seemed, the less likely I could get anywhere. I had hoped that, with the arrival of my diaries, I would be equipped with a wealth of material for my first novel. Not a single word kept in those diaries ever reached me from across the ocean. I felt as if part of my heart had been wrenched out of my chest. I would sit in silence and pain for days.

By the time I wrote my third novel, again unpublished, I had begun internalizing the diaries to such an extent that I found myself writing bits and pieces dating back to the 70s, recalling details as if they had happened to me only yesterday.

Was this recalling or was it imagining? I think it is both but I am not sure. The memory fades with the passing of years and if I put it down now in my computer, is my past brought any nearer to me than what is already there in my head, one of fading remembrances? I do not have any friends; or should I say, I do not have many friends, with the addition of a mere 'm'? I sometimes do feel it is the former, rather than the latter. One entry, at this juncture, 11.08 p.m., in bed, emerges from the depth of my oceanic, sleepwalking memory:

11/12/1973: I find myself alone in bed. Yang has gone out hunting for dogs. After I turned down his invitation he left in a huff, although he did not seem to get upset with Long who had also said no. He left with these words that are still ringing in my ears: When I bring back the dog and stew it, you guys won't have anything to eat!

It is 11.10 p.m. now, another day, another night, another one that will disappear like all the previous happenings.

Only last week, you said to me that going past 50 was like returning to zero. You said you did not know anything anymore, a feeling growing daily intense that there was nothing worth striving for anymore: love, fame, fortune and all the rest of it. You wondered if that was the approach of death or the first sign of dementia. You wrote little. Of the huge backlog over the years, you said you did not care to select any for submissions. Perhaps, you wondered, chucking them out on a weblog might be the best way to give them an existence otherwise denied, the thought of a posthumous hand going through the pile for other purposes, any purposes, almost too painful to bear.

I had thought you were right till I came across 'the loveliest of trees' poem.1 I realised with a start that the thing could be re-written so that it read, 'Now, of my threescore years and ten / Fifty will not come again'. When I told you that, you were absolutely devastated, once again reminded of a similar saying from the other country that goes, 'Seventy years is rare in human life.' You really did not have much longer left in this world, you thought and I thought, too.

'Some people', one of your very few good friends says. 'resort to drinking when they get beyond 50, their lives taking a downturn.' That sets me thinking. If life is only meant for pleasure seeking, then wine drinking must be our best excuse for 'pouring wine over worries', as another saying from the other country goes. I, for one, however, still want to keep cool-headed and clear-eyed despite the surrounding hedonism, underneath which lurks a deep gloom.

'That's your stupidity,' I heard you say one day. 'for, unlike the other country, people here will only pursue two things in life: mammon and mating. Not that there's anything wrong with it but, to me, a nation intending to overwhelm its guilt with wealth is one that will overwhelm its wealth with guilt. You can always become grass-eating animals but the guilt will one day have you kill yourselves in droves even though the sky will never be overturned.'

---

1 See 'Loveliest of trees, the cherry now' by A. E. Housman, at: http://www.bartleby.com/123/2.html

I find you getting further beyond me, not belonging to this country, not belonging to that country, not even belonging to yourself, not even wanting to, whereas I, the slight idealist, still cling to something that did not even exist, such as my 40-odd diaries. A few years ago when she went back to that country, I asked her to mail whatever was left of my diary box and this one, the only one, recovered by her and brought back to this country, is a green plastic-covered notebook that contains entries written in two languages, the English of which, randomly selected, is one as follows:

27 June, 1980, Friday: Now the question is that if I am to have a good knowledge of English, any carelessness should be avoided.

The idea of the examination seemed to follow me everywhere, when I read it punctuated me from time to time; when I was having a nap it caused me to dream it. I endeavoured to throw it away, but in vain.

The whole afternoon was spent by the East Lake side in reviewing political lessons, a most tame lesson. Mr Brown and I were good crammer(s) then. We burdened ourselves with so many useless facts that I forgot one item immediately we went on with another. I swore that I would never study them after the exam was taken. I was attracted by the boats passing us in the lake, while he was reading aloud to me.

It is Friday today, too, Friday the 14th, not the 13th, a day of death in that country's terms and a day of resurrection in this. The question a character asks in a DVD film that I have watched today is unanswered by the addressee: If I know I do not have long to live what is it that I should do as a matter of necessity or urgency? A range of possibilities flashes across my mind: finding new love in rejecting the old, visiting new places that I have never been before, spending all my savings on things I never have any need for, such as a caravan or motor-boat or, strangely, a villa by the sea, even though I could hardly afford any of these.

None.

I shall lie in bed, like this, thinking into the keyboard, thinking with tentacles reaching out across the past which will become present when I go, merging into one with me. Literature, now, is nothing but this desire to become small, so small one is invisible to anyone but oneself. Like the crickets out there in a dying autumn. When I stand near them they go silent. Someone dead many years ago comes back to me in that instant: words on the tip of his tongue, till I go.

It is not true that no man is an island. Everyone is, as you told me the other day. Only a word is not: No word is an island. You said, laughing, when I noticed the glint of something metal in your mouth. For no reason at all, I remembered this line: 'love is love, in beggars and in kings.'1 'But everyone is a car,' I said, in return for the joke, seeing the city in the shape of endless cars, each occupied by a single individual. 'What I would like, though,' I continued. 'is put these diaries together in a book and find someone to publish it.' As the thought struck me, I drew another scrap piece of paper and began writing when someone honked behind me, urging me to move on. I raised my head and saw that the lights had turned green and the car, right in front of me a minute or so ago, had gone ahead, leaving a wide empty space in between.

Ten hours later, I looked at the paper to see that I had meant to write a preface to the book. Ah, I found it in a corner of my memory:

You won't believe this if I tell you that these are diaries of memory, retrieved from a past that lives even in the present. As one becomes terminally old, one seems to realise that one is no longer punishable by silence, no longer penalizable by time, a mindful body increasingly deleted of its toxin, both personal and social, in its daily search for something deeper if only higher, something unutterable if only

1 Sir Edward Dyer, 'The lowest trees have tops,' *The Oxford Book of Short Poems*, chosen by P. J. Kavanagh and James Michie, OUP, New York: 1987 [1985], p. 11.

unsexible. Perhaps only by engaging in the impossible could one hope to attain that which lies beyond the reach....

My mobile phone hardly rings these days. Early in the night, my left thumb presses the key to switch it off, realizing that I could have started off on a much lower plan if I had known that it would be like this. Why don't people make sculptures featuring people walking or sitting while holding a mobile phone to their ears, their eyes looking elsewhere inside their own eyes? Perhaps F is right when he says he does not need one for communications as there are more intimate and physical ways that deserve better.

By now, like you, I have delayed the process of submission. The significance of being accepted for publication, then read when published, diminishes with the passage of time. After all, it is not as though one's life is captured and kept there in those pages if one gets published. As I told you the other day, I'd probably keep writing without getting published, writing just a daily need for removing the toxin. I'd probably, I further stated, publish them in my head and start imagining readers.

And there is nothing that will stop you from growing old. One night, as we sit in the couch watching television, she mentions more than once that the couple in the television drama splits up for no reason at all and she wonders if that has something to do with the fact that they no longer find anything in their shared life that excites or even interests them. Sooner or later, one comes to one's death prematurely as one sits before the computer, completely lost in one's own undoings, not wishing to check into a cable-enabled email address only to receive one more junk email or saunter into an over-trotted porn site, only to find oneself unable to erect anymore, over-sexed to the degree of obesity.

Past grammar is unfixable despite the strong urge in me to edit, to correct my previous life, a youth as beautiful as ugly, as syntactically erroneous as structurally. Who are we to judge? Random should as random be, a final entry:

Sunday June 22, 1980: Yesterday evening I did not go to bed until one o'clock. I wrote a number of poems during the past two months, but did not bring them to perfection, for being pressed for time, how could I? So I spent much time copying all of them down and changed some sentences here and there if necessary.

This morning I went to the library with the intention of reading some *B.B.C. Modern English* and *Reader's Digest*. But I found it so interesting that I just could not put the B.B.C. magazines away, and one followed another. I read two magazines all told the whole morning, then left the room half contented, for if situation permitting, I would sit there reading for hours together.

In the afternoon after a short nap, about half an hour, I went to the building No. 8 to watch TV. We, I mean Lionel and I, were a little late, so when we got there it had begun. The film was titled *Carve Her Name with Pride*. I once saw it a year's ago, but this time when I saw it, I had got a different impression. Great changes have taken place on me, so to speak.

This person is no longer there. I realise with a sigh as I finish keying in the last word 'speak'. I can't revise him; it would be like trying to revive him. If these diaries containing him won't be published, publishable, I'll give them a space here in my heart where, paper-less, they shall remain evergreen, or, better still, evergrey, as grey as the matter.

Chapter 3: Field Work: a Man and a Woman Fought

Pan Dalin, a possible ancestor of the villagers with the same surname, was a poet in the Song dynasty, who is known throughout history for an unfinished poem with a single line that survives. Legend has it that he replied, in a letter, to a poet friend enquiring if he had written any new poems, that he was writing a poem when a creditor arrived urging him to pay his rent in arrears, when he managed to only produce that single line he now is famous for. It goes, 'The city is filling with wind and rain as it approaches the Double Ninth Festival'. Zu, growing up in a family with a father that was a great lover of classical poetry, loved such stories. He wondered about the poet's ability to survive the centuries with a single line. He wondered if this was a feat deserving as much praise as volumes of poetry by famed poets. His father thought differently. History is a person with a long memory who never forgets, Zu Senior said. It remembers the bad as well as the good, even if what is good is a mere line of a poem never finished, because if it is a star it will shine the only way it knows: singly and brilliantly, refusing to be obscured by the rest of the crowded stars. Read Du Qiuniang, a woman poet, whose name survives because of her one and only poem while her own life remains virtually unknown.

As he said so, he did what he would normally do, reading aloud from memory 'Gold-threaded Garments', by this one-poem Tang dynasty woman poet:

Treasure not the gold-threaded garments,
Treasure your own youth.
Pick the flowers when they are fresh,
And not wait till the branches are bare.

Vaguely aware of the significance of what his dad had said and of the poem itself, Zu nevertheless had his own life to live, in the small village where fate had taken him. On a night, by the oil lamp, he found himself sitting in bed and writing his entry for the day:

When I refused to go chicken-hunting with him, Han got very upset. He threw tantrums and said he'd go alone and when he got the chicken, he threatened to eat it alone and not share it with anyone. I first expressed my doubts about hunting for chickens as they were not wild ones; they belonged to the peasants. I didn't say that to him. I just said that I wasn't familiar with the surroundings. And I was tired. He went out, quite annoyed, with a lit cigarette stuck to the side of his mouth. Whenever he got angry or wanted to show his manliness, he would light up a cigarette and put it between his lips, always in one corner or the other of his mouth, with his head lifted back in defiance. He had just got back, chucking something onto the earthen floor with a loud thump. 'Got it!' I heard him announcing his achievement in that usual tone of his, overbearing and aggressive. I don't know if we can get along well with each other in the future. But we'll see. I'm not afraid of anyone.

The next day, Cui was the one to cook. Dutifully, she prepared the chicken by soaking it in hot water, removing its feathers and washing it clean. After carefully taking out its gall without breaking it, she cut it into pieces and stir-fried them in a wok, with sliced ginger and chopped spring onion. She did all that efficiently as she had learnt the skill at home from watching her Mum do it. She then put in some soy sauce and vinegar. Zu could hear the clicking and clanging of her turner. But he did not give her a hand, ashamed with the thought itself. Nor did Han and Len help, either. Boys grew up without mastering or even wanting to master the kitchen skills; women were supposed to be the cooks. Xi was the one who insisted that they all share the work. Because of Han's strong opposition, it was eventually decided that the boys do the dishes by turns and that they shoulder-pole drinking water in barrels from the nearby pond while the girls cook the meals.

When she served the chicken, along with bowls of steaming rice, Cui went back to her own room shared with Xi, with the stir-fried bok choy on top of her bowl of rice, but not touching the chicken. That enraged

Han, who thought this was a sheer affront directed at him, meant as a criticism of what he had done in stealing the chicken from the peasants. He said, in a voice audible enough for all to hear, that some Party members wanted to gain credit for themselves so they might eventually end up getting out of the village earlier than the others. Len smiled a tolerant smile, knowing what he was like, a man of fiery temper who had difficulty controlling it sometimes. Zu, for his part, knew his charges to be true or partly true. He had observed how Cui had tried to be nice to everyone, including the village elders and leaders, always presenting everyone with a smiling face, in an attempt to set a brilliant example of moral uprightness as a Chinese Communist Party member. But, on this occasion, she maintained a solemn face, looking straight as she went back into her room, not sharing the meal with the others, showing by the very act that she was a woman of principle, a Party member who did the right thing, though not saying a single word of criticism. Xi got the best part of the chicken because Han liked her enough to keep it for her. But she didn't even take a second look at it. Instead, she simply refused to eat, protesting in a whisper to Len that she was not feeling well. She certainly looked pale, as far as Zu could tell. But she had always looked pale. She was tall and delicate, and moved about with grace. Out of the five living under the same roof of this newly built house, she was a presence that was absent, for she seemed to be hardly ever there, preferring the world outside in the village rather than the one within the house. When the lunch—Zu ate it with guilt because he had declined to join Han in the hunt the previous night and now he was enjoying the chicken—was over, the bowl of the best bits of chicken was left untouched and it left Han fuming. He stormed into the kitchen, making his stomping loud enough for the girls to hear, with the bowl, which, in a blind fit of fury, he could not find a spot to stow away, so he came out with it again. Seeing that the other men were watching, he said, more to himself than to them, that he'd eat the lot if no one wanted it. Then he said, casually ignoring Zu, to Len: Would you like to share this with me? Len looked up in surprise and said, stammering a bit, But you can take the lot, can't you? Seeing that Han was about to lose his temper again, he quickly changed his mind and said, Well, I'll have it then.

祖

The village pond lay, like a mirror, in the arms of Clear Water Village. It served as a huge communal basin for the villagers to do their laundry and to wash their night pots in, and to drink from. Early every morning, Zu would go down to the pond-side, with a face towel and a washbasin, and his toothbrush and toothpaste, to wash his face and brush his teeth. It never occurred to him that the place lacked in hygiene. After he finished doing these usual things, he would go to the toilet, a wooden affair built on the other side of the pond, with part of it extended over the water, for the purpose of letting things excremental slide into the water as food for the fish. As he squatted over the hole through which he could observe the water below, with occasional ripples when a school of fish swam by, his thoughts went homeward. At the back of the compound attached to the work unit where Mum worked and lived, there was a toilet, used by the staff and their family members. Mum would often complain how much it stank whenever she came back from it; she would complain that even her clothes smelt. Zu found the comparison amusing although his experience was different. He would often go there with a book. The one book that moved him immensely was *Les Misérables* by Victor Hugo, in Chinese translation. He was one day squatting there doing his bowel movements while reading it when he found, without knowing why, he was much moved. The miserable ups and downs of Rang Ah Rang, or Jean Valjean, were such, mixed with the strong stench that wafted from down below, that he was moved to the brink of tears. In that instant, he achieved willy-nilly a full identification with Jean Valjean as if he was the ex-convict cum mayor himself, overwhelmed with a desire to do good the way Valjean does in the book. He was brought back to the reality by a loud call by Pan Da, the village head, so loud that it rang throughout the village: Get up! Get up! All to the fields!

In the misty semi-dark morning, villagers were up and about, with their hoes and their tools, going out into the rice paddies in front of the village. There were dogs barking. And there was an undulation of cocks crowing, setting in motion a chorus of cocks crowing from the surrounding villages. It was spring, time for pulling up rice seedlings in bunches before planting them in the empty waiting paddies, filled with water.

The work was never inspiring. As Pan De, the returned soldier from the Korean War, said as soon as the group of students arrived at the village, You guys are not here to stay long; you'll have to return where you come from pretty soon. For this reason, he'd caution them to not work too hard in the fields. He didn't have to worry about Han because he could see in one glance that he was not the sort of guy cut out for hard labour despite his humble background with both his parents minding a curbside stand, selling fruit and vegetables. All he wanted was a good time, doing as little work as possible. Right now, when bunches of the pulled seedlings were carried to the ridge of the rice paddies and were laid in a row, for the barefooted peasants to pick them up one by one, holding it like a grenade and throwing it to where the women peasants were in the water, their backs bent and their hands busy separating the bunch into smaller bunches before planting them in the soil, in nice and neat rows, he was nowhere to be seen. Zu knew that he had one of his usual excuses: going to the loo, his toilet visits more frequent than the rest of them.

Remembering his own tainted background, Zu was determined that he would work hard and do a good job. Obviously, the way he worked impressed the peasants. Some of them exchanged glances and whispered to each other, saying, This bookish boy looks like someone hard on the job, willing to put in an effort. That's very good.

The work, on the other hand, was great fun for the peasants, apparently. Standing on the ridge, the men were aiming at the women when they chucked the seedling bunches towards them. The bunches seemed to have grown eyes; they didn't land on the backs of the working women, nor in front of them or far behind them. They always seemed to land right between their legs, wetting their lower-downs instantly, making the men laugh out loud among themselves, some jumping for joy, others holding up their hands, wildly waving, like kids. But the women didn't take it as an offence. Instead, they joined in the fun, and hit back. One woman, by the name of Spring Flower, took hold of a handful of mud from underneath her lower-downs and, stealing close to the standing men, chucked it right in the face of Pan An, a handsome man of a broad face, heavy brows and big eyes, with a row of grinning teeth, white against his sun-tanned skin. His laughter, loudest among others, was instantly choked back in. It was now the women's turn to laugh their heads off. Zu watched this and laughed along with the others. But he never had the guts to do the same, as these people were not familiar to him. He was thinking one of his thoughts about living and working this way for the rest of one's life when he heard a loud thump. Before he knew what was going on, the man and the woman were already down in the water, the man cursing, and the woman yelling abuse, more ferocious and dirtier than the man, when all the male hands were set upon them, trying to separate them, green and yellow with mud and water and ragged rice seedlings.

Chapter 4: Mother's Letter

Zu received a letter from Mother. At home when he was alone with her, the son and his mother would often fight over trifles. From when he was a little boy, Zu recalled, he liked reading lying in bed, with a book popped up against the wall in front of him. Mother would come over, pick up the book and put it width-wise, the way you read a book when you stand. Zu tried to read but found it hard unless he twisted his head sidewise. But that caused pain and discomfort. After Mum went away, he put the book back the way that went more along with the eye movements where he lay. Mum chastised him but he wouldn't listen. There were conflicts with table manners, too. Mum wanted him to make no noise when eating, not even when eating noodles, a noisy food. Zu was astonished to observe how people were chomping and chewing noisily at that first village lunch where no one seemed to care how much noise they were making. In contrast, he seemed to be the only one who didn't make any eating sound. Then, Mum made sure that he put his chopsticks next to the bowl of rice he was eating, not on top of it, because one would only put the chopsticks over the bowl in lunch or dinner prepared for a funeral. She would also forbid him to talk over a meal because it was considered poor manners. And she never liked him to ask any questions when she and his father were discussing matters concerning their own colleagues, her motto being, When adults talk, kids listen, not cut in. On one occasion, they were talking about someone Zu happened to know of, one expression kept popping up in their conversation, which literally meant skin stumbling or *pipan*. When it was too much for him to suppress his curiosity, Zu found himself wondering aloud what that meant. Then came Mum's warning: Stop asking that question. You are not supposed to know as a child. Even Dad, who was normally tolerant enough with new words or expressions, even with English—in fact, his passion was English—did not relent. But a child had his own way of finding out and Zu managed to do so eventually, even though, at the time, he resented Mum and Dad for not being willing to tell.

Mum's letter, hand-written in the calligraphic style of Lin Feiqing, began thus,

Since you left, my son, I have begun missing your footsteps. You know how you would always run back home instead of walking, the length of the outer corridor echoing with your footsteps till you reached the entrance to the inner hallway. There, you would pause and, your heavy breathing audible, you would jump down the step. On quite a few occasions, when I was in the room, I would hear your footsteps outside approaching, in the wider corridor. I thought they were yours. But they disappeared. Or sometimes, it was the footsteps of Auntie Hong or Auntie Chang. I don't know how to express myself. Isn't it strange but it is these footsteps that made my heart leap for joy. Now that you've gone to the country, I find myself missing them constantly.

How's your life in the village? In your last letter, you said you had to share accommodation with the other students in your newly built earthen house. How do you get along with them? Whenever you live with more than one person, it is essential that you try to get along well with them. Be generous. Be tolerant. And, most important of all, do not easily throw tantrums as you would at home. Your own Mum wouldn't mind it much. But others may not take it too kindly. While you can cope with the physical labour in the village, you still have to mind your own health. Wear warm in spring to avoid catching cold. Or else when you have another asthmatic attack, it won't be as easy as here to seek medical attention.

Everything here is as usual and good. And I am quite fine, too.

The letter and her calligraphic style, often admired by her colleagues, deeply impressed Zu because of the sentimental note it struck, something he had thought Mum was incapable of. His own 'footsteps'? Living at home, he'd never taken note of his own footsteps. How strange it was

146

that she would miss his footsteps. Unlike most of her women colleagues, she smoked, she didn't cook, and she liked to hold conversations with her male colleagues as much as she did with their female counterparts. Curiously, though, in his early teens, she had wanted him to dress up as a girl because, Zu recalled, she had always wanted a girl; a boy was a mere accident, not willed into existence. As he grew up, he became rebellious. His rebellion coincided with the advent of the Cultural Revolution when he was a mere pre-teen. For the first time, he saw how people died before his very eyes. In one single year, everything seemed to have happened. It was the year Dad taught him to learn by heart the poem by the decadent king-poet Li Yu. He was captured after he lost his kingdom and ordered to be poisoned by Emperor Taizong of Song, reputedly because he wrote the poem, remembered ever afterwards for the line that goes, 'a river runs eastward carrying spring waters.' Without prompting, Zu could recite it off the top of his head,

The Beautiful Woman Yu

So many things have gone, turning into the past, but when will the end come for spring flowers and the autumn moon?

The east wind came to the little pavilion, last night, when I couldn't even begin to recall my old kingdom in ruins, facing the bright moonlight

The carved balustrades and the marble steps must still remain the same except that their red features have changed

If you ask how sad I am, I'm as sad as the river that runs eastward carrying spring waters

It was indeed a sad time, not in the sense of Li Yu, the king-poet, but in the ushering of a time no one had expected. School was suspended, all of a sudden. Streets were thronging with peasants; armed with *chongdan*,

147

shaped like a bamboo shoulder-pole with either end as sharp as a horn; staff of various work units; primary school students having nothing to do; and people from all walks of life. Zu was wandering on the street like a lost soul, not knowing whether to go home or linger a tad longer before he did. Just then, he found that people were streaming into the department store in the centre of the town, its gates wide open, no shop-assistants minding their counters. In fact, all the counters were under thick covers of cloth. The place had lost its usual glitter and glamour, instead becoming a cold, dark and desolate human jungle. In no time, he found himself standing on the open top of a three-storey building, where kids were running around, uttering loud, excited cries as they did so. Zu went to the low retaining wall surrounding this open top and took a look at the street below. It was normally lined with street stands selling vegetables, fruits, fish, pork, eggs, tofu, tobacco, brooms, soaps, rice, but now they were all gone. As he watched and wondered, Zu heard a noise coming from below, not from the street but from the bowels of the building. The noise was amplified because of the spaciousness of the rooms in the building; it sounded almost as if they were not rooms but a large empty auditorium. The kids had stopped running. They followed Zu's example by coming to the low wall. But it was too high for them to see anything. A voice said behind him, But they are coming to blows. Zu turned his head back and saw that it was Hei, a local boy from his neighbourhood. How on earth he was there and why didn't he see him first thing was beyond Zu. But he said, Who's fighting whom?

Hei said, Well, you know, it's the two different groups. Then he entered into a prolonged monologue about the struggle between the Rebels and the Loyalists, to which Zu only lent half an ear, until a loud bang went off, like the crack of thunder, below them in the hollow hall that those rooms resembled. A chorus rose all around him as kids were jumping for joy, without knowing why: Someone's got shot! Someone's got shot!

The atmosphere became taut with increasing tension as invisible beings began throwing things from inside the windows, out onto the street down below. Things got started, and people followed, getting thrown out, too. As this was happening, careful and caring hands on the street found a ladder from nowhere and put it up against one of the open windows because someone was climbing out of it. With his own eyes, Zu saw how the man let himself out foot first, going down rung by rung, his hands holding the ladder on either side when a hand, of an invisible being, shot out and pushed the ladder outward. By then, the man had got down half the way, level with the second floor. That push alone landed him on his back, together with the ladder, which was lying on top of him. He went down head first, his back hitting the cement of the street with a dull plop. Hands were scrambling to remove the overlying ladder but other hands were quicker. One pair of hands, in particular, had found a brick nearby and raised it high. As Zu saw it poise in midair, he held his breath and dreaded what was going to happen. No one came to the man's rescue. They stood watching. The man, too, knew what was going to happen. He must have seen the brick raised above his head. But all he could do was put his arm around his head to protect it. The brick came smashing down, and down again. And again. Years after, in his memory, Zu could never decide whether the man was lying face down or up. But the detail recalled was unmistakable that the brick either smashed the back of the man's head or his face, till the man stopped stirring, lying in a pool of blood.

What closely followed was even more terrifying. A group of peasants, tall and strong, their muscles brown, bulging, and shiny with sweat, came rushing into the street with their *chongdan* balanced in their hands, like bayonets, pointed to the crowd. Instantly, all disappeared, not a trace of humanity left, except the armed peasants, yelling abuse and looking wildly for victims, in a deserted street.

Zu read the letter by the kerosene lamp, recalling the past. By his side, in his bed, was a copy of *Goya: A Biography*, in translation, which he read whenever he could find time. There was much death in the man's paintings. But he was particularly intrigued by one Goya did, portraying one of his enemies in the shape of an enormous penis. He was so amused that he shared the detail with Len, his roommate. Len had to laugh. But it was obvious he wasn't impressed. It was a dirty detail, not something to be broadcast, least of all for one to be proud of sharing with people. Seeing that people seemed shy after he told a few others of it, Zu ceased the adventure of sharing his discovery, if it could be called one, and kept his private thoughts to himself; he admired the artist for his invention and daring and that was that.

He went on to record that day's events in his diary, a habit he had formed since middle school during the Cultural Revolution. On this spring night, he recorded how, when Pan Da, the production team leader, chastised Han for not working hard enough, the latter retorted that he was having a bellyache while muttering a well-known rhyming couplet that goes, '*Guantian guandi, guanbuzhu wo lashi fangpi*', that means, 'You can control the sky and the earth but you can't control me wanting to shit and piss.' He also recorded, in an entry, how Xi became the talk of the village when she was found swimming in the reservoir behind the village up in the hills where the villagers were shocked to find that she was swimming naked, well, almost naked, because she wore a swimming suit that exposed large parts of her body, her bare face, her bare arms, her bare legs and her bare feet, everything bare except what was hidden beneath her swimming trunk. That, in the eyes of the villagers, was tantamount to going naked. Never in the history of this village had any men gone swimming in the open, let alone a woman and in such a scantily clad manner. Zu recalled, though, how happy she seemed, when she entered into the house in the early evening, followed closely at her heels by two village young men, about Zu's age, Lin and Shun, both her admirers. For some reason, Zu didn't like the latter the first time he set his eyes on him. This was a man who seemed all smiles. But there was something going on underneath that Zu found hard to fathom. He was the production team treasurer and, in that sense, was an official. He greeted everyone like he was an official, too. As he strutted around the house, he poked into every corner, wondering how things were and admiring the city things they had brought with them to the country, particularly the polyester shirt Zu was wearing, clicking his tongue like he was impressed. But, out of the corner of his eye, Zu could see he was thinking otherwise as he seemed to have a mind of his own. Lin, on the other hand, was lean, whose mouth had lips that never met, thus leaving his teeth constantly exposed in a perpetual grin. He stood in the middle of the house, a large space flanked by two rooms on either side, like a village idiot, smiling a stupid smile that seemed to be eternally etched on his face. But Zu, for some reason, liked him enough to chat with him and, in the meantime, he noticed Xi going back into her room shared with Cui, not to come out again till he and Len went to bed. She seemed to prefer to go about her own thing in a secret manner, not wanting to be placed under constant scrutiny by the others.

Chapter 5: Sha's Story

Soon it was getting warm. The rice paddies were a vast green expanse of growing rice stocks. Chirpings of rice birds were heard everywhere. In the sky, there were cloudlarks, and peasants were seen in twos and threes, doing the *haoyang*, weeding the rice stocks twice the length of one's middle-finger. They did it without any support, unlike Zu and the other student-peasants, who had to use a bamboo stick to support themselves. It was a simple enough job. You had to tell the weeds and the rice stocks apart, weeds that, by the very look, were darker coloured and harsher textured. Then, as you inched along between the rows of the stocks, you separated the weeds from the rice and pressed the former, first with your toe, then the rest of your sole, into the soil, thus stopping them from growing. At first, Zu got laughed at because he would occasionally press the wrong thing into the soil. That is, he would press the rice stocks down, leaving the weeds standing. Gradually, he learnt to separate the good from the bad and managed to do a few long rows back and forth in the morning, though not as many as a full labourer could do. They, as student-peasants, were spared the heavy duties, such as scraping the cow dung off the floors of the cowsheds, shoulder-poling barrels of it to the fields and picking up handfuls to chuck them all over the fields. The result was general stench. Pan Da was considerate enough to give them a miss as he thought it harsh to put the student-peasants through this dirtiness.

But there were other pains, though minor, such as the leeches. Despite the fact that they wore long trousers, with the ends tied around the ankles, leeches found their way right up to their thighs, sometimes even to the crotch. During recess, Zu was horrified to find his legs covered with them when he untied the knots around his ankles. He tried to pull one off, cigarette-long. But the leech didn't come off even as it was being stretched to the limit. Someone came along and said, Let me do it. It was Pan De. Instead of picking the leech off, he patted Zu on the leg near it, with a moderate amount of force so that, one by one, the leeches fell, leaving spots of blood all over Zu's legs.

You know what? He said to Zu. If you pull hard at it and break it, it'll leave the leech's poisonous head buried inside your leg. That may lead to diseases. You either wait till they, sucking, and filled with your blood, fall off, one by one, by themselves or you pat to shock them off.

Carefully, he sprinkled some salted water over Zu's legs, saying that it would help the wounds heal quickly. Pan De, generally known as Brother De among the other male peasants, was someone Zu found not only helpful but also knowledgeable and experienced. He had fought against the Americans in the Korean War, when China sent 200,000 troops to North Korea on 25 October 1950. His two kids, one girl and one boy, were named after the War effort, the girl called Kangmei, Fighting the Americans, and the boy, Yuanchao, Supporting the Koreans. He would, from time to time, talk about his days in North Korea, particularly things he had experienced himself or people he had heard about. One story he told was horrifying. According to him, his life was saved by a piss. He was travelling with a truckload of soldiers when he felt the urgent need to pee. The military truck went on its way without him, the driver telling him to hop onto the next one. That's what he did when the next one arrived. No sooner had he got onto the truck when they heard a huge explosion ahead and saw a ball of fire shooting into the sky. Shortly after, the news came that a bomb had hit the truck, killing all, including the driver, when they arrived on a bridge, which was destroyed by the bomb as well, from an American bomber.

In school, Zu had heard about gruesome stories of war heroes such as Qiu Shaoyun and Huang Jiguang. The former let himself be burnt alive to avoid any slightest movement that would attract the enemy's attention to his mates lying around in an ambush and the latter blocked an embrasure in a fortress held by the enemy, so that his comrades could successfully launch their attack. Such heroic stories had been moving enough for Zu to want to be a soldier himself. But it was not going to be because of his tainted background. Before the regime change in 1949, when the Communist Party took power, his father had worked as a low-level official in the Kuomintang government. What future he might have in the way of promotion turned out to be impossible after the change, when he was locked into a category known as 'Pseudo Officials', officials of the defeated and dispelled Kuomintang, which meant there was no hope for him to ever rise above his current position of a factory accountant, and meant his children had no hope of advancing in any future career. The only hope was to apply for a Party membership, which Zu had done on numerous occasions at school but had been knocked back each time, because of the shadow cast from his father's past.

Listening to Brother De talking about his past and recalling his own, in the shadow of his father, Zu didn't reveal his thoughts, finding no one to share them with. His only friend was his diary, that much he knew, and he stayed up late with it whenever he could find time. The entry he made that night went as follows,

> The girls were assigned a much better job, of chasing the ricebirds off the rice paddies, because they were considered unused to the hard labour, their city-bred hands incapable of handling heavy duties. Cui reported that she had almost caught a bird with her straw hat. But just as she thought she'd got it and was about to reach under for it when it came rushing out, right beneath her eyes. While she was enthusing about this, Xi was dismissive. She looked glum. The only thing she let out was a 'the sun was too strong.' It was indeed strong. Despite the straw hat, it touched one's face to a degree that the skin instantly turned brown. I didn't have a problem. I am not afraid of the sun. As a boy, I went barefoot and bareheaded in high summer on the Yangtze River bank, and let myself get so suntanned that my skin peeled, and peeled again, covered with the white residuals, till a new skin replaced the old, that was dazzling in its new colour, commonly known as the ancient bronze colour, which I was proud of. Xi is withdrawn. She doesn't talk to anyone. Of her I know little, except that her father is a banker and is under a cloud because he is a capitalist roader. As for Cui, she is well-grounded because she herself is a Party member and her parents seem both Party members, too. Han, as soon as he finished dinner, prepared

mainly by Cui and occasionally assisted by Xi, went back into his own room, one he occupied alone because he didn't like the idea of sharing, without offering to do the dishes as if he had no part in it, his part being an eater, not a dish-washer. Len and I did them alternately because that seemed to be the right thing to do. After all, work like that should be shared equally among us. I did mention that Han should do the work. But he was angry and didn't like my suggestion.

祖

While he was interested in *Goya: A Biography*, Zu did not touch *The Journey*, a big novel of 480,000 Chinese characters by Guo Xianhong, of which everyone received a complimentary copy from the government, supposedly to encourage the student-peasants to use it as a good example for them to learn from by sticking to the countryside. But he didn't read it; he couldn't. He was later to know that three million copies had been printed. But he didn't read it; he didn't even open it. He just let it lie on his desk by the window, gathering dust. Out the window, he could see an open space between their house and those of the villagers'. Although he had been in the village for many months, he had not stepped into any one of their houses; he hadn't been invited. The only one he had ever got near to was occupied by a single man, known to be the son of an old landlord. He was Pan Chang, a smiling man, disgraced by his past. Whenever there was a political struggle meeting held at the commune, to which members of the production team in Clear Water Village and in the surrounding villages would go, Chang would be struggled with, along with other surviving landlords or their offspring, to keep the memory alive that these were class enemies notorious for their past exploitation of the poor and lower-middle peasants, who had to be constantly struggled against, lest the people relive the past misery. It also served the purpose of instruction that the present was a glorious one, thanks to Chairman Mao and the Party.

Once, Han pulled a reluctant Zu out of a book he was reading, whispering into his ear that he'd go and get a chicken. But Zu had made his mind up that even if he went, he wouldn't do anything; he'd just watch, which was exactly what he did, not wanting to incur anger on Han's part. They came to a stop in front of a chicken coop against the hillside, beside a ramshackle house. As Han motioned for Zu to stand still and not make a sound, he went up to the coop and put his hand inside it, starting to grope. Just then, a coughing sound was heard as a man emerged. Han quickly withdrew his hand and, featuring an instant smile on his face, he made to offer a cigarette to Chang. But the latter refused, smiling his constant smile, and said, in a humble voice, But that gesture you made is so terrible.

Han lit his cigarette, which he left between his lips to one corner of his mouth in a threatening manner, much the way a street hooligan did, and said, in a falsetto voice, What did you say?

Chang backpedalled. Holding up his hands, as if to ward off an imaginary impending blow, he said, Nothing, nothing really. But Zu distinctly heard what he had implied in his remark about the 'terrible' act of stealing and was moved enough by his terrified look to say to Han, Let's go.

祖

Ever since his pre-teen years, Zu had known one political campaign after another, till now when another one was ushered in by the central government under Mao. Called the Criticise Lin, Criticise Confucius Campaign, it aimed at destroying the inimical influences of Confucius and, by extension, of Lin Biao, his follower. A local of Zu's, in the same county, Lin was one of the best ten Chinese field marshals, known for his war strategies and fighting skills as a military commander. One of the widespread stories about his personal life detailed when he was stationed with his army in northeast China, in the Liaoning-Shenyang Campaign, and Lin would make sure that the peasant's house he was going to stay in had no women, either wives or daughters, that were good-looking, to avoid falling into pitfalls of possible love affairs, either natural or set up, as many of the other military officers were known to have been trapped in. For this, Zu much admired this fallen leader, fallen because he had fought against Mao, plotting to bring him down from power. Instead, he ended up dying in a plane crash in Ondorhaan of Mongolia, after a failed coup attempt. When the news was read out to all the students in his class, Zu was shocked. In that instant, someone he had grown up to admire, had turned into an enemy that he was now told to denounce and criticise. Decades after, he would still keep that admiration. But, at an impressionable age of 16, when coercion and silence were the order of the day, he could do nothing but follow the herd. Family advice against rashness and stories about the downfall of outspoken people had served well to manage his own mouth properly, never saying anything improper and, better still, keeping it tight shut.

This campaign, at a village level, was reflected in the big posters that Zu helped put together. He essentially did it all by himself, as the rest of this student-peasant household were reluctant to join in the effort, with excuses of being busy or sick or not skilful with the brush, even though Len and Cui wrote a few small pieces of criticism. Han, the oldest, and the strongest he thought he was, wouldn't do a thing. And no one dared raise a brow. As for Xi, looking so pallid and wan, no one dared make a suggestion that she write either, although later on she contributed a drawing of her own, showing Confucius and Lin Biao cowering under the iron fists of the people.

Zu wrote his own, with a brush dipped in ink, on a large piece of white paper spread out over a wooden table, their dining table. Then he copied the pieces hand-written by Len and Cui on the same before he, with the help of Han, who enjoyed doing that rather than writing itself, put the paper onto the wall. Many years after, Zu would feel ashamed of what he had written then, all slogans copied from such newspapers as *People's Daily*, words and phrases commonly seen in the media. But his calligraphic style, written with the brush, drew attention from someone from an adjacent village. This was a learned man by the name of Bao, who dared call himself Bao Xueqin, after Cao Xueqin, author of the famed novel, *A Dream of Red Mansions*.

He came striding into the house, standing before the posters on the wall and admiring them while he clicked his tongue, making the sound of tsik, tsik, tsik. Then, without even asking Zu, he fetched a roll of pieces of paper from his pocket and thrust it into Zu's hands as he said, Read them. Read them.

Zu, his hand holding the roll, took a look at Bao and saw a broad head, covered with thick straggly hair that looked dirty, in clothes that were tattered here and there. He quickly glanced through the pieces, littered with poems written in the classic style of 4-line, 5-line or 8-line poems, each poem with either 5-character lines or 7-character lines. The poems were plain. Nothing out of the ordinary. He passed the roll back to Bao, without a word.

This seemed to hurt Bao so much that it set him talking at once. He said, You must come to my place one day and I'll show you a novel I have written. Then you'll realise how good I am because I can do as well as Cao, perhaps even better than him. As for the poems you've just read, they are mere trivia. I've got much better stuff at home. I'll show you if you come.

Without knowing why, Zu found himself bursting into laughter as he glanced around at the others, finding Len amused, too. Peeved, Bao left, without as much as saying goodbye.

祖

One early morning in spring, Zu lay awake in bed. He didn't know if he was woken up by the cuckoo flying across the rice paddies in the distance, the crowing of the cocks, one after another, in his own village, or from the surrounding villages. Or if this had something to do with Sha, his schoolmate from the Middle School days. At school, she had fallen in love with a music teacher, many years her senior. Their love quickly developed into a passionate love affair, so passionate that stories were told of how they were having sex everywhere, on the sports ground at night, or underneath the wooden planks of the stage in the auditorium until they were found out. The harsh punishment that resulted saw them transferred separately to two primary schools in two separate small towns, far away from home. There, in that primary school, she worked as a teacher, even before she graduated from middle school. When she learnt about his whereabouts, she wrote him a letter, inviting Zu to visit her.

It was a woman who met him at her door when Zu arrived after a long walk through the spring fields. So matured the woman was that Zu could not believe his own eyes. He made a mental comparison of her as she was now, with the one back in the old school days when she was indistinguishable from the other schoolgirls, in her own flowery cotton jacket in winter and blouses and skirts in summer. But now she looked like a married woman, except that she lived alone, with no husband or kids in sight. When he came inside her room, he could see in one glance that there was a desk against the wall, a bed by the desk, and a deep brown leather case. That was all. Because she had only one wooden stool, she had to borrow another two lower and smaller ones to sit on, with the higher one serving as the table.

Zu and Sha started talking about the old days, even as she was preparing the meal, a simple affair cooked on her kerosene stove. They talked about how they were deeply impressed with the North Korean films shown, such as *The Girl Who Sells Flowers*. Many of their classmates burst into tears while watching it although, according to Zu, he remained unmoved, never shedding a single tear, finding it much less moving than *Beican shijie*, Victor Hugo's novel, *Les Misérables*, although the Korean music was wonderfully fresh. Sha had to laugh, perhaps out of curiosity, or because of the fact that she knew he was an oddball, someone one would see doing things entirely on his own, never in the company of others, and given to asking strange questions that would embarrass his teachers. Zu himself didn't know that he was to record Korean songs in longhand he had heard on radio in numbered musical notation, and offer them to the girl he had fallen in love with, hearing her sing them in a beautiful voice, years after his country days ended.

When asked how, Sha reminded him that she saw, with her own eyes, how Zu asked a mathematical question that upset the math teacher, with the result of him physically dragging Zu out of the classroom, not allowing him to come back in, a scene Zu remembered clearly, but without rancour and without remembering any exact details. His memory was a strange one that tended to be a mass of impressions instead of details. He remembered he was dragged out of the classroom and that he was angry. But he forgot why.

On the other hand, Zu had to carefully avoid mentioning anything in relation to what had happened between her and the teacher. Instead, he talked about his passion for listening to Enemy Broadcasting on his radio by stealth, a passion he cultivated whenever he had time while his mother was not nearby. He would turn the radio knob from one station to another, his ear glued to it, turning the volume to its lowest so that no one might hear the sound. With practice, he had trained himself to distinguish between Asian languages and European languages, the musical Vietnamese, the hyperactive Korean, the highly-strung notes of Thai, the nasal sound of Russian, the familiar speech of English that he had heard his father use, and the staccato German, without knowing a single word of any of those except English, which he had learnt at school. He recalled how well he had done in the exams, winning 100% in marks twice, even though, as he recalled, the sentences constructed were no more than 'Learn from the Workers, Peasants and Soldiers!' and 'Long live Chairman Mao!' and he was proud of himself, when a remark came from Sha that froze him, after she had brought all the dishes she had prepared onto the stool-table.

What do you think I should do to handle this matter between him and I? said she.

Zu was struck speechless. He had been pretending, shamming forgetfulness. But the question was confronting, and he found it hard to skirt around it. He raised his eyes and saw her stained teeth, once again, on many occasions, too many occasions, a detail he never failed to notice but had not mentioned to anyone else.

I'm not sure, he confessed, honestly, then quickly added, What do you think?

In tears, she began telling him how much she had suffered since she and the teacher she loved were chased out of the school and were put down in this tiny place far from home and loved ones. For many days, shortly after her arrival, she said, she could not sleep for nights on end and she could not eat anything, her eyes swollen from crying. But for her enduring love of the teacher, she would have taken her own life.

Would you like to get back to him and can you? Came the question from Zu.

I'd love to, said Sha, her eyes red. But not for the moment because that would attract attention from the authorities and result in even worse punishment.

Like what? Zu was surprised; he couldn't understand why love was cause for concern and why it had to be punished even when it was made known that they were in love with each other. The simplest thing would be to allow the two of them to live together and get married.

With a deep sigh, Sha dropped the subject. Avoiding his eye, she picked the choicest part of a stewed pork rib with her chopsticks, and put it in his bowl, over the rice.

Sha didn't bring up the matter again.

Chapter 6: Double-rush Time

This place, Zu began, I'm telling you, is far, far away, from anywhere, so far away one does not even know what it is called. Let's just call it the South.

The night was falling. The peasants stood around him, listening. The kids were running around inside the house, giving each other chase, laughing and shrieking with shammed terror. Len was sitting on the edge of his bed, doing nothing, just staring, out of the window. Han was again looking at himself in the mirror, trimming his moustache, which he thought made him more manly and handsome. The other two girls were inside their own room, where Zu had never stepped in, occupied with things Zu had no knowledge of and didn't wish to know, either. Lin had a cotton jacket on, broken in places where you could see the white cotton bursting out, like flowers. He listened with his mouth agape, as if he couldn't close it. An was there, too. He was passing by when he noticed the noise from inside, so he popped in to see what was going on. But the first thing he asked was, But where are the girls? Zu paid no attention to him, as he knew his interest was not in him or any other boys. An went up to the wall, covered in big posters, and began reading them aloud, character after character. He got most of them wrong but Zu didn't correct him. He let him pretend while continuing with his imagining.

He said, They have a habit in the South. They don't give you a handshake. Instead, they grab your balls as a way of greeting.

As he said so, his eye fell on Lin, his mouth wide open. If a fly happened to fly by, it might find its way inside there before it was too late for him to act; he might shut his mouth with the fly in it. Zu made a gesture that surprised even himself. He reached for Lin's lower-downs. But Lin was nimble enough to get out of the way with a jump backward and came back for his, his hand shooting out at Zu's. Unused to the situation that he himself had caused, Zu beat a quick retreat, fending off the assaulting hand, as a detail emerged deep from his memory.

Many years earlier, in his early teens, Zu had visited his Dad alone, in another town upstream of the Yangtze. Known as Black Dragon Town in ancient times and now as Round Wind, this town had an area of slightly over 100 square kilometres. Each year, when summer vacation came, Mum would urge him to go and visit Dad. The thought, a swift one, came to Zu once: 'Why does she not want to come together with me?' before he gave it up. He went alone on board 'East is Red', a ship that plied between Wuhan and Shanghai, along a long wooden plank that linked the bank to the ship, picked a place on the second-floor deck, sitting on a low wooden bench, among the other passengers, and traveled upstream for half a day, arriving usually after night had fallen. He would sit there, a teenager on his own, watching the others. No one would speak to him, nor would he speak to anyone. He saw how a peasant woman was taking a nap, sitting in the middle of her shoulder-pole, with each of its end baskets full of golden persimmons. His mouth watered instantly. But he looked away, trying to ward off the temptation, to where the river was, a thoroughfare of yellow waters, rolling eastward ceaselessly, set ablaze where the sun struck it. He had heard that Dad had been struggled with, at his work unit, with a big wooden board hanging from his neck, with large black characters streaming across it, to this effect: 'Down with the Kuomintang Official, a Tired Bourgeois Running Dog!' He didn't like such things. He didn't tell anyone that he didn't like it. He imagined that his father must be a tired man. But he wasn't when he met him. Instead, he seemed in high spirits, talking and laughing with his colleagues, telling them that Zu was his son and asking him to call this man, Shushu (Uncle), or that woman, Ayi (Aunty), something he did not like to do because he was embarrassed, but that he felt he had somehow to do, under the circumstances. One Ayi, in particular, had impressed Zu as she spoke Mandarin with a perfect Beijing accent, so perfect, indeed, that Zu thought she was a radio broadcaster, the one who would always make important government announcements and make her voice heard throughout the country. When he asked Dad where Zhan Ayi (Auntie Zhan) was now, Dad frowned and, with an impatient wave of his hand, stopped him, then and there. It was not till much later, when he returned to Dad's tiny room, allotted by his work unit, that

Dad revealed what had happened, in as few words as possible: She had committed suicide because she had committed the *pipan*. Subsequently, he wouldn't be drawn out, however much Zu tried. But he had already guessed it as it must have been as a result of something similar to what had happened between Sha and the teacher she loved. What he couldn't work out was why she should have killed herself. She could have managed like Sha, couldn't she?

He kept these private thoughts to himself and was content enough with the smallness of Dad's room, so small, in fact, that when his own bed was set up in the middle of the room, it was filled to capacity, leaving a narrow gap between his bed and Dad's bed, and the desk against the wall. Here, in the cramped space left for him after Dad went to work, he did what a newly formed habit inclined him to do: combing his hair backward while looking at himself in the hand mirror, a tiny one Dad must have used for his daily appearance. Unlike most of the other boys in his class, Zu's hair was straight, standing erect and hard on his scalp, which he could neither press down or back. However, when he tried to comb it backwards, his comb dipped in water, a feminine look appeared, much in the same way actors in the 1930s films looked, and he was aroused, his penis standing erect, strangely and magnificently, as he was swept over with a sense of pleasure, tenderness even, as if he had become two in that instant, a woman in a man that the man fell in love with. Out of shame, though, he would put his hair back in its original straight manner, for fear this secret might be found out, and as soon as that was done his erection subsided.

The very first thing that happened after he did that and went out onto the street, was that he bumped into someone who happened to be passing by. It was a boy much younger and shorter than him. An argument ensued, in which he told the boy off in a threatening manner, when the boy, looking unafraid, went straight for Zu's balls, taking them in his grip without letting go. This unexpected act of violence took Zu aback. He was about to hit back when the boy tightened his grip. The pain was so much that he 'ah'ed and had to give up resistance with the boy's threat that he'd squash his balls if he fought back. This experience left Zu humiliated and disconsolate for days on end although he couldn't even share it with anyone else, not even his father. He hid his shame as he always did, deep in his own heart.

祖

Soon it was double rush time when the whole village came alive, going to the fields before sunrise and returning home after sundown. It was harvest time and seeding time, harvesting the ripened rice and planting rice seedlings in late July, both at the same time. With the girls agreeing to stay home cooking, the boys went to the fields and learnt to do the real thing. This consisted of cutting down the rice stocks with a sickle, putting them together and tying them up in large bundles, carrying them to the threshing ground with a *chongdan*, and thrashing them up before getting the grains in.

It was the hottest time of year. The sun, once risen, never seemed to fall, and it was not one sun, but two, the second one much bigger and wider, reflected in the golden colour of the ears of rice extending as far as the eye could see. Zu, new to the job of cutting the rice, was so slow he could never catch up with the rest of the peasants; but, even as he was slightly better than Han and Len, he was determined to do a good job, following his father's motto that one should excel in what one does, however trivial it is and wherever one finds oneself. Han had no intention of competing with anyone. He'd work for a while, then stop, going to the bank between the two rice paddies where he'd pause and drink from a large bowl of tea. Len was happy with the way it went, taking his time. He didn't want to be seen as lazy nor did he like to apply himself too much to the work. Zu was the one who thought he could do better. He went slowly with the job, getting used to the way the sickle swept from one side to the other as bunches of rice stocks, grasped in his left hand, fell to the side, and lay next to the standing stocks in a row, like a long, paved path of gold. The colour of the ears of rice, their smell, mixed with the aroma of the soil underfoot, and the delight in the act of harvesting as well as the excitement of work itself, left Zu wanting for more, instead of otherwise. Gradually, he quickened his pace as he got the hang of it, working with rhythm, not taking too few or too many bunches in his left hand before his right hand took a swipe at them with the sickle. By noon, he was happy to find that he was able to work as fast as some of the women peasants although the male ones left him far behind as they were really adept at the job.

Years after, Zu would remember the sun, of all the things. He would remember it as a fiery ball, in the middle of the sky, taking years to move an inch, never seeming to move even. Unlike the sun, one never stopped moving. It was always one rice paddy of fallen stocks after another till the sun was blown up to many times its original size as it edged towards the Western skies, hanging there like a huge lantern, bloody red. People heaved a sigh, not because how beautiful it was, but because it was finally time to go home. By then, they would have worked 15 hours or so.

Things followed one another in quick succession, in which Zu saw a pattern: Rice stocks, standing, then fallen, then standing again in bundles, then all gone, leaving the stubbly fields, a pattern that seemed to suggest something significant. He didn't dwell long on this because something else caught his attention as now it was time to carry the *caotou*, or the rice bundles, to the threshing ground.

Despite the peasants, particularly Pan Shun's warnings against the heaviness of the bundles, weighing 25 kilograms at either end, Zu insisted that he do the job. He was handed a *chongdan*, with which he thrust one end, like a bayonet, into the bundle, right beneath where it was tied with a straw rope, and, holding the *chongdan* up on the elbow between the left forearm and the arm, with the bundle on the end, he thrust the other end into the other bundle. But it was here that he faltered because he found himself on shaky ground, as the bundle was too heavy on the other end, making it difficult for him to thrust the other end in properly. It was Lin who came over and helped him steady himself. Then, with his strong hands, Lin put the end of the *chongdan* inside the bundle as he lifted it for Zu. In that instant, Zu felt as if his feet, under the heavy weight, were sinking into the soft earth. The load was so much that he could not hold himself steady and he began swaying from side to side. But for Lin's help again—he took hold of the *chongdan*, lifting it up a bit, to ease the load—Zu might have fallen face down then and there, under the load. Still, he managed to bear it with magnanimity and, after a few steps, he could walk with more ease. Lin, worried for him, carried a load himself and followed him not far off in case something happened. But he breathed a sigh of relief when he saw that Zu managed to get to the threshing ground along the narrow bank, by mentally muttering to himself the words of the now disgraced leader, Lin Biao, a battle hymn that had inspired many in the wars before Liberation: Set my face like a flint / Be afraid of no sacrifice / Overcome all difficulties / till a victory is won.

The letter Zu wrote back to his mother was a brief one. He wrote,

> Life here is so busy. I work all day, cutting the rice and carrying it to the threshing ground. It's so tiring I fall asleep as soon as my head hits the pillow. The villagers here are kind towards me and I have no problems living with the other students. Don't you worry about me. I eat well, sleep well and work well. I get praise for my work from the other villagers. Everything's fine.
>
> Son

There were so many things he could have written into that letter, the resultant pain in his limbs from the physical labour, the skin of his arms, legs and face so suntanned it looked like scorched, the one occasion on which he did so fast cutting the rice that he'd almost cut his left little finger off. As the blood spurted out, unstoppable, he grabbed a handful of rice stocks, trying to stop the bleeding by wrapping them around his little finger. But the blood kept flowing out, dyeing the golden stocks red. Brother De happened to be arriving on the scene just then, with a piece of cuttlefish bone, which he ground with his sickle into powder, that fell on a piece of newspaper that he had spread over the rice stubbles. Then he took a pinch of the powder and spread it over the cut. Almost instantly, the bleeding stopped. It was not till then that he realised that drops of his blood had stained the newspaper below, one that was published on the 1st July, 1974, with the title of a headlined editorial that thus ran, **It is the Party that will Take the Lead in Everything**, accompanied with a standard photograph of Chairman Mao and followed with these words, The Chinese Communist Party is the core leadership for all the Chinese people and the socialist cause will not achieve victory without such a core.

Curiously, something Brother De had joked about months before returned in his memory. Zu recalled how De, unsmiling, remarked to all present, including the women villagers, during a break, on yet another playful tussle between a woman villager and a male, this time An again, that he had met people who found women's thing so tender and soft that they could go right through till their own thing came out at the other end. That set the whole crowd laughing. Zu didn't balk at such lewd remarks, as they were facts of life one grew up to know, to learn even, although such things were never written in a book. But there were people in his life who said worse things, Ca Ayi, for example, wife of a staff member of Mother's work unit.

This was a fat woman who, as a rule, wore black, an all-weather, all-season colour of attire. She was nice and all smiles whenever she met the young teen Zu, enquiring after him with an invariable 'Have you eaten?', thus always leaving Zu well-impressed. He didn't know why she wore black. But, with a boy's instinct, he found her pretty, her face round and creamy above her night-black garment, and he would invariably return with an 'Ayi!' He was surprised, though, on a number of occasions, that this woman had a ferocious tongue when she got upset, so ferocious, in fact, that she would shout abuse at anyone who had done anything untoward that made her angry. She stood on the compound of Zu's mother's work unit, surrounded by all the two-storey staff dormitories. Her voice was loud enough to raise the dead, but her words were hardly intelligible to Zu as she spoke a dialect that was not local. Zu would walk past her, his eyes lowered, looking abashed, and he was not noticed as otherwise he would have been, as the woman, standing akimbo, directed her abuse in a certain direction at someone only she knew she had in mind. A few words here and there made sense to Zu as he could tell that they meant 'cunt' or 'fuck' or 'dick' or 'stealing a man'. Curiously, not once did anyone come forward by openly acknowledging it and challenging her. She seemed to always have her own way. Even more curiously was the fact that the woman was never discussed at Zu's home. As soon as he arrived home he forgot her and whatever she had said. Later in his life he would wonder why he had never even asked Mum why the woman behaved the way she did. Nor had Mum talked about the woman, not even when Dad came home for a visit, when they would talk about anything and everything.

祖

It was around this time that Zu began writing a short story, his first one, the only one he had attempted while staying in Clear Water Village. At middle school, he had done compositions as part of the assignments handed down by the language teachers. His written pieces, as a whole, were commended. One in particular was so well-written, that Hao, the tall, elegant man, always with a smile on his face, handpicked it and read it aloud to all the rest of the students, along with a piece by Sha. He read Sha's first, praising her for her fine description of rain that hit the ground before it turned into running, gurgling creeks spreading everywhere. He then picked up another one and, without introduction or warning, started reading, merely saying this was the one that he liked and thought that it stood out from the rest. A few sentences into it and Zu realised that it was unmistakably his own, a long piece of self-criticism on something that he regretted having done. His face was flushed. He sat stock-still. And he dared not look at anyone, proud as well as ashamed, and, at the same time, resentful.

The incident had happened a while ago, during a time when general teaching in all subjects was suspended, in favour of education received from peasants, workers and soldiers, as part of the new education policy that denounced the bourgeois educational system, in which things of the feudal (from the Chinese past), the capitalist (from the West) and the revisionist (from the Soviet Union) were taught. In one of the activities, known as 'Remembering the Bitter and Thinking of the Sweet', organised by the school, meant to negate the past steeped in bitterness brewed by the landlords and capitalists, in honour of the present that was all sweetness brought to the people by the Great, Glorious and Correct Party, all the students went on an outing to a nearby village. With their quilts bundled up the way soldiers did, they went in a rapid march in military style, with their infantry packs on their backs, till they arrived at the village, stopping in a row outside on the threshing ground. There, a huge wok, many sizes larger than a large washing basin, was cooking over a brisk fire. The students were told that the food being cooked consisted of what even a pig could not keep down, let alone the poor peasants in the past, simply because the wicked landlords had treated them so harshly, feeding them the uneatables. The students, dutifully, sat on the ground and waited. When the lid was removed, the steaming wok gave forth a smell so pungent that their nostrils were assaulted, a smell they had never smelt before. One classmate, by the name of He, whispered his complaint to Zu, But how can one eat it if it smells so horribly? Zu smiled and didn't say a thing. His parents had told him stories of how people said negative things about the socialist system, only to be reported to the authorities by the bystanders who shammed interest, egged them on, and took notes, with accurate information about date, time and place when these things were discussed. Having parents with a black past, Zu was not someone who could afford to wreck his future with wayward remarks.

Soon, it was time to eat as each one of the students went to the wok to receive a bowl of the porridge, mixed with vegetables, wheat bran and soybean curd residue, a black, gluey and smelly affair, accompanied with a *mantou*, steamed bread, each, to soften the impact and to help with the food. Bowls in hand, Zu and He went back to their row and began eating.

However much he tried, Zu could not eat the whole thing. Instead, he managed to eat up his steamed bread when he noticed another piece of steamed bread by his side. His peripheral vision told him that this had come from He behind him, so without a word he pushed it back and went on eating the remaining dark stuff.

A commotion rose somewhere that caught Zu's attention, still hesitant if he should eat the rest of the difficult porridge, when he noticed the approach of quick steps. He looked up in surprise, to see Political Instructor Lang, a thin man in yellow military uniform, come up to him and demand, in a serious tone, Is this the bread you have thrown? Zu was taken aback as he saw that the half-bread he had pushed behind him was now in the extended hand of Lang's, like evidence of crime committed. But I didn't throw it, he mumbled his protest.

All the eyes were fixed on Zu as all the heads were turned towards him, as the political instructor, with the half-bread in hand, went to the front of the congregation, strode to the foreground and made the startling revelation, in a denunciatory voice,

> This is a serious occasion, an occasion on which we have all come to learn from the peasants by eating the Remembrance of Bitterness Meal, lest we forget the past bitterness at the hands of the evil landlords, as compared with the happy lives we now are living, when something so horrible has just happened. A student among us has discarded a piece of priceless steamed bread, to the amazement of everyone, flying in the face of all the regulations and rules. And, by so doing, he has callously shown himself to be someone who does not appreciate the treasured food that peasants have worked to produce, toiling and moiling all their lives.

When he gave the name, singling Zu out, as a quintessentially bad example of wanton waste, contempt and disgust were shown on every face. Zu, for the first time, found himself in total isolation. Even though his heart was seething with protestations because he was so wronged, he did not have a voice; his voice was squashed by the loud voice of the political instructor who wanted everyone, on their return back to the school, to write an article of criticism, and this included Zu himself who should write one of self-criticism, to give a full account of the incident and to explain why his mind was so corrupted by bourgeois ideology.

Chapter 7: Raising a Pig

Years after, Zu was to know that the literary world was one as corrupt as any other, hinged on money matters, accepting or rejecting manuscripts based purely on commercial viability or political restraints, and few editors would ever bother replying, instead trashing hand-written submissions by the bag-loads at the waste-paper recycling stations. But, shortly after he posted his story, of a young man pining for a girl faraway, Zu received a letter from the literary magazine, *The Yangtze Literature and Arts Monthly*. Though the editor did not accept the piece, he recognised its merits and praised Zu for his bold approach. In his letter, beautifully written in a flourishing hand, the editor encouraged him to write more and keep submitting as he was sure Zu would achieve his goal if he kept trying. Zu was touched and he thought of how Hao had encouraged him in his middle school days by reading his writings aloud, not once, but a few times, to the rest of the classes. He was determined that he would go on writing. But other things that happened made this unlikely.

The student-peasant household, like the rest of the village households, had been raising a pig because it was one of the few sources of meat, apart from chickens and ducks. The girls were against the chickens and ducks as they were running all over the place, sometimes jumping onto their beds, making a mess of them, spotted with chicken or duck shit. After a debate among themselves, it was agreed that they purchase a piglet in the market, but it had to be kept outside, not allowed in the house. There was a hole dug in the ground, immediately outside the door, where one dumped rubbish and garbage, then covered with soil, supposedly to turn it into manure, later to be used on their vegetable plot by the creek. When Lin, commissioned to do the buying job because he knew how to select them, came back from the town with a young grey piglet, everyone was excited. They saw it run and scream, tied to the doorpost with a string, stretching the string, its body arched with strain, and talked about how they could raise it to its fullness. Lin told them that a pig was the easiest thing to raise. Give him leftovers, let him lie in the hole, wallow in the water, sleep in a corner, and you'll see him grow to a full-sized pig in no time, usually within four to five months.

Pigs were nothing new to Zu. In his Mum's work unit in the small town, next to the staff canteen was a pigsty, where five or six pigs were kept, exactly on the daily leftovers from the kitchen as well as the husks and chaffs, mixed with hogwash. When Spring Festival approached, a pig would be butchered, on the compound, right in front of the canteen, and between the canteen, the staff dormitories and the two-storey office building. There, Zhou, the chef, a man known for his extraordinary abilities to produce the best-quality steamed bread in a most careless manner, sometimes wiping his nose into the dough, would stand in his leather apron, a sharp knife in hand, waiting, while the others, led by Uncle Yang, Uncle Tan and Uncle Xiong, the three strongest staff members, opened the door to the sty, and let out one of the fattest pigs. The pig, aware of its impending fate, would rush out with a shriek and started running wildly around on the compound, which tightened the noose around its neck and stretched the string taut until the strong three caught him. Tan, reputedly a bandit that had lived and fought in the mountains, was the bravest as he would hold the pig in his arms by the neck, with its feet taken by the other two. They would wrestle the pig onto the ground, its feet skywards, still shrieking as hell, and drag it to the steps that led to the building, where a large wooden basin was placed. Zhou, his knife at the ready, would take one pig ear in his left hand as he thrust the knife right into the pig's throat, in such a lightning speed that few, let alone Zu, could clearly see how he did it. Almost instantly, the blood spurted out of the pig's throat, hot and steaming. But someone had already raised the basin to receive it. Beautiful blood, Zhou sighed as he wiped the knife clean, and, using the same dirty bloody towel, he wiped the sweat off his forehead. Everyone knew what he was sighing about, because the pig blood, when congealed, served as one of the best dishes, as soup or stir-fried with tofu or leeks.

This piglet, unlike cats or dogs, did not have a name. In fact, there were no cats in the village. A few dogs were there, but not as pets, only as guard dogs. Their names were unknown to Zu, either, as he hardly ever visited the villagers' homes. Everyone was so busy working during the day that they wouldn't come home till nightfall. Then it was time to go to bed. To save on kerosene, people were wont to go to sleep as soon as they ate their dinner. The only fun that existed between husbands and wives, according to Shun, was what he referred to as *yindan*. And when he used the expression, people laughed. But it was lost on Zu till someone else explained it. In the village, every household kept a chicken coop, built next to the house. The local habit was for the woman of the house to go and put her hand inside it through a narrow opening every morning, to feel for the number of eggs the chicken had supposedly laid the previous night. Hence the expression *yindan*, literally, feeling for the eggs but, figuratively, groping for (the man's) balls. The more he thought on it, the more Zu found it dirty and funny, and quite vivid, too. He was thrilled to imagine how the women, in the saving darkness, went about their business *yindan*ing their husbands whose balls were being handled at ease. It was an experience beyond him. He was only 18. And he had never had any women to *yindan* him. When he was very little, lying on top of his mother one early morning, his hands cupping his mother's naked breasts, in that tiny little room of theirs, large bundles of quilt batting hanging on the walls, the only way to put things away in the snail space when days became warmer, he found his little body afire with something hot that was running underneath, so unutterably pleasurable that he was amazed and remained silent, while his mother answered his question about where babies came from with this remark that went, But you are so *hou chuizi* tiny, you don't understand. I'll tell you when you grow up. 'What is *hou chuizi* then?' Zu found himself wondering. Mother explained that it was the monkey's balls, so called because their balls resembled the weights of a steelyard. Tiny.

The piglet grew up so fast that in no time it turned into a half-sized pig. When the villagers went by the student-peasants' house, they would say, Well, I'd say the pig weighs about 50 or 60 *jin* now. Or they would size it up and say, Pretty soon when it grows up to its full-size, you can take it to the market and sell it for 120 or so bucks. It was a fairly big sum. It meant that on average each member of the household would receive 24 kuai. Not bad. The thought was so pleasant that Zu found himself one day stroking the pig with his foot, along its hair, while it lay sunning itself in the hole just outside their house. It felt comfortable, so the pig turned on its back, its feet pointed skyward. Afterwards, satisfied with the thought of the pig grown to its marketable full-size, Zu left for the fields, carrying his *chongdan*, and did not return till late afternoon, to fetch hot water for the men working on the threshing ground.

Once inside the empty space separating the two rooms on either side, Zu found the pig lying in one corner, looking content and happy. He was happy, too. The labour in the fields, though tiring, was exhilarating as he had managed to *chongdan* the heavy stacks of rice stock from the fields to the ground, without wobbling from side to side. He could in fact walk all the way, with the heavy stuff on his shoulder, as any male peasants categorised as members of *quan laoli*, 'full labourer-force', did, accustomed to the rhythm of the *chongdan* as it upped and downed under the weight, which, according to the skilled and experienced peasants, would ease the load, making one feel as if he was carrying less weight than it really was.

He was taken aback when he entered the kitchen at the end of the hallway that served as the space separating the rooms. It was a total mess, everything turned topsy-turvy. The dinner, long prepared by Cui, who was now working in the fields, was upset in such a way that the rice had been spilled out, strewing the floor, with its snow-whiteness, topped with a blaze of yellow, red and green colours, yellow being the yolk, red being the tomato and green, the vegetables, all pre-stir-fried and ready to serve. And, on top of all that was the fallen kitchen cabinet, all its doors crashed open, and a few broken china plates.

The violent sight set Zu's blood running hot. Who did this? As soon as he swung out of the small kitchen and saw the content pig, its mouth oily with food, he understood. The pig had ruined the dinner for the day and after they came back from work there would be nothing to eat; the pig-touched food wouldn't be any good, even if picked up from the earthen floor. He was upset with Cui for not putting their two-leaf door under lock and key when she left; he was more upset with the pig for daring to break in and spilling the food beans of everything by turning the cabinet upside down. He must teach him a lesson now. Thus thinking, Zu snatched up a shoulder-pole leaning against the wall as he went to the door in hastened steps, latching the wooden latch on, before he went straight for the pig. The brute, sensing the impending danger, raised its head as it stood up to its feet, before breaking into a run. When the first swing of Zu's shoulder pole hit the pig on its broad back, the animal shrieked. It headed for the door but, seeing that it couldn't snout it open, it swung back and headed towards Zu. This head-on charge left Zu nearly off balance. When he regained his balance, Zu hit harder. But each time he hit, he missed because the pig was nimbler than him, dodging him this way and that, shrieking so loudly that Zu felt his eardrums were being split. Just then, the old wife, the slit-eyed one, who lived next door, came to the door and, through the crack between the two leaves, begged Zu in a whispered voice to let the pig go, saying, Zu, don't hit him. It's just a pig. It doesn't understand. Let him go, let him go, please.

Her voice was drowned amidst the pig shrieks and Zu's curses until, all of a sudden, Zu was tired and thought better of it. He threw the pole onto the floor, and went to the door, unlatching it. The pig, as soon as it saw its chance, rushed out, screaming all the way. In that instant, Zu thought, with foreboding, that it might run away, never to come back and then he might have committed a worse crime. The old wife next door kept ensuring him that a pig was like a human being and if it was well fed and kept it would turn up whenever it felt hungry. Sure enough, at dinnertime, it came sauntering back. By then, Zu's anger had long died down. He, along with Cui, picked up the broken pieces from the thrown food and gave it to the animal while the rest of them ate a much simpler meal in total silence.

That night, before he puffed out the kerosene lamp, Zu made an entry in his diary:

Lin made a remark hinting at my relationship with Xi. I just laughed it off. Then again, his instinct is as right as mine. To me, Xi seems to have come from another planet. She's never part of us. She doesn't belong and doesn't want to belong. Since we arrived in this village, we have not even exchanged a single word, except an occasional nod of our heads. She's not exactly pretty. But she's tall and graceful. Although I never venture into the room she shares with Cui, one glance assures me that the neat bed and the fresh flowers, plucked from the fields, on the bedstead must be hers, something that bespeaks a cultured background. What gets me, though, is that she seems to enjoy the company of the village teenage boys more than ours. Those rough boys with the names like Spring Born, Iron Eggs and Big Roots follow her everywhere and one hears her talking and laughing with them all the time. As soon as she enters into our house her face falls, all her smile gone. I don't think she even likes it here. I think I like her. But I don't think she likes me. And I do not know how to make her like me.

On the other hand, every advance made to Xi by Han has met with frustration. All she offered him was a cold demeanor and few words. I heard from elsewhere that she had no interest in Han at all, not in his abject background nor in his pretentious polished manners. Somehow, her displeasure with favours shown towards her by Han made me happy for her. The other day, I saw with my own eyes how she turned him down by refusing to drink from a bowl of cold water he offered her, instead scooping a bowl of hot tea from a wooden barrel and drinking from it herself. Han's face turned ghastly instantly, muttering darkly. But Xi acted as if he didn't exist. Well, I must stop here. But if there's anyone I can warm to and will find as a friend, Xi might be the one.

The days were hot. The work was harsh. And the student-peasants were kept busy day in and day out. They were left without time to do anything else. Books, untouched, were gathering dust. The pig grew fatter each day, the two-leaf door constantly under lock and key, to prevent the same havoc from happening again. Han kept complaining about the need to work that hard, saying that he'd got no time to go hunting for dogs or chickens and there was little money to be earned from the work, only 7 points a day as compared with 10 points out of 10 for the 'full labourer-force'. Len was the quiet guy. Outwardly, one saw nothing that could suggest displeasure or unhappiness. He was, if anything, the quintessential example of taking the rough with the smooth. Though he shared the room with Zu, he was not a talker at night after the kerosene lamp was blown out, something Zu enjoyed. Len would often quote an ancient saying that goes, *Chi buyan, shui buyu,* which means one doesn't talk over a meal or in sleep, to silence Zu when the latter found it hard to fall into immediate sleep. Zu would often lapse into reminiscences about the past, his past, in which he would spend summer nights with friends on the open top of the staff dormitory building or wandering along the embankment of the Yangtze, talking about things of general interest, particularly of war and philosophy. One absentee was Qian, a former classmate before he was enlisted in the Army, sent to fight the Americans in the Vietnam War. Zu had kept correspondence with him for years since the early 1970s when China sent the troops over to Vietnam. He would relate bits and pieces revealed in the letters about Qian's life as a telecommunications soldier, having to work the nights till his health was deteriorating to such a degree that he suffered constant insomnia and anorexia. Zu told the stories with mixed feelings. On one hand, he resented the fact that he had been rejected by the Army in his application because of his *jiating chengfen,* the class origin of his family, a classification that would mean he would never be accepted into the System, not as a soldier, not as a university student, not as a Party member, the only way to officialdom, not even as a worker with a coveted job in a factory, the way to avoid having to go to the country, like millions of others, and, on the other, he was secretly pleased that things didn't turn out to be that fantastic over there as he imagined it would be. Even though Qian didn't have to fight and run the risk of losing his life, his was a hard fate, too. The son of a printing worker, this thin man of reticence had to quit school at an early age of 16, having hardly finished his second year of junior school, while Zu managed to finish his four years of formal schooling, a plus on his part as compared with a minus on Qian's because of the latter's lack of schooling in the middle school. Whenever he came back to Yuwang Town, his hometown as well as Zu's and Qian's, Jia would invariably catch up with Zu. He, too, was one of the lucky ones because he had secured a job in a factory making military weapons in the depths of the mountains; such job opportunities were denied the likes of Zu. About his age, Jia was a handsome, sallow-faced young man, who, even in his tender age of 16, had had numerous affairs with women and he would occasionally share some of the stories with Zu, making the latter jealous and feel incompetent. One of the exploits he would relate was how a fellow woman worker, much older than him, seduced him, only to give him the go-by the next day, immediately following the night of sex. According to him, that was humiliating. But it was also revealing because it gave him the signal that things like sex were not as forbidding as people wanted us to believe; instead, they were one-night stands one could barge in and out of quite by accident or by choice as long as both parties were happy together when they were together. Much as he found it shocking, Zu could not help resisting thoughts of seeing himself in such affairs with diverse women, only to end up in masturbating himself, never picking up enough courage to make advances, for he was ever the imagining type, thinking, not doing.

Among others, Jia stood out as a pessimist. Zu could never work out how he was so pessimistic while always managing to successfully get the women's attention. It was true that his father had committed suicide when he was little. But he had got a good job earning a salary and he was not unhappy about it or in it, while Zu was facing the bleak future of working in the fields with peasants in a village possibly for the rest of his life. Both of them read but each of them read different books. While Jia preferred the ancient classics, Zu preferred foreign literature in translation. They had got their books from the recycling station near their homes, where people who stole them after they broke into school libraries in the chaos of *wudou*, armed fighting, at the height of the Cultural Revolution, sold them for a song. Zu read, then forgot, his memory like a sieve, only remembering what was the most essential. But Jia had a memory that retained much of what he had read. He would scorn book writing by citing the example of Yang Zi, an ancient philosopher no one had heard of but him, who, according to him, had remarked on the pointlessness of writing books. Jia would recite tracks of what was attributed to Yang Zi, which made things worse because Zu's knowledge of the ancient script and of its density was so scanty he could hardly understand it, except the main message that one's main purpose in life was enjoy it to the exclusion of aiming for fame and achievement.

When I checked about what Yang Zi had to say, I found the passage that convinced me probably what Jia had quoted in classic Chinese language and it goes,

One hundred years is the limit of a long life. Not one in a thousand ever attains it. Suppose there is one such person. Infancy and feeble old age take almost half of his time. Rest during sleep at night and what is wasted during the waking hours in the daytime take almost half of that. Pain and sickness, sorrow and suffering, death (of relatives) and worry and fear take almost half of the rest. In the ten and some years that are left, I reckon, there is not one moment in which we can be happy, at ease without worry. This being the case, what is life for? What pleasure is there? For beauty and abundance, that is all. For music and sex, that is all. But the desire for beauty and abundance cannot always be satisfied, and music and sex cannot always be enjoyed. Besides, we are prohibited by punishment and exhorted by rewards, pushed by fame and checked by law. We busily strive for the empty praise which is only temporary, and seek extra glory that would come after death. Being alone ourselves, we pay great care to what our ears hear and what our eyes see, and are much concerned with what is right or wrong for our bodies and minds. Thus we lose the great happiness of the present and cannot give ourselves free rein for a single moment. What is the difference between that and many chains and double prisons?[1]

Lying in bed in the total darkness, Zu had endless thoughts, such as this that came to him and kept him awake till he fell asleep. His life was nothing like Jia's or Qian's; that much was obvious. He had to find his own way out and endure it for the moment. Only the other day, a very hot day at noon, he was carrying two heavy *caotou*, two stacks of rice stock, on his *chongdan*, from the furthest rice paddy to the threshing ground, under the scorching sun, when he found he could no longer stand the weight and the strain. It nearly broke his back; if he didn't stop then and there it would. Besides, his throat was parched. Looking around and seeing no sign of anyone coming, he found a ditch with water in it, between two rice paddies. The water was stagnant, covered with leaves and overgrown grass. He was so thirsty that he couldn't help stooping himself, on his hands and knees, to put his mouth to the water. It felt hot on first contact although there wasn't any bad smell. Emboldened by the discovery, he, parting off the leaves and the grass, started drinking directly from it, taking a sip at a time, then drinking mouthfuls, till his thirst was slaked. The experience, ever afterwards, had left him with a mixed sense of elation and humiliation, instilling in him a steely determination to do whatever he could to rise above the circumstances.

祖

[An inter-textual insertion: When I checked with Old Zu about its authenticity, he had this to say by way of reply that the character of a person was formed in much the same way as a piece of metal which, after a process of tempering and self-tempering, turns into steel. That sort of put the matter to rest as I think I can understand.]

1 Quoted from the entry under 'Yang Zhu': https://en.wikipedia.org/wiki/Yang_Zhu

Chapter 8: The Tung Oil Incident

The Double Rush was over, and the rice paddies filled with water again and were ploughed, for the next round of seedling planting. Here and there, one saw the dark water buffalos with the ploughshares behind them, handled by the elderly peasants, elderly because they were the skilled ones and knew how to properly handle them. As they went over the paddies, rows of ploughed soil turned up like dark waves, burying the stubble underneath as manure. A rich smell, mixed with the cow dung and the newly broken roots, was in the air. Once or twice, Zu got so interested that he wanted to give it a go, finding the work so easy at the hands of Hua. A frail old man and gaunt, Hua looked like someone a blow of wind might fetch down. But, with his whip and his yelling, and his hand on the ploughshare going straight in a row, the buffalo listened and obeyed, working hard for him. When it was Zu's turn to do the handling, he could not even maintain his proper balance, let alone put the buffalo under control. However hard he tried to yell at it by imitating the sound of Hua, it refused to move. And the ploughshare, so heavy, became as stiff as stone. Not only did it not go straight forward but it wobbled. All the peasants, standing and watching, laughed. This infuriated Zu but he could not do anything except give it up, crestfallen. Hua was kind enough to say to him, You'll have plenty of chance to try this once you get more used to it. One of the peasant women said, But they won't have to learn it as they won't stay long. This is a place where not even birds shit. When Zu saw, in one glance, that the remark came from a woman by the surname of Wang, who had married one of the peasants in this village from another village and was known for her sharp tongue and tantrums thrown towards her husband whenever things went wrong, he felt even more humiliated.

That evening, at sundown, when they headed back home for dinner, something happened. Rain had just fallen. The air was fresh. The soil was aromatic with birdsong. The ploughed rice paddies, in dark rows and filled with water, were steaming in the still-strong setting sun. Zu, carrying his hoe and a basket, went around to their vegetable plot, half neglected but growing strong nevertheless, and picked fat fingers of green beans, and quite a few broad leaves from the bok choy. He stood there for a while, looking down at the poorly cultivated plot, wondering what he could do to improve the lot when he realised he could at least fertilise it with his own bodily fluids, so he loosened his pants, took out his penis and spread the hot urine that came rushing out of his body over the bok choy and the beans, wondering at the same time if he should make a suggestion that they tend to it by turns. Afterwards, he went back, along the ridges of the paddy fields, and the road, the only one, that separated the village from the fields, skirting around the pond, and arrived back in their own house.

The first thing he noticed was a tableful of food, set right in the middle of the house. Prepared by Cui, it looked fresh and shiny with oil. When all except Xi, again excusing herself with one of her many ailments, sat down and set to, they found the dishes delicious beyond belief. Cui, who had just returned from a short visit to her parents in Yuwang Town, explained that the oil she had used from a bottle left in the house was particularly good, aromatic and tasty. Because everyone had been working so hard over the last few weeks, she thought she'd give them a treat. Even though there were only things from bok choy to broad beans and green beans and tomatoes to tofu, with little meat, they had a hearty meal and were surfeited. Han commented that they'd never had such a wonderful meal before. Len didn't say anything although he looked happy. Afterwards, when it was dark, everyone retired to their own separate rooms, lit their kerosene lamps and went about their private business, or simply doing nothing, just sitting by the window and watching the gathering darkness.

Not long after, Len cried in pain, complaining about bellyache, as he ran towards the toilet over the pond. Zu found it odd but didn't comment. Soon, he found a pain developing in his stomach, too. Then it was Han's turn to do the same. In no time, everyone except Cui and Xi, profusely loosened their bowels and vomited hell out of them. Something terrible must have happened. But what was exactly the problem? No one knew. As the problem persisted, suggestions were made that they go to the nearest country clinic to seek medical attention. As it was five kilometers away and they had to walk in the total darkness between the rice paddies, they, bar the two girls, as Cui had eaten her own food she brought back from home and Xi hadn't touched anything, carried an electric torch each. The tortuous journey tired them out and, yet, at one stage, Zu found himself strong enough to support Len on his arms as he seemed the frailest by the look of it.

When the doctor asked them what they had eaten, they couldn't come up with a proper explanation, all saying how wonderful the dinner was. Unable to diagnose the exact condition and seeing that the boys were recovering, the doctor prescribed them some anti-diarrheal medication and antibiotics before they walked the dark distance back and fell asleep immediately after, like logs. It was not till the next morning when Liu the carpenter came to their house to take his large bottles of oil that the truth came to light. The previous afternoon, when he came back from the town with his tung oil, meant to repair barrels, tables and wooden joints or surfaces, he left them in their house. An unsuspecting Cui, on her return, went straight to work, preparing the dinner, with all the good intentions in the world.

The villagers, when they had learnt about the news, came to enquire about their health but, seeing that everyone had miraculously recovered, laughed out loud and told them that dishes, when cooked with tung oil, had the best taste in the world.

As it was a rest day for them, Zu read a story about Confucius in an old book left by Bao, the poet from an adjacent village. Many of the stories, written in the traditional script and in the classical language, were hard to understand as quite a few characters were no longer in current use. Still, he managed to work out the meaning of one story, in which Confucius, along with his disciples, watches how a man jumps into a waterfall that is 90 meters high and runs as far as 45 kilometres. When he wonders how this man can manage to jump into it, swim and get out of it, where no fish or turtles survive, the man tells him that it is *chengxin* (honesty and faith) that enables him to do so. Confucius, impressed, tells his disciples to mind what the man says, adding that if a man can achieve that in such dangerous waters by sheer good faith, what else can he not achieve?[1]

That plunged Zu into a profound reverie of thinking. Mrs Zu, his mother, had always stressed the importance of honesty since he was little. She wanted him to behave properly, never tell lies, never cheat, and to always be faithful to his parents at home, to his teachers at school, and to his superiors at work if and when he ever got a proper job. Her words held sway, but only up to a point. In his mid-teens, an incident had taken place, in which he broke a young tree on the compound. One day, when Huang, Bureau Chief of the work unit, saw him idling away outside the collapsible grated door, he casually asked who had done it. Zu, prompted by Mother's words about never telling lies, told him that it was he who had done it, not without a sense of pride because he was sure Huang would praise him for his honesty. A few days after, at home, Mother started chiding the boy for his wanton behaviour, much to the boy's bewilderment and chagrin. A conversation ensued.

But I did nothing wrong, Zu said. Why do you always criticise me?

Tell me what you have done recently? said she. I want to know.

Nothing, Zu said.

Nothing really? said she, her voice raised.

This questioning met with a silence, suddenly fallen.

Tell me: What happened? said she.

The silence, continuing, became obstinate.

All right, she, relenting, said. If you don't want to tell me, I'll tell you.

Then, in an angry voice, his mother revealed how unhappy she was when told by the leadership of the work unit that her son had broken a young tree, worth hundreds of yuan, that they had recently purchased and planted, and how her son had admitted to Mr Huang himself that he was the culprit.

But I wasn't in the wrong, was I? Zu protested. Because I told them the truth.

You told them the truth? His mother was furious. And you know how

1 See *Liezi quanyi* (A Complete Translation of Liezi), trans. by Wang Qiangmo. Guizhou People's Publishing House, 2009, pp. 191-2.

much that is worth? I had to—

Abruptly, she stopped, choked on her own words, and knowing that the son wouldn't understand if she told him that they had slammed a fine on her worth half of her monthly salary.

The boy was angry, too, because he could never work out why he was fined instead of being rewarded for telling the truth. And what he found most baffling was also the fact that Mother, instead of pleased with his righteous behaviour, got so upset. The young boy, certainly, had much to learn.

祖

With the arrival of autumn, there came a short hiatus when there was nothing much to do. The working buffalos were lying around in the cowshed, their broad mouths moving, ruminating. Villagers were mostly engaged in field management, involving weeding, manuring and irrigation. Da wasn't too much concerned when he noticed that the students from the city weren't participatory, preferring to stay in the comfort of their own house, or only working for a few hours before they stole back. He, like the rest of the villagers, knew that these students weren't here to stay, being not native to the place and their homes in a city far away. He, for one, didn't want to work them too hard, even though he noticed that Zu, unlike the rest of them, seemed intent on going it alone with them, day in and day out. He had recently received an application from him for Party membership, in which the young man confesses he is from a family background of denounced origin but is determined to rise above it by working hard, as hard as any other Party members until he is accepted. Da, a Party member himself, knew by instinct that chances were slim for such a person as Zu. The Party line was clear-cut: You were either Party members or you were not. Only those who were from the poor peasant or lower-middle peasant background were eligible while the upper-middle or well-off middle peasants had little chance. As for those categorised as landlords, rich peasants, reactionaries, bad elements and the rightists, they all belonged to what was known as *lingce*, or the other category. Zu's family background would probably be fitting into that category, somewhere between a landlord and a rich peasant, people who would never be recognised as full citizens. Mere dregs of the society. Still, it wouldn't hurt if he wanted to give it a go.

On the other hand, Zu's effort in applying for the membership was half-hearted. Deep down, he knew, for someone like him, the chance would most likely be nil. Dad had worked as a senior officer in the Kuomintang government, managing personnel affairs, whose counterpart, according to Mum, was that of Organization Department under the Communist Party, an important body that assessed the quality of government officials through examinations and assigned them work at all levels of government. Mum had also come from a middle-class background; her parents, dead even before Zu was born, had worked as clerks in the Kuomintang government as well, which was why Qiao, a childhood playmate in the same work unit, had made insidious references to 'the Landlord's Daughter' in Zu's presence when they went fishing in the Yangtze. Though deeply hurt, Zu didn't say a word, nor did he even dare ask Mum about it. He was, unlike most boys of his age, so used to the humiliation that, instead of raising a voice, he would internalise it and bear it in total silence, taking it for granted as part of things natural, even unnatural. All he was told, by Mum at least, was to do his utmost and be a good boy. To this day, many years afterwards, he could still recall what she had once said to him, as he lay beside her in bed, If you do well in the future, Mum shall be able to die with her eyes closed. Although he did not know what that meant, he could sense the significance of the remark. And he would murmur, in his heart, that he would live up to her expectation, without knowing what exactly her expectation was and without even asking her about it.

祖

Because things had slowed down a little, the instinct for wandering returned, an instinct buried inside everyone, waiting to blossom at the drop of a hat should someone hint at it. Zu, the shy, white-faced young man, with ugly buck teeth, also gappy, restless and adventurous by nature, the young man who would not normally run comments on the state of things, offered one evening over dinner to the other boys that they should explore the surrounding country in order to see the world at large. When asked how they could travel around without a vehicle, Zu revealed his idea, one that he had been sleeping on for quite some time. He had dreamed of covering the length and breadth of China in a random manner, his idea being that they stand by the roadside, hailing the first truck that went past, whichever way they went. If the truck happened to go north, they would go north. If it went south, they would follow south until it reached its destination, wherever it was. Then they would repeat the process, going on and on, ad infinitum. As soon as he revealed this idea, everyone's imagination was set afire even though they had initial doubts and reservations. Len said, But what if we run out of money for food and accommodation? Han, the ever adventurous, countered by saying, We could work for the truck driver by helping him upload or download his cargo, thus earning a meal or two. Zu applauded the idea with a cheer although the girls laughed it off, saying things were pretty organised and the drivers might have their own helping hands without having to seek extra help. As they talked, Han became even more enthusiastic than Zu, saying, I've got a friend in Xishui. I think he'll be delighted to see us and put us up for a night or two. Besides, Han said, we may even run into pretty girls and have a fling with them, you know? That remark struck a chord with these boys, in their late teens, who, except Han who had just gone past 20, were human deserts that had never been enriched with women waters, each and every one of them having a secret desire somewhere in them for bumping into a girl after his own heart. This, though, was something they would rather keep to themselves. Except for Han, who would openly flirt with any pretty girls he happened to spot, not in the village, for there simply wasn't anyone worth the effort, but in the town of Upper Bahe, as he had done on a previous occasion when the three boys went for a visit, Len and Zu never exchanged their hidden thoughts girl-wise. Occasionally,

Zu would talk about a girl in his senior middle school class, as the quiet one and the good looker who was so shy she would never pose a question or answer one in class, instead preferring to sit by herself and walk to and from school alone. That casual remark about the girl, once said, was hint enough to the other two that this was the one Zu was after, so they laughed at him for being so chicken as not even dare to court her by writing to her. Han said, If I were you, I'd take action because you would never know who'd rush ahead of you if the man set his sights on her because of her pretty looks. Zu, whose face was flushed at this, would deny wanting to have anything to do with her, excusing himself by saying that he was only making a running comment on who was good-looking, while, deep down, he was aching for the possibility of seeing her one day.

It was soon agreed that they would go on a journey and see the world, the drudgery in the paddy fields too much for them. It in fact helped, too, that the village wasn't particularly concerned with whatever the student-peasants were on about, as long as they could survive on their own family support and rely on themselves, not having to overconsume the production team's resources. Meanwhile, there was someone else who wanted to join them. His name was Qu, Old Qu, who, at a similar age to Han's, looked much older than him, with a large body that floated about like a loose barge, and a face that, when smiling, broadened to twice its size. The first words he said, when he barged into their house, were, So I heard you guys are going abroad, right? Can I join you? Han immediately said, Oh, yeh. Why do you want to join us? You can't even play Three against One. This sounded like an open affront. But Old Qu took it lightly, saying, Oh, but I can always learn, can I not? Zu didn't know him. But after a brief introduction in which he was described as the son of a professor, Zu immediately showed admiration, believing a professor's son had much to offer by way of learning. And he could see how Han, even Len, bantered with him, joking about the way he was dressed, nearly in tatters, and how he didn't seem to get upset at all, always smiling, always saying kind words in return, admiring the good order in their house and the number of books Zu had in his possession. One, in particular, caught

190

his attention. It was *The Brothers Yershov* by Vselod Kochetov.

Did you read it? said Qu.

Oh, yes, said Zu.

How did you find it? said Qu.

I thought it was good, said Zu.

Oh, yeh, I thought so, too.

It was then that Zu recalled how he had been moved by the lines of a poem in the novel when he read it night by night in his tiny little room shared with Mum. It was so plain, so simple. But, then, it was somehow evocative and moving, without him knowing why. He recalled how he had read the lines again and again, finding in them a quality that was palpable. From memory, he read them out loud to Qu,

> If it was a momentary passion
> It would pass away like the flitting clouds in the sky
> But you'll understand
> That even a drifting cloud
> On a hot day
> Would bring delight to the labouring people.[1]

How amazing, Qu exclaimed. That's exactly what's said here, Qu said, admiringly, his fingers pressing where the lines were. Unfortunately, Qu said, sighing, although I've read it, all I can remember now is the clouds. How odd it is, that a big book of that size leaves one with only the clouds.

Now, Han announced, we'll be the clouds, drifting from place to place, never stopping, and never coming back.

---

1 The Chinese translation, on which the English translation is based, is found here: http://blog.voc.com.cn/blog_showone_type_blog_id_667874_p_1.html

Chapter 9: The Accidental Travelers

When they arrived at the outskirts of Upper Bahe, by the roadside, darkness had fallen and it was raining. Traffic was light but the headlights when a truck went by illuminated the rows of trees flanking the roadside and their shadows in a dazzling shower of light. Each and every one of them—Zu, Han, Len and Qu—were in a state of uncertainty as well as expectancy, not knowing what lay ahead of them. They took immediate action as Han had organised it in such a way that two of them stood on one side, the left side, of the road and the other two, on the other side, the right side. If someone took them on the right, they might end up in Xishui, a big town twenty-odd kilometres west of Upper Bahe. And, if by chance, someone took them on the left side, they might end up home, in Yuwang Town, fifty-odd kilometres south of Upper Bahe. Either way was fine as long as they ended up somewhere else, anywhere else, except where they were. As Zu had said, If you take the first step, it will lead to the next, then the next, till you arrive and don't even know where you are. The more unknown, the better. Those words were inspiring enough to get everyone going. They had put their resources together, the pool of money consisting of 1 yuan from each, plus a bag of eggs, a bunch of white turnips and a bundle of bok choy, fresh from the soil, as gifts for Han's friend in Xishui.

As they stood in the rainy darkness, one holding an umbrella for two, they waved to every passing vehicle except the Beijing jeeps, which were too small to accommodate the four. After a futile attempt to stop any trucks going in the direction of Yuwang Town, they decided to switch to the right side of the road, focusing their attention on one direction only because Zu thought that when a truck driver saw people lining the road he might get scared, thinking they were highway robbers. Sure enough, as soon as they switched sides by standing all on the right side of the road, the first truck that they waved at came to an abrupt stop, right in the middle of the road, its headlights on, cutting through the darkness like a shining sword. The driver, though sounding rude, was kind enough to let them on, saying, Quick, fuck, quick! And, after they had scrambled on, from both sides, bags and all, and before they could even settle themselves comfortably, the truck had got in motion. Through the windshield, over which the wipers went swiftly from side to side, they could see nothing but a dim view of the road ahead, cut through by the headlights, in a narrow strip of pale yellowness. As soon as they got on the way, the driver said, What do you want to do? Where do you want to go?

Zu was about to say something when Han cut in, saying, Oh, Master, we were buying stuff in Upper Bahe because it is a market day today and had to go back to Xishui where we are based, having to till the fields, you know, as educated youths. As we poor student-peasants don't have much money, we have to do this. No one but you stopped for us. You are so kind. Please, take this and I'll light it for you.

As he said so, he had already extended his hand, with a cigarette-lighter thrust underneath Master's mouth before he quickly changed his mind. He took the cigarette from Master's mouth and put it back between his own lips, lit it and, taking a deep suck on it till he made sure it wouldn't die out on its own, put it to Master's mouth in such a manner that made the act familiar and likeable. Master, whose name was never made known to them, looked straight ahead of him on the road, taking a deep drag on the offered cigarette, seemingly content, mumbling about their rashness in doing such things. He had a way of holding the cigarette between his lips while talking without losing it. Watching him, Zu was fascinated. What a great thing it would be to drive a truck, from city to city, from town to town, across the country, to go anywhere one liked, never stopping at one place for more than one night, but always on the move, going places till one saw the whole country.

The other three were smoking and talking among themselves about how lucky they were to have flagged down the truck when, with a sharp screech of the tires and a loud cracking noise, the driver braked. His act of braking came so suddenly it threw them all forward, out of their seats, like heavy gunny bags of rice, head first, right onto the windshield, as the truck lurched sidewise, scraping the sidelong branches, breaking a large bough with its side rear mirror, on its roadside swerve, till it came to an abrupt stop by the roadside trees.

In the pouring rain, the driver, cursing nonstop, got off the truck and walked around it, back to front. It was not till he had checked that everything was fine that he went back to his seat, with a question thrown to the boys, Are you all okay?

No one dared say a single word of 'not', afraid that the driver might throw them out, but everyone chimed that they were fine. The upshot of this incident left Zu's forearm bruised when he held it up to protect himself in his forward movement. And the bag of eggs, clutched in Old Qu's hands, was now lying in a pool of cracked eggshells, yolk and white, oozing out of the broken bag onto the back seat where he was sitting. Han ended up having a big bump on his forehead, which he kept messaging.

Meanwhile, the driver kept muttering under his breath, saying, The fucking idiot was overtaking the other car when he should have slowed down and followed it. If I had not swerved sidewise we would most certainly have had a head-on collision. Mother-fucker. Son of a bitch. Dog-fucker. His mother's cunt.

The boys had a great time listening to the guy cursing as the string of dirty expressions rolled off his tongue. Judging by the accent, Zu was sure that he had come from Qizhou, about 60 kilometers downstream of Yuwang Town. But he kept his mouth shut, for fear of incurring more fury on the part of the driver after what had happened. The place was not unfamiliar to him as he had once been there, on a visit to his dad, who was working as an accountant in a factory. Whenever summer vacations came, Zu would be packed off by his mother and went alone by ship to visit his father wherever he happened to be. Dad seemed to be always in transition, working in small county towns like Round Wind and Qizhou. But before he could indulge more in his memory of the past, he heard the driver say, Here we are. You need to get off, all of you.

It was nine o'clock sharp at night when they got off the truck by a river. The rain had stopped. This must be the White Lotus River, Zu's heart told him. He had heard about it many times. Now, standing by the side of it, the river was a luminosity in itself, expansive and surging, cutting through the darkness. Han's remote relative, Gao, a factory worker, was living in one of the rooms in a factory dormitory along the river. He welcomed them into a spacious room on the second floor, where he had arranged four mats and quilts, side by side, on the floor. When he heard their story, Gao, a young man in his mid-20s, with a grave face, said to them, But you were lucky to have survived the accident. According to him, the road between Upper Bahe Town and Xishui was narrow and dangerous, prone to accidents, particularly at night in a rain, where trucks carrying yellow sands from the White Lotus River plied between the place and Yuwang Town and many other smaller towns. Why do they carry yellow sands? Zu ventured, wondering about the use of such sedimented sands at the bottom of the river. Oh, Gao said, but this is very precious because it is quality material that, mixed with concrete, can be used for any buildings. Trucks from all over the country come here and go away, with loads of yellow sands. There is much demand for the sands in South-east Asia as well.

It took them no time to find out that Gao was not working in a factory; instead, he worked as a labourer shoulder-poling bamboo gabions from the sandbar to the waiting trucks. It was heavy work but he earned much more than a peasant. He didn't like the work. But there wasn't much he could do about it as he had a family to support, a two-year-old son and his wife pregnant again. Before he left them to themselves, Gao warned, saying, Your idea is a good one but it is not practicable. For one thing, there are too many of you. What if another accident took place? Only a few days ago, a truck plunged headlong down into the Bahe River right on the bridge, breaking the railings. Didn't you see the gaping gap when you went past the bridge? And, for another, it would be best if you were only one or two travelling on the road, provided you are good friends with the driver, say, someone that comes from afar, such as the Northeast. But because it's so far away, you'd have to wait for days before you can catch one. What if the guy refuses? Then it's all wasted. No, I'd say, it's not worth it.

The excitement over, the four boys, now lying in the darkness, were talking about their impressions.

I'll get married as soon as I find someone after my own heart, Han said. And have lots of kids.

Well, that, Len said.

You wouldn't have a problem, I don't think, Qu said, because you are so handsome.

Oh, no, no, no, Han said, but I'd like to have fun, you know. It's a pity we arrived too late at night. Otherwise, we could have gone out into the town and seen it for ourselves.

I heard that girls here are pretty, with very white faces, Qu said.

Because the water is good, Len said.

Because the lotus root is good, Zu, after a long brooding silence, said. They are brought up on the lotus root starch, which is supposed to make the skin creamy.

Oh, how much do I wish to have such a girl? Han sighed.

Are you feeling yourself? Qu said.

No, I'm not, Han said, are you?

Ha, ha, Qu said.

I'm sure he is, Zu said.

What are you talking about? Qu said. I don't even know how to do it.

A noise came from the middle of them, one that sounded like the clearing of a throat, cracking, before it rose and subsided, in a happy and content rhythm.

Oh, my, Han said. Buck Teeth's gone.

I'm going too, Qu said. I'm so sore and tired.

What do you think of Xi? Han said.

She's fine, Zu said, knowing the question was directed at him.

I think she's arrogant, Han said.

You do? Zu said.

Why are you pretending? Han said. You know better than anyone.

I have no idea what you mean, Zu said.

Well, I don't know, Han said. I just hate the way she acts as if no one else existed in her eyes.

I don't care one way or another, Zu said. I really don't.

I thought you did, Han said.

You must have fallen in love with her, Zu said. Have you?

Oh, no, Han said. How is that possible? I don't even like her; I hate her.

People only hate those they love, you know, Zu said.

Have you got someone in mind? Han said.

No, not yet, Zu said.

What about the girl in your middle school class? Han said.

It's all hearsay, Zu said. Nothing real.

If there ever is a chance, Han said, gnawing his teeth, I'd pay her back for her arrogance.

Zu knew who he was referring to. But he didn't say anything in reply. Instead, he said, I'm going to sleep now.

祖

Back in the village from Noisy Water Pool, life went as usual. Villagers were busy preparing for the autumn harvest. But things had subtly changed, with the arrival of two visitors, one Liu, a burly man of a broad smiling face, and Fu, a reed of a man who walked like a wind, with the quality of wind, too, both from Wuhan, a big city upstream of the Yangtze, and both speaking the city accent, the epitome of sophistication on one hand, and of rascality, on the other. As soon as they came, Fu hit it off with Han, out of nowhere, entering into a lively chat about where to find dogs to hunt and how to get chickens. They agreed to take immediate action by going to the nearest village that night. While they were chatting, Han assuming the Wuhan accent as if he were also from the big city, Liu, like a big brother, introduced himself to Len and Zu, as one of the educated youths from Wuhan, put to work in a farm with many others. As the farm work wasn't overtaxing, they'd begun on a journey, known as *caidian*, treading spots, from village to village, to see how other educated youths, like themselves, lived. The idea was fascinating, of a nature similar to Zu's travelling idea, but more manageable. All you needed was your own legs. You traveled to a nearby village where a *zhiqingdian*, Educated Youths Spot, was based, stayed a few days before you wandered onto another, then another, till you did the rounds. This, Liu said, is much better than roaming the country and running the risk of being rejected by the drivers.

Months of labouring in the rice paddies had left the three Clear Water Village boys hankering after new acquaintances and new friendships, and this whirlwind arrival of the two older boys from the big city came just at the right moment. Despite the doubts of Len and the disinterest that Zu was showing, Fu and Han threatened, cajoled, and persuaded, with belittling or sweetening or emboldening words that eventually led to a dog-hunting night, joined by all. Fu and Han, each had a broken bough in their hand, and the other three waited in the darkness, until they came back empty-handed.

There are no dogs in this village, Fu said.

But I heard them barking, Zu said.

Yeh, you did, Han said, contemptuously. The hurting remark reduced Zu to silence.

But they are all chained to the houses, Fu said.

If we kill one, the whole village will turn out, Han said, and that will be the end of us all.

What shall we do then? Len said.

Go to my place, Fu suggested.

Thereupon, they all headed for Fu's place, a village somewhere, where he was sharing accommodation with another two girls, also from the same big city, walking in the darkness till they saw a house, dimly lit, into which they entered.

Two girls, looking tired, emerged from what looked like a peasant's dwelling, and, after the introduction, retired to their own room. Han commented immediately after, Nice looks.

You can have her if you like, Fu said.

But isn't she yours already? Han wondered.

Not my type, no, Fu said.

Nor mine, Han was dismissive. Too fat.

The girl in question was Xiang, fragrance. Her fat features, to Zu, were nice enough to cause his thoughts to wander. How could I have never bumped into someone so nice and from a big city? Wouldn't it be lovely to make the acquaintance of her and go from there? But his train of thoughts was interrupted as they were led into a room, bare of anything except a table, with a kerosene lamp, and a bed, covered with a single quilt. That, Fu told them, was his own bed and it was there that they were going to stay for the night.

The idea of sleeping with the others under one quilt was anathema to Zu; from when he was little, he had always slept by himself except when he was tiny and needed to fall asleep with his hand cupping Mum's breast. Under the circumstances, though, he, seeing that the others seemed quite happy about it, couldn't even begin to raise an objection. Han, spotting Zu's scowling look, said, But you can share the bed with Xiang since you seem quite taken to her. Amidst the laughter that followed, Zu vehemently denied having anything to do with her, let alone share the bed. Afterwards, without washing, they all crept onto one bed, Fu and Han on one end, and Len, Liu and Zu, on the other, Zu next to the wall.

This crowd-bedding made Zu uncomfortable in the extreme. Sitting up alone, in the total darkness, would have been infinitely better. The feet, obviously those of Fu's, which poked out from his end and by his face, made the whole thing worse because they stank. To fend for himself, Zu had to turn on his right side, facing the wall, while listening to them subject-surfing, from the difficulty of catching a stray dog and killing it, to how easy it was to steal chickens from the peasants, a skill that Han was now passing on to Fu, until they brought Xiang up again when Fu was heard saying,

You know what? I wouldn't even want to touch her. There were so many pretty ones in Wuhan. In my life, I've gone through so many hot ones that this fat one falls far short of my expectation. Besides, when you share a peasant house with her day in and day out, you simply become indifferent. No *ganjue*, feeling, whatsoever.

I must go and catch one of them one of these days, said Han.

You've got to speak the local lingo, though, Fu said, wearily.

That's right, Liu chimed in, they'd dump you as soon as they realise from your accent that you are a country yokel.

What about the other one? Len said.

She's no good, not even worth a second look, Fu said. Xiang's only problem is her fatness and small eyes. Otherwise, he whispered something into Han's ears and the latter burst out laughing.

Zu knew what they had in mind when they laughed. But he pretended not to have heard it; in fact, he couldn't care less. None of the girls he had met so far, in his own village or in Upper Bahe Town, or even in Xishui, were his type, to use Fu's expression. Although Xi stood out among them, she was too emotionally standoffish, preferring to befriend the other country boys to the three young men sharing the house with her. Because of a casual remark someone had made that he should target her as a possible catch, Zu had started thinking of her, watching her every movement, making diary entries about her, and imagining him in a possible relationship with her, only to find that there was little enthusiasm in his heart, to say nothing of passion. Xiang seemed approachable. While she was cold towards others, she seemed kind to him, even glancing at him once. That glance, lasting no longer than a second, melted Zu. A fat girl is a fat girl, Zu thought to himself. There's nothing wrong with it. If she likes me, I don't think I can't like her; I probably will, given time. After all, she's from a big city and that makes it worthwhile.

Thus thinking, he drifted into sleep, only to be woken up by a loud song.

> We are walking on the big road
> When a group of girls come towards us
> Some so fat they resemble the winter gourds
> Others so thin they are like wood sticks
> Just beneath our notice

Just beneath our notice
When we go back to the city
We'll find someone better[1]

That night, no one had slept well, all excited, singing and chatting. But Zu was the only one who had fallen into a sound sleep from which he didn't wake up till the sun shone through the latticed window, shedding light on the other four sprawling figures, sound asleep, underneath a dirty flowery quilt. Judging by the look of it, it hadn't been washed for months. Zu got up, went to the kitchen, scooped water from a large vat with a water ladle and went outside, where he took a few mouthfuls to gargle and, using his right hand, patted his face with palmfuls of water. At the touch of the cold water, all his senses came alive. He could see a similar arrangement of the village to his own, Clear Water Village, with houses of black tiles and white walls surrounding a pond, and vegetable plots in front of the houses. There were cocks crowing and dogs barking, particularly when there were footsteps approaching of early rising villagers who, with hoes on their shoulders, were walking towards the rice paddies.

Just then, someone said, Here you are. He turned to see a grinning Xiang behind him, a dry towel in her extended hand. He 'oh'ed, and took it from her, feeling grateful.

Did you sleep well last night? Xiang said.

Yes, I did, Zu said, avoiding looking at the slits of her eyes.

They were so noisy, Xiang complained.

But I didn't join in, you know, Zu said, speaking in the Wuhan accent.

Are you from Wuhan? Xiang said.

But I have relatives there, Zu said.

Oh, you do? Xiang said, eyeing him.

Zu was embarrassed under her stare. He didn't want people, least of all girls, to see him as a country yokel, and because both his parents spoke the Wuhan dialect, he had learnt to speak it fluently from early on. But he always had a feeling that it was fake and people knew that it was

1 The original Chinese lyrics are found here: http://bbs.tianya.cn/post-45-1391012-1.shtml

fake. But Xiang was kind enough not to dwell on the topic; instead, she asked him about his family, what his father did for a living.

Their conversation was cut short by the guys coming out of the house when Zu heard Han say to Fu, What did I say? See how they hit it off, like that?

Xiang did not say a word and went back into the kitchen, never to come out again.

Chapter 10: Treading Spots

Not long after that failed dog-hunting adventure, Fu came back one day, to borrow a suitcase from Len. This happened when all the rest of the household were down in the paddy fields, working. He kept saying to Len that he would return it as soon as he came back from Wuhan until Len softened and gave in, unpacking it and handing him the empty suitcase.

As soon as he heard of this, on his return from the fields in the early evening, Zu said, But you can't trust these people. Wuhan is a city that abounds in hooligans. When these people come to the country, they do nothing but idle away their time, stealing chickens, killing dogs and looking for pretty faces. How could you have trusted him enough to lend that suitcase to him? I don't even believe he has, as he said, lost his own suitcase. How could he even have lost it? I'm sure he sold it when he ran out of money. These things do happen, you know.

Len was in a contemplative mood, neither saying yes nor no to whatever Zu had to say. He had a mind of his own. Having grown up a fatherless child, this man would rather keep his own counsel than listen to someone he didn't particularly trust, as he found Zu a rash man himself, as attested by his suggestion about the truck journey and its subsequent coming to no fruition. On the other hand, because he had known Han for many years, living in the same neighbourhood, he looked more kindly on those who were closely associated with him, than with Zu. When he said that it was fine and that he was sure Fu would return the suitcase when his business, whatever it was, was done, Zu realised, once again, as he had many times before, that his own kind-heartedness was mistaken for intrusion, therefore deciding not to be bothered again. Mum's words, repeated numerous times at home, came, Don't you worry about others; worry about yourself and conduct yourself well. It was this and other pieces of homely advice that served him well later in his life.

A month went past. Then another. And another. Nothing was heard of Fu again. It was almost as if he had never been there in the first place. The suitcase and the wisp of a man who chain-smoked and spoke the fashionable Wuhan accent were gradually receding into memory, along with a song he had sung when he first visited their house,

> The Yangtze waters rolled eastward
> day and night, never turning back
> but, my girl, where are you?
> where can I find you?

Carefully, Zu took down the numbers as he listened: 332356, 616535653, 566132, 2321656.

It was a simple enough song. To Zu, who was widely read in classical literature, particularly poetry of the Tang dynasty, it was too simple. The tune was simple; the words were simple, and the guy simple, too, having not even finished his junior middle school. But Len and Han loved it. Fascinated by the simple beauty of it, they sang it almost every day despite Zu's indifference. The message in the song, though, was unmistakable: the girl, and where is she? Where can he find her?

The instant he thought of the word 'girl', a girl appeared in his mind, with a round ashen face and thin lips, a girl whose eyes he had never directly met, never managed to, and who had always remained silent in his presence, in or outside the classroom, but a girl he had pursued deep into the night with thoughts, to the exclusion of any other girls. He had not told anyone of his thoughts, not his Mum or Dad, not his closest friend Jia, even though he had once blurted out that he was impressed by the looks of a girl in his class. Afterwards, Jia joked about it for days, laughing at his lack of guts in making a move.

Timid by temperament, when it came to matters of infatuation, Zu had been a boy who easily fell for the looks, in his middle school days. In his teens, he fell in love—he didn't know it was 'love'; he was just fascinated—with a number of girls, in and outside his own class. Zhi was such a girl. The mere mention of her name, Golden Branch, was fire to his timber. In fact, he had fallen in love with the words of the name even before he saw the face of the girl, a plump one with slit eyes. When she appeared in class, Zu was disappointed. The girl was no match for her name or vice versa. In her flowery spring clothes, Zhi looked exactly the country type, nothing attractive whatsoever. Quickly, Zu's attention shifted to a petite girl with a bright name, Mi. He liked her oval face, her sprightly gait, her brisk movements and the way she looked, alert and agile. Whenever they met on their way to school, she from the opposite direction, Zu would sense her approach and hear his heart beating fast, so fast that he could hardly breathe. He kept walking, his eyes lowered, looking at the part of the ground before him, wondering if he should raise his eyes and meet her stare. But there was no stare. By the time they went past each other, his eyes had never picked up enough courage to look and there was pain felt by his heart that had been beating overfast. This went on for quite some time till he found another object of desire, this time in a girl from another class, whose name was Juan, a word that denoted gracefulness. True to her name, Juan was a walking ray of sunshine. Whenever or wherever she appeared, hearts stopped beating, breaths were suspended, and eyes were downcast. Zu knew, because he had heard people talk. Hei, a friend, for example, would enthuse how white her face was, a quality that outshone any other. He would go on and on about her, as if he knew everything about her, that she had a sister, Yan, also pretty but not as pretty as she herself because Juan was more like Yang Yuhuan, one of the four great beauties of China in the Tang dynasty, a musician and dancer, an imperial concubine. Zu suspected that he had somehow set his sights on her by the way he talked, even though he himself never mentioned a word about it; instead, he kept his admiration to himself, secretly nourishing a fondness for her that went beyond daydreaming. It was at this time that *Swan Lake* was shown for the first time in Yuwang Town Cinema. Zu, along with other students, went to see it. He was amazed by the dancers in the shape of white swans, flitting across the stage like butterflies, to the accompaniment of the unearthly music. That's as far as it went; he left, content and impressed. But, shortly after, a student in a senior class was singled out for attack because of a remark he had made: 'I love the best three minutes of the film in which vast tracks of thighs are shown, so fascinating. Absolutely gorgeous.'

The Party Committee of the school was shocked. They took the student to task by forcing him to confess his crime of bourgeois indulgence in immoral thoughts and to apologise for having made the shameless remark. The incident reduced the rest of the school to silence, which didn't mean that everyone agreed. Zu, for one, admired Qingye, the tall guy, for having the guts in speaking his mind. He, too, found the three minutes, indeed, the whole ballet performance an unforgettable experience. He only wished that there could be more such things.

Meanwhile, in Clear Water Village, these things of the past, even though they had happened only a few years earlier, lay like forgotten memories and were hardly ever talked about. They flickered in Zu's mind, like a candle flame in the wind, for a fleeting second, at the thought of girls, before the daily realities set in again.

The harvest season now over, there wasn't much left to do. Han was itching to do something again. One day, he said to Len and Zu, Can you go and *caidian* again?

Having done that once with Fu, both Zu and Len agreed, thinking it a fitting idea.

Might be an interesting thing to do, Zu thought and said.

Let's do it, Han said, emboldened by Zu's agreement. How about we invite someone to come first?

I think we should go and see what others are doing, Len offered.

Agreed, Zu said. Let's go and see the ones in the nearby village.

They all knew what he meant by the 'ones'. More appropriately, they could be called 'the old ones' because they were older than them and had settled in the adjacent village one year earlier. Called Shiba Po, or Eighteenth Slope, the village was situated at the bottom of a valley, with hills on all sides. When they came downhill on a winding path, they could see roof after roof of black tiles spreading from one end to another, with more houses than they could count. Han admired the density of humanity in the village, as his own village was a mere forty households while Len said it was probably better that way as it was easier to handle and less labour intensive. Zu, though, noticed a tree of red leaves and a couple of white geese swimming in a pond where women were doing their laundry. Kids, again, as soon as they noticed strangers coming, appeared from nowhere and followed them right to the doorsteps of the house that the old ones occupied, raising delighted shouts of admiration and wonder.

Old Xiao, a smiling man in his early 20s but who looked much older, appeared at the door and welcomed them. This was a house similar to the one they themselves had built and lived in, except that it was smaller, with three rooms only, as there were only three occupants, all male. As soon as they entered the house, Han got busy offering cigarettes to everyone, including Old Zhao and Old Tang, Old Xiao's two roommates, also student-peasants like them. Zu, in one glance, could see that the other two were not very welcoming, as he thought he had detected a note of displeasure swiftly sweep across their faces, replaced by an instant change of attitude as soon as the cigarettes were offered. While they were standing in Tangwu, or the main hall, Zu had a quick look inside each and every one of their rooms and was amazed by their orderly cleanness, a bed and a table next to it, with an oil lamp on the table and a carefully folded quilt on one end of the bed and a pillow on the other, not a spot of dust seen on the bed-sheets, very much in an austere military style they had been trained to keep at the middle school.

When Han revealed that this was their first attempt to tread spots, Old Zhao, a stern-looking man of a stocky figure, expressed his uncomfortableness with the idea.

What's the point of doing that? He said.

Isn't this the in thing that everyone is doing now? said Han.

Not that I know of, said Old Zhao.

But it's so boring working in the fields, day in and day out, said Han.

Well, said Old Zhao. That's probably the only way out, working in the fields, and hard.

Stung by the remark, Han could do nothing but smile a curt embarrassed smile as he blurted out with a 'But I must go out and have a look around.'

What did he mean by that? Looking at Han's departing back, Old Tang, the tallest man among the three, who wore tattered but clean clothes, said.

Oh, Zu said. He's probably looking around to see if there are pretty girls in the village.

He might as well go elsewhere for that, Old Zhao said, with contempt. We don't do that kind of thing here, you know.

Soon enough, Len and Zu were made to know that this was a dedicated family of three males, as they were shown around their kitchen garden, a little paradise of delicious verdure, where there was a trellis scaffolding hanging with towel gourds, each ending with a wilted yellow flower, plots of bok choy, so green, were sending forth a sweet tasty smell, and a number of baby pumpkins were peeping out of the fat leaves. According to Old Xiao, they could never finish eating the lot because of the abundance and had to give part of it away to the villagers in need. When the time came, he said, this would stand them in good stead as the villagers would not frown on them wanting to leave for home, having worked so hard and being so generous.

Han did not come back till lunchtime and, when he did, Old Zhao and Old Tang kept silent, not wanting to know what he'd been up to. It was not till everyone sat down by the table, laden with large bowls of stir-fried bok choy, fresh from the field, and of egg drop and tomato soup, sprinkled with chopped spring onion, that Han launched into a tale about his wanderings in the village and he said, There really is nothing much to see in here. The villagers are working their ass off, like they do in Clear Water Village. A couple of girls I saw on the village road were old before their time, sun-scorched and almost black. And—

Oh, Old Zhao said. Don't you say that. Our production team is the best around the place, with the highest rate of productivity. If it is the girls you are looking for, there's plenty in town.

A silence ensued, a hostile one, in which the clinking of the spoons against the walls of the bowls, the chewing of rice and the eating of soup as it was being swallowed became audible. To ease the obvious tension, Zu thought of something and said, Have you guys heard of the song, 'Eighteen Gropes'?

You didn't mean 'Eighteen Slope'? said Han.

No, no, with an impatient wave of his hand, Zu said, it's a folk song, popular among the country folk.

How do you know? wondered Len.

I just do, just a little bit, came the answer as Zu began chanting,

> Let me touch Sister's hair on the side
> A dark cloud flying across half the sky
> Let me touch Sister's forehead
> It's so full and high I'm drawn in instead

Oh, I know that one, Old Xiao said as he sang a stanza,

> Let me touch Sister's brows
> Thick in the middle, thin on either side
> Let me touch Sister's tiny eyes
> The white whiter, the black, blacker

Keep going, the stern Old Zhao said, his interest aroused even though he still looked glum. But neither Zu nor Old Xiao could come up with anything more as it's a song that was found only in memory, and, as such, existed only in bits and pieces.

Well, Han offered. I think I've heard it somewhere before although I can only remember this much. As he said so, he sang,

> At Grope 16, I reach the thighs
> Two lotus roots that are so fat and white
> The more I grope, the more I like
> Ai-yo-yo, the more I like

> And at Grope 17, I reach below
> Like a ploughing buffalo
> In a deep grassy ditch
> Ai-yo-yo, in a deep grassy ditch[1]

1 Based on the Chinese folksong: http://zhidao.baidu.com/question/352186708.html

That's all you know, Old Zhao said. I gather.

Oh, I know much more, detecting the contemptuous tone in Old Zhao's voice, Han retorted and said nothing more. But one could see that he wasn't happy.

These two, Zu thought, might come to blows at any moments.

But nothing happened. Instead, Old Zhao launched into a harangue about how hard they had worked to get where they were, with their vat full of rice that would last a few seasons without any fears of rationing, their tank full of drinking water, their vegetable plot cultivated in a variety of goodies, such as loofah, cucumber, pumpkin, string beans, winter melon, bottle gourd, edible amaranth, red chilies, and whatnot, and, on top of that, they were raising two pigs, one of which was big enough to take to the market, and a number of chickens, with enough eggs to collect for daily food. It is here that he stopped, throwing a meaningful glance at Han, before he went on and said, The eggs here are safe and sound; no one else ever touches them or dares to.

Like a firebomb, Han exploded. Deeply hurt by the veiled attack directed at him, he said, But that is nothing. You guys are doing this only because you want to get out of the village and back to the city as soon as possible. That's so tame!

Tame? Without even looking at him or raising his voice, Old Zhao said. Who among you have ever carried *caotou* of two hundred jin nonstop to the threshing field?

I did, Han said without batting an eye.

No, you didn't, Zu said, remembering how Han would always try not to do any heavy duties if he could ever find a way to evade them.

What did you say? He turned on Zu, furious with him for exposing the lie. I can easily throw you onto the ground if you don't believe it.

Come on, someone said. Let's give it a go.

What I said was only the truth, Zu said. I saw with my own eyes how you staggered under the weight of the *congdan* till you could no longer hold it and fell—

Han shot out a hand, clenched into the ball of a fist, which caught Zu full in the face, right between his eyes, slightly to the left. And, with the push of another hand, he sent Zu sprawling onto the earthen floor. All this happened so unexpectedly and quickly that everyone was surprised. But when Zu picked himself up and tried to hit back, he was held by the others while Old Zhao pushed Han back, saying as he did so, You should be ashamed of yourself as you are bigger and stronger than him. Why, I mean, he was only telling the truth, wasn't he? You can't stop people speaking their minds, can you?

Han, his face livid with fury and his hand trembling, lit a cigarette for himself, trying to look calm.

祖

That night, Zu made an entry in his diary that went,

> Whenever I come to blows with people, I fail to achieve any success. Mum or Dad never taught me how to fight. On the contrary, they always told me to avoid fighting with anyone. When I was in my early teens, I had the misfortune of being kicked hard on my shin by Hei's older brother. It caused so much pain that I felt as if my body was shrinking back onto itself, turning into a tiny ball. I didn't fight back because I was trying to convince myself that he was much bigger, taller and stronger than me and if I fought back I'd be hit even harder, and I would lose the battle. On another occasion, I was walking home at night, pleased with myself for having made a string of rubber bands, with a self-made wooden pistol attached at the end underneath my clothes, when I was attacked by a number of local boys. They not only snatched off my treasure but also stuffed something, a handful of glass fibres, down my back. The itch it caused nearly killed me.
>
> Did I bawl? I don't think I did. But, on that winter night, when I stood in her office, Mum stripped me bare, right down to my waist, as she removed hundred if not thousands of tiny little shiny fibres off my pink swelling skin, itchy beyond relief and expression. As she did so, she kept saying, Who did that? Why

were they so cruel, so devoid of conscience? I was totally crushed, my pride and joy all gone. I stood there, letting her work on me, like I was a ruins of itchiness, alternately shivering with cold and convulsing with the unbearable discomfort. It was also the first time I ever experienced something close to motherly love.

Chapter 11. Hong and Xin

Hong was a tall man with a pallid face as if sick with some unknown condition. The standing joke about him was that he would easily be the *xiucai* (scholar) among the country yokels without him even uttering a word. Put him in a grey gown, have him hold a *jiaobian* (teaching whip or pointer), and you have a quintessential village teacher in the flesh, which is exactly what he did, bar the gown and the pointer. Shortly after he began on his spot-treading, Zu caught up with Hong in his one-bedroom dorm, built on a slope, overlooking a vast expanse of rice paddies. There were no farming tools in his room. But what caught Zu's eye was a small blackboard, hanging on the wall in a corner. On it were two expressions written: 'Rui Dian' and 'Ao Da Li Ya', two extraordinary country names that sat uncomfortably with the rural ambience.

Why did you write those names there? Zu wondered aloud.

Oh, Hong said as he regarded Zu smoking, obviously with disapproval although he did not say a word of objection. His objection would most often show itself in what he didn't do instead of what he did, as Zu was to find out shortly. I was teaching them geography.

You are lucky because you don't have to work in the fields, said Zu and, as he said so, he looked around for any signs of farming tools, finding none.

Not as lucky as you guys, said Hong, because I can't run around doing nothing; I have to teach, you see.

Teaching is an easy thing for you, isn't it?

I suppose so, said Hong, looking sharply at him before he turned his large grey eyes elsewhere.

But why Sweden and Australia? What's that got to do with China? And what's the point of teaching about these far countries?

Oh, just part of what they need to know about the world outside, you know.

Mere place names, though.

You may say so, but don't you find it odd that these two countries are poles apart?

But what about Norway? What about the Soviet Union, with its most remote city, Arkhangelak?

Arkhangelsk, said Hong. The authoritative tone of his voice had a forbidding quality in it. It's less the distance than the mind.

What did you mean? Zu was lost and hated himself for being so browbeaten. And did the kids know the difference?

Not if you don't teach them, said Hong as he waved off the smoke blown in his direction, and coughed. That was occasion enough for Zu to joke about what he saw as part of Hong's effeminateness.

Nonsense, said Hong. They plucked me out of the rice paddies and planted me in this one-classroom and one-student school, not because I was like a woman, but because I had qualities they thought were fitting for a teacher.

Where's the school then? And on learning that it was Hong's own dorm, Zu burst out laughing but was cut short by a stern remark from Hong, who said, In the beginning, Confucius had only one student, and no classroom.

I didn't know about that, surprised, Zu said. I thought he had three thousand disciples.

Haha, Hong laughed one of those rare laughs he had, revealing a row of tiny, inward-drawn teeth. What does it matter if he had three thousand students or one? Lao Tzu had none. People went to him as they pleased. And they taught in the open, no classroom. He said the last two words emphatically as if it were some rare virtue, completely lost in contemporary times. That, to me, is ideal teaching.

Never heard of such things, Zu laughed it off.

Oh, there's a lot of things you haven't heard of, I'm sure, said Hong. But it doesn't mean they didn't exist.

This conversation left Zu disconsolate. As he stood outside Hong's dormitory, smoking a Jingji, the cheapest of the cigarettes, costing 8 cents a pack, his eyes swept across the autumnal rice paddies after the harvest, stubbly with an air of indolence, on which sparrows hopped about as they went picking the dropped rice grains. He recalled how he was ill with asthma on one occasion, whooping all night, kept awake with the difficulty of breathing, only to feel better with the rising of the sun, as if its light had a curing effect, when he went to the fields again but was told by Pan Da to not worry about it. Instead, he went in search of ears of rice along with the frail and the old in the village. This felt better than when he went picking cotton as the smell of the green cotton leaves and the fluffiness of the cotton itself would invariably set him off on a string of asthmatic attacks. The dry paddies with stubble in autumn was a perfect golden brown colour, with paddy ridges, overgrown with green grass, snaking through the paddy fields, looking pleasing to the eye. His back bent, he would wander from stubble to stubble, its roots blackened with the recent rain, looking for any ears of rice grain between them. As he faced down, his back towards the skies, getting close to the earth, he could smell the aroma of the earth, mixed with that of the stubble, the grain and an occasional wild flower, usually blue. It was a job that he enjoyed most, not the least because there always was a conversation going on somewhere between the pickers, one in which he learnt much about the village and its past. The aged peasants, such as Pan Hua, would shock him by saying that landlords were not wicked in the so-called *jiu shehui* (the Old Days) as they were quite humane and caring. It was true that they were wealthy landlords. But they had to rely on the long-term hired hands for farming-related work, had to pay them well and treat them with respect. On festive occasions, these hired hands, long-term or short-term, would be entertained with sumptuous meals to *dayaji*, literally to fatten their teeth, but figuratively to wine and dine. Pan Hua paused, threw a cautious glance around him, and, making sure that no one was watching and lowering his voice, said, Unlike now, when we can't even stuff our bellies as there's never enough to eat. You are lucky because the government subsidised your resettlement here until it's time for you to return to the city.

From casual conversations like this, Zu also learnt that farm labour in the old days was never as strenuous, harsh, and backbreaking as now because there used to be only one season of planting the rice seedlings and one season of harvesting the ripe rice, with the rest of the year spent in doing nothing except lying idle in the comfort of their homes, playing

Mahjong, or drinking and eating, wearing and tearing time as one pleased until the Party took over the country.

祖

After his visit to Hong the village teacher, Zu traveled on to a farm where Xin lived. This was a heavy man with tiny eyes. He was taller even than Hong but more burly, steeped in books, because his father was a scholar-teacher, in a nationally well-known secondary school, called Yuwang Town Middle School. Immediately when they met, Zu noticed how he quickly blinked his eyes whenever something book-related was brought up as if the very blinking was his way of thinking. Zu talked about a detail he had read in a book by Mao that he found in a wooden box containing many books his father owned. He said that he was shocked that Mao, the supreme leader, should have remarked about women in a way that didn't seem proper.

What did he say? said Xin, his eyes blinking hard.

I don't remember exactly anymore, said Zu. But I came across that in one of his volumes Dad had and underlined it because I found it quite odd.

There shouldn't be anything odd about the great people, said Xin.

Oh, really?

Good people never pipan; great people do.

Pipan, said Zu. I know that one.

Do you? Said Xin, raising an eyebrow, his tiny eyes blinking, thinking.

Not that I pipanned but that I know many did, and, as a result, they fell from their high positions.

Didn't you find the word intriguing? Xin offered.

Yes, but I don't know what it exactly means.

It's as plain as one glance taking all in. *Pi* is skin and *pan*, which actually should be correctly pronounced 'ban', is stumbling. Simpler than simple.

One could see that Zu's eyes glazed in a moment of contemplation, of failed understanding. Instead of laughing at his incomprehension as Zu had thought he would, Xin had a face that was growing serious and his eyes blinked, as these words poured out:

You stumble across the skin of someone. If you are a man and stumble across the skin of a woman—.

I know, I know. Zu cut him short.

But you said you didn't. Xin stopped blinking, his eyes opened wider than the slits they were.

Zu didn't say anything in reply. Images flashed across his mind of big posters stuck on the walls in his hometown, at a time when every usable public space was plastered with them, aimed at exposing the darkness of human action and human thought, along the lines of class struggle. He would see the two-character expression pop up everywhere that led to the downfall of the man or the suicide of the woman, as was the case with the Beijing Ayi in Round Wind where Zu Senior worked. What shocked him was the fact that someone who spoke a perfect Putonghua, equivalent to RP of the UK, of a kind findable only in Beijing, should be the one to have committed adultery and, worse, suicide.

As if in answer to his puzzlement, Xin's voice came that said, 'As far as I know, women's skin is so slippery that it leads to men stumbling and tumbling along, eventually falling.'

How do you know? Said Zu, wide-eyed.

Ah, said Xin, his eyes blinking harder and faster, like an ophthalmological stammer. And he said, But it's a long story.

That night, over a dinner prepared by Xin, with a chicken that Han had stolen from a neighbouring village, they drank the local *baijiu* till each of them got quite tipsy, when, prompted by Han, Xin began telling his story of how he once stumbled across a slippery skin. As Xin rattled on, Zu found it hard to keep his eyes open. The kerosene lamp flickered in front of him. The shadows of the other two lengthened, then widened, as the story sank in. A man and a woman. Their skins touched. But nothing much else happened. It all sounded so abstract that, presently, Zu found himself half asleep while Han begged Xin for more lurid details till the latter had to invent more as he went. Zu knew at heart that what little Xin had said was as interesting as what he goes

217

through in his mind when he masturbates.

A detail emerged out of a forgotten past and part of Zu's mind. Living alone in his one room of two beds, one window and a desk, Zu had a sole companion that was a Chinese parasol tree. It stood like a huge spreading umbrella in a walled-up courtyard outside down, below his window across a cobbled lane. From his desk by the window, Zu could see most of the courtyard. A clothesline between the trunk of the tree and a wall had constant laundry hanging out to dry. There was a girl, too, who would occasionally saunter out into the courtyard from her family home on the other side of the tree and take in the laundry when dry. Zu watched the girl. She was short and wore flowery clothes. Her face was not the prettiest kind. But the more he looked at her, the more Zu was drawn to her. When she was gone, he found himself missing her. Then one day he managed to catch the girl's eye and she returned his glance. A slow simmering fire was set off that led to more frequent eye contact until sometimes the girl would wander in her courtyard, apparently having nothing to do, the laundry on the clothesline already taken in. By instinct, Zu knew that she knew that Zu wanted her to be there with him. Their eye contact, once maintained, lingered and lengthened till it sparked. It was on one of those dreary days, minus Mum who had gone to the hills with her colleagues on a tea-investigating trip and minus Dad who was away at work in Round Wind, on which Zu fell into a revelry so entrancing that he thought he found music, faint notes of beauty that were pouring out of the sky, into his ears by fits and starts. His head, buried inside the hook of his arms, was dizzy with the drunkenness of it till he raised it and grabbed a fountain pen, lying next to him on the desk, ready to put the notes down on a piece of paper when his eyes were lit up by the appearance of the girl right behind the wall down below, her eyes intent on his, so intent, in fact, that he had an instant hard-on. He would have rushed out the window, jumped across the lane, climbed over the wall and joined the girl but for his faint-heartedness. Instead, he tried the idea that came to him instantaneously, by hanging a bronze-framed mirror on the mosquito-net hook, tilted in such a way that he could see the girl inside it, looking up at him as he looked down.

The girl, unaware of what he was doing, moved in the backyard in a leisurely manner, pretending to look up at the Wutong tree leaves above her, looking for the loud cicadas, while turning her gaze back, from time to time, to where Zu was. Zu held her gaze in the mirror, and, in that instant, he quickly masturbated himself until he came. The girl, obviously a virgin, did not know what was going on. She waited and waited for him to return her gaze. But Zu was done and was so ashamed of himself that he took down the mirror, hiding himself in his tiny room, away from the window. Besides, after he did what he did, he grew weary of what he had done and of the girl, too.

That night, Zu and Xin slept in the same quilt in the latter's bed, in a synchronised way. If Xin lay on his right side, Zu turned also on his right, his face millimeters away from Xin's nape. He would have preferred to lie on his back, turning on his left, facing the ceiling. And, better still, he would have preferred to lie back to back, turning on his left and facing away from Xin. In the circumstances, though, inside the cramped quilt, lying still and facing the other's back was the only way he could manage or else half of his body would be exposed outside the quilt. By now, he had known a thing or two about Xin's family history. His dad had died in the early days of the Cultural Revolution as a result of the violence meted out by the Red Guards. His librarian mother brought him up alone, among the books available from the library or stolen from the school library when it was ransacked by the Red Guards. One thing Zu kept repeating to himself was a remark Xin had told him, that he attributed to a name he had never heard of: Cioron. It went something like this: 'Nothing proves that we are more than nothing.'[1] He didn't really understand what it meant, although he found it appealing to him. He kept repeating it to himself in silence when Xin, whose face was turned to the wall, said to the wall, interrupting his train of thought: I find you someone to whom I can have a heart to heart talk.

Umh, said Zu.

Can we become close friends? said Xin.

Umh, said Zu, feeling moved but not untipsy and unsleepy enough to

1 Qtd in E. M. Cioron, *A Short History of Decay*. Penguin Books, 2010 [1949], p. 54.

answer coherently without stumbling among the words. He would have said 'yes sure' or 'how delighted I am' but.

In no time, he fell into a sleep so unbroken only the light of the day could break.

Chapter 12. Watching a Film in the Open and Huishu

On a moonlit night, a film was shown on the threshing ground of Production Team 9. It was an Albanian film, titled, *Gjurma*, dubbed in Chinese translation as *Hai'an fenglei* or *Wind and Thunder on the Coast*. Because the rest of the household had seen it before in the early days of the Cultural Revolution when there was still school, Zu found himself late and alone, watching it from the other side of the silver screen. Villagers from the adjacent villages were mostly sitting on the right side, watching the film under the full moonlight, talking and laughing, sometimes very loudly. A breeze rose, cool and comfortable, that set the screen billowy. Sitting on the wrong side, Zu saw everything in reverse. If someone had a cigarette in the left corner of his mouth, he had it in the right corner now. When one of the characters chucks a 5-cent coin onto the floor, and a hand reaches for it, a foot comes down right on the hand, with an accompanying remark, 'How could you have sunk so low?' That remark, while setting the audience howling with laughter, left Zu wondering about his own situation. Musical composition, his favourite pastime, and his passion, too, didn't seem to lead to anything fruitful. After that mirror incident involving the nameless girl when the first impulses of music stirred in his heart, he had composed many songs based on lyrics that he wrote himself and had only received rejections after submitting them to a variety of magazines, including *Songs and Lyrics*, a nationally distributed magazine, published on a monthly basis. Occasionally, he would pause to think of other alternatives, like writing another short story or turning his attention to poetry.

He did so, back in the room he shared with Len and by the still burning kerosene lamp, where he went through a grey-covered notebook, with *Gongzuo Biji* (work notebook), in red, across the top part of the cover, that was full of poems and song lyrics he had written since he came to the village. He found one of his lyrics written prior to his graduation from the middle school:

In the fine skies
Happy little birds are flying
People are working hard in the fields
Feeling so good
With warm blowing breezes
And the sun shining on them
Oh, what a beautiful winter!

After he set that to music, he had only himself to sing it to, a habit that Mum contemptuously referred to as *gufang zishang*, solitary fragrances for self-enjoyment or indulging in self-admiration. On such occasions, a fight would ensue, between the mother and her son. So what if it is *gufang*, solitary fragrances, as long as I can do it myself? retorted Zu, his face flushed red.

Confronted with such young ferocity, Mum would mutter darkly and say things like, You are stinking and stiff, like a stone in a shithouse, because whatever she said in trying to bring him to his senses, that one had to receive training in order to become a professional, he just wouldn't listen, going solo as he always had, listening to no one but his own heart beatings.

Old Zu would realise how romantic he was in those days, his lyrics and poems full of words like 'ambitious youth', 'an ideal road to a beautiful, happy future', and 'rock-like hardness'. In one particular poem, he went so far as to claim, in an outburst of passion expressed in the moment of departure from his mother, that, unless he reached 'the peak', he wouldn't see her again. The man in his old age didn't remember what young Zu had in mind when he talked about 'the peak' or if ever there was one. The Cultural Revolution, in its heyday, dumped these youngsters, aged 19 or 20, as soon as they graduated from middle school, in villages across the vast land of 96 million square kilometres, without giving them any hope of ever rising above the village level. Romanticism, it seems, was a way of self-comforting, like masturbation, when hope was lost against hope. When the paradigm was a national political 'Sword of Damocles', hanging over everyone's head, one tended to wax lyrical about vague ambitions that acted as a dosage of comforting imagination, like weeds.

祖

Then, there was love that was never there, a mere thought that, like a gentle breeze, would ripple the waters of his heart. Except his mother, there had never been any other women in Zu's life, his physical life. He'd never touched a woman's hand; never been near a woman of his age; never seen any pictures even remotely close to what is now so easily available online, even on baidu.com, and, yet, he'd seen women, women of his age, in their mid-teens or late teens, at school. He'd spotted faces so pretty his heart went pit-a-pat, and one recently spotted was just that, a face that altogether turned his head, quickened his heartbeats, lengthened his daydream and made him expectant. Life was worth living now. There was something to look forward to, day after day, and week after week, in that construction site at Noisy Water Pool where Zu was temporarily stationed along with a team of peasant-workers, working on a pipeline that went across from one hilltop to another, part of what was known as hydroelectric projects that peasants were assigned to do in winters when work in the rice paddies was finished for the year.

It was after work. They had just had dinner, rice and stir-fried vegetables and towel gourd soup. Zu was walking back towards the work tent with his workmates, bowl and chopsticks in hand, past a small hut that housed the office of the worksite headquarters, and was about to light his cigarette between his lips when he stopped, his hand holding the lighter frozen in the air and his eyes fixed somewhere that his workmates did not see. They got impatient and hurried him along because they wanted to start the usual card game inside the tent, by their beds.

While they were sitting in Pan Lin's bed, in a circle, playing a poker game, Zu went to his own bed, lying down, hands behind the back of his head, staring into the ceiling, thinking he was gazing into a pair of eyes, the eyes he had just seen, by the hut office, that were gazing back to meet his. The eyes were so dark and beautiful that they set the tip of his heart aquiver with thrills and longing. He had never seen anything quite like that. They seemed to make her face whiter and her whole person perfect beyond expression. And, most mysterious of all, the eyes didn't seem to show any contempt when they met his, a guy who looked no different from all the other peasant-workers and a guy he himself habitually regarded as ugly and unworthy of a woman's second glance. He fell into a reverie in which he found himself talking to the owner of the eyes, in words he was the only person privy to: But who are you? Why are you so beautiful? What business do you have here with all these peasants, including myself? Are you someone from another world?

He was thus musing when his train of thought was interrupted by a yell from Pan An, who said, Come over, Zu. We need you here to help us win.

He turned on his side, with his back towards them, pretending to sleep. But Pan An's voice was persistent as it became suggestive, audible enough for all to hear: This guy must have fallen for the girl. When all expressed their ignorance, the voice continued, But she's from the big city and she's a secretary here. The voice lowered itself into a whisper that set every listener bursting into lurid laughter. Zu rolled out of bed and threw something on as he walked out of the tent in quick steps.

Darkness had fallen. Rows of work tents, all lit up, dotted the open valley, like a huge spreading fan of lights. A cigarette in hand, he went along the Sibai River, a meandering river of 30-odd kilometres originating in Macheng and emptying itself into the Bahe River. Aimlessly, he went along the riverbank, a slowly moving mass of shimmering water. It was a moonless night. A cold wind was rising. Leaves were rustling. And he felt cold. Perhaps a few months ago, he recalled, he had seen two girls emerge from nowhere. Although he could not see their faces distinctly, he was instantly turned on because the girls wore their trousers tight enough to show the line between their buttocks. He watched them till they disappeared inside a house in a nearby village.

Long after that, he kept wondering who they were and why they wore their trousers like that. And, on more than one occasion, he reminisced about the sight, telling his roommates and classmates, particularly Luo, of what he had seen, till Luo blurted out, You must have fallen in love with them then and there? That was when he realised he must have revealed too much of his inner thought that others found prurient. Afterwards, he kept mum.

Somewhere, something plonked in the river. Zu raised his head and thought: It must be a fish. His memory was set alive with fish, fish that he had caught as a child in the Yangtze where he would go fishing every summer, particularly the *can*, pronounced 'tsan', schools of them habitually swimming around the end of an anchored ship or boat. All you do is whip at them with your line and rod, with half an earthworm on the hook. The second the hook hits the water, the *can* would come and snatch at it. You lifted the rod and you got it, a flash of white in the sun that was curling and flipping and flapping. On one good day, in less than half an hour, he fetched dozens of them, silvery chopsticks the length of the distance between the tip of the thumb and that of the middle finger when extended.

The fish-related thoughts kept him warm despite the late autumn cool. As he retraced his steps and neared the tent where his bed was, he thought of the secretary and how the glance, like a meteor, cut open the night of his heart and left an indelible trace there. As soon as he arrived back, to a tent where most had gone to bed, he took out his notebook and scribbled something across the page:

They say her name is Huishu. It is a beautiful name. Everything about her is beautiful, like the film I saw when a child. When the woman appeared on the screen, her stunning beauty struck me with awe, admiration, like an abyss into which I was irresistibly sucked. I had no idea what beauty was when that young. But I knew by instinct, if ever there was one I'd like all to myself, it would have to be her; I'd give all the world to have her. This Western woman of pure whiteness.

I'll think so much of her that Huishu will come to me in my dream all by herself. I'm not sure if that is what people commonly refer to as love. But ancient stories, particularly those written in the Qing Dynasty, often tell how women die, only to revive after men make love to them. The meeting of our glances is the first step that I don't know where it will lead. But I hanker so much after love that I think a woman like her is all I have that could sustain my courage in continuing to live.

A year after that exchange of glances, Zu still had her in mind, so much so that he found himself transmitting his memory to a poem, in which he wrote,

> Last year when we met outside the hut
> Your beautiful features left me intoxicated
> And hankering after you no end
> The road to love breaks
> Although your pretty shadow remains
> Years flow, like water
> When shall we meet again?

Chapter 13: The Water Project

As soon as the job was finished in the construction site where Zu met the beautiful secretary, they moved further into the mountains, to work on yet another hydroelectric project. In a rented house that smelt of cow dung that they had recently moved into, next to the construction site, ten peasants slept in a row, one by one, in their quilts of assorted colours. Some slept with their heads towards the wall and others slept the other way. But all slept side by side, wrapped up in their cotton quilts. In the early morning, when everyone was still asleep, Pan Hua, the village elder, was always the first to rise. He didn't immediately get out of bed; he sat against the wall, smoking, with his thick cotton-padded jacket thrown on his shoulders, knees drawn up, wrapped inside his quilt printed with loud-coloured peony flowers. Zu woke up from the pungent smell and coughed. And he coughed again. As if on cue, Hua started coughing, too, a cough that was so fierce and continuous that Zu feared that everyone might be woken up. No one was; they all seemed to have sunken into a blissful slumber from which not even a crack of thunder would have extracted them. The coughing did not stop till a mouthful of phlegm was spat across part of the bed onto the vacant spot near the threshold. The old man, in his mid-50s, looked like someone in his 70s; he had spent all his life in the fields. After his wife died of pneumonia, he lived alone with his only daughter, a scrawny girl of 14. This girl, Zu recalled, had called him Bajie, after Pigsy in *Journey to the West*, probably because he looked like one, with his protruding teeth. The appellation displeased him no end. But he couldn't possibly do anything about it. The girl was a bundle of energy despite her slight figure. She would attack anyone who tried to provoke her, calling them all sorts of names, and they just had to laugh it off, dismissing her as unreasonable and tempestuous. Of all the names, though, Bajie was the one that stuck and his fellow educatees soon picked it up and applied it to him, although the villagers were cautious enough to avoid it; they, the lowest of the low, had a decent sense of decorum and propriety, inculcated through tradition, carried down the centuries.

Zu watched Hua sitting and smoking in silence. Neither spoke a word. Zu closed his eyes. He wanted to fall back into sleep but couldn't, his mind a mess of fragmented dreams, none of which was even close to complete. By and by, one detail emerged. The boy, by the name of Ben, who was about his age, was aggressive enough to challenge him to a game of wrestling yesterday which he flatly refused. On the surface, Zu acted as if he was not afraid of anything or anyone. Underneath, though, he was a man who was verbally aggressive but physically inept. The guy seemed to have spotted it in one glance and made the challenge. Inwardly shaking, Zu knew he wouldn't meet it. In fact, he was never good at wrestling. In school, when he was a boy, he had had a number of fights with other boys and he was always the first to be wrestled to the ground. No matter how he tried to learn, by watching others wrestle, he was just not nimble enough, his body too clumsy to tackle. This is probably why he loved reading stories about people fighting with skills. A novel he read but forgot the title of features a figure who can wipe people off their feet with a mere sweep of his leg. A story he read but also forgot the title of features a wrestling champion who ends up by being thrown onto the ground by a green hand only to tell him later on in a whisper that he's an old friend of his father. When it comes to real fighting, however, he was a hard mouth (a local expression that refers to being stubborn and reluctant to admit defeat in the face of a challenge) who'd invariably come to grief.

As it happened, the next day, while they were all sitting by the roadside, waiting for the work to start, Ben came over and said, Shall we give it a go? As he said so, he threw a contemptuous look at Zu while scanning the others in a triumphant manner, as if he had already won. This was a lank guy of rough features and rougher manners. Zu remained silent, looking away. He's scared, said Ben. I've scared the shit out of him.

Before he could finish his words, Zu leapt to his feet and pounced on Ben. It was over in a second. Without making much of an effort, Ben threw him off his back and onto the ground, the way he put down a heavy sack of rice grains. All the rest of them started laughing when

Hua, team leader, who liked Zu enough to stop this going, stood up and said, Stop fighting. Let's get down to business. Humiliated and hurt, Zu went along with the team to the truck to carry concrete slabs, not looking at anyone.

祖

It seemed a most unpleasant period in Zu's life but, as Old Zu found out years after, a lone poem that Young Zu wrote records an optimism that didn't seem to match the mood, with such lines as 'we, grinning, looked at each other / your finger was bruised / and his sweat was a river / but this slab was a great fellow / that gave me a thorough bath/and made my fingers itch'.

On a Sunday after an intense period of working on the aqueduct, everyone was exhausted. Most were sleeping in. Han and Len went to the local market to have a look around. When they asked him to come along, Zu declined, saying he was too tired, ignoring the lewd suggestion by Han that he must have exhausted from masturbation the previous night. He waited till they left, then rolled out of bed and threw on the dark-blue cotton-padded jacket Mother had hand-made at home for him. There was something he had always wanted to do; he wanted to take a long walk along the Sibai River. If possible, he wanted to walk as far as possible, till he reached where the river joined the Bahe River, known in ancient times as the Ba Water, of 151 kilometres in length.

It was a winter day. The sun was a pale ball the size of an egg yolk, hanging distant in the sky. The stubble fields in the valley were grey and silent, awash with morning dew. Houses of white walls and black tiles dotted the landscape. There was no one around. Winter was a time that put people to sleep or rest. An occasional late cock crowed, followed by a number of other cocks crowing in other villages. Otherwise, there was no sound, not even the sound of the river running. As he went further away from the construction site, the river-scape became bleaker and more somber until he came to a place where the river plunged, deep down a gully, creating a sonorous noise that was booming somewhere down below. He didn't know how long he had been walking. He didn't know where he had come to. But the sudden change in the landscape and the river-scape had the effect of a dream that took a firm hold on him, wrapping him up like a cotton-padded quilt. All around him were walls of sandstone, like in a museum built with sandstone of yellow and grey. Not yet complete, this sandstone museum had broken walls here and there, the wall faces hanging with nothing but troughs of rain and traces of wind. The sky, indifferent so far, now seemed keen on observing how the small guy would react to this new dream of reality. As the sky saw, the guy was bewildered, wondering to himself if this was a practical joke that the scape of the land and of the river had played on him. How come everything—the stubble fields, the river, the village houses, the valley, the crowing cocks, the surrounding hills—was so placid and peaceful till it was turned upside down, presenting, as it were, a picture only a mind at sixes and sevens would have been capable of producing. The sky went on to see the little man raising his head in contemplation, gaining no response from the earth's counterpart, the sky, before he lowered his head, again in seeming contemplation, not stopping for a single moment in his exploring steps.

Long after that experience, Zu could never rid himself of a sense of parachuting. It was almost as if he was parachuted to the place, but to what purpose? Just so that he was made aware of another world existing in parallel to his own? Or that the shape of future was presented the way it was, bleak, barren, and unpromising? Or simply that it was the other side of his mental landscape, thus far hidden from his own view? Such subsequent wonderings, by fits and starts, frequently led to a void in his mind that nothing could fill, a cerebral hole whose backfilling must needs be done by the imagination of a woman.

And that woman was Huishu whom he had met and had written into a poem. At this stage of his life, the 18-year-old Zu had masturbated profusely whenever he was inspired but had never had any physical experience with any women. As he once joked, perhaps the only physical experience he'd ever had was with female mosquitoes, in an absolutely uninvited, passive way. In the tiny village world formed of kids, peasants, a pond, rice fields, a creek and houses, there was little inspiration to be had, no one worth him setting his sights on. But Huishu opened a totally new world to him. Reputedly, she was from a big city upstream of the Yangtze, and her dress and manners showed it. Everything about her was right. The dark of her hair, the white of her face, the tone of her eyes, and the seduction of her whole person that acted as a disturber of his nights. He would see her eyes wherever he went. If he went to the edge of the river to wash his hands after work, he would see her eyes emerge out of the muddy water. If he closed his eyes when the last candle was blown out at night when everyone went to bed, he would see her eyes shiny and bright, burning a hole in his soul. Already, the insides of his quilt were a dry crust of semen, all shed for the thinking of the girl, near at hand but impossible to gain access to, as far as the edge of the sky. Curiously, though, whenever he took his desire Huishu-wise, and emptied it the way a river does as it rushes towards a bigger river, he experienced the way a river would not have possibly felt itself; his body, vacated by the variety of images in connection with the girl, felt hollow and empty, like a grain sack with no contents. Afterwards, all he ever wanted was to fall into sleep. Thus, the process repeated itself, at irregular intervals.

祖

One day, he received a letter from someone. He couldn't tell who, by the look of it. But when he opened the letter, he realised from the familiar handwriting that it was from Hair, a nickname given to Chen, a short man of agility whose main interest was in soccer, and who otherwise had little interest in studies at school. It was a short one that he wrote:

> If you have time, come to visit me. [Address given]. We shall have a good chat about the old days.

So it was the following Sunday that Zu went alone to visit Hair in Yiliuhe, an over-spilling river, somewhere in the bluish hills. The journey would cover a few kilometres but he wouldn't mind. He'd like to try the old trick: Stop a truck or something right in the middle of the road and get onto it from the back. That was his plan and it was with this plan in mind that he set out, on a bright sunny day.

He followed the bend of the river part of the way, then he turned onto a *gonglu*, a public road, that got higher as it wound its way into the hills. There was little traffic. An occasional jeep or truck went by, raising a cloud of dust behind it. The sun struck down, directly on him. But he didn't feel hot. He walked for some distance before he stopped. He let the wind blow dry the sweat on his forehead and face. Then he started moving again. This went on till he reached a bend in the road when he noticed something gone wrong. A house on fire! Right inside a compound by the roadside. He took another look and decided that it was not the house that was on fire but a stack of rice straw. People were running around in the compound. They were passing bucket after bucket of water in a line till it reached the end of the line when someone poured it over the fire. Outside, cars or trucks went by, no one noticing, or paying any attention to what was going on. Without a thought, Zu went in and joined them. He picked up a bucket, walked with it to where it was closest to the burning stack and, raising it overhead, poured directly into the fire. People noticed this new man's arrival. There was no time to greet. In silence, they accepted him as part of them and went on with the extinguishing work. In less than half an hour, the fire was put out.

Seeing there wasn't much else to do, Zu turned to go, when the man at the head of the line, who looked like a leader of sorts, went over to him and took his hands in both his hands, shaking them and thanking him profusely, then asking him for his address. After he gave the man his address, Zu left the compound and got on his way again.

It was midday and hot now. Zu was pleased with himself because he had done something worthwhile; he had literally helped put out a fire. The intensity of this pleasant feeling was heightened when he saw a truck appear in the distance. It slowed down considerably as it came uphill, its engine coughing and complaining like an old man. Taking his chances, Zu waited till the truck was at its slowest and climbed it from behind its back. When he sat down on a pile of sacks of rice, he was even more pleased, congratulating himself on yet another success. But no sooner had he settled himself comfortably between two fat sacks than the truck pulled up to the side of the road, coming to a complete stop. The door swung widely open as an angry face appeared behind it, yelling, What the fuck did you do? Get off this second!

Mumbling about the need to go somewhere and trying to appease the driver, Zu got off the truck reluctantly. Thinking he might win him over by bribing him with a cigarette, he walked around to the front, a pack of cigarettes in hand. But the truck had got in motion. The driver threw a remark at him, like a stone, Don't you ever do this again. Pretty dangerous.

Like a lost soul, Zu stood in the middle of the road, bewildered, his hope shattered. A bird whistled at him from a roadside tree, its eye seeming to wink in mockery. He shook his head and cast around for a stone. But the bird took flight.

He plodded in despondency for a couple of hours till he reached the place, a restaurant in the middle of nowhere.

Hair was already there, waiting for him. After graduation from the middle school, Hair seemed to have matured overnight. There was still that big grin, with a neat row of teeth revealed. But the teenager of uncertainty, who had had loads of questions to ask even when the fullest explanation was given, was no longer there. In his place was a man with real hair, a half-ring of black down over his lips. They sat down at a table and ordered food. There was no food left. Only *baijiu*, or white liquor, made of grain. This Hair bought after much fighting with Zu because he insisted this was his shout. It came in two large earthen bowls, the liquor as clear as water one could see the fine cracks on the bottom. But it smelt good. The restaurant had no customers but Hair and Zu. All food had been sold out by 12 and it was past 1 p.m. now, so they sat there, drinking as they chatted. The restaurateur, a middle-aged peasant, sat behind the bare counter, occasionally raising his head from his nap before lowering it down again after making sure that the two were still there.

A few mouthfuls of the *baijiu* and Zu started feeling heady; he had never drunk liquor on an empty stomach like this. And now the unexpected turn of events made him even more heady as their conversation moved into more murky waters. If there wasn't money, there were always women. But how to get them remained a thorny issue. Everything seemed a dead end. Long hours of labour in the fields, alternated with long hours of playing poker games to gamble away cigarettes, was followed by long hours of dead sleep. Future was never there, no prospects whatsoever. The problem was exasperated, on Hair's part, because his old mother, an invalid at home, needed support but his dad, a street sweeper, did not earn enough money. Zu could do nothing but sympathise. And he was getting more and more heady as the conversation turned one-sided, becoming a soliloquy of bitter complaint on Hair's part. Zu wanted to sleep. He wanted to lay his head in his hands. Better still, he wanted to lay his heavy head in his arms. He did so as his head hit his arms crossed on the table.

A long time went past. It felt like a century. It was only a few minutes before Zu raised his head and held the scenery, through the door of the restaurant, of bare hills in his vacant gaze. He wondered why he had come all this way to drink the *baijiu*, foodless, in a restaurant bare of anything, except empty tables and chairs, and why Hair was full of complaints but did nothing to fix them. The thought reduced him to utter silence. Outside, it was silenter, the hills huddling helpless under the sweep of a wind that seemed to scatter the sunlight into dark stains. He rose to go. But something held him. His stomach turned, churning inside. He staggered towards the door as his gorge rose. Then he puked, throwing up everything he'd drunk, with little food in it but yellow liquid mixed with the remnants of what little he had eaten at breakfast.

His diary entry that day ran as follows,

> Life isn't worth living as it is. Even though it's full of sunshine and occasional pleasure-seeking, the ultimate result is darkness. I recalled, but forgot, to tell him an incident that had happened at one stage in my life. Flathead, a school friend, and I, along with

a few others, had a night out on the riverbank. We went to the usual meeting place, the water lock that sat between the Yangtze and a channel, acting as flood retention and sluicing. But we couldn't gain access to it that night as it was occupied by a couple petting and necking, right at the entrance. Flathead paused as an idea came to him. He pulled Hei aside and whispered something into his ear. Hei nodded his head, saying nothing. But soon everyone intuited that something was going to happen although no one knew what. It was obvious that the couple were enjoying themselves under the moonlight. I stood looking, admiring them, as it was a sight I'd like to be part of myself. Then, Flathead took action. He rushed towards the unseeing couple, hit hard at the back of the man's head and, with a blow, fetched him onto the ground. Without a word, and before the woman had time to turn her head back and see us, he started running as he yelled, in a suppressed voice: Let's go! Everyone, including me, followed him, running as fast as our legs could carry us, until we reached a dark spot, the darkest spot in fact, where we stopped, panting, and laughing. But, abruptly, the laughter stopped. A sense of sadness swept over me, an unspeakable sense.

Old Zu sent me a poem, written in Chinese, by WeChat and said, Have a read and see if there's any connection to what you imagined, and the poem goes, in its entirety:

Beating

We ran to the bridge
Our hearts beating hard
The sound of slapping, just now
Still roaring in the ears

By the moonlit riverbank
Couples sat, coupling
Despite a distance kept in between
To avoid hearts' whisperings being overheard

Where did the madness come from
That prompted us to rush onto them
In an instant, ghastly faces lay on the ground
Reflecting a bled moon

I, shivering all over
Saw the heads and faces twisting under the fists
The ruthless pointed leather shoes
Kept kicking where the hearts were

I, standing wooden on the bridge
Staring into the flowing moonlight under the bridge
As they laughed out loud, pleased with themselves
My heart-tears gone, flowing with the moon

祖

After saying goodbye to Hair, Zu went on his way to Jigongshan, the Cock Mountain, to visit his friend Jia, whose two outstanding facial features were the whiteness of his face and the movement of his ears. Yes, his ears could move, the way a rabbit does. Whenever friends gathered together, they would invariably say to him, Show us how you can move your ears. And when he did, everyone's eyes popped out, staring in amazement at his ears that erected themselves, pointing forward, then flapping backwards, while his face remained unmoving, a mask of white features, like those of an albino. Amidst an outburst of laughter, he would mutter, with total aplomb, about the absolute ease with which he could do that, saying it's nothing out of the ordinary, little worth laughing about, not a trace of smile on his face. He, as far as Zu knew, had great ambitions; he had wanted to be a writer of fiction and he had wanted to be a soldier as well. But none of those was possible for him because he had suffered a stigma. His father had committed suicide by throwing himself into the Yangtze. That was all Zu knew about, as Jia never gave any details; perhaps he himself didn't even know, because his father had killed himself when he was young. His reason for not giving any detail was that his mother never told him why he killed himself. Instead, he got a job straight after he graduated from the junior section of the middle school and seemed to have matured overnight. Zu was a close friend because both shared an avid interest in reading. Books passed between them in a flow of exchange wherever and whenever they could lay their hands on them. When Zu expressed his regret that he had taken all his father's classics to a waste paper recycling station and dumped them there, including *Fables* of Ivan Krylov, *And Quiet Flows the Don* by Mikhail Sholokhov and *The Captain's Daughter* by Alexander Pushkin, in response to a call by Mr Song, his Chinese-language teacher, for confiscation by the authorities or for dumping, because they were part of what's labeled the feudalistic, the capitalistic, and the revisionist, Jia told him that it was a stupid thing to do and he did none of that; instead, he hid all his books away and lied about them, saying that when his father died he left a will that all his books be burned with his body. Zu was thus able to read some of the books he had in his possession, such as *The Gadfly* by Ethel Voynich and *Cement* by Fyodor Gladkov. When Zu expressed his amazement how he got those books, Jia said, I stole them from the library.

You did, did you? said Zu. But how?

Well, you know, Jia tipped one ear forward as the other went backward, and said, I just did.

Arthur is interesting, said Zu. He's so clever.

He's got a sharp tongue.

He writes under the penname of Gadfly and he attacks his own views, sounding so convincing as well.

But I like the way he faces death, so unafraid. And he says, 'They kill me because they are afraid of me; and what more can any man's heart desire?'[1]

I, though, like this remark that he makes, 'We are all fit for better things than we ever do'.[2]

Thus it went on, from one book to another and from one thought to another. Whenever Zu expressed romantic feelings about love, Jia would dismiss them as trash, saying, That's not for me. I don't feel it the way you do.

Right now, as they were walking on a path that went through tall grasses towards the top of a hill, known as the Cock Mountain, Jia said something similar again, his eyes gazing into the distance across a row of lower hills, in a wave of verdure. One had difficulty realizing what he was saying because the way he was talking was like mumbling to himself, his lips tremulous, in a shape of no.

When they reached the top, they saw what looked like the remains of a burnt house. No roof. No contents. Only half walls over which one could see the surrounding hills in wave after wave of trees. But the few clusters of withered grass within the compound ignited an old passion in Zu for fire.

Can I set fire to this? Zu wondered aloud.

No, Jia said. Why do you want to do that?

Don't know, said Zu. But just feel like doing it. In fact, I'd like to set the whole mountain afire. Wouldn't that make a beautiful scene?

Well, Jia started mumbling again. Zu was familiar enough with his lip-syncing to understand that he was disagreeing. Then, as if emerging out of his dream-like depths, Jia said something loud and clear, We'll both die if you do that.

No, we won't, said Zu. We'll both run quick enough out of danger.

No, you won't, in a cold voice, Jia said. You won't run out of danger. You'll run into it.

Into it?

Yes. When the whole hill is on fire, we'll both die in it, burnt to death, like the remains of the house on top of the hill. There's no way

---

1 See it here: https://www.goodreads.com/author/quotes/799335.Ethel_Lilian_Voynich
2 Ibid.

you'll run out of the engulfing fire when it starts spreading from one hill to another, across the valleys, reducing all the villages to cinders. No, you can't do that. Let's go.

It was not till then that Zu told Jia what had happened when he set fire to the silvergrass grown along a river near his village.

It was a morning, on a Sunday, their only rest day. Len, Han and Zu were walking their pig to Bamao Town along a river thick with silvergrass on either bank, so thick it stood like a wall, erect and swaying, even when there was little wind. From afar, the Bamao River, along with its two walls of silvergrass, looked like two fallen columns of smoke, dark green, that lay prostrate and serpentine, extending as far as the eye could see. While they were walking the pig and talking the talk about things that drifted to mind, things of little importance that were daily and minor, that were little more than a conjecture about how much the pig would sell for and if Han might bump into another pretty girl in town, Zu stopped in the middle of the road. The other two stopped, too, watching him take up a bunch of the broad-bladed silvergrass in hand and wondering what he was going to do with it. Zu held the bunch in his intense gaze as the thought, long present in his mind, became ignited. 'Can I set fire to this?' He wondered aloud, not looking at anyone, but hearing a giggle from Han, who said, 'Do you dare?' Without a second thought, he took a cigarette lighter out from his trouser pocket and pressed the button with a click as it spat a plume of fire that instantly made one of the green blades of the silvergrass curl. At first, it didn't seem to catch fire. When he was about to press the button again, Len said, in a trembling voice, It's on fire!

Sure enough, a tiny ball of fire leapt, flashing pale in the sun, eating into the leaf the way a silkworm did, before it spread, leap by fast leap, onto other blades. Mesmerised, Zu stood there, watching the fire grow as more leaves of silvergrass wilt, melting away in a heat that was getting more intense each passing second, till a voice thundered in his ears: Run, quick!

It was Han who yelled the warning. And that prompted them all to take to their heels, beating the pig as hard as possible, making him run with them. The pig shrieked, feeling the pain, pulling the rope tight, dragging Len and Han behind him.

祖

As they were reaching the foot of the hill and nearing the factory compound, Jia interrupted him with a 'I don't like the place at all.'

What happened? said Zu, too wrapped in the excitement of his own storytelling for this.

Oh, nothing, said Jia, nonchalantly.

Zu wasn't able to finish the rest of his story as Jia's remark permanently diverted his attention to a subject whose significance far exceeded his understanding. According to Jia, a woman older than him by 20-odd years had seduced him. But as soon as he thought he had fallen in love with her, the woman gave him the go-by, after the night of love. It was a huge blow to his self-esteem, Jia said. Being a young man barely out of his teens, he found it hardly understandable. Even though Jia gave no more detail, Zu was able to work out something for himself from the expression, *pipan*, that this must be one of the skin-stumbling instances in which men and women got physically involved. Not to hurt Jia, he kept his mouth shut and said nothing. His entry that night was brief,

> Didn't end up lighting the fire on the hill. But heard Jia's story of a woman who dumped him the minute they did it. Would have been pleased myself if that had happened to me, if only for once.

Chapter 14: Selling the Clothes, and Another Girl

The construction work was over after the winter and it was time to head home. They—Len, Han and Zu—were trudging on their way to Clear Water Village through a tiny town called Dandian. It was springtime. The sun was warm. They were feeling warm from the walk, too. Zu took off his cotton-padded jacket, carefully folding it together, and put it in one of his bags that he was shoulder-poling. At a curbside fruit stand, Han stopped, staring at a row of apples, mouth agape and watering.

So, you want to buy them? Len said.

Yes, said Han. But I've got no money. What about you? He turned to Zu.

I don't have money, either, said Zu, fingering the money in his pocket.

Well, I think I can have them if I sell my coat to them, said Han, looking at Len.

I don't think it's a good idea, Len said. You'll need it when it gets cold again.

I don't give a damn. If I want them, I'll get them. With that, he said to the man minding his stand, 'What do you say if I give you my cotton coat for these apples?'

The man raised his head and said in surprise, 'Are you sure?'

'It's a good coat,' Len chimed in while Zu looked away, feeling awkwardly ashamed. He could have bought them if he had wanted to. But he had lied about the money in his pocket. Han obviously had guessed it because he said to the man, 'Just give me the lot, or half of it, because I am at least generous enough to give it away to people in need.' While they were haggling about it, Zu wandered away to have a look around the place. There was a grocery shop, a few peasants squatting by the roadside selling their local produce, and a muddy street that ran through the village town.

When he came back, they were done. Han was minus his coat but he'd got a small bag of apples. He handed one to Zu who declined, saying he didn't like apples. Han laughed, quickly withdrawing his hand. In that laughter, Zu realised a contemptuous tone but he ignored it.

Back in the village, Zu received a thank-you letter that filled him with delight. It was from the village where he had helped put out a fire. He hid the letter away, afraid that the other two might see it and get jealous. He had done what he should and they did the same. That was that. No need to let anyone else know.

That night, Zu made an entry in his diary,

> The women never appeared. When they were haggling about the worth of Han's cotton coat, I kept looking for them everywhere, thinking they might disappear if I didn't look hard enough. An occasional woman that appeared on the street was either a peasant woman or an old aunty, nothing like those two fresh-looking girls in tight buttock-clinging trousers. Life, to be honest, is really boring. I've never felt happy, for some reason. We have never talked about happiness in my family, either. Why talk about something that simply is not there?

News came that there was hope that one could return to one's own hometown; it echoed with the peasant's prediction, made long ago, when the educated youths first arrived in the village: We are sure you won't be staying for too long. You don't belong here. The government would want you all back where you come from. At the time when they said that, Zu could only offer a wry smile. He bore Mother's words in his heart: Be a good boy. Work hard. Get along well with others. He was a good boy. He worked hard. And he managed to get along well with the others, peasants and educated youths alike, even though getting along well with the others seemed the hardest thing to do. He would rather have a little room of his own, like Han, mind his own business, and live alone like Pan Chang, the despised landlord's son. But he had no choice. He had to live with the other four under the same roof. He had to listen to Len eating noisily but did not say a thing, as much as he hated the noise. He had to bear with Han's stupidity in behaving preposterously

242

towards Xi, getting upset when he failed to arouse her attention or becoming overjoyed in thinking she was showing favours towards him when she did the same to everyone else. He disliked the way they, including himself, wasted their lives playing poker games night after night, smoking, winning or losing cigarettes. But there was nothing he could do about it. Like a boat without a rudder, set adrift on a river, he watched himself cut loose, unloved, and un-liked even. Despite what they said about him being liked by Xi and him liking her, nothing ever really happened between them apart from the first entries he had made in his diary. He was watching himself watching her, from the pages of his uncomfortable record of daily events, and missing her, too, till it went dead because he heard that there's a crowd of country youngsters following her everywhere, with their hands, if not with their eyes, or perhaps with both. They helped her carry her luggage when she came back from her hometown; they helped her do the work in the fields, so she did not have to work hard, no, she did not even have to work, just standing by, watching, and complaining about the heat, like a lady. Zu was disgusted. But he was not jealous. The kind of love they said that he could try to aim at simply did not exist and he couldn't possibly have made it happen, either. Wishing, he was just wishing, that something could happen.

But nothing happened in a long, long time, not till when he went back to the country town again one day, where they were watching how the other educated youths from other villages recruited, went through the registration processes before they set out on a journey back home. Zu was aware of the nationwide movement from the country back to the city, and he was seeing with his own eyes what was happening as part of that movement. A pang of sadness washed over Zu as he saw how boys and girls, like him, poured in from the surrounding villages, wearing their Sunday best, their faces lit up in delight, and their luggage laden with stuff: bundles of quilt, bags of rice, a couple of cackling hens or quacking ducks here and there, and strips of salted pork, too. Zu watched them with envy. He saw how interviews were being conducted in a roadside hotel, temporarily put aside for the purpose, into which people went and out of which they came, talking and laughing. He could intuit how these people were feeling: In a few days they would leave all the bad years behind, join the workforce in the city, stay home with their Mums and Dads, enjoy a comfortable life with good food and perhaps marry.

As he thought so, Zu found himself carried in the stream into the hotel-office, and, further, in a room. It felt like he had entered into a dream: a bright young girl was sitting on the edge of a bed, in a room without anything else, except a large window.

The girl, smiling, said to Zu, So, are you also leaving?

No, said Zu, noticing that she was holding something in her hand. And you?

Yes, said she. Very soon, actually, in a few days.

Her smile was so sweet that Zu's heart was moved. He looked out the window and saw people moving around. He looked back at the girl, in a simple flowery dress. He found her so pretty that he managed to pick up a courage that he never had experienced before in front of a woman. He asked what her name was and where she was based. Ah Bao, speaking the Wuhan dialect, told him everything. He was just wondering if he could have her address so that he could write her letters when someone called her name and she had to go.

Back in the village, he kept hating himself for not waiting till she was done. He could have then found out about her address and he could have probably chatted with her a bit more. The girl was like a sunshine that lit up his life, elevating him, as it were, to the skies, only to drop him back into the mud of paddy fields in Clear Water Village. The moment was simply too short. What wouldn't he do to have her back? In his diary that night, he wrote, untypically, just one sentence:

Ah Bao, where are you?

祖

The road home was long and bumpy, particularly when Zu was lying on top of a jeep of apples; literally, he was lying amidst the apples in the back of a jeep, heading home. The vibration of the car, the roaring of the wind and the continuous mechanical noise from the engine made it impossible for him to sleep or to think in a clear-headed manner. He picked up an apple and put it to his nose. There was a faint aroma and it smelt good. In the semi-darkness, the apples heaved, rolled, and sighed, as if hankering after watering mouths that weren't there. As soon as Zu closed his eyes, trying to be swayed into sleep, the girl's face emerged on the insides of his eyelids: an oval face with wide smiling eyes, and a faint body odour, perhaps of sweat, that resembled that of the apple. Like all the other girls he had been fascinated with, this one was a goner, too, disappearing the minute she appeared, allowing for days, weeks and months of missing. But, then, what about the other girl, the girl who found her way into his poem? And what about the other two girls who had induced him to one of many wet rains between his bedsheets? It was all nothingness. All dreams, never meant to be realised. He thought of how Xueqin had told him of a Pu Songling story in which a woman allows herself to be loved by a man and a year after hands him a baby as she dumps a bleeding head onto the floor, saying that her mission is now over because she's killed the local judge that had taken her father's life three years before. As the jeep bumped along the road, with him lying prostrate on top of the apples, rising and dropping, as if on a rough wave, one thought led to another. He thought of Fan, one of Mum's colleagues at her *danwei*, work unit, a poet of sorts, who had shown him poems about his youthful aspirations and exhorted to him about the worth of poetry. He thought of Mum's words, uttered when he was a little baby and she held him close to heart: *tongren, tongren,* pain person, pain person. He thought of how the peasants described the flatterers as being *gua er tian, di er ku,* melon-sweet, melon-stem-bitter, ones who were capable of painting a word picture of whatever they wanted to be sweet or bitter. He thought of how the peasants would refer to the ignorant person as a *bai bizi,* white nose. He couldn't suppress a chuckle to himself when he thought of that expression, so odd he had never heard of it used elsewhere. Then he thought of *caishui,* vegetable water, that Mum loved, juice left of stir-fried bok choy that she would pour a small amount of hot water in and drink, like soup.

All this time, the apples that surrounded him and that lay underneath him, a thick layer of them, like thick bedclothes, were rolling hither and thither, giving an occasional jump when the tires of the jeep slid into a hole in the road or when the jeep swerved on a bend. To steady himself, Zu dug his hands deep into the slits of the apples underneath him. They were loose in a way and felt warm. He could have picked up any one of the apples, cleaned it with his sleeve and eaten it. But he didn't. A sense of dignity and honour held him from it. After all, he had never gone out on an adventure with Han, stealing and killing chickens from the peasant houses, nor had he ever gone on a dog-hunting trip with him, either. He was halfway between Cui who agreed to cook the stolen chicken or dog-meat but declined to eat a single morsel and Han who went all out on a killing rampage, night after night; he just ate the cooked meat, listened to Han's stories of his achievement and laughed or brooded. That was that.

About midnight, the jeep came to a screechy stop outside the unit where Mum lived, in a room allotted her by the *danwei*, on the second floor, at the end of the corridor.

Zu thanked the driver, picked up his stuff and went home.

祖

When I told Old Zu I didn't remember what exactly happened afterwards, he said to me, Don't worry. Keep inventing.

I said, Do you think I made all this up?

He said, Of course I don't. But what can you do if you don't remember?

I said, Did you read Raymond Carver?

He said, No. Then he said, Why?

I said, Then there really isn't much to talk about.

He said, I heard about him, though.

I said nothing.

He said, Come on. You can't be serious. Tell me about it.

I said, Well, reading him, I got a feeling that his male characters are all reflections of him to varying degrees.

He said, That's life, isn't it?

I don't know, I said. My past seems dead. Stark dead.

What doesn't die, though, is in your memory, or is that right? he said.

I don't know about that, I said. I only remember what I don't forget and forget what I do forget.

Ha ha, that's funny, he said.

That's not funny, I said.

Why not? he said.

No idea, I said. It's just that I find it a near impossibility to connect one thing to another many decades after it happened. If anything, there are events, like the jeep of apples, that stand out like tiny islands in an ocean of time. One wonders if one is allowed to stick to the truth about these isolated islands regardless of whatever happens in between, the same way one doesn't worry about each and every wave that comes churning up around the ship on its way to its destination. Then one wonders who is there to allow what to write and what not do, and for what purpose. I could, as you said, keep inventing along. But the point?

For me, the point remains that if one didn't put down a single word in writing, one might have not lived at all, he said.

That may be the case, I said, but my memory fails me or I fail my memory, so I'm sorry.

You'll let that go, you mean?

Exactly.

祖

A diary entry, as yet unwritten, that I found from the memory of my character is uploaded here about something that I realise, as an after-thought, that this book has hardly ever touched upon, a snippet of a life that Zu had lived but had forgotten himself:

Pan Da invited me to his home after my return from the Spring

Festival. I was served an earthen jar of pork-rib soup, with pieces in it of *ciba*, cooked glutinous rice, pounded into paste and molded into round shapes, then dried up. I not only ate the soup, the pieces of *ciba*, but also the pork-ribs, right to the bottom of the jar. Pan Da watched me eating, not saying a word, a smile I found mysterious on his face. It was not till afterwards that I realised the mistake I had made. A villager, Pan Shun, I think, told me that the custom here is that people get a treat after they get invited. But, instead of eating everything, they only eat the *ciba*, have a taste of the soup and leave the rest untouched because the remaining soup and the pork-ribs will be re-heated with new pieces of *ciba* added, as a way of keeping the precious treat lasting longer. When I wondered if this was too stingy of them because the city people would never do that for reasons of hygiene, Pan Shun said, simply, 'But that is the way. Besides, we can't afford it.' I noticed that he avoided using the word '*qiong*' (poor).

In retrieving this entry from my character's mind, I did something I shouldn't. I explained the word 'ciba' because I had to or else my readers wouldn't understand. But would Zu have done that when he made the entry?

Chapter 15: The Cows Did Come Home

On his return to Clear Water Village, Zu was beginning to hear voices. One voice was distinct and persistent, particularly when night deepened and sleep was impossible, which was rare for the nineteen-year-old. Once was a time when sleep was rare because of what one staff member at the Bureau jokingly referred to as 'the Cat' that sat inside his throat, hulu-hulu-huluing, as he was suffering from asthmatic attacks. The boy hated the world and the people around him, looking with pleasure at him in pain. He sat crouching in a chair, obviously too large for his person, in a corner, in his mother's office, raising a sullen eye at the staff coming in and out of the office while listening to his own wheezing breathings, often with the explosive effect of choking. His mother didn't comfort him with soothing words or babyish sweet nothings. After administering him his medications, she went to work and left him to himself. This, in one of his asthmatic deliriums, led to a discovery about flowering in solitude. 'Flowering in solitude?' the future voice said. 'What is that?'

He turned around in his bed and was now facing the wall as a blob of spit came surging to this throat. He cleared the throat and spat it out. The blob of spit hit the wall with a dull thud and, with it, came another voice: In forty years, someone will record all this and more. He listened. Even though you no longer practise it but a parallel memory in the universe had begun the second you did it, without even realizing what you were doing. He turned on his right, facing Len in the opposite bed, continuing to listen. You, in your extreme solitude, coupled with the suffocating asthmatic attacks, brought your own erection to ejaculatory offerings that you swallowed up, believing that, in doing so, you've served yourself well. He tried to shut his ears the way he shut his eyes but couldn't and the voice persisted, One day you'll have to watch yourself doing it again and again in immeasurable time that time itself is not even aware of. Nothing dies once it comes into existence.

In his diary, Zu made an entry after a long absence:

> They never reject me. But they never reply. Which probably
> means they will never accept me. Bao's words are interesting:
> One's life is pre-determined. It is useless trying to rise above
> that. You think you are a new person with a name that is not
> duplicated for miles around and you are headed for a new life that
> no one else has experienced, while in fact you are living a life that
> has been lived, multiply. You get born, you grow up, like weeds,
> or a plant, you eat, you shit, you accumulate, like an ant, then you
> die, like a bird falling out of the sky, and disappear from the face
> of the earth. It's all been repeated ad infinitum. He talks about
> emperors with huge reputation and enormous power, enjoying
> endless women of stunning beauty, only to be reduced to dust that
> is not even tangible in history. One in particular, by the name of
> Hailing, was so obsessed with beautiful women his single most
> ambitious desire was to turn all of them on earth into his own
> wives. The end result? He's had his sexual surfeit but was finally
> defeated by his own people and was posthumously demoted
> to a commoner. A life of utter pleasure and a death of utter
> commonness.

It was early spring, not yet time for spring ploughing. There was a
discussion about the cows. Production Team Leader Pan's idea was that
the boys—Len, Han and Zu—ought to look after them because it was
the lightest kind of jobs, one that could tie them to the fields when there
wasn't much else to do. He was the boss. The others had little say about
it. Besides, according to Pan Shun, the village treasurer, these boys were
a real pain in the arse. One ought to pack them up and send them home
for good. Prompted by the thought, Pan Hua dropped a remark about a
suggestion jokingly made by the boys sometime ago, that they take the
cows to their hometown because there was a hill, known as the Dragon
King Hill outside the town, with good grazing hillsides. That way the
boys would enjoy the comfort of their home while keeping the cows

fed. It was then decided that the three boys walk the cows back to their hometown, one cow for one person to manage, and stay there for one month. No advice was given except that they must keep the cows healthy and fat.

祖

If this scene were to be shot on location today, it would not be possible. Given the strict road regulations over the highway and large volumes of traffic today, three adolescents, walking ahead of their cows, or after, or alongside them, would find it impossible to even get onto the road. In those days, though, a public road was for the public, carrying a motley traffic of wooden one-wheeled hand-push carts, two-wheeled hand carts, tractors, hand-held tractors, bicycles, Liberation trucks, peasants carrying fresh produce in their baskets with shoulder-poles and, occasionally, jeeps with important people sitting in them. When they set out early, at daybreak, there was little traffic and the road was like a newly spread bedsheet, welcoming and expectant. Before they set out, they had been told by the old peasants in the village that there was no need to carry rice straws to feed the cows as long as they remembered to let the cows drink water from the roadside ditches, from time to time or else they would refuse to move.

Thus, they set out on the road, each with a yellow cow walking in front of him, in a single file, along the cogongrass bank, where, reminded of the fire Zu had set, Han joked about Zu's fear and attempt to escape, while Len was more careful about the well-being of his cow, stopping for him to graze where there were clusters of last year's grass that remained half green and new grass that had just sprouted. The speed was slow because of that, and with the rising sun, they managed to get out of town and onto the main road.

Memories thronged as Zu went along. When he went past the bus station, he recalled how a man he had met sometime ago used a penknife to scrape the plaque from his teeth, of which he had a mouthful. Glancing at the man in disgust, Zu could see sparks coming out from under the knifepoint. The man went on relentlessly about his tartar-cleaning job as he spat out phlegm mixed with tartar fragments that were yellow and sticky.

Not long after, they went past a hill where crowds of people were working, cutting the hilltop in an attempt to flatten it and turn it into a field. People were kept busy, even on a winter day like this, following Mao's slogan to learn from Dazhai, the quintessential mode of agricultural production at the time. A flitting thought went through Zu's mind, that in a little while all the surrounding hills would be gone, turned into rice-paddies. That would make a pretty sight. He did not let himself dwell on these things because his own cow kept moving on the road and he had to make sure he arrived home with him safe and sound by nightfall.

In the afternoon when they reached Lukou, more than halfway between Upper Bahe and Yuwang Town, the three stopped with their cows. On the way, they hardly exchanged a word, the distance between each of them and of their cows making it a near impossibility. Besides, Han was not persistent. He would walk and stop, walk and stop, constantly complaining about the exhaustion and the boredom. On occasion, he would simply refuse to go, letting Len and Zu handle his cow for him as well. Finding it unfair and knowing the kind of person he was, Zu bit his lip and went resolutely on, prompted by the thought that the girl he lived in hope of meeting one day might be living somewhere close to the road they were traveling on. He remembered her lovely pallid face that was moon-shaped. And he liked the eyes that were deeply set in the face and always found it a mystery that the girl seemed to avoid social contact, preferring to keep to herself. She seemed interested in him but he was not sure; he could only guess and that guesswork was largely part of his self-aggrandisement. His cow, a nameless one, was unaware of what was going on in his mind and went on her way, in a leisurely and relaxed manner. As he tagged along after the cow, Zu found the slowness of time too fast for his liking. Soon it was nightfall when they found themselves arriving at the foot of the Dragon King Hill where each of them tethered his cow to a tree before they separately went home.

祖

The days that followed were daily visits to the hill, which, to put it simply, was a literary hill, famous for its precinct housing the historical and literary relics associated with Su Shi (1037-1101), left after his 4-year exile as a result of a poetry-induced political case against him. The politics, and the poverty the poet suffered, were a long-forgotten memory. But his poetry remained, and that was what left Zu impressed. He would, for example, lead his cow to the grass in the green dale as his mind ranged through lines like '*qingye wuchen, yuese ru yin, jiuzhen shi xu man shifen; / fuming fuli, xiuku laoshen, si xi zhong ju, shi zhong huo, meng zhong shen.*' (No dust on a clean night when the colours of the moon are silvery, and if you fill a glass with wine, fill it to overflowing; / but floating fame and floating profits / are not worth laboring my mind on, as they are like a horse that goes past a gap, a fire in a stone or a body in a dream), lines that he grew up with and could readily call to mind without referring to a text. The stillness of the mornings and the solitude, with only the companionship of a cow, were inducive enough to a meditation that was not to be had back in Clear Water Village. Zu liked the morning dew before its drops evaporated. And he chose to be near the Red Cliff where he could see, through leaks of foliage, the Yangtze River winding its way towards the East and the West Hill on the other bank of the river, like a windowless high-rise *pingfeng*, windscreen, or screen, that turned tender-green in spring and dark-green in winter. Zu would set his cow grazing on its own while he sat on a stone, watching the cow graze, moving from tree to tree, her tongue thrashing at the grass, curling up, as tufts of grass were sucked into his mouth. Occasionally, the cow would stop, her head raised as was her tail as a large chunk of dung came out between his hips, steaming in the early spring cold.

Zu's plan was better than his action. Always he made sure that he'd take a book or two with him when he went to the hill. But once there his eyes turned lazy and he did not even want to touch the books. The surrounding scenery was enough to put his mind to peace as he roamed in it, getting lost sometimes and losing his cow, too, at other times. It gave him a huge fright when, having wandered to a pagoda facing the Yangtze River through a clearing on top of the hill, he returned to the dale where he had the cow grazing on her own and found that she was nowhere to be seen. He was so worried he sweated and went in search of it, climbing the hill till he reached the other side of it. Breathlessly, he was relieved to find it lying down by a tree stump, looking at him unperturbed, without emotion, without recognition even. If it were the pig he had raised back in the village, he would have recognised him straight away and he would have come running towards him, full of joy, aware of the food that Zu was going to feed him. Even when Zu gave him a good beating for spoiling his food, he bore no grudges against him. He would always present a happy face on seeing him, giving him grunts of content and, sometimes, when really satisfied, would lie in the sun, letting Zu rub him along the hair with his foot, the pig's tiny eyes closed in a blissful state.

The cow, though, acted completely unlike a pig. She was ruminating, her jaws moving, her big head seemingly full of thoughts and her eyes looking at him as if at a total stranger. Even when he went up to her, putting out his hand and doing what he did to the pig, running his hand through her yellow hair, the cow would remain unmoved, with no response or reaction. Zu picked up the rope that went through the cow's nose and tied it up around the tree next to him. Then he went home, forgetting his books once again.

祖

His diary entries became haphazard and fragmentary. One went, 'One sleeps most of the time and never seems to tire of it.' Another went, 'Will the cow find me boring?' A third went, 'The Yangtze flows all day and all night long. But it never seems to tire of its own energy. All I ever want to do is go away.'

It didn't take long, though, for his going away to happen. Shortly after the three of them finished the business of grazing the cows in the hills surrounding their hometown, they went back with the fattened cows to Clear Water Village, spending another day on the road, walking. The morning after their arrival back in the village, Zu remembered something. He took out his nail clippers and cut his fingernails and toenails in one go, taking his time. And he was having a rest now that the cow-grazing days were over when the news came from none other than the landlord's son Pan Chang, who happened to be passing by, shoulder-poling a pair of *fentong*, shit barrels, containing the night soil as manure for the fields. When he raised his head, Zu met his eyes and smiled. It was probably that smile that won the day, for Chang stopped in his tracks and beckoned him to come over. When he got closer, Chang whispered into his ear something that pleased him immensely. He waited till Chang disappeared in the field beyond the creek and made his mind up.

He went to the local shop and bought two cartons of cigarettes, of the *guangrong* or Glory, brand. Then he sought Pan Da, the production team leader, out. Normally, he would be out in the fields, not back till sundown. But, on that particular day, he was home, sorting out some domestic matters, and when Zu came, he made him welcome, asking him to come in and fetching him a stool to sit down on. To his mind, this young man was an oddity. Even though they hardly ever spoke to each other, and never really had a decent face-to-face conversation, he seemed to know this guy all his life: a man who was cut out more for a scholar than for anything else, bent as he was over books whenever he got a chance, and, unlike the other students, this was a man who worked hard in the fields with the rest of the peasants, too. He liked him for that. He pulled a stool over, sat down, and listened.

Zu first thanked Da for his leadership, saying how diligent he was, rising early every morning, his voice of calling people to work carried loud and clear throughout the village. He also praised Da for his care and concern for the students including himself. As he said so, he gave the two cartons of cigarettes to Da and went straight to the point, about recruitment of students in a school. In a hurry, he said how delighted he was to hear the news and how much he'd like to study; in fact, his ideal life was one devoted to study for the rest of his life. As he said so, he could see Da's face become interested, hanging on his words, nodding his head with approval. The minute Zu finished, Da said, I'll have a chat with them and let you know.

祖

Nothing came as easy as this. Zu had applied for Party membership and his application was never accepted; no one had bothered even inviting him to a meeting. His one lone submission of a short story was rejected even though the letter from the editor was encouraging. His hope of becoming a songwriter was dashed as his numerous submissions of songs with lyrics composed had all met with rejection, which he kept a secret and never told anyone about. And, of course, there was that woman he was secretly, and, hopelessly, in love with, who, he realised in despair, would never ever be his except in his dream or daydream. But this came so easily that he was surprised: he had been accepted by the school and the new term would begin in early March. Stars showed in his eyes. Birds sang in his ears. The sun struck his face with full light, and delight. But he was alone, as he always had been. Walking alongside Lin, he was empty-handed, all his luggage carried on a shoulder-pole by Lin, on one end his wooden box, packed with books and clothes, and, on the other, his cotton quilt. He had expected that people might pour out of the village to see him off. No one did. Even as they walked, one after another, with a safe distance between them because of the shoulder-pole, down the ridge, in full view of peasants working in the paddy fields, no one raised their heads to look, let alone greet him and say bye. He walked away with a feeling that people were somehow treating him like a stranger. He thought to himself that this probably wasn't wrong because he had never really been part of them, living side by side, as it were, with them, confirming their view that these people, these students, would be temporary, here for a couple of years, and there to go forever. His existence here was like that of a bird. When it arrived and sang, people paid attention. When it left at the end of the day, people weren't even aware of its disappearance and they wouldn't have bothered anyway. Not interested. Period.

Zu and Lin were now walking side by side, on the bigger riverbank road, overgrown with head-high silvergrass. In total silence, Zu heard the footsteps of his and Lin's own. He was disappointed by the reaction on the part of the villagers on this day of his departure. There was nothing he could do about it and it was beneath his dignity to share his dismal thoughts with Lin. Already, he was looking forward to the day when the new school life began. And it was here that he thought of the apple jeep, and he told Lin so.

Oh, did you eat any? said Lin.

No, said Zu.

Why not? You could have eaten a few and pocketed a few more.

No. But why would I do that? said Zu as he scanned the river through the silvergrass, seeing tiny squares and rounds of water through the seams of the grass blades.

Lin said nothing, panting as he went along, carrying Zu's luggage. In that instant, in which Zu was made acutely aware of himself walking side by side with this peasant carrying his luggage, on his way home, perhaps for the last time in his life, he realised that friendship was absolutely impossible in this world. Lin was a 'friend' only because the team leader had organised for him to do the job, for which he would get a credit for the day, earning his work points. But he dismissed the thought the instant it arose, as too dark for his liking. He ought to be an optimist as his mother had recommended on one occasion when she observed him sighing. She said, 'What's there to sigh about for a young boy like you? Be brave and bright. And never lose hope.'

An Interlude

That night, after he got home, Zu had a dream. In the dream, he visits a far, far away country. There is a lake on the plain. Only a single tree stands on a nearby hill. Trees that stand naked in the water are all dead. A voice says to him: But this is not a lake. It's what is known as a lagoon. He is pleased that he is being noticed and that a voice is speaking to him. The voice continues, You won't find hope here because hope, like despair, is as high as despair is low. I have been struggling for years without getting anywhere. Nothing seems right. Everything seems wrong right from the beginning. But, then again, the only one you can blame is yourself.

As the voice is speaking, Zu sees himself getting airborne, feeling light and dizzy. He finds the voice boring, and he wants to get further away. But all he sees are dead trees covering the land. Spirits they are, the voice is insistent. If you chase after it enough, you'll have it.

'After it?' he wonders to himself what the voice means and who bodies forth the voice. When he looks down, he sees a huge tree trunk lying over a creek that runs with a noise underneath a thick cover of snow. Trees, hundreds of meters tall, spread around, forming a vast dark green cloud. The voice says, But you'll not be happy wherever you go, even when you are considered somebody someday, which is meaningless. You see the tree? How enormous it is!

He wakes up, finding himself lying in a pit that is another dream, in which happy heads are full of praise for each other; they are particularly fond of themselves in that they photograph themselves the best way they can and share them. They no longer work as sharing things for praise is part of their daily work. When he wonders why, his secret wonderings are overheard by people. They treat him as a laughing stock, directing the squares in their hands at him, giggling, chuckling or chortling, their skies heavy with a mechanical haze.

'Wake up, Bin, wake up!' When Zu finally woke up, he found Mother shaking him. He rolled out of bed and said, What happened? Mother said, simply, I have just picked you up from the floor. You were so heavy in my arms. I could hardly hold you.

At breakfast, Mother said, smoking, How are things in the village? while Zu was eating a steamed bread over a bowl of *xifan*, liquid rice or congee.

Fine, said Zu.

Getting along with everyone? Mum said, looking into his eyes.

I suppose, said Zu, looking away.

You sure? said Mum.

Of course, said Zu.

I don't believe it, said Mum.

Alright then, it's up to you, said Zu.

Nothing untrue can escape a mother's eye, said Mum, inhaling a deep breath of smoke.

You don't know anything, said Zu.

I do because I am your mother, said Mum. I watched you grow up. Even if you are a big boy now, I know what you are like. Sucking hard on her cigarette, Mum thought of something and was about to say it when she held her tongue.

[The editors's note: We feel reluctant to include Part III as intended and written for two reasons, one that what is contained in it has been covered in another book, already published, by the author, and the other that even though it's new material the English it's written in is nearly 40 years old, written at a time when the author, in his mid-20s at a university, had not gone overseas to an English-speaking country. Hence an English our potential readers might find uncomfortable reading. Our suggestion to the author is that he replace Book III with Book IV so that the book is more focussed on Zu's life as a teenager and an educated youth in the country during the Cultural Revolution.]

Book III. 'His Long Travels in Pursuit of Tense'[1]

On this Greek island of white walls and sky-blue houses, they lay in bed, facing the sea through a window large enough to contain the sea from end to end.

'Do you still remember the saying?' said she.

'What saying?' said he.

'The saying that goes, *zhongren jiezhu wo du qing, zhongren jiezui wo du xing*,' said she.

'Oh, that one.'

'Wasn't it something constantly on your lips when you were an ambitious university student?'

'Ambitious was probably not the right word.'

'Well, you certainly had ambitions when young.'

'Not really. I was just like anyone else, a bit tormented.'

'How would you turn that saying into English?'

'I wouldn't have a clue.'

'Can I give it a try?'

'By all means.'

'The whole world is dirty but I remain clean; the whole world is drunk but I remain sober.'

'Not bad. In fact, very good.'

'Or perhaps I should delete the word "whole" and add a word "alone"?'

'Might as well.'

'The world is dirty but I, alone, remain clean; the world is drunk but I, alone, remain sober.'

'Sounds very poetic, like the poem by Liu Zongyuan in the Tang dynasty.'

'Which one?'

---

1 Quoted from Roy Fuller, *Collected Poems Roy Fuller*. Andre Deutsch. London: 1969 [1962], p. 30.

'The one titled, "River Snow"', said he.

'I know that one.'

'Can I recite you the English version I rendered?'

'Oh, yes, please.'

'"birds have vacated a thousand mountains / footsteps erased from ten thousand paths / an old man in a boat, with a straw cape and a bamboo hat / is fishing, alone, the cold snow"', said he.

'That's beautiful,' said she.

'That's because you are beautiful.'

'I'm not beautiful. I am beautiful only because you love me.'

'That's what love is all about.'

'But, by the way, do you think by continuously writing thus you'll eventually achieve something?' After a long pause, this was the first string of words that tumbled off her tongue.

'I do not care any more,' said he.

'I didn't mean to hurt you,' said she as she touched his hand. 'But I actually had a dream last night in which I spot a book of yours that has become a bestseller.'

'That would be nice,' said he. 'But are you sure dreams are not the reverse of what they are?'

'Don't know if they are,' said she. 'although it's true that they are, from time to time.'

Both fell silent and into each other's wasted arms, only the whites of their eyes glinting in the dark, visible to one another, their nostrils inhaling each other in regular rhythms that timed with the rise and fall of the waves.

'Let me light a cigarette,' said he, as he reached for his lighter on the bedside table. Then, as he smoked, he found the passage by the fiftul light on the end of the cigarette he was smoking and started reading aloud. '"He hated Julia and her flat bird. He hated the walks on asphalt. He hated the South Kensington Museum. He hated Eden, who was his sister...."'[1]

'A hate person but unlike you,' said she.

1 Patrick White, *The Living and the Dead*. Eyre & Spottiswoode, 1962 [1941], p. 85.

'There is commonalty in the word "hate", with details that are vastly different.'

'Details? Where?'

'In my head, not yet written.'

'Can't wait to read it, the novel.'

'You've already got the genesis.'

'You mean the paper manuscript?'

'Yes.'

'I'm enjoying parts of it—do you mind?'

Silence.

'Love?'

'I was trying to remember, or forget, a poem I wrote multiple decades ago that was steeped in hate.'

'Perhaps it was because you wanted so much to be loved?'

'There was so little love.'

'Yes, there is. I am love for you.'

'Perhaps, when I die, you'll put all my early writings in English together in a collection, called something like juvenilia.'

'Please don't mention the word, ever! But I hate the word "juvenilia"; it sounds so patronizing and unfair, almost as if one's youth was a crime and nothing one does in one's youth is worth anything except sexually as in the relationship of a younger woman with an older man. In my opinion, a writer's work is not complete without the early part when he's young, inexperienced, rebellious, experimenting, unaccepted, unacceptable, unrecognised, unrecognizable, and, in your case, the budding of a linguistic genius in the use of a foreign language without even going to the country where the language was used. The thought has, from time to time, visited me that some of the writings done in one's twenties are often one's best, such as Ernest Hemingway who had published *The Sun Also Rises* when he was 27 although he may have started writing it at 25 or 26, Emily Brontë who had published *Wuthering Heights* when she was 29 although she may have started writing it around 27 or even earlier and Wilfred Owen who had written his best poetry before he died at 25. But, with your permission, I shall certainly compile a collection of your writings in English done in your mid-20s, some 40 years ago. If no one accepts it for publication, I shall publish it at my own cost.'

'No, forget about it. It's not important.'

'Youth is important. Love is important. Youth and love, combined, are most important.'

'I'm getting old.'

'No, you are not.'

'Yes, I am.'

As their sham bickering intensified, the walls listened, the sea breathed in a quieter tone, and a bird, somewhere in the hills behind them, twittered in its sleep, like a reminder that the night was too far gone for any such tiffs.

'How about have a listen to music?' he suggested. 'Or you prefer to sleep?'

'I prefer to go with you wherever you go, to the end of the earth.'

'Is that the title of a song?'

'Yes, sung by Jessica Mauboy.'

'I haven't heard it before.'

'Here you are,' said she, as she put an earphone in his ear while inserting another in hers, the cables between them like a 'Y', its faint whiteness holding the shape of a dark heart in its crotch.

When the song was over, they remained silent for a long time before he said, 'Can we listen to something else please?'

'Oh, yes,' said she.

'Let me find something for you, for us,' said he as he started searching on his phone. Then he said, 'How about this?'

'Can I have a look what you've chosen?'

'No. Please close your eyes and just listen. Let your eyes turn into ears. Let your ears turn into eyes. Then tell me what you see.'

'I see a river of white waters shining in the distance. Far, far away, birds fly like piano, like cello, musical notes so small, smalling, the eye is hungry to catch them, to retain them in its retina. An open plain as broad as the joined pieces of paper you wrote words on many years ago, as green as our joined youth and when the wild grass becomes wilder your kisses, like fire flames, transparent in their purity, intense in their desire to burn themselves out and. White mountains, white mountaintops. Water, white and shiny, is pouring down, from the cliffs, the cracks, the crevices—' she stopped, breathless. 'Did I sound too romantic?'

'Love, for all eternity, is romantic, meant to be, still is, centuries after the passing of romanticism, until.'

'Until what?'

'Until mundanity and banality of it all set in.'

'That's life.'

'That's love and that's life, the two so incompatibly compatible and so compatibly incompatible.'

'Absolutely.'

Cadences, harmonic cadences of the night, thought the man.

'I heard your thought,' said the woman.

'What's it?'

'You were thinking of your old manuscript.'

'Right. But there are so many of them. Which one you had in mind?'

'The one you wrote in English at the university.'

'Perhaps you want to find something for me and read it?'

'I already did,' said she as she, closing her eyes, recited a passage. 'We went out to the ditch, a shallow trough that cut through the Yangtze near its bank. It was in the morning when we skipped the classes and went straight to the trough. There, a group of us stripped us bare to wearing only shorts, we formed a line, crouching and groping in the mud, each was a few meters off from the other. Zhao, who was a sort of a teamleader because of his reticent ways, was most adept at the game for, every few minutes, his hand would shoot out of the water with a whoosh and one would see a fish flapping in his hold, springing drops of water around in a spray of light. I was the one who clamoured but missed the catch for each time I felt the stir of a fish in my hand it would instantly escape from my slippery fingers, causing the others to burst out laughing close to their chin-high waters. In the end, I never caught one. I only managed to produce one exclamation after another as the fish came and went.'

'I don't remember ever writing that although it's part of my memory. Thank you so much,' said the man.

Second Night in Ag Nik

The man and the woman continued their conversation after a long day spent in sleep.

The man said, I got a feeling that you didn't sleep during the day.

The woman said, Your guess is as good as mine.

The man said, What did you mean?

The woman said, I translated your novel.

The man said, You did? Which one?

The woman said, Just a paragraph with a keyword that very much resembles the place name here.

The man said, Yes?

The woman said, Ugly.

The man said, Oh, Ag Nik.

The man said, Read it. Read it aloud to me. As he said so, he directed his gaze through the sunflower embroidered tulle curtains past the tip of the small island extended into the blue ocean now turning darkblue after the sun had set.

The woman said, But you still have your earpieces on.

The man said, I know. But nothing is turned on, neither music nor I.

The woman smiled in silence and started reading from her notebook where she had spent most of her day translating a paragraph from the man's novel, self-published about twenty years ago but that contains material written at the university 15 years prior to that; there was a tacit agreement between them that neither wanted to mention the title of the book:

She lets herself ordered about by me. That's the beginning. It gradually transitions to a stage where I allow myself to be ordered about by her. Ugliness has a power, which, unbending, will definitely overcome you. I meant it will definitely overcome me. It's a weird pleasure to allow oneself to be dominated in sex, in which you present yourself like a sacrificial offering, along with a wakeful consciousness, to completely indulge in a consciousnessless imagination to a degree where the person is not ordering you but someone else about while you yourself have transcended to a state of complete nakedness. There, things are stripped off their camouflage or decoration, like trees that are denuded, revealing their smooth and tender skins, abandoning themselves to the gentle touch or kiss of a breeze. Men and women, fully naked, are strolling along the streets, sunning themselves on the beach or dancing a simple and slow dance, each embracing the other. The feeling gets stronger and stronger until the sun blinds one as masses of red fog emerge on the inside of one's eyelids and the eyeballs are feeling the pressure of the red fog. One's body, in the final moment of thrills, gives a violent leap, like the lava, long suppressed, that bursts the thin crust of the earth, in a rushing surge, followed by the silence of the sea, like death, after the storm. What's more, when you allow yourself to be swayed by her, you can call and recall, in your imagination, all the beauties imaginable in the world, standing in front of me, their legs spread open, waiting for me to enter, and then, only then, that intense feeling will grow the more intense. I shall have completely lost my sense of guilt. Why should I be feeling crestfallen every day as if I had stolen someone else's key? Whenever we feel like doing it, we shall do it, never having to feel guilty again. Obviously, she didn't think as much as I do. But as long as I want it, she'll satisfy me because this satisfaction is mutual. Besides, she does not have any other needs, such as childbirth. She doesn't want offspring, her thought being that if the child is an ugly monster it would be better to go without. And my thought is that if everyone hates ugliness then let ugliness have no posterity. Still, my instinctual love for ugliness (the way I love eating stinking fish and stinking tofu and the way I love my stinking bodily airs, such as bad breath and foul armpits) is not something anyone can destroy and will remain till death.

Afterwards, neither spoke a word. The walls seemed alert, listening for more. The sea outside in the far distance was a spread of flickerings of light and sound. They had shifted their positions side by side on the bench outside in the corridor. The air was suffused with the fragrance of a flower neither could work out the name of. As the man lit another cigarette, the woman said, Can I have one?

The man hastily looked inside the pack, saw it was empty, crumpled it, produced another one of Chunghwa, carefully opened it, took one out, put it between her offering lips and lit it for her. It was not till then that he thought of something and said, My Mom smoked all her life, you know.

'In my family, only my father smoked,' said she.

'My mother is a very strong woman,' said the man.

'In what ways?'

'She never cooks. She never wears makeup or anything flowery. She plays table tennis like a man. And she smokes.'

'That's real lovely.'

'That's the style of the times that Mao encouraged women to cultivate, in Mao's own words: "Love the military uniforms, not rouged cheeks".'

'Why's that?'

'Because, in a way, he wanted the nation of men and women to be fully armed against the American imperialists and the Soviet revisionists.'

'Someone I knew didn't even know who Mao was.'

'You are joking.'

'I'm not. In a restaurant in Hainan Island that I went to a few years ago, there was a party and people were talking about Mao. When the waitress, about 18, I think, brought out the dish, a man asked if she knew who Mao Zedong was. The girl said no, in all seriousness.'

'That's like what happened when a young male speaker said in answer to a question asked that he had no idea who Lenin was in an academic conference I went to years ago,' said the man. 'But that's the balancing power at work. People with supreme power and influence will one day go out of currency and memory.'

A wind from the sea ruffled their conversation and their shortening, burning cigarettes, leaving a brightening reddish circle around their nose tips.

'You know sometimes,' the man began. 'I'd love to have a cigarette so long that one can smoke nonstop till both the smoker and the cigarette run out of their own lives, the cigarette reduced to a heap of ashes and the man, a heap of bones.'

The woman looked up at the man in surprise, but, at the same time, she was amused. 'It almost sounds like a sexual innuendo,' said she.

'Oh, yes,' the man said. 'I'd love to stay there forever, as I do here on this island.'

'I like you like that,' said the woman.

'When we were young and had no experience, we were fascinated by the act. In sharing our fantasies, we thought how wonderful it would be if one stayed inside a woman for the whole night every night and night after night.'

The woman laughed out loud in spite of herself.

'And even when there was little literature available, there was the occasional book stolen from the ransacked libraries, such as *Ku caihua* by Feng Deying.'

'Not that I know of.'

'He's that rarest writer who never writes about love without fleshing it out with vivid physical details.'

'Do you still remember any?'

'No. I can only remember how we teens read the novel together, fascinated as well as abhorred by what he described of the man and woman engaged in the act, something, forbidden and rare in those days, that we now find so mundane.'

'Are you going to write all that down in your novel?'

'Probably not.' Then, 'No idea.'

'Can we write something together?'

'How?'

'Don't know.'

'Then why mention it?'

'Just a thought, on your advice that if one has a thought that drifts past across one's mindscape, one'd better catch it and write it down or else it's gone forever.'

'Did I say that?'

'You did. I never forget.'

'That sounds like someone who never forgives, too?'

She hit him with her fists, raised in a shammed fashion, as he dodged. Then, both stopped and gasped as the moon, large and round, rose out of the sea, in all its golden rotundity, its edges dripping, like a familiar stranger who suddenly turned up on their doorstep. If there was someone watching from inside the room, the eyes of this person would see them sitting side by side in the moon, as if embedded there.

The Third Night

For a moment, he wondered if he was a dead man walking, minus even her. The night wrapped around him, like a dark cloak of thoughts. He heard his own footsteps, like in a dream. All his dreams, it seems, were about classrooms, teaching, being taught, most of the times the latter, and most of the time, in Mandarin, despite years in the diaspora.

Footsteps. Urgent calling. And a shadow emerging from the night. When its cloak was lifted, he had arms to cloak up instead, twin and entwined.

'Nothing will be anything,' said he.

'Meaning?'

'You know what I mean, don't you?' The man said, eyeing the invisible sea in front of him, where nothing was really anything. Just

270

wind and waves.

'Can I ask you to tell me another story please?'

'I've run out of stories, as a matter of fact.'

'Are the words waves?'

'Meaning?'

'Just a thought.'

'Yes?'

'Nothing, really.'

'I love you, although the three words have been said so many times that they cease to mean anything.'

'I still like to hear them, the most beautiful words. But they have to be said over and over again. I love saying them, always, its meaning in the very saying of it, particularly when one is in heat.'

'In heat?'

'Yes, in the very middle of the heat.'

'We are wasters of time, and, in some way, of words, too.'

'You are, I am not.'

'I am. And I am a liver of lives, too.'

'A liver of lives? You are a liver of me when you are inside me.'

'I like the way you describe it. You really have a silver tongue.'

'A silver tongue that is a silver bullet.'

'A silver tongue bullet.'

'Listen, to the sky falling.'

'I thought you said the height falling.'

'Not much of a difference anyway.'

'In a little while, we shall take that blood bath.'

'Oh, yes.'

'To be forgotten; to be oblivioned, as you once put it.'

'Did I? But that's a verb.'

'You always verbalise the unverbable. You said: Let's they them.'

'Ha, ha, ha.'

'You know it is. But you did it.'

'Why not? Let's night it.'

'We've dayed it so many times we might as well night it and, hopefully, survive it. Or survivre it.'

'You really think that is the way of prolonging a thought?'

'What if there is not a single reader left in the world?'

'I thought you said "a single word"; that would be nice.'

'See that road over there, that little path that winds its way between the houses till it disappears behind that blue building?'

'Sure. But that's what you said over the last few days.'

'You said that, too, yourself.'

'It'll be tonight, our last night.'

'I don't believe these things. But I'll do it. I have long wanted to do it and it's never as perfect as this.'

'Just as you said in that story you told me a couple of days ago.'

'Which story? I've told you so many.'

'The one in which the abbot dies sitting with his legs crossed, entering into what is known as the "seated transformation" or 坐化, *zuohua*, only to have a woman by the Yangtze pregnant in a dream the same day, giving birth to a boy the next morning. It sounds so fantastic, so unreal, and, yet, so wonderfully believable.'

'Oh, yeh. But why not a daughter?'

'That would be even better, wouldn't it?'

'And the daughter may grow up to become the president of the country or an accountant, or dozens and dozens of possibilities.'

'Sure. What is not impossible in this world?'

'Even nonfiction has become fiction, don't you think?'

'Oh, nonfiction has always been fiction, right from the start.'

'And failure?'

'Fai that is Lure. Sounds like a name, a good name, actually.'

'That's what you call me, from time to time, like this: Fai Lure.'

'Surname Lure, given name Fai.'

'You must come with me to Stockholm,' said she, her voice sounding uncertain, unsteady, like a boat in the face of a coming storm.

'We'll perhaps meet in Copenhagen.'

'That would be super.'

'We'll meet in a new country every time we see each other.'

Silence, for the first time, on her part.

'Sorry but I was just joking,' then, 'If I die, I hope you can come and visit me in my country.

'I shall one day join you,' she said, resolutely.

'I'm sure you will,' he said and, after a short pause, added, 'We shall meet in The Delightful Pagoda.'

'Where is that? Brisbane?'

'No, it's on the Yangtze, built by Zhang Mengde in Qi'an.'

'Tell me about it.'

'There's nothing more to tell you. Go and read the essay by Su Zhe.'

It took her only a few minutes to find it online on her mobile phone and finish reading it while he smoked another cigarette, outside in the hotel compound.

'I like this.' As she said so, she quoted the line that goes, "张君梦得，谪居齐安，即其庐之西南为亭，以览观江流之胜，而余兄子瞻名之曰'快哉'".

'Qi'an is the ancient name of my hometown where Zhang, in his exile, built a pagoda on the Yangtze that Eastern Slope Su called, "The Delightful Pagoda".'

'How lovely!'

'Both Zhang and Su were exiles,' said the man.

'Both of us, too,' said the woman.

'You know why I came here with you?'

'To love me, to love me to love you.'

'That and also—'

Her face lifted, her lips expectant. Beyond her face another moon, the moon of the third night.

'I'd like to dispose of my life's manuscripts in the sea.'

'You might as well destroy me.'

'But after I met you, I've changed my mind.'

She looked into his eyes, her soul impinging on his.

'I'll give you password to access all my work on iCloud when I returned to the country,' the man said.

'Give it to me here,' said she as she opened her mouth. 'by way of your tongue.'

As he did so, a passage, written long ago but long forgotten, emerged from underneath the bedrock of his memory,

> We sat at the edge of the bed, a little apart, her eyes intent upon me, never winking or moving away and so were mine. A desire stewed, simmered, stirred, boiled, surged until at last it became so strong that I could not help kissing on her voluptuous lips, filled with intoxicating charms and dreamy spells. My tongue on her teeth and hers on mine. Her mouth was an abyss of love, into which I felt I was gliding, trembling and shivering, just as if—

Sources used:

《＜人民日报＞社论：党是领导一切的》（1/7/1974）：
http://club.kdnet.net/dispbbs.asp?id=11413635&boardid=44

《"志愿军"老兵回忆点滴》：http://www.huanghuagang.org/
hhgLibrary/july2008/zhiyuanjun_laobing_huiyi.htm

Acknowledgments

'Zu or Part Thereof', published in *Meanjin*, Autumn 2022, pp. 52-59.

A big thank you to David for publishing the book, to Bruce Sims and to Erin Symes for editing it, to Li Lu for typesetting it, and to Zhao Baokang for the cover image.

www.ingramcontent.com/pod-product-compliance
Lightning Source LLC
Chambersburg PA
CBHW031115030726
47496CB00002BA/559